D0197626

DOOMI GOLO

The Hidden Notebooks

DOOMI

AFRICAN HUMANITIES AND THE ARTS

SERIES EDITOR

Kenneth Harrow

The African Humanities and the Arts series mirrors the agenda of the African Studies Center at Michigan State University and its commitment to the study of Africa. The series examines all aspects of cultural research—including art, literature, film, and religion.

EDITORIAL BOARD

Simon Gikandi, *Princeton University*

Eileen Julien, *Indiana University*

Manthia Diawara, *New York University*

Carmela Garritano, *Texas A&M University*

Jane Bryce, *University of the West Indies, Cave Hill*

Akin Adesokan, *Indiana University*

Moradewun Adejunmobi, *University of California, Davis*

Jonathan Haynes, *Long Island University*

Frieda Ekotto, *University of Michigan*

Teju Olaniyan, *University of Wisconsin–Madison*

Olivier Barlet, *Africultures*

Keyan Tomaselli, *University of KwaZulu-Natal, South Africa*

Nicolas Martin-Granel, *Institut des Textes et Manuscrits Modernes, Centre National de la Recherche Scientifique*

Nasrin Qader, *Northwestern University*

Gorgui Dieng, *Université Cheikh Anta Diop*

GOLO

The Hidden Notebooks

Boubacar Boris Diop

TRANSLATED BY Vera Wülfing-Leckie AND El Hadji Moustapha Diop

MICHIGAN STATE UNIVERSITY PRESS | *East Lansing*

Copyright © 2016 by Boubacar Boris Diop

♾ The paper used in this publication meets the minimum requirements
of ANSI/NISO Z39.48-1992 (R 1997) (Permanence of Paper).

Michigan State University Press
East Lansing, Michigan 48823-5245

Printed and bound in the United States of America.

25 24 23 22 21 20 19 18 17 16   1 2 3 4 5 6 7 8 9 10

LIBRARY OF CONGRESS CATALOGING-IN-PUBLICATION DATA
Names: Diop, Boubacar Boris, 1946– author. | Whulfing-Leckie, Vera, translator.
| Diop, Moustapha, translator.
Title: Doomi golo—the hidden notebooks / Boubacar Boris Diop ;
translated by Vera Wulfing-Leckie and El Hadji Moustapha Diop.
Other titles: Doomi golo. English | African humanities and the arts.
Description: East Lansing : Michigan State University Press, 2016.
| Series: African humanities and the arts | English translation of Les petits de la guenon (2009),
"a liberal French adaptation of the Wolof original."
Identifiers: LCCN 2016027977| ISBN 9781611862140 (pbk. : alk. paper)
| ISBN 9781609175016 (pdf) | ISBN 9781628952742 (epub) | ISBN 9781628962741 (kindle)
Classification: LCC PL8785.9.D56 D6614 2016 | DDC 896/.32143—dc23
LC record available at https://lccn.loc.gov/2016027977

Book design by Charlie Sharp, Sharp Des!gns, Lansing, Michigan
Cover design by Shaun Allshouse, www.shaunallshouse.com

Michigan State University Press is a member of the Green Press Initiative and is
committed to developing and encouraging ecologically responsible publishing
practices. For more information about the Green Press Initiative and the use
of recycled paper in book publishing, please visit *www.greenpressinitiative.org.*

Visit Michigan State University Press at *www.msupress.org*

To Janis Mayes and Arame Fal Diop

For Aminata Asha and Evamaye

INTRODUCTION

Vera Wülfing-Leckie

THE PUBLICATION OF *DOOMI GOLO* (2003),[1] BOUBACAR BORIS DIOP'S FIRST novel in Wolof, was greeted by Nasrin Qader as "a veritable literary event in the landscape of Senegalese culture,"[2] an accolade that Diop's select but growing readership echoed with enthusiasm.

However, with his readership unable either to decipher or to understand Wolof, it wasn't long before the author was inundated with requests for a translation. Eager to allow *Doomi Golo* to fend for itself for a while, he waited, but eventually gave in and personally produced a liberal French adaptation. When it appeared under the title *Les petits de la guenon* (2009),[3] certain scholars claimed it was a new novel that merely bore close similarities to the original.[4] The title, in both Wolof and French, can be translated as "The Children of the Monkey" or alternatively "The Offspring of the She-Ape." *Doomi Golo—The Hidden Notebooks* is a direct translation of *Les petits* into English.

In each one of its incarnations, *Doomi Golo* is a complex, multi-layered narrative contained in a deceptively simple framework: Nguirane Faye, an old man in the fictitious Niarela district of Dakar, in Senegal, decides to compile a "chronicle of everyday life" for the benefit of his absent grandson Badou. He hopes that one day in the future, probably when he is no longer alive, Badou will return and dig up the *Notebooks* that are waiting for him, buried under the mango tree in the courtyard of his house in Niarela.

Prima facie, Nguirane's chronicle consists of six *Notebooks*, different narrative strains that alternate like the movements of a symphony. His cinematographic techniques let him zoom in on different locations, real or imagined, from this vantage point under the mango tree. They give him the freedom to skip back and forth between past, present and future, as he sees fit. However, there seems to be a mysterious seventh *Notebook, The Book of Secrets*. . . .

With seven published novels to date, Boubacar Boris Diop, who was born in Dakar in 1946, is one of Senegal's most celebrated Francophone writers. *Murambi, le livre des ossements* (2000), was nominated as one of Africa's 100 Best Books of the 20th Century,[5] and for his second novel, *Les tambours de la mémoire* (1987),[6] he won the Grand prix de la République du Sénégal pour les Lettres (1990), while *Le cavalier et son ombre* (1997) was awarded the Prix Tropiques (1998).

In 2000, Boris Diop received the Grand Prix Littéraire de l'Afrique Noire for the entirety of his oeuvre, which has grown since then. In addition to the novels, it comprises numerous short stories, three plays, several screenplays, and an opera libretto.[7] His political engagement finds expression in nonfiction titles like *Négrophobie* (2005), co-written with François-Xavier Verschave and Odile Tobner; *L'Afrique au-delà du miroir* (2007),[8] a collection of essays and articles; and *La gloire des imposteurs* (2014), an exchange of letters with coauthor Aminata Dramane Traoré, the former Malian minister of culture.

In the course of his dual career as author and journalist, Boris Diop cofounded *Sud,* Senegal's first independent daily paper, before being appointed editor-in-chief at *Le Matin,* another Dakar daily. He was adviser on the editorial staff of the bilingual Pulaar-Wolof monthly *Lasli-Njelbeen,* and in 1990 he started contributing articles to a number of quality international newspapers, in particular *Le Monde diplomatique,* the Swiss daily *Neue Zürcher Zeitung,* and *Internazionale,* an Italian magazine. In 2004 and again in 2008 Diop was visiting professor at Rutgers University, and in 2014 he taught a semester-long course on "Novel-Writing and the Duty to Remember: African Writers Faced with the Genocide of the Tutsi in Rwanda" at the ETH (Eidgenössische Technische Hochschule), Switzerland's most prestigious academic institution. A project launched by the International Parliament of Writers took him to Mexico for a three-year stint as Writer-in-Residence in 2006, and in 2010 he spent six months at the University of the Witwatersrand in Johannesburg, South Africa, also as Writer-in-Residence. His desire to gain a better understanding of the differences between the Maghreb region and Sub-Saharan Africa motivated his relocation to Tunisia in 2008. In the three years during which he was based in Tunis, he gave frequent lectures and made guest appearances at Manouba University.

As the indefatigable traveler, sought-after teacher and public speaker he is, Boris Diop has lectured at many of the world's top universities including Harvard, Yale, Stanford, and the Sorbonne, to name a few. He is a popular participant and guest of honor at conferences, literary festivals, book fairs and other cultural events in all four corners of the globe. But, never oblivious of the ultimate purpose of his manifold activities, he regularly spends time back home in Senegal. While there, after his return from Tunisia in 2011, he held a teaching post at Gaston Berger University in Saint-Louis, where he introduced a unique new course called "Senegalese Literature in the Wolof tongue."

Jointly with two other Senegalese writers, he has acquired a Dakar book-shop, which also forms the venue for book launches and debates, and he cofounded Jimsaan, a new publishing venture based in Senegal. In collaboration with Éditions Zulma, he has launched Céytu, an unprecedented series of selected texts from world literature translated into Wolof. In January 2016 Diop took up a visiting professorship at the American University of Nigeria, where he is currently teaching courses in African literature, creative writing, and journalism.

Unlike the scores of African intellectuals who leave home without appearing to feel much regret when given the opportunity of a life in the West, Boris Diop has purposely always kept a foothold on the African continent. This makes him the perfect embodiment of his own maxim, conveyed by Nguirane Faye, the main narrator of *Doomi Golo*, to his grandson: "I am perfectly aware, Badou, that turning one's back on the outside world is tantamount to the kiss of death. It's bound to be a good thing if a nation lets the winds that are blowing from all corners of the globe expand its chest, but not unless we do what we can to preserve the crucible destined to receive its breath when they are blowing."

The remarkable breadth and depth of his oeuvre in French does not prevent Boris Diop from describing *Doomi Golo* as the best he has written.[9] In *Africa beyond the Mirror* (2014) he explains that "writing in your mother tongue makes you experience feelings . . . you would have thought absolutely impossible before . . . The words I use to write *Doomi Golo* do not come from school or from a dictionary. They come from real life. These words rise up to me from the very distant past, and if their sound is simultaneously so familiar and so pleasing to me, it is because I belong, with every fibre of my being, to an oral tradition."[10]

Only a few African writers freely admit to such sentiments, and even fewer decide to follow the example of Ngũgĩ wa Thiongo, who, in the 1960s, pioneered politically motivated mother-tongue writing in Africa.[11] Most are reluctant to turn their backs on a prosperous, educated audience in the developed world, only to withdraw into the virtual ghetto of one of more than a thousand African languages, some of which have never been codified. When Diop's compatriot Cheik Aliou Ndao (1933–) was courageous—or should one say foolhardy?—enough to write his debut novel, *Buur Tilleen* (1967), in Wolof, the manuscript languished in a drawer for thirty years, unable to find a publisher. Its French translation, *Buur Tilleen, roi de la Médina* (1972) on the other hand, was an immediate success.

Even if for Boris Diop the final push to start writing in Wolof did not come from Senegal but from Rwanda, the reasons that prompted him to ignore the risks of abandoning French as his literary language and composing *Doomi Golo* in his mother tongue are closely linked to the incongruent political and cultural landscape of post-colonial Senegal.

By the time Dakar, where Diop spent his formative years, became the capital of newly independent Senegal in 1960, it had played the role of official headquarters of French West Africa for nearly six decades. Like the ancient trading post of Saint-Louis farther north, it was one of the country's famous *quatre communes* or "four municipalities" (the other two were Gorée and Rufisque). The assimilationist colonial policies peculiar to France meant that anyone born—like Boris Diop—in one of these municipalities before independence was technically a French citizen. The colonial master plan was to foster an educated, Francophone urban elite whose members, the so-called évolués, would be plucked from these chosen districts, while the rest of the population, referred to as *originaires,* remained illiterate. It was precisely this illiterate section of Senegal's population that remained dependent on, and faithful to, the indigenous languages, thereby keeping alive the rich African oral tradition.

As a member of the privileged minority, Diop went to the exclusive Lamine Guèye secondary school in Dakar's Plateau area, where the teachers were French and French was the sole medium of instruction, while African languages were banned. With this educational background, and steeped in the classics of French literature from the personal library of his francophile father, he would have corresponded admirably to president Leopold Sedar Senghor's ideal of a "Frenchman in a black skin," had he not had a mother who was an accomplished storyteller and only spoke Wolof.

In "Brief Escapades," the fifth of the six *Notebooks* that make up Part One of *Doomi Golo*, the author paints a masterful *tableau vivant* of the split society he remembers from his own childhood and adolescence:

> You should have seen us on our way into the city center after the prayer of *tisbaar.* I am talking about a time, Badou, when the horse-drawn carriage was a means of transport reserved for the privileged few. Picture them looking down on us from their seats up there, like royalty, while we, the riffraff, were trailing along behind or next to the horses, forming a kind of guard-of-honor for those fake Whites, without even being aware of it. I still see them in my mind's eye, my évolués: shipping clerks, bookkeepers, the black elite, if you like. They used to go to their offices in jacket and tie, wearing pith helmets. Some of them were reciting verses by Lamartine or Victor Hugo from their lofty position, while those too shy and reserved for that simply kept their faces buried in *Paris-Dakar,* the only daily paper available to us in those days.

The next few lines are unequivocal proof that Diop has chosen to position Nguirane Faye, the narrator-cum-protagonist of Part One, firmly outside the ranks of the "*négraille*" or black middle class, the sector of Senegalese society where the French language and European dress style were *de rigueur*:

> As for me, I was a worker at Air Liquide, the gas factory near Kayes-Findiw. I'm sure I became a militant member of the Parti Africain de l'Indépendance out of contempt for those conceited idiots who were so proud of being slaves.

Early on in *Doomi Golo,* the reader learns that Nguirane Faye admires figures like Grand Makhou, a simple but charismatic street fighter, the Koranic teacher Mbaye Lô, the Sufi poet Serigne Moussa Kâ (1890–1926), and Cheik Aliou Ndao. What they all have in common is their non-acceptance of French cultural norms, with Wolof as their chosen language of expression. While Moussa Kâ and his contemporaries belonged to an older generation that wrote Wolof in the Arabic script, the so-called *Wolofal,* Cheik Aliou Ndao was a member of a group of Senegalese university graduates in France who, in the late 1950s, westernized the codification of Wolof by transcribing it from the Arabic to the Latin alphabet. Even before then, Wolof words were often spelled phonetically by the French, which explains some of the variations in Wolof spelling one still comes across today.

The inspiration for the new Wolof syllabary, the "Ijib Wolof," originally came from *Nations nègres et culture* (1954),[12] the seminal work by Senegalese historian and anthropologist Cheikh Anta Diop (1923–1986). Aimé Césaire called *Nations* "the most courageous work by a black author to date,"[13] and it is no exaggeration to say that it has inspired not only Cheik Aliou Ndao and Boris Diop but also a growing number of other contemporary writers and intellectuals to help resurrect Africa and give it back its history, its culture, and above all its dignity, after the ravages of colonization.

Throughout his life, Cheikh Anta Diop not only focused his attention on two central issues, African languages and African identity, but he also showed how closely they are interlinked. Picking up on Frantz Fanon's concept of internalized self-rejection, Cheikh Anta was the first to tell Africans they had to "learn to look at themselves in the mirror." While this is also one of the central themes of *Murambi,* the Rwanda novel, its treatment is much more explicit in *Doomi Golo.*

In Part Two of *Doomi Golo,* for instance, this idea is dramatized in the gruesome scene where two gorillas mistake their own mirror image for enemies. One of them tries to attack the perceived intruders, without realizing that he is actually attacking himself. When he then turns on his companion, they both inflict injuries on each other so grave that they end up dying a slow, agonizing death.

A human stereotype who personifies this internalized self-rejection is Yacine Ndiaye, one of the two main female characters in the novel. She is the widow of Assane Tall, the narrator's only son, who as a professional footballer went to France and later died there. After his death, Yacine arrives in Niarela with their two children, Mbissine and Mbissane. Yacine's one and only wish is to be white, hence the comparison with the eponymous monkey, a creature viewed by humans as an inveterate imitator. When Bigué Samb—Badou's mother and Assane's first wife—co-opts the magical powers of a witchdoctor, her wish is finally granted, but she has to pay a heavy price. Through Yacine Ndiaye, the monkey-symbolism in *Doomi Golo* juxtaposes the multitude of those who blindly copy "the Other" against those courageous enough to resist foreign domination and expose its pernicious consequences. A few famous examples of these Men of Defiance are listed in *Notebook 5*, where, at the end of Grand Makhou's story, Nguirane concludes:

> Looking back on it now at my age, Badou, I realize we had a lot of people like that here, people just as proud as Grand Makhou. Cheikh Anta Diop. Amilcar Cabral. Mongo Beti. Samory Touré. Thomas Sankara. Lumumba. You know all those names. Each one of them was a Man of Defiance in his own right. And for that reason and for that reason alone, the White colonizer killed them or at least reduced them to silence.

In Part Two of *Doomi Golo,* Cheikh Anta Diop makes a cameo appearance. The description of a political rally in Niarela where Cheikh Anta, President Senghor's[14] most fervent ideological adversary, is addressing the crowd in Wolof, conveys the sense that author and narrator are speaking with one voice.[15] While Cheikh Anta Diop comes across as completely genuine and free of ulterior motives, the other two politicians in the novel, the fictional president Daour Diagne and his mirror image Dibi-Dibi, are the usual opportunists. Strangely enough, the satirical manner in which they are depicted makes them all the more realistic. By representing Dibi-Dibi as president Daour Diagne's simulacrum—and it helps to know that Daour Diagne himself is based on Senegal's third president Abdoulaye Wade—the author uses a technique borrowed from the visual arts. The postmodern social theorist Jean Baudrillard (1929–2007) argues that when an image is created by copying a copy of the original, it becomes truth in its own right, "the hyperreal."

The mirror serves as a versatile tool in this novel. Whether it takes the form of the perfectly smooth surface of a lake, or the eyes of a passing stranger in the street, a mirror is normally a "Truth-Teller" who does not lie. But when it distorts or magnifies, it can turn into an instrument for caricature.

On par with Cheikh Anta Diop, the novelist and pioneer of African cinema Ousmane Sembène (1923–2007) was a brilliant, sharp-witted opponent of Senghor's neo-colonial style of government and repressive language policies. Sembène's feature films, e.g., *Xala* (1974), *Ceddo* (1977), or *Moolandé* (2003), are classics; *Mandabi* (1968), based on his own novel *Le Mandat* (1966), was shot twice, first in French and then in Wolof. The prize-winning *Camp de Thiaroye*

(1988) deals with the same notorious French army attack on a transit camp for Senegalese soldiers that Boris Diop had made the subject of his play *Thiaroye, terre rouge* seven years previously.

In *Notebook 1*, the author lets Sembène appear under the guise of Ousmane Sow, a Niarela cart driver. Similarly to Nguirane Faye himself, nobody in Niarela seems to take any notice of him: "He's just a wretched old cart driver, they think . . . and yet, the good man has very clear ideas about everything . . . You could call him a forceful spirit, our friend Ousmane, no matter that he is only a simple working man."

Even taken at face value, the encounter between Ousmane Sow and Nguirane Faye is one of the standout scenes in the novel. But to realize that this *boroom saret* is actually Ousmane Sembène adds a whole new dimension. The intertextual reference here is to Sembène's first film, *Boroom Sarret* (The cart driver, 1963), a twenty-minute black-and-white fictional documentary about a day in the life of a cart driver from the Medina, the part of Dakar that Niarela is modeled on. Sembène himself was constantly in trouble with the authorities, just like the cart driver in his film.

In *Doomi Golo*, Ousmane Sow, alias Sembène, lambasts Nguirane Faye for his docility. When Nguirane questions him about his horse's Swahili name, wondering why a modest cart driver from Niarela would go and search for a name for his horse "at the other end of the world," he shoots back:

> That's terrible, Nguirane, to see how so many years after his liberation the slave in us still hasn't managed to cast off his shackles! There really is no need for the Master to put us in chains anymore! He may as well let us roam around freely as long as we come trotting back to the plantation every night like so much cattle to their stable. Our chains are in our heads, you see.

Like the concept of internalized self-rejection, the idea of a deep-seated slave mentality, inculcated into generations of Africans by the colonizer, also goes back to Frantz Fanon and his essay *Peau noire, masques blancs* (1952).[16]

For Boris Diop, these are the very issues underlying the 1994 Rwandan Genocide of the Tutsi. In an interview in 2003 he commented as follows:

> For me, the genocide is a profoundly cultural issue, associated with self-rejection, the inability to look at oneself in the mirror. You might think that the Tutsi and

the Hutu despise each other because they are different, but in my eyes, it is because they resemble each other. What I saw in Rwanda has perturbed me very profoundly. I needed my language to help me make peace with myself.[17]

It was at the fifth convention of Fest Afrika, a literary festival in Lille in 1995 that Boris Diop and a group of nine other African artists—including Abdourahman Waberi from Djibouti, Véronique Tadjo from Ivory Coast and Tierno Monénembo from Guinea—decided to visit Rwanda, hoping to gain a better understanding of the circumstances surrounding the last genocide of the twentieth century and its aftermath. Between 800,000 and 1,000,000 Tutsis and moderate Hutus lost their lives at the hands of extremist Hutu militias during the Hundred Days of Rwanda, while the international press was indifferent, largely depicting it as "just another civil war" in Africa. For Diop, the harrowing journey that took him and the other artists to Rwanda in 1998 was a decisive watershed. Finding conclusive proof that the French government not only did nothing to prevent the mass killings of the Rwandan genocide but was actively involved in their preparation and execution, in order to preserve the country as a Francophone stronghold in Africa, could not fail to have a profound effect on him. His feelings of critical ambivalence toward the former colonizer turned to revulsion and disgust. *Murambi, le livre des ossements* is Boris Diop's literary tribute to what subsequently became known as *The Duty of Memory Project*. It bears no trace of the exuberant, sometimes playful, experimental style that is the hallmark of his earlier novels, especially *Le cavalier et son ombre*.

For the first part of his career as a novelist—until Rwanda, in other words— Diop used to delight in the solitude and creative freedom conveyed by his favorite saying: *When the memory goes out to collect wood, it brings back any bundle it likes.* He felt no need to stick to the facts, couldn't really understand those for whom writing was "all about telling the truth," and found it much more exciting to stir up "doubts and uncertainty."[18]

All his earlier novels, including *Le temps de Tamango* (1981) and *Les tambours de la mémoire,* with their focus on lost or suppressed episodes of Senegal's history, convey this delight in stirring up doubts and uncertainty. The last page of *The Knight and His Shadow,* where the ferryman announces that he is sailing towards an unknown destination with only the clouds as his compass, represents the climax and endpoint of this phase.[19]

A comparison between *The Knight* and *Murambi* illustrates the drastic change Diop underwent as a writer post-Rwanda very clearly. In *The Knight*, reality and fantasy intermingle, eventually becoming indistinguishable. *Murambi*, on the other hand, with its sequential arrangement of eyewitness accounts, is much more austere and structured, in an attempt by the author to establish some sort of order in the underlying chaos.

The theme of broken identity and cultural alienation is the umbilical cord connecting *Murambi* and *Doomi Golo*. It culminates with the long, intense monologue by the old man in *Notebook 3*, a passage also known as "The Search for the Ancestor." The common ground between *The Knight* and *Doomi Golo*, on the other hand, lies in the enduring gap between the African oral tradition and Western print-based culture, a gap still waiting to be bridged.

The Knight vividly depicts this dilemma through Khadidja, the heroine. When she finds employment as a professional storyteller, she is forced to do her work sitting in front of a half-open door, unable to ever find out whether there is anyone on the other side.

The absence of the listener in *The Knight* not only functions as a parable for the situation of the storyteller who has lost his audience, Charles Sugnet suggests, but it also symbolizes the predicament of the author, especially an African author "who has chosen to write in an African language and whose audience is so small as to be invisible."[20] The Wolof oral tradition is based on an age-old ritual that binds the *griot*, or storyteller, to his listeners in a mutual agreement or pact. The performance cannot start until the storyteller has pronounced the word *Leboon*, "Once upon a time," or, more literally, "Listen to my story," to which the audience replies *Lepoon*, "We are listening." With the transition from orality to the written word, there is no longer anyone to legitimize the *griot*, now a writer, by saying *Lepoon*.

"I would have preferred to talk to you face to face, of course, like any storyteller worthy of that name, but, I am writing to you, because it is my only option," Nguirane Faye tells Badou in *Doomi Golo*. With this statement, Nguirane, the narrator, clarifies his attitude towards orality versus writing, reading, and books. Face to face contact would be preferable, he says, but the written word, however unsatisfactory it may be, can bridge time and space. Orality and the written word should not be mutually exclusive, as Muslim traditionalists think, but complementary. As repositories of knowledge, books fulfill a useful function. At this point, *Doomi Golo* enters into dialog with Cheikh

Hamidou Kane's landmark novel *L'aventure ambiguë* (1961). Steeped in its author's Sufi background, *L'aventure* paints Western culture as seductive but ultimately incompatible with traditional Islamic practices that restrict reading and writing to the realm of the spiritual. Samba Diallo, the main protagonist in the book, is catapulted from a Koranic school in rural Senegal straight to the Sorbonne where he grapples with the need to reconcile the cultural influences. His tragic accidental death at the end is symbolic of his failure to do so.

By leaving his *Notebooks* to Badou as his personal legacy, Nguirane Faye passes on his knowledge and experience to his grandson like Elders have done in Africa—and elsewhere—since time immemorial. With their excursions into Senegal's distant and more recent past, their acerbic social and political commentary, interspersed with philosophical meditations and passages of exquisite lyrical beauty, the *Notebooks* are intended as a replacement for the formal education Badou has lost out on. "Maybe it was your dream, too, to become a civil servant or an engineer one day. You never had the chance to go to university, and you weren't ashamed of washing cars at a petrol station . . . or working as a street hawker," Nguirane tells Badou in the first pages of *The Tale of the Ashes.* "I pass [what I write here] on to you, so that when, on your return, you read through everything, it's as though you had never left Niarela." Ultimately, having this knowledge conferred to him by his grandfather is an act of initiation for Badou.

The suggestion that orality and the written word can coexist and even complement each other is not the only indication that Nguirane Faye is no ordinary African Elder. When he was young, he says, adults were only capable of "giving orders and issuing advice"; he calls this "a path that was a bit too narrow for a young man who had fallen in love with freedom." These simple words, so casually expressed, are a discreet hint for Africans who have been accused of having a tendency to stagnate in the straightjacket of outdated traditions. Another writer who has made this point more or less indirectly was Chinua Achebe (1931–2013) in *Things Fall Apart* (1957).

This literary masterpiece, the first novel by an African specifically aimed at a Western audience, demonstrates how the traditional way of life in a Nigerian village is surreptitiously, but irreversibly, undermined by the presence of the colonizer. The fact that in *Things Fall Apart* nearly every action taken, every event that occurs, is punctuated by a maxim or a proverb, adds authenticity, but Okonkwo's suicide at the end is a stark reminder that preconceived ideas—even those rooted in ancient wisdom—lack the flexibility that is necessary to help us deal with the modern world.

Doomi Golo, written by an African for an African audience, is also spiked with popular sayings, but, in typically "Borisian" fashion, there is a twist.

When his search for the ancestor in Mbering-Saaj does not turn out as he had hoped, Nguirane initially finds solace in the reminder that *If you insist on playing the drum with an ax, you will only be able to obtain a single sound from it, no matter whether it is sweet or unpleasant to your ears.* In the cemetery, enveloped in total darkness and feeling "as if I was suddenly both blind and unable to breathe," he defuses the tension with a delightfully inappropriate aphorism: *If your enemy prays that you should starve to death, burp loudly every time he walks past you.* Later on, when that tension returns and builds up to a fever pitch, he admits to Badou that "I very quickly forgot all my aspirations to heroism, and not a single one of Wolof Njaay's proverbs came to my rescue."

The subtly ironic message that there simply isn't a fitting proverb for absolutely *any* eventuality becomes much less subtle in the last third of *Notebook 1,* where "Veritable salvoes of Wolof proverbs were flitting through the air. There was the one about the camel's fart, which, as we all know, is positioned as high up as the anus from which it escaped . . . and the one about the murderer who should not be too surprised that his hands are stained red from the blood of his victims."

Here, Boris Diop reminds his fellow Africans with humor and wit that many of the thousands of African proverbs that are held in such awe are mere tautologies and thus not particularly useful in a tricky situation. Tradition and ancient wisdom may be valuable, but in the final analysis, only thinking for oneself—as opposed to blindly following the crowd—will lead to personal growth and maturity. This is precisely what the old man from Mbering-Saaj is trying to get across. It is a lesson that can also be learned from Kocc Barma Fall (1586–1655), the "subtle and irreverent philosopher" from Cayor. After a meeting with the grandees of Cayor "one sunrise in the year 1619," Ali Kaboye describes him as a typical intellectual in the Sartrean mold who "pokes his nose into everything, especially when it's none of his business." Kocc Barma Fall is credited with having coined the phrase "Shame on the nation that has given up listening to its old men." "I'm sure you have heard our people solemnly repeating this age-old maxim over and over again," Nguirane Faye tells Badou in *Notebook 1,* "perhaps it's true to say that this strange fellow from

Cayor who never took anyone seriously—himself included—would have been amused to see that, so many centuries later, we still think of him as practically infallible."

Of the many old men that appear in Nguirane's seven *Notebooks*, some are worth listening to, while others are not. The legend about the Women of Ndeer, for example, shows that sometimes it is a little girl we should listen to. This is so important that it has become the motto of Part One of *Doomi Golo*.

Jean Sob in his monograph *L'impératif romanesque de Boubacar Boris Diop* (2007) characterizes Boris Diop as a parodist.[21] This may well apply in a generalized fashion to the earlier novels, but in *Doomi Golo,* it is no longer true. Here, Diop handles the full range of different moods and registers from subtle irony to savage political satire all the way to the earthy Rabelaisian burlesque of the palace scene in *Notebook 1,* not as a mask to hide behind but as stylistic tools that fulfill a specific purpose. While he is listening to the old man's monologue in *Notebook 3*, for example, the narrator's gently teasing irony in describing his own reaction helps to lighten the gravity of the atmosphere.

Two mirror scenes deserve special mention. One that by conjuring up eerie images of an "entangled mass of bodies, twisted and intertwined like the gnarled branches of a baobab," evokes Rwanda, and more specifically Murambi, the technical college that lent its name to *Murambi, the Book of Bones.* Having been lured there by the local bishop and mayor under the pretense that French troops would protect them, more than 45,000 Tutsis lost their lives at this site in a single night. Here, the mirror acts as a kind of camera obsura, offering glimpses of a nightmarish scenario with figures that are "warped, their faces hideously blurred, grimacing, and seemingly attached to the wrong bodies." When the massacre was finally over, most, but not all of the corpses were thrown into hastily dug mass graves. The rest were simply "left abandoned where they lay." Today, Murambi has been turned into a genocide memorial, and the victims' remains, preserved in lime, have become its exhibits.[22]

The second, equally striking scene could hardly be more different. Here, multiple, shifting mirrors are the theatrical machinations used by the witch-doctor Sinkoun Tiguidé Camara to bring about Yacine Ndiaye's transformation from a black woman into a white woman. The way the author suffuses both dialog and drama—the mirrors, the comings and goings, the opening and shutting of curtains and doors—with his own personal brand of acerbic black humor and sense of the surreal, is masterful. It is a passage that deserves to be acknowledged as one of the great metamorphosis scenes of world literature on a par with Kafka's.[23]

These examples are ample proof that the simplicity of form and austerity of style that mark *Murambi, the Book of Bones,* have been left behind and that Diop is once again making full use of his creative skills. But, as the Senegalese scholar Ibrahima Wane has observed, post-Rwanda, Diop's words "have a different ring to them, and he appears to be more vigilant and demanding with himself."[24]

As if wanting to compensate the reader for the seriousness of what has gone before, the narrator opens *Notebook 4,* the story of *Ninki-Nanka, a Fiction* with the announcement to Badou that he wanted to amuse himself a little and that "nothing you read about here has actually happened." Almost overnight, Nguirane Faye, who started out as a mere diarist or "minor scribbler," has become a writer of fiction.

With its talking monkeys and the cardboard characters Dibi-Dibi and Commander Zero, *Ninki-Nanka* initially comes across as completely fantastical, but on second glance, it reveals itself as a sharply critical commentary on colonization and the senseless civil wars that afflict African countries at regular intervals. As in Part Two, where Ali Kaboye tells "the most improbable and therefore the most truthful part of the story," there is a great deal of truth in the surreal plot of this chapter, which, by being placed at the center of Part One, creates a cesura, an exact symmetry in the book.

Part fable, part political satire, *Notebook 4* is the story of Atou Seck. The town of Gouye-Guewel is the epicenter of a seemingly interminable civil war between Dibi-Dibi and Commander Zero, and Atou Seck is the last remaining inhabitant who hasn't fled. The narrator remarks that

> it is not the first time that Atou has felt sympathy for the victims of catastrophes like this one who don't even get the chance to find out *who is coming to kill them or for what reason exactly* they have to go through such excruciating suffering and die.

Why, one might ask, this portrayal of such a generic civil war, where "nobody knows exactly how many armed factions are attacking each other or who is fighting whom"? Unlike in Rwanda, where the massacres started after an explosion, and a flash of light in the night sky signaled a deadly plane crash, Dibi-Dibi's war begins almost imperceptibly with a harmless student protest.

The most plausible answer to this is the fact that Rwanda was a cataclysmic event, hopefully never to be repeated, whereas wars like Dibi-Dibi's are seemingly endless; they smolder on and on, in several countries at any one time.

The story zooms in on a single victim, describing the individual suffering caused by each one of these senseless, arbitrary conflicts. Every such outbreak of violence destroys too many lives like Atou Seck's, while the perpetrators remain unscathed.

With its animals acting like humans, and its burning political relevance, *Ninki-Nanka* resembles George Orwell's allegorical, dystopian novella *Animal Farm* (1945). Closer to home, it brings to mind Cheik Aliou Ndao's Wolof novel *Mbaam aakimoo* (1997), the story of an unidentified African nation that gets rid of a ruthless dictator by asking a witchdoctor to transform the dictator into a mute donkey.

In *Ninki-Nanka*, the eponymous she-ape—the mirror image of Yacine Ndiaye—deposits her two young in the courtyard of Atou Seck, Nguirane Faye's doppelgänger. To complete the picture, Yacine's children Mbissine and Mbissane are mirrored by the two little monkeys, affectionately called Ninki and Nanka by Atou Seck. To start with, he thinks the monkey-mother has brought back his grandchildren, who, together with the rest of his family, have perished in the civil war. But when they turn into his captors, he discovers their sadistic tendencies. They expel him from his house, tie him up with a rope, humiliate him and force him to starve while they are living like kings. In essence, they do to Atou Seck as the colonizer did to Africans.

While working on *Les petits,* the author decided to interpolate the tale of "Baboon on the Rock of Gibraltar," which is absent in the Wolof version. Here, the versatile monkey is not a generic representation of the colonizer but impersonates black Africans. Inserted into the plot as Atou Seck's dream, the Gibraltar story gives Baboon the chance to treat his friend Rodrigo Mancera to a thumbnail sketch of the ravages of colonial history, reminding him of the Spanish conquista, the Massacre at Wounded Knee, the Algerian War of Independence and more. Rodrigo is the typical "non-racist" *Toubab*, full of the usual prejudices about blacks.

When Baboon launches into his fable about Lion and the Monkey Army, the whole of *Notebook 4* reveals itself as a hall of mirrors. However, it would be a mistake to think that fables and miraculous events told in the manner of magical realism are restricted to this notebook only.

When making provisions for his imminent death, Nguirane Faye appoints Ali Kaboye, a vagrant lunatic, as his successor. By the end of Part One, Ali Kaboye has been killed and come back to life twice, and by the time he takes over as narrator after Nguirane Faye's death, he has undergone a remarkable rebirth. The ragged, smelly vagrant reappears as a vociferous, omniscient, but invisible sage in Part Two.[25]

In the manner of the oral tradition, both Nguirane Faye and Ali Kaboye constantly instruct, criticize, and hold up real and imaginary mirrors to their audience. This differs sharply from the equalizing, democratic approach of modernist and postmodern literature with its polyphonic narration, reminding us that in a society where a large proportion of the population is illiterate, the storyteller enjoys a certain status and authority.

After the catastrophic events in Rwanda, the author's priority is to create a stable framework for his novel. This he achieves by means of the two narrators who don't alternate but each narrate one of the two parts of the book, addressing a known and named audience in the form of Badou, Nguirane's grandson.

Nguirane Faye is an old man; like Mansour Tall in *Les traces de la meute* (1993), he no longer has anything to hide and promises to get to the bottom of things.[26] This makes him a reliable source of information.

In his essay "The Storyteller," Walter Benjamin (1895–1941) states that it is the natural authority of an old man close to dying that stands at the beginning of the storytelling tradition:

> So it is that in a man who is dying, more than anywhere else, not only his knowledge or his wisdom takes shape, but first and foremost the life he has lived, because that's the raw material that stories are made of.[27]

Ali Kaboye shouts out his admonitions and reprimands not only to Badou but to the whole of Niarela. Unlike Nguirane Faye, Ali Kaboye is a larger than life character who is immortal and omniscient, "precisely like a storyteller."[28]

The true nature of Part Two is never revealed, but if it is indeed the seventh *Notebook* or *The Book of Secrets,* Ali Kaboye has to be understood as a figment of Nguirane Faye's imagination. This, in turn, makes the latter the one and only narrative voice in *Doomi Golo.*

By addressing Badou, who has secretly left the country and functions as his clearly defined audience, Nguirane restores—at least unilaterally—the ancestral narrative pact. Thanks to the fictitious scenes of dialogue with Badou, as in the tea ceremony in *Notebook 3*, the narrator can assume that his audience has said *Lepoon*.

For Nguirane Faye, writing his own life story and interweaving it with the many digressions, reveries and ruminations that make up *Doomi Golo* means getting ready to confront his own death. As Francesca Paraboschi states with reference to Lat-Sukabé in *The Knight*, "To prepare himself for this last journey, he has to submit to the arduous task of reconstructing his personal past . . . and to accept the full weight of his cultural identity."[29]

The idea that the act of writing helps the writer come to a deeper understanding of him or herself and thereby construct his or her own identity, is discussed in *Une si longue lettre* (1980), the epistolary novel for which the Senegalese novelist Mariama Bâ (1929–1981) became the first recipient of the Noma Award.[30]

Within the first three *Notebooks*, Nguirane's self-assessment changes from the lighthearted optimism of the opening pages to a deeply probing and rather despondent mood later on. Having introduced himself as "one of the most popular dancers of my time," "a fiendish womanizer," and someone with the confidence to claim that "all in all, I have lived a good life," in *Playing in the Dark*, he wistfully draws the conclusion that his life was a series of "lost battles and faded hopes" that are making him feel "like a hollow gourd swept away by the waves."

This is the point in the novel where, after the sudden appearance of a cat whose gaze has unsettled him, he starts questioning who he, "the man by the name Nguirane Faye," really is. He realizes that the sum total of what he knows about his own and his family history is negligible, and that the political activism in a workers' union that took him all the way to Ghana to petition support from president Kwame Nkrumah has come to naught.

In his state of aporia, he sets off on a trip to Mbering-Saaj, his native village. The end result of this difficult journey is that instead of finding his ancestor's grave, as he had hoped, he learns that ultimately, our own actions count for more than an illustrious pedigree. While he is daydreaming on the bus, Mame Ngor, the ancestor, appears to him and says: "Let those people talk, Nguirane. Just be aware that every single word that comes out of their mouth is a lie. The truth is this: if I am your ancestor, it is because you yourself have given birth to me."

To his consternation, the village seems deserted, and the inhabitants are anything but welcoming. After staggering around in the local cemetery in vain, he is forced to spend the night out in the open. Eventually, an old man joins him and announces that he has brought him a gift: "nothing that would weigh heavily upon your shoulders, Nguirane . . . [just] some words."

In the monologue that follows, the man explains the reason for the villagers' reticence; too often before have they welcomed strangers with open arms and ended up paying a heavy price for their hospitality.

Mame Ngor, Nguirane Faye's putative ancestor, is the prototype of any stranger-cum-colonizer and could therefore have been either an eleventh-century Islamic invader or someone from a neighboring town. All of these strangers, as the man points out, came with "prophecies" and "doctrines" they were peddling as The Path leading to the Truth. All too often they demanded with brutal force that the locals adopt them. In the course of the old man's speech, Mame Ngor temporarily takes on the features of Daaw Demba, a cruel despot and former ruler of the Cayor, but he also speaks in a "weird, incomprehensible language." This blurs the line between foreign invaders and locals, and conveys the message that the issue is not as clear-cut as it seems.

Not only is Badou warned against falling prey to false prophets but Nguirane also dismisses scientists' attempts to unravel the mysteries of "the earliest hours of humanity," implying that their speculations cannot be but false information and misrepresentation of the truth.

The question *What is truth?* has become much more urgent for Boris Diop since Rwanda. Initially, in the passage about Nguirane Faye's love for the written word, it is presented in a predominantly esthetic light. Without the "make-believe of signs and symbols," he states in *The Tale of the Ashes*, "there would be no truth on this earth, neither good nor bad." Subsequently, however, much of the debate about truth and falsehood carries ethical overtones.

Nguirane's final message to Badou before he dies is the strongly allegorical discourse about Truth, alias "the Miracle-Maker," in his constant battle against the Lie, "the favorite weapon of the Evil One." The narrator tells Badou: "I consider it my duty to protect you against the Evil One. Yes . . . I'm talking about the Evil One. Cheytan." Cheytan is Arabic for "evil demon," or "Satan." This passage in *Notebook 3* harks back to Birago Diop's short story "Vérité et mensonge" in the collection *Contes d'Amadou Koumba* (1961), where Truth personified, due to his sense of moral superiority, becomes haughty and arrogant, even corrupt. One very important lesson not only Badou but everybody needs to learn is that not many of the so-called "Truth-Tellers" are free of ulterior motives, and as so often before in *Doomi Golo*, the lines between binary opposites such as good and evil, truth and lie, black and white, local and foreigner, are blurred.

If they weren't, everything would be much less difficult. Through the narrator(s), who act as his mouthpiece, the author is more outspoken in this novel than before, without ever being simplistic. The stance he wants his reader to adopt is that of the Kierkegaardian existentialist—instead of remaining comfortably perched on the fence for all eternity, the existentialist is encouraged to reflect carefully before he acts, but act he must, and this is how, just like the writer by writing, he creates his own identity.

In *Africa beyond the Mirror*, Diop has made the following statement: "When I write in Wolof, more than anything, it makes me feel that I am taking my place in an emerging national literature. And when I compare my earlier novels to *Doomi Golo*, I realize now that the words of "the Other" helped me articulate as much as they reduced me to silence or a pathetic stammer."[31]

The same article re-articulates Cheikh Anta Diop's suggestion that "Franco-African literature may well only represent a brief period of transition in a more complex historical trajectory."[32]

Boris Diop took the "painful, difficult, ambiguous decision" to write in his own language, perfectly aware he was essentially writing for a future audience.[33] Since unlike Ousmane Sembène, he remained faithful to fiction writing, he tried to give the contemporary, largely illiterate, Wolof audience access to *Doomi Golo* by turning it into an audio book, re-oralizing it in a way.[34]

"Text shifts as it is translated," Kathryn Batchelor writes in *Decolonizing Translation* (2009). "The translated text is not, and never can be, simply the original text in another language; rather, the shift in language engenders a new text, usually strongly related to the original, but nevertheless a distinctly different entity."[35]

This is particularly true for Afrophone fiction that is translated into a European language and vice versa, first and foremost because each new version in a specific language is aimed at a different audience. That it is vastly easier to translate from French into English than it is to translate from Wolof to French is obvious. In the former language combination, "the sounds are the same," Diop explains, and "the cultural codes are harmoniously in tune with each other." Translating *Doomi Golo* from Wolof into French, however, was a challenge, he continues, since he had to "create correspondences between two radically different conceptual worlds."[36]

The opening passage of the book, the traditional farewell ritual after there has been a death in the family, shows how difficult this really was. The three words in the Wolof version—"Addina. Dund. Dee." (Down here. To live. To die.)—are a kind of shorthand; every Senegalese will automatically fill in the dots, "the silence that follows, the sudden gravity of the atmosphere, and that moment where everyone, whether he likes it or not, seems to recall the extraordinary precariousness of human existence."[37] When writing *Les petits,* the author-translator had to fill nearly two pages to explain this "shared meaning" and thus make it accessible for a Western readership.

By comparison, the transition from *Les petits* to *Doomi Golo—The Hidden Notebooks* was much more straightforward. It was simply a question of finding the *"mot juste,"* that is, of not deforming the text, of welcoming "the Foreign in all its foreignness," and not betraying its Alterity, as the French translation theorist Antoine Berman postulated.[38]

African authors have used a variety of strategies in the attempt to subvert the "foreign language" they had imposed upon them. The Ivorian writer Ahmadou Kourouma (1927–2003), who received the Grand prix littéraire d'Afrique noire for his novel *Les Soleils des Indépendances* (1968), became famous—or perhaps rather notorious—for inventing "his own French" by rejecting grammatical norms and suffusing and enriching it "with the rhythms of his vernacular Malinké." Boris Diop criticized Kourouma harshly, calling his linguistic experiment "the refusal to submit to any sort of restriction [of style]," suggesting that instead of being "innovative, or even subversive, ['the Kourouma model'] was born out of inadequacy." While the Africanization of English has become a frequent, perfectly legitimate phenomenon, Boris Diop did not want to see this happening to French out of fear that it might become even more deeply entrenched in the Francophone countries, rather than just being "a tool that history has *temporarily* imposed upon us."[39]

For this reason, and presumably also because in linguistic matters he is a purist, Diop is not in favor of creolization. To ensure that *Les petits* remained a recognizable palimpsest of *Doomi Golo,* its original avatar, he had to use other methods.[40] Besides the close links, not only to the griots of the oral tradition but also to the ancient Arab scribes, who were compilers of chronicles, there are frequent "visible traces" of the Wolof language and culture in this novel.[41]

At the very beginning of *Notebook 1,* Nguirane Faye quotes two verses of a popular Wolof song, which is not translated but casually paraphrased later on in the same paragraph. In *Notebook 5*, in the passage about Senegalese wrestling, we equally find some untranslated Wolof expressions and turns of phrase.

By contrast, all the proverbs in *Les petits* appear in translation. They are always italicized, and therefore count as "traces within traces." The same goes for the excerpts from the writings of the Sufi poets Serigne Mbaye Diakhaté (1875–1954) and Moussa Kâ (1895–1926). These passages form a direct intertextual connection between *Doomi Golo* and the older West African literary canon in the Arabic script, also known as *ajami*.

Terms denoting items from everyday life, such as *cere baasi, fonde, tengaade, kel,* and *turki,* occur in the text as untranslated visible traces. While they were left standing in *Les petits,* in *Doomi Golo—The Hidden Notebooks* they are listed and explained in a glossary that has been attached at the end.[42]

Visible traces not only occur within the novels but can also be found within the titles of the novels themselves. *Les petits de la guenon* is a straight translation of the Wolof title into French and can be rendered as "The She-Ape and her Young" or, more literally still, "The Offspring of the She-Ape," meaning that in this case, the title has been completely "domesticated," and no visible trace of its Wolof origins remains.

Not so in the English version; *Doomi Golo—The Hidden Notebooks* is a mixed-language title where the foreignizing Wolof element has been restored and para-tactically linked to a short explanatory clause in English, allowing the text to orient itself "towards a Western readership whilst simultaneously affirming [its] Senegalese . . . identity."[43]

Foreignization, or at least a more judicious approach to the inevitable domestication of a foreign language text, is an indispensable tool in tempering, or even annihilating, the hegemonic, exclusionary "linguistic imperialism" of the past.

One of the hazards translators have to grapple with are well-meaning but poorly briefed copyeditors who will do everything they can to re-domesticate a carefully primed text. A thorough copyeditor will attempt to wipe out every "visible trace" in the interest of the reader, totally unaware of the importance of these intentional ambiguities.

By "welcoming the Foreign in all its foreignness" the practice of translation must become more hospitable, states Berman, also stressing the moral aspect of this important activity.

Having annexed and appropriated nearly the whole of Africa, the West initially dismissed its languages as minor and irrelevant. Although this has changed, similarly to Badou and the Hidden *Notebooks*, it has taken the outside world decades to unearth the hidden treasures that constitute African and particularly West African literature in this case. With the invaluable help of my co-translator El Hadji Moustapha Diop and the author himself, I have tried to produce a new hybrid of *Doomi Golo* that, while being a recognizable descendant of its Wolof-French ancestry, is vigorous enough to fly with its own wings and continue its odyssey that began in 2003 with the publication of *Doomi Golo*.[44]

NOTES

Unless otherwise stated, all translations from French are my own.

1. Boubacar Boris Diop, *Doomi Golo* (Dakar, Senegal: Éditions Papyrus, 2003).
2. Nasrin Qader, Foreword to Boubacar Boris Diop's *The Knight and His Shadow*, trans. Alan Furness (East Lansing: Michigan State University Press, 2014), vi (from the original *Le cavalier et son ombre*, 1997).
3. Boubacar Boris Diop, *Les petits de la guenon* (Paris: Éditions Philippe Rey, 2009).
4. Cullen Goldblatt, "Lëndëmtu: Réflexions sur Doomi Golo et Les Petits de la Guenon," in *Des mondes et des langues, L'*écriture de Boub*acar Boris Diop* (Paris: Présence Africaine, 2014), 66.
5. Africa's 100 Best Books of the 20th Century is a list conceived by Ali Mazrui at the 1998 Zimbabwe International Bookfair. *Murambi, le livre des ossements* (Paris: Éditions Stock, 2000) is now in its second edition, which includes an added afterword by the author (Paris: Éditions Zulma, 2011). The English translation by Fiona Mc Laughlin, *Murambi, the Book of Bones* (Bloomington: Indiana University Press, 2006) is currently being re-edited with the afterword. *Murambi* has also been translated into Italian, Spanish and Slovenian; adapted for the stage with performances in France and Senegal; and incorporated into a play about Rwanda called "Hagati Yacu/Entre Nous" (Uz et Coutumes). In collaboration with Kota Yamasaki from Japan, the Senegalese choreographer Germaine Acogny turned it into a ballet, *Fagaala,* first performed in California in 2004, and followed by several world tours.
6. Boubacar Boris Diop, *Les tambours de la mémoire* (Paris: Nathan, 1987).

7. Short-stories: *La nuit de l'Imoko* (Saint-Louis, Senegal: Éditions Xamal, 2000), a collection; others have been published separately elsewhere. Plays: *Thiaroye, terre rouge* (1980); *Grandakar-Usine,* with Oumar Ndao (unpublished); *Ibu Ndaw, boroom jamono,* in Wolof. Screenplays: *Une si longue lettre,* by Mariama Bâ, with Angele Diabang; *Fowukaay* (Best Humorous Movie Award at the festival in Oberhausen, Germany); *Le prix du pardon,* by Mansour Wade (Carthage: Tanit d'Or, 2002); *Un amour d'enfant; Les feux de Mansaré* Opera: *Leena* (2010).

8. Boubacar Boris Diop, *L'Afrique au delà du miroir* (Paris: Philippe Rey, 2007); Boubacar Boris Diop, *Africa beyond the Mirror,* tr. by Vera Wülfing-Leckie (Banbury: Ayebia Clarke Publishing, 2014).

9. Interview with Jasmina Šopova, "Les langues, ça compte," in *Le Courrier de l'UNESCO* no. 1 (2008):3.

10. Boubacar Boris Diop, *Africa beyond the Mirror,* 117.

11. At the "Conference of African Writers of English Expression" at University College in Kampala in 1962, Ngũgĩ wa Thiongo protested that the conference automatically excluded those who write in African languages. He sparked off a discussion that prompted him to start writing in Gikuyu, his mother tongue. In *Decolonizing the Mind* (1986), the Kenyan novelist declared his "Farewell to English."

12. Cheikh Anta Diop, *Nations nègres et culture* (Paris: Présence Africaine, 1954).

13. Aimé Césaire, *Discours sur le colonialisme,* (Paris: Présence Africaine, 1955), 41.

14. Leopold Sedar Senghor (1906–2001), Senegal's first president from 1960–1980.

15. The essay "Senegal between Cheikh Anta Diop and Leopold Sedar Senghor" in *Africa beyond the Mirror* provides interesting background information on these two key Senegalese personalities.

16. Frantz Fanon (1925–1961), *Peau noire, masques blancs* (Paris:Éditions du Seuil, 1952), 81, 139.

17. "Le français n'est pas mon destin" (French is not my destiny), a conversation by Taina Tervonen with Boubacar Boris Diop, October 2003, www.africultures. com.

18. Diop, *Africa beyond the Mirror,* 10

19. Boubacar Boris Diop, *The Knight and His Shadow* (East Lansing: Michigan State University Press, 2015).

20. Charles Sugnet, *Des mondes et des langues, L'écriture de Boubacar Boris Diop* (Paris: Présence Africaine, 2014), 166

21. Jean Sob, *L'Impératif romanesque de Boubacar Boris Diop* (Paris: Éditions A3, 2007).

22. The Murambi Genocide Memorial Centre website on Wikipedia explains: "On

April 16, 1994, . . . after the victims were told to gather [at the Murambi Technical School], water was cut off and no food was available, so that the people were too weak to resist . . . the Tutsi were overrun on April 21. The French soldiers disappeared and the school was attacked by Hutu Interahamwe militiamen." After some 45,000 Tutsi were murdered at the school, "the French brought in heavy equipment to dig several pits where many thousands of bodies were placed." But Through a Glass Darkly (www.genocidememorials.org), describes more specifically what must have inspired the images thrown up by the big mirror: "on the occasion of the second anniversary of the genocide, when the mass graves . . . were opened, the remains of some 5,000 victims were exhumed and hundreds of intact skeletons (many frozen in the positions in which they met their gruesome fates) laid out in dozens of the school's classrooms."

23. See Franz Kafka's novella *Metamorphosis,* originally *Die Verwandlung* (1915).

24. Ibrahima Wane, "Du français au wolof: la quête du récit chez Boubacar Boris Diop," Éthiopiques 73 (2004):10.

25. In *Des mondes et des langues, L'*écriture de Boub*acar Boris Diop* (Paris: Présence Africaine 2014), 59, Souleymane Bachir Diagne writes: "Ali Kaboye [is] a strange fellow who transforms himself from an insignificant, simple fool in the first part into an 'individual with superior knowledge' (un individu supposé savoir), to use an expression coined by Michel Foucault. He stands out because he knows everything about everybody and due to his strange ubiquity, has all the specific features which characterize the storyteller."

26. Boris Diop, *Les traces de la meute* (Paris: L'Harmattan, 1993).

27. Walter Benjamin, "The Storyteller," in *The Novel: An Anthology of Criticism and Theory 1900–2000,* edited by Dorothy J. Hale. (Malden, Mass.: Blackwell Publishing, 2006), 369.

28. Souleymane Bachir Diagne in *Des mondes et des langues, L'*écriture de Boub*acar Boris Diop* (Paris: Présence Africaine 2014), 54

29. Francesca Paraboschi, in *Des mondes et des langues, L'*écriture de Boub*acar Boris Diop* (Paris: Présence Africaine, 2014), 137.

30. Mariama Bâ, *Une si longue lettre* (La Madeleine-De-Nonancourt: Le Serpent à Plumes, 1979).

31. Diop, *Africa beyond the Mirror,* 117.

32. Ibid.

33. Www.africultures.com, "La langue en question," Interview with Virginie Andiamirado in cooperation with Alain and Bérénice Ricard, 6 December 2007.

34. Work on what subsequently became the *Doomi Golo* audiobook (ebook-africa. com, Joseph Gaï Ramaka), started in 2007. It took Boris Diop three weeks to make the recording in his own voice. It is very disappointing indeed that due to technical problems, this ebook is currently no longer available. It is our sincere hope that this situation will be remedied in the near future.

35. Kathryn Batchelor, *Decolonizing Translation: Francophone African Novels in English Translation* (New York: Routledge, 2014), 1.

36. Boubacar Boris Diop, "Écrire entre deux langues. De Doomi Golo aux Petits de la Guenon," *Repères DoRif* n.2 Voix/voies excentriques: la langue française face à l'altérité—volet n.1—novembre 2012—Les Francophonies et Francographies Africaines face à la référence culturelle française, November 2012.

37. Ibid.

38. Robert Maggiori, "A. Berman, L'Âge de la traduction. "La tâche du traducteur" de Walter Benjamin, un commentaire," on Fabula, La Recherche en littérature , 30 November 2008.

39. Diop, *Africa beyond the Mirror,* 114.

40. Chantal Zabus, author of *African Palimpsest: Indigenization of Language in the West African Europhone Novel* (Atlanta: Rodopi, 2007), uses the palimpsest metaphor. A palimpsest is an inscribed surface from which "the original writing . . . has been effaced to make room for a second [and/or third] . . . [West African texts] are indeed palimpsests in that, behind the scriptural authority of the European language, the earlier, imperfectly erased remnants of the African language can still be perceived" (3).

41. In *Decolonizing Translation,* Kathryn Batchelor defines "visible traces" as "direct borrowings of African-language words by the main language of narration . . . In her study of indigenization of language in West African Anglophone and Francophone texts, Chantal Zabus . . . terms such borrowings "visible traces," stating that "visible" African words, phrases, and, at times, whole sentences seep through the cracks and crannies of the Europhone narrative" (49).

42. Glossaries, introductions, endnotes and other paratextual additions "shift the book away from fiction and towards factual writing and represent a marked contrast to the presentation of the original text," Kathryn Batchelor cautions in *Decolonizing Translation* (13).

43. Batchelor, *Decolonizing Translation,* 50.

44. Boubacar Boris Diop, "Écrire entre deux langues. De Doomi Golo aux Petits de la Guenon, " on Do.Ri.F. Università.

DOOMI GOLO

The Hidden Notebooks

CONTENTS

PART 1

NGUIRANE FAYE

Shame on the nation that doesn't listen to its little girls . . .

THE TALE OF THE ASHES

FOR GENERATIONS, THE FAREWELL RITUAL IN OUR FAMILY HAS REMAINED the same: one by one, we enter the room where the dearly departed has been laid out on a mat, and there we each say our silent prayers for the peace of his soul. The faces are grave and the bodies solemn, as befits the occasion. But almost without fail there will be someone—often the closest friend of the one who has passed away—more devastated than the rest, and he will try to brighten up the atmosphere a little. He will gently tease the deceased who thought it so clever to make a quick getaway from our trivial worries here on earth. And he will tell him, "You are mistaken, old chap, if you think it's all over between you and me. I am never going to leave you in peace. I'm already on my way, in fact, and I promise I will give you so much hell in heaven that you'll regret ever having gone there!" And when he implores him to keep a cozy little spot for him in Paradise, some of the others manage to flash a quick smile, gone in an instant.

Such moments are precious, Badou.

We do need to remind ourselves from time to time that life isn't really such a big deal, even if we all make a huge fuss about it, this flickering little flame that the wind can snuff out at any moment.

But don't get me wrong: I haven't opened the first of my seven *Notebooks* with these slightly somber, doleful words to fill you with disgust for life.

It's quite the opposite. When it comes to living life, I, for one, have never been shy.

Right now, for example, as I write these lines to you, a piece of music that was very popular some sixty years ago is rising up in my memory. *Àddina amul solo ndeysaan / Ku ci dee yaa ñàkk sa bakkan ndeysaan.* And so it went on, this joyous and exuberant song, so rich in its flamboyant colors, if I can put it like that. It's about the time we spend on this earth, about these days and nights, so empty and uncertain that one has to be really dumb to put up with dying in the end without even having been happy! We really loved that tune. And then there were the pachangas . . . In those days, we used to play a lot of Cuban music at our soirées in the Plateau district. Sizzling hot it was, and the drink was flowing. I can still see us all, a mass of wriggling bodies under a sweltering and dusty hangar. Imagine dozens of girls and boys gyrating like crazy lunatics and making enough noise to drown out the tumbas and the maracas!

I was—and I say this in all modesty—one of the most popular dancers of my time and, I must confess, a fiendish womanizer. Girls were always chitchatting about me, and the name Nguirane Faye was on their lips from sunrise to sunset. Yes, there were certain young ladies, slightly older than myself, who hadn't remained entirely indifferent to me. They never missed a chance to badger me in the street, "Hey, Nguirane, you're such a show-off! Who do you think you are? May the Almighty fling you into the flames of Hell!"

I wasn't lost for words, I assure you, and when I was certain we were out of earshot I would notify the naughty lady I was going to make her clitoris sing loud and clear, adding, "You'll love that kind of music, hehe!" Then she would cover her mouth with her hand in mock indignation, calling on all the saints in Heaven.

Yes, we were the Niarela Boys! Everyone knew our little gang of hooligans. We used to go completely wild from time to time.

I had my heroes, of course, such as Grand Makhou—you will come across him again later on in these *Notebooks*. But adults, quite frankly, I didn't really trust them. All they ever did was give advice or orders. Seriously, that was all they were capable of doing, giving advice and issuing orders. Such a path was a bit too narrow for a young man who had fallen in love with freedom; you quite simply couldn't get away from it, and you couldn't just say to them, "Hey listen, hold on a moment, I don't agree!" which ought to be the easiest thing in the world. If you just wanted to have a normal conversation with these people, it never worked. They hardly ever agreed among themselves and I thought they wanted to hoodwink me, not only regarding the small, petty things in life, but also when we started talking about God, Destiny and the Speed of Light. They invariably got caught up in endless contradictions, something I actually found quite amusing.

I was then, roughly like you are now, in my late twenties. If you read these seven *Notebooks*, you will see that I haven't been keeping my mouth shut later on either.

So, all in all, I have lived a good life, and I wouldn't hold it against you if you did the same.

Now I am old and quietly waiting for the end, right here in the courtyard of our house in this part of Niarela you know so well.

I'm not in perfect health, that I know—and how could I be at the age of nearly eighty?—but I am pleased to say that so far at least, my body is not a total wreck. I certainly don't relish the thought of becoming completely decrepit.

And you, Badou, the child of my deceased son, are now the focus of my life.

Sometimes I close my eyes, trying to guess at least the name of the country where you are living now. But I always give up very quickly. It's so frustrating not even to have a vague idea.

Which sunrays caress your eyelids when you wake up in the morning, Badou Tall? Your friends in the area initially reacted very badly to the news that you had simply gone abroad one day, just like that, without saying a word. So I told them that even your mother Bigué Samb and I didn't know which country you went to after leaving Niarela. That calmed them down a little bit. They all shook their heads: *That his mother Bigué didn't know, that we can believe! But you, Nguirane . . . you were so close, you two . . . How could he . . . ?*

I am not sure what to reply to them, to be quite honest. Here in Niarela, people were never really able to work you out. We are simple folk, we stick together when the going gets tough, and we don't have a lot of time for those who make a big song and dance about things. But you used to be so reserved that some people decided you were selfish and arrogant. You may have been taciturn, secretive even, but you never hesitated to help those in need. To this day, people in Niarela haven't stopped talking to me about your integrity and your spirit of sacrifice. In order to help your mother Bigué Samb and me survive, you took on the sort of menial jobs most of your mates would have found humiliating. The girls here in Niarela have of course always been keener on young men who sit in air conditioned offices with two or three telephones positioned very visibly in front of them. They were brazen enough to make up horribly callous songs to tease you, these women, but you didn't seem to mind. Maybe it was your dream, too, to become a civil servant or an engineer one day. You never had the chance to go to university, and you weren't ashamed of washing cars at a petrol station in Ouagou-Niayes or working as a street-hawker on the big HLM market.

And now there are those who claim you have traveled east. Rumor has it that you are in Algeria, in Morocco, or perhaps even further away—in Lebanon. Everybody here is dreaming up places where you may be living in exile, without rhyme or reason. The other day, one of them actually had the audacity to say, "Mark my words, everybody! Badou Tall has answered the call of the blood. We all know blood is thicker than water. Sooner or later, someone will come and tell us he has seen this boy in France. Badou has followed in the footsteps of his father Assane Tall who passed away in Marseille! And on the day when we hear this news, don't forget that I was the one who said it first!"

Wherever you are, the only thing that really matters is that you are feeling well there. Someone with your degree of courage and staying power deserves a dignified existence. You are not the kind of person who would settle in a place where you're not wanted. And if there is one thing no one has even the slightest doubt about in Niarela, it is that one day, sooner or later, you will come back here to take your rightful place among us.

I, alas, shall no longer be on this earth by then. The thought that we will never see each other again is very hard for me to bear, I can't deny it. That is the reason why, for some time now, I have been talking to you so much through my *Notebooks*. Everything I write there is addressed to you. Initially, I merely wanted to compile a chronicle of everyday life in Niarela for you. You know, everybody here thinks I'm talking gibberish and that I am probably going senile. As a result, they're not really paying attention to me and they forget to put on their usual masks when I am around. When you are a man of nearly a hundred you barely count for more than a newborn baby in a cradle. That allows me to observe without being seen and to eavesdrop everywhere. And I pass it all on to you, so that when, on your return, you read through everything, it's as though you had never left Niarela.

There was just one small problem, quite difficult to resolve for an aged novice writer like myself. Since I cannot count myself among the famous poets our nation is so proud of—names like Serigne Moussa Kâ, Mabo Guissé or Cheik Aliou Ndao—I have felt totally at sea when, as the weeks went by, other events somehow demanded to be told as well. If I had to express myself in images, I might say they were banging on the door and making a hell of a noise, while at the same time trying to jump onto the pages of my *Notebooks* and staking their claim to a place in there. The end result was a huge shambles. Out of sheer battle-weariness, and undoubtedly once again due to my lack of experience, I decided to give in and let them have the last word.

One of these *Notebooks* I have called *The Book of Secrets*, and that is the one to which I would like to draw your special attention. You will easily recognize it by its red cover. There, I reveal things that must only be known to you and me, things that can often be downright embarrassing. Sometimes I feel like tossing those pages straight into the fire. What they contain isn't pretty, far from it—it's pure, unmitigated hatred, jealousy and slander, a snapshot of unadulterated life in the raw, if you like. I have heard neighbors malign you—you, who are so gentle—and I have repeated their malicious words back to you. I think I know you well enough to trust that you won't get too worked up about my silly gossip. You must watch out, when the time comes, that *The Book of Secrets* doesn't fall into the wrong hands. It could sow discord in Niarela.

I would have preferred to talk to you face-to-face, of course, like any storyteller worthy of that name. Then I could have made your heart beat faster and challenged you with my perplexing riddles. You would have had to look for clues buried deep under the ocean and spend many nights patiently searching for them to unlock their secrets.

But, I am writing to you, since that's my only option. I must confess that without that, I wouldn't give a damn whether I was alive or dead.

．　　．　　．

It was on a Thursday, if my memory doesn't deceive me. We were back from the airport with the mortal remains of your father, Assane Tall, who had died in Marseille a few days earlier. After the corpse was prepared for burial, Imam Keita invited you to go and say a final prayer before the body. You simply shook your head and declined, and immediately everybody started staring at you.

Something like this was unheard of in Niarela, but no one made any comment. You somehow seemed so different from everyone else that people were always slightly unsure of you. News of the incident spread like wildfire, and a few minutes later, Ndeye Sylla planted herself in front of you with her massive body and said emphatically, but without raising her voice, "Badou Tall, there is no need for you to try so hard to convince us that you're not an ordinary human being like the rest of us. Now go and explain yourself to Imam Keita."

Everyone in the tents was eager to see how you would react. In your usual taciturn manner, you simply reiterated your refusal by gently shaking your head again.

Someone came up to me and complained, "Nguirane, this time, your grandson has really gone too far. Go and tell him that he simply won't get away with this. You are the one and only person he has always listened to."

I don't even remember who said this to me, but my reply was, "Just give Badou Tall a break, will you? If you don't know why he is behaving like this, then he certainly does."

Ndeye Sylla erupted, "I, Ndeye Sylla, am telling you that this boy is going straight to Hell! Who does he think he is, your Badou Tall? How can you let him publicly humiliate his father on a day like this?"

That was enough; now it was my turn, and I yelled back at Ndeye Sylla, "You are just a simple mortal, Ndeye, you can't send anybody to Hell! Badou Tall may be young, but I know him better than the whole lot of you, and I have never seen him do anything without good reason!"

But between you and me, Badou, I have to admit that even though I did my best to excuse your behavior that day, I was just as baffled as everyone else. Even I couldn't understand what this was all about. When it runs that deep, a son's hatred for his father becomes quite simply intolerable. And yet, when I think of that scene, which I do now and again, I feel you were right. After all, they asked you to go and look at your father, Assane Tall, for the first and the last time in your life, half an hour before he was to be taken to the cemetery ˜ That really didn't make much sense.

This incident, I think, reminded all the friends and relatives present that our family has never quite fitted the mold.

Of course nobody had any idea at that point that your father's death would—years later—cause such serious trouble in Niarela and that it would even, in some way, shake up the entire country.

You were already abroad by then, which is why I am going to go now, to write a chronicle of these rather unusual events for you.

.   ■   ■

Visitors had to walk across a sandy courtyard and take a seat on the small veranda that served as a waiting room. Mbaye Lô, our master of Koranic studies, would then receive them in the dimly lit room where he lived like a recluse. People came from all over the country to seek his advice and his prayers, and he graciously obliged in exchange for a few coins, or a handful of biscuits. He used to spread out these offerings in front of him to show his gratitude, but we all knew that he didn't really care about the money. He was a man of great austerity who fasted for a large part of the year. Despite my tender age—I was five or six years old at the time—I understood perfectly that Mbaye Lô was unlike—actually *very* unlike—any of the other adults.

I just didn't know exactly why I found him so special.

Day after day, he opened our young hearts to the Word of the One and Only God. We would form a semicircle around him, and while I was reciting verses from the Koran with my classmates, I watched him out of the corner of my eye. Although he was prematurely aged and slightly hunchbacked, Mbaye Lô's face was smooth and handsome. He always wore the same caftan, which must originally have been dark brown but was now so faded that the color had turned into a murky café au lait. He was probably not in the habit of spending his nights on his bed, because that was cluttered up with all sorts of objects, including pages from notebooks covered in Arabic texts he had copied out in his own hand. It happened that mice came out of their holes and scampered around between our legs before taking refuge under the bed, and whenever Mbaye Lô had squashed a cockroach with an old issue of *Bingo*—this seemed to be the only use for the dozens of copies of that once famous magazine lying piled up next to a wooden wardrobe—one of us had to go and drop the creature into the latrine. There was no denying that our master lived in filthy conditions and his lungs were in a parlous state. We often saw him spitting blood into a bowl reserved specifically for that purpose—in brief, Mbaye Lô was some sort of a human wreck.

His *daara* was in Rebeuss and if you had asked one of the notables who lived there, right next to Niarela, about him in those days, he would have pulled a scornful grimace and replied, "Oh hell, you should stop wasting time on this

Mbaye Lô of yours, his life is worth about as much as a dead rat in a pile of rubbish."

I, Nguirane Faye, would never have said anything so outrageous about this man, anything so full of arrogance and foolish conceit. If I am telling you about Mbaye Lô today, it's because no Son of the Earth has made a more vivid impression on me in all the many days I have lived. Although I never saw him again after my childhood, I've been unable to forget him. He was one of those people whose impact on us is all the more indelible, the more fleeting our encounter with them. Someone may remain etched in our mind forever, even though we have crossed his path in the street but once. Looking into his eyes may make us feel, for a fraction of a second, that this stranger is somehow not of this world.

That's how it was with Mbaye Lô.

If God were to offer me a second life and the chance to decide my own destiny, I certainly wouldn't hesitate to choose that of Mbaye Lô. If one day the Almighty were to say to me, "Nguirane Faye, I made you come into the world for the first time in 1922, and I know you haven't been a happy man. Year in, year out, you have struggled from morning till night, trying to keep the wolf from the door. Yours has not been a glittering existence; a few moments after your death, the world will have forgotten all about you and it will be as though you had never lived. But it hasn't escaped me, Nguirane Faye, that being poor has not hardened your heart and that throughout your life you have remained a man of great generosity. That is a rare virtue and to reward you for it, I will grant you the exceptional favor of letting you reenter your mother's womb and the privilege of being born a second time. And this time, before I let you come back into the world, you will pick your own destiny. You can say to me, "The ruler of this country is President Daour Diagne, I want to take his place, I want to be so filthy rich that I no longer know what to do with my money, I want to be the one and only topic of conversation in the whole country from dawn till dusk, I want those who don't love me to feel petrified in my presence and I want to be the sun that no Son of the Earth dares to look straight in the face."

"Is that your wish, Nguirane? I can grant it. You know full well that I am the Omniscient and the Omnipotent, the Almighty God. This very night I can make the walls of Daour Diagne's palace crumble, I can send his power crashing to the ground, and surrender him to the howling mob in its frenzy of wrath. Then you will quite simply become President Nguirane Faye. You will receive messages of friendship from all over the world, and you will be the equal of the most revered personalities of your era. At times this glamorous life you yourself have chosen will seem so improbable that you'll bounce out of bed in the middle of the night, asking yourself whether it's actually true that you are one of the most illustrious leaders on the planet, or whether you're just a poor devil lost in a cruel and preposterous dream. If you want to wield power in this world, let me know and I will make it happen instantly. But if, unlike most of the other Sons of the Earth, you want to be reincarnated into the life of Mbaye Lô, your erstwhile master, a life full of hardship and anguish, I can grant that, too. You will be lonely and destitute, vermin will ravage your body, and you will be denied the enjoyment of even the most basic of life's pleasures. I am listening, Nguirane Faye: who do you want to be?"

Take the place of President Diagne? I have absolutely no desire to do so, Badou. Ah, Daour Diagne . . . ! In my eyes, there has never been a man as vile and despicable as you, Daour Diagne! You have plundered Senegal, insulted the poor and sowed hatred in every heart. Be damned, Daour Diagne. I am the mouthpiece for the whole country, and I am telling you to go to Hell!

If He asked once more, "I am listening, Nguirane Faye. What is your decision?" I would beseech Him to bring me back to life in Rebeuss, in Mbaye Lô's shack.

Malice and meanness were completely foreign to that man who managed to live in abject poverty without ever losing his dignity. As a child, I used to watch him with fascination as he was tracing symbols for hours on end. His body remained perfectly still while the quill at the end of his right hand performed its unhurried dance. Sometimes he would look up, and his eyes, lost in the distance, suddenly shone with a peculiar glow. It was as though he could hear the echo of his own silences coming back to him from another universe. I never went to the school of the *Toubabs* and I owe my love of the written word entirely to Mbaye Lô. The same applies to my genuine faith in God and my conviction that without the make-believe of signs and symbols, there would be no truth on this earth, neither good nor bad.

■   ■   ■

He advised him to be patient. The mystery of the Seven Paths unfolding in front of his eyes would soon be revealed. The time had come to put an end to being nothing but a flimsy mirage in the desert, to this constant desire to run away from himself. Telling himself incessantly that the mirror is an out-and-out liar would lead nowhere. And since he couldn't bear to look at his own face, he kept aping the other nations. At that point, the Asians were the last ones who still eluded him, but soon he would amaze them with his boldness: "For millennia you have been trying to be yourselves and now you think you've achieved it, but you are mistaken! Let me show you how to act like a real Chinese or a true Japanese, since I know the secret formula for all the transformations."

.   ■   ■

Which one of God's creatures can claim to know the dimensions of the universe? There are those who pretend they can give us the exact measurements of the Infinite: they are impostors. They draw lines that go on forever, and they are the first to get confused by their foolish equations. Question any one of them about his occupation and he'll reply, "You mean me? I am a scientist."

Then, if you tell him you are impressed, you'll immediately see this idiot puff up his chest and say, "You are not the first to be amazed by that. Yes, we great scholars, you see, we're always far too modest! As you see me sitting here in my miserable little garret, forgotten by the entire world, I am working on revolutionizing our knowledge of the universe. Whatever you want to know about the sun, the moon, the stars or the movements of the celestial bodies, I can explain it to you in a few words. My name will cut a swathe across the centuries—oh yes!—my name will be echoing in the memory of mankind for a long time to come."

But as soon as you ask these morons a few perfectly simple questions you see them hesitate, scratching their heads and mumbling some nonsense about heaven knows what probabilities, margins of uncertainty and hypotheses. Now and again, however, one can't deny that their ramblings have a touch of the poetic: "If the black cat right here in front of me circles the acacia tree on this vacant piece of land ten times, followed by the chicken over there on the left, and if, but only if, they both start barking like dogs, then, in all likelihood, a devastating collision between Pluto and Jupiter will ensue and it logically follows that we can expect to see incandescent lava spurting from the top of Kilimanjaro . . ."

If that isn't what you call talking drivel, I don't know what is, Badou. Really, it's not surprising that almost without exception, such individuals end up in a lunatic asylum. Too bad for them. They would have been better off sticking to what they know. Not one of us was present when God decided to create the universe. Only He knows why He did it and where this whole story—which when you think about it is really quite strange—will lead us in the end, and by that, Badou, I mean the mere fact that things exist and that they move right here in front of our eyes in the very place where we have all been forever perfectly still in the immense vastness of nowhere.

. . .

And yet, even if they reach all the way to infinity, neither places nor hours will ever be able to encompass the seven days of the week entirely.

Isn't that marvelous, Badou?

Most of the time, the days do their rounds peacefully, even monotonously. They whirl about like dead leaves under a clear sky, following one another without causing too much trouble, and they stretch and they yawn with boredom. People ask, "What day is it today?" That means the contours of time have softened and the hours making up day and night have gone limp and lost their sap.

At other times, fire and bloodshed reign supreme. Every mouth shouts the word *freedom*, and the big boulevards reverberate with it. One barricade. Another barricade. And then another and another . . . Flames shoot up into the sky, followed by thick black smoke. Whole towns come crashing down. Bodies are floating on a river of blood, and there's a smell of gunpowder and cannon shot in the air. Days of rage. Nights of fury. The intersections, piled high with corpses, are off-limits for VIPs. The King and the Queen were trying to flee the country—shame on them!—when they got captured by a gang of angry young partisans. The great National Throat Slitting took place three days ago, and the dead bodies were left abandoned where they lay. The scavengers that gouged out their eyes are still here now, circling in the air on silent wings above the open mass graves.

The battle between the seven days of the week is ferocious. Only one of them is destined to outlive the Son of the Earth and all his tribulations.

Even the cowards boast about their imaginary feats on the battlefield: "I was there myself, you know! How I wish you could have seen me that day!"

A voice echoes back, "Yes, we all saw you spreading panic in the enemy ranks, like a leopard among a herd of gazelles! No doubt you were the most courageous of all, you, whose ancestors made entire kingdoms tremble with fear!"

Each day wants to be the scar that remains after the great blaze. What's left, for all eternity perhaps, is two days unlike the rest, and no more.

Gouye-Ndiouli, the Baobab-of-the-Initiates, one Sunday. The Tuesday of the Women of Ndeer.

Dibéeru Guy-Njulli.
Talaatay Ndeer.

■   ■   ■

He had been walking on a carpet of dry grass for hours before it started getting more and more sparse. Some patches of cracked earth looked as if nothing had grown or germinated there for a very long time. In certain parts the earth had a whitish hue, suggesting this must be the location of ancient salt marshes. On closer inspection, the grass seemed calcified and stiff, but when he turned back, he saw it all around him, not very high perhaps, but of a beautiful golden yellow color and bowing gracefully in the wind.

Gouye-Ndiouli, the Baobab-of-the-Initiates, was visible in the distance. They say it was born of a seed embedded in a flash of lightning, hurled into the ground eons ago by Saa-Ndéné, the Founder. Whether or not that is actually true was completely irrelevant. All that was left in peoples' memory was the gruesome, barbaric impending battle that nobody wanted, especially Macodou Fall—the Damel of Cayor brutally slain at the behest of Pinet-Laprade or some other *Toubab*—and Samba Laobé Fall, his opponent on the battlefield, and also his own son. Never have two enemy armies been so fond of one another. Legend has it that even during the fighting the warriors' faces bore an expression of profound sadness, showing no trace of the usual eagerness to win and to shed blood.

But could there have been another heart in Kahone, the capital of the kingdom of Saloum, as torn as that of Queen Mother Latsouk Siré Diogob Mbodj? The son was born of her marriage to the man he was about to face in combat. Even after many years of separation from her husband, for Latsouk Siré

Diogob Mbodj, their marriage remained the happiest time of her life. Secretly, deep down inside her, where quarrels for the throne—the madness of men, in other words—had no place, her heart was still beating for Macodou Fall.

How she cursed the day when messengers came to report that the old Damel of Cayor, haunted by a preposterous dream, was on his way to the Saloum! While normally this news should have filled her with joy, on that particular day it carried in its wake nothing but death and despair.

Once the time and place of the battle were fixed, the people of the Saloum addressed Latsouk Siré Diogob Mbodj, the Queen Mother, and said, "Tomorrow will be a very strange day for you, since the son born of your entrails and his father will face each other in combat."

Calmly, Queen-Mother Latsouk Siré Diogob Mbodj replied, "Tomorrow, whatever the outcome, you will see tears of joy on my face mingling with tears of pain."

It was written that the battle would take place. And take place it did, for the will of humans is often powerless to prevent the most dreadful disasters from coming to pass. All we have left now is a few words: *Gouye-Ndiouli*, one Sunday. Terrible words that speak of the ceaseless wanderings of a humiliated sovereign, horrific bloodshed, and two kingdoms in disarray, the Saloum and the Cayor.

∎　∎　∎

Sadani Thiam and her cousin Yaye Mati wouldn't have known how to explain why they always found the silence in midmorning so deeply disturbing. They were too young to be able to untangle the confusion of their feelings. It was the time of day when they could be particularly sure Ndeer belonged to them—just two little girls—and to no one else in the world. The thought also frightened them. Was it because all the adults had gone to work in the fields and the village was deserted? Perhaps, but that was even more so at other times—before sunrise, for example. It's possible they neither felt the same tension nor the same fears at sunrise since they both knew the Trarza horsemen would never cross the river at that time to attack the well-guarded capital of the kingdom of Waalo. Early in the morning, Ndeer was always in a state of high alert, either ready to counter an invasion, or preparing to unleash its own men on one of the Trarza villages.

In truth, the main reason why the middle of the morning filled them with so much dread was that all of a sudden, Ndeer felt like an abandoned village.

On that Tuesday, the fifth of March 1820, the men had gone to plow the soil and prepare it for sowing, leaving the women behind in Ndeer. Not even the slightest gust of wind swept the air. Well before reaching its zenith, the sun became so violently hot that it made everyone dizzy. The leaves of the trees took on a milky hue and curled up as if to protect themselves against the rays of the sun. Within two or three days, they would have fallen off the branches and lie scattered all over the ground.

"Let's go to the river," Sadani Thiam said all of a sudden.

She was always the one who decided what they should do.

While they were on their way, they came across Mbarka Dia, a young woman, not very tall but with fine, regular features. One could sense that she was vigorous and strong-willed, with her feet firmly planted on the ground. Her force of character and innate sense of authority had helped her rise to her present social rank, making her modest background irrelevant. Aged thirty, she was part of the retinue of the Queen of Waalo who treated her more as a confidante or friend than as a servant. Although our records don't prove this, it has been said that the Queen of Waalo used to regularly seek her advice when faced with certain delicate political decisions.

Partly as a matter of principle, Mbarka Dia scolded the two little girls who always seemed to find an excuse for shirking their domestic chores, but above all she asked them to be cautious, because for once, the riverbanks were completely deserted. At the same time, she urged them to keep an eye on the opposite shore, which was Trarza territory.

Did she have a premonition of what was about to happen that Tuesday, the fifth of March 1820? On that specific issue, the chroniclers are divided, but on one point at least they all agree: having been constantly on the watch, Mbarka Dia knew that on that day, Ndeer was in danger of an enemy attack. She had even just aired her concerns in an audience with the queen. The Brack, as the sovereign of the Waalo is officially called, had absented himself for no more than a few hours, but that was enough for the Trarza warriors. Their spies had given the go-ahead the night before, and the raid went off without a hitch.

The moment she heard the two little girls scream, Mbarka Dia, with a flock of village women trailing behind her, hurried to their rescue.

Before she even had time to question them, she spotted the Trarza army in the distance.

The Queen was in such a state of panic—that at least is what several reports imply—that she consented to Mbarka Dia's every decision, sobbing quietly all the while.

This is how Mbarka Dia spoke to the women of Ndeer: "The Moors of Trarza are coming to attack us in the absence of our men, but under no circumstances will we allow them to take us home as their booty. We will do everything in our power to make sure the Brack of Waalo is not greeted with this news on his return to the kingdom. Death is preferable to suffering such a disgrace!"

On hearing her say these words, some of the women cursed her in secret.

But Mbarka Dia continued, "We must fight the Moors, but if they discover we are women, the certainty of their victory will make them invincible. Therefore, let's all dress up to look like our warriors."

According to the chronicle, the women disguised themselves as men and went valiantly forth into battle. They made the enemy take flight and started pursuing him. At that moment one of those small incidents happened that can change the course of history. On the way out of Ndeer, one of the women on horseback lost her bonnet and it fell to the ground, revealing her dark braids. Upon seeing this, the Trarza Moors suddenly realized with horror that they were running away from women, and one of them called out to his companions, "Where are you off to then, gang of cowards? Would you dare admit to the Emir of Trarza it was women who made you turn tail and flee from Ndeer?"

The battle started raging again. When it was clear that all was lost, Mbarka Dia raised her voice once more and said, "Come what may, but let no one tell our king, the Brack, that we, the women of Ndeer, were enslaved by his enemies. We have no choice but to set ourselves alight in the Great Hut."

The flames shot up high into the sky, and with their attackers looking on in shock and disbelief, the women of Ndeer started chanting a farewell song to the land of Waalo.

And now, Badou, are you going to ask me, in the skeptical manner of the young people of today, "Nguirane, since there were no survivors on that Tuesday in Ndeer, where do you get your story from? Or do you expect me to believe you simply because you are my grandfather?"

My answer to you is that my story is not yet finished.

When all the women had gathered in the Great Hut, Mbarka Dia said to little Sadani Thiam, "You, Sadani, are not going to die with us. One of us must live to tell the world about our sacrifice, and that will be you."

She showed her how to get away unheeded by the Trarza army and added, "I, Mbarka Dia, am telling you to go, Sadani. It's an order. When our Brack returns, you will tell the Waalo all about the women of Ndeer who preferred death to slavery."

And so it was that the first person to inform the world about the sacrifice of the women of Ndeer was a young girl by the name of Sadani Thiam.

At this point in my story, Badou, I would like you to permit me a digression, although in actual fact it isn't one. You know Kocc Barma Fall, our subtle and irreverent philosopher. "Shame on the nation that has given up listening to its old men," was one of the things he used to say. I'm sure you have heard our people solemnly repeating this age-old maxim over and over again. Perhaps it's true to say that this strange fellow from Cayor who never took anyone seriously—himself included—would have been amused to see that, so many centuries later, we still think of him as practically infallible. But let's not forget that in the history of our country there was a figure bold enough to take on this devious and sarcastic dialectician. For isn't that exactly what Mbarka Dia did in making Sadani Thiam the only survivor and the memory of that day? Engulfed by flames and about to be reduced to ashes she still found the strength to declare, in bold opposition to Kocc Barma Fall: "Shame on the nation that doesn't listen to its little girls."

It's obvious that Mbarka Dia was an extraordinary woman. First, she defended the Waalo on the battlefield, wielding weapons with her own bare hands, and then she chose a glorious death, but not without first presenting the redoubtable Kocc Barma Fall—the man even our boldest young thinkers have never dared contradict—with one final challenge.

And you, Badou, which side are you on in this controversy? Are you on Kocc's side or do you want to support Mbarka? From my grave whence I will speak to you a few years from now, I see you scratching your head and looking confused. I understand your dilemma—having to choose between our two giants isn't exactly easy.

．　　．　　．

You hear a noise. Where does it come from? You look up. In the distance, a dust cloud. The bright sunlight makes you shield your eyes with your right hand. You wonder who the two well-nigh identical human forms might be that are coming toward you. They must be old friends, you think. As they are getting closer, you see them splitting their sides laughing and giggling and tickling each other like little girls on the way to school. They can't stop quarrelling about trifles. Soon they have drowned out every other noise. They have been inseparable since the birth of the seasons, and it's impossible to tell which of the two is the other one's shadow. Let me tell you, by the way, that they are as old as time itself. They are called Yesterday and Today. They are so fidgety and so full of themselves that nobody wants to pay attention to their crazy antics. But be on your guard, Badou. If you see them whispering secrets into each other's ears, don't be shy, be indiscreet—position yourself in such a way that you can hear what they are saying to each other. If you listen carefully, you will learn a lot from them about yourself and your fellow human beings.

· · ·

I hear your voice. It's far away and barely audible.

From the foreign country where you are, but which is unknown to me, you ask, "What could they possibly teach me that's so important?" I like your curiosity, Badou. At your age, this is a good sign. Let me answer you. But be warned, nevertheless—if we carry on rambling like this, I will never find the time to tell you the true story that binds together the seven tales of these *Notebooks*, a story that's more important to the two of us than anything else: the life and death of your father, Assane Tall.

But let me say just two words about Yesterday and Today, and that'll be the end of my quixotic little escapades.

I do not know if our universe is tens or hundreds of millions of years old, and to be honest, I don't really care. The fact nobody can doubt is that there was a beginning. The day God created the universe, that day which was not preceded by any other day, was called Today. That's the only day to have deserved that name, since the following morning it was already dead. Yesterday emerged out of it like the chicken emerges out of the egg. Since that day, these two clever fellows haven't stopped dying and giving birth to each other. Who is the father? Who is the son? The reason they never stop bickering is because they can't settle that question. And one of them always has the last word. He taunts his companion, calls him pretentious and reminds him that he can give him whatever color and shape he likes; he's like clay in the hands of the potter. In a nutshell, he tells him: You are just an ordinary tree trunk that has fallen to the ground, and I, a Laobé artisan, am the only one who can make your body shed tears of joy or tears of pain. And it's true, isn't it, that Today is constantly messing about with Yesterday, molding and shaping him as he sees fit. We feel like shouting, Bravo, well done! He doesn't lack creative imagination, that fellow, and his admirers are right in praising his genius for forgery. Without taking the whole thing too seriously, he quickly cobbles together a life story and a soul for his alter ego. It's hardly likely that someone who saw it all with his own eyes will come back from the dead and accuse him of plagiarizing reality!

And anyway, everybody always ends up forgetting everything. There have been times when this country—and I mean Senegal—was on the brink of disaster, and we are not alone in this. We have seen our people getting hurt, and their voices were full of fear when they said, "We came within an inch of ending up in the abyss."

Everyone is so shaken that day that words to describe what happened aren't even necessary. But from the next day onward, nobody remembers it the same way as his neighbor. Each person tries to impose his version of the facts upon everybody else, and the argument may well end in a savage fight. If it's that difficult to agree on recent events, why should we believe those who claim they can tell us all about the earliest hours of humanity?

These things are complicated, and I like our ancient local wisdom, which demands from every storyteller that he confine himself to reporting only what he himself has experienced. When a stranger arrives in town and pronounces the words *Once upon a time . . .* he gets asked just one single question: "Stranger, are you sure you were there on the day when it was once upon a time?"

■   ■   ■

Dakar, the shambolic city.

Still exactly as you left it on the morning of your departure. Chaotic. Hectic. Unpredictable, like those disheveled, haggard lunatics dressed in rags that you come across at the street corners and who make you flinch, from fear as much as from disgust. All the smells mixed together. Petrol. Exhaust fumes. Fried fish and peanut sauce, that's what office staff, factory workers, and artisans have for lunch around here. Everywhere you see signs saying "Urinating prohibited" since people piss all over the place and the odor is strong, quite overpowering in fact. It makes a curious cocktail when it mingles with the delicate perfumes of the ravishing girls you see sauntering up and down the streets, each one of them dolled up to the nines. You just need to follow your nose, that's how delicious they smell, the little honeys. They know exactly how to keep the young men on tenterhooks, one can see that, and day in, day out, cops and taxi drivers get caught up in these mad speed chases down the streets and avenues leading to Colobane or the city center. All this adds up to the daily hustle and bustle, vendors selling roasted or boiled peanuts at one corner, green mangoes and Chinese trinkets at another, and even little bits of our democracy: with quivering voices they will tell you that the country may be bankrupt, but its freedom of expression is still unsurpassed.

At every traffic light, newspaper sellers are holding up copies of *La Tribune*, *Les Dernières Nouvelles*, *Le Progrès* or *Dossiers classés*, and on the front pages you see the same politicians who are so good at making our lives a misery—I'm sure you know the type I'm talking about. Each one of them tries to convince us that he alone can finally bring us health, education and justice. They make me so angry, these impostors, but I should not get worked up about them; they couldn't care less about me. It's crystal clear that a man my age is worth less than nothing to them, or certainly no more than a piece of dead wood. No, it's you they are targeting, the young, since you are still foolish enough to hope and strong enough to fight.

And then there are the tourists with their straw hats and Bermuda shorts, their *anango*, and their sunglasses. They're the only ones who don't seem to mind being out in the open in a sandstorm, but then they never seem to know where they are going. They wander around here and there, then they stop before walking on again and turning round to go back to where they came from. They spend hours going round and round in circles all day long, and you frequently see them with their cameras dangling on shoulder straps, always in the same parts of town, looking up at the sky. Has somebody perhaps told them our city is all the way up there, somewhere behind the clouds? Maybe they're hoping to pick up its secret vibrations that way. I guess it's perfectly normal for people who've come from so far away to be curious about everything. They already imagine themselves back home, happily reunited with their friends.

And they talk.

They talk about the mountains of garbage. The land of Africa, a land where it's so hot that your feet get burned. "If you ever take off your shoes, you'll immediately leap up into the air, shrieking with pain. And then those narrow little streets full of potholes with rivulets of greasy green water trickling down them . . . The stench is unbelievable, my friend, I have no idea how they manage to survive in all that filth. But the women down there, they're so hot, I tell you, they can drive you insane. Those lacy little bits of nothing they wear when they get laid, damn, I've forgotten the name, but who cares what they're called, what matters is they're simply fatal. All this is true, believe me; I've knocked about in a lot of places, but I've never seen anything like it anywhere. So all in all, it's been a great holiday, my friends. I'm just not sure I understand what's really going on there. They have nothing but famines and tribal warfare, killing thousands of them every day. And then there's AIDS, of course, but that's just the latest one of the endless epidemics they have to grapple with, and still, they sing, they dance and they laugh all day long."

And this is just the beginning, Badou.

■   ■   ■

As I have told you before, I am not in the same league as our world famous authors with their powerful, fertile imagination. My modest little trips from one *Notebook* to the other are all I really need to get fired up. And yet, even a minor scribbler like me must never forget that his worst enemy is the very person he is going to so much trouble for. Your reader is trying to make you believe that those signs you write down turn into people more real than actual human beings. Don't listen to him. He's just flattering you so he can ruin you. In reality, his heart is brimming over with hatred and he hates no one on this earth as much as you.

■   ■   ■

I can't shake off the idea that you must miss Niarela terribly. For this is where you were born, where you played soccer, running half naked under the rain, and where you first felt the pangs of love. Those moments from your early youth must still be very fresh in your memory.

How come, Badou, that at so early an age one goes off to settle in a foreign land? Tell me? Ah, times must have changed, indeed. I could have never done that. Even here, in Senegal, I can't picture myself living anywhere but in Niarela.

Yet every now and then one of my Fulani friends will taunt me: "What are you doing here, damned Serer? Why don't you to go back to your native Sine and take up your fetishes again?"

For all answer, I just shake my head, smiling a little. Yes, I know nothing about the world at large. Niarela is the only place on earth that I can boast of knowing inside out. You bet that I know this neighborhood! Even with my eyes closed, I can still see it, I can feel its inner pulses. All I have to do is cock my ears to certain familiar sounds. When I hear little bells jingling through the silent dawn, I know Ousmane Sow, the cart driver, is harnessing his horse, Tumaini, right around the corner of our sand-blown street. In the wee hours, the soil is still wet with morning dew. Mango and lemon trees are visible in the distance, inside the enclosures, their wet foliage dangling in the wind. The early morning chill seeps through the bones, and Ousmane Sow must sometimes rattle his teeth. He's tightening the amulet around his arm while muttering long prayers. He is not asking heaven for the impossible, our cart driver. *Would the Almighty assist me in finding many clients today.* These are his words. Nothing more. Ousmane says his prayers with a throbbing heart, and I know exactly why. For people like him and me, times are hard and it is getting more and more difficult for us to feed our families. So no, he can't afford to drive around with an empty cart. Nobody in Niarela pays any attention to Ousmane Sow. He's just a wretched old cart driver, they think . . . And yet, the good man has very clear ideas about everything, and these ideas of his are not as banal as you might expect, believe me. You could call him a forceful spirit, our friend Ousmane, no matter that he is only a simple working man. One day I questioned him about the meaning of his horse's name. "Tumaini means 'to hope' in Swahili," he replied, as he fixed me with his open, intelligent gaze. "So if you hear this word in countries like Tanzania, Rwanda or Kenya, Nguirane, be aware that it means 'to hope.'"

We looked at each other silently for a few seconds, and then, without taking his eyes off me, he added, "I'm sure you can guess why I chose that name, Nguirane . . ."

"Of course," I answered, "of course, Ousmane. Hope, that's what we, the little people of Niarela, all live by. But *Tumaini*, that's quite a complicated word, don't you think, Ousmane? Why would a modest cart driver from Niarela go and search for a name for his horse at the other end of the world?"

With an abrupt movement, Ousmane Sow's upper body recoiled very slightly, and he stared at me in utter amazement. It was crystal clear to me that he was putting on an act, that his surprise wasn't really genuine. This devil of a cart driver was impossible to pin down; he must have anticipated my reaction. In any case, what I remember most vividly right now is that he was roaring with laughter. He was completely doubled up, holding his stomach, quite literally incapable of restraining himself. What on earth could I possibly have said that was so funny—or so stupid? When he saw me getting irritated, Ousmane said with a straight face, "That's terrible, Nguirane, to see how so many years after his liberation the slave in us still hasn't managed to cast off his shackles! There really is no need for the Master to put us in chains anymore! He may as well let us roam around freely as long as we come trotting back to the plantation every night like so much cattle to their stable. Our chains are in our heads, you see. And so you, Nguirane Faye, ignorant as you are of the language of the whites, want to tell me that it's closer to us than Swahili?"

I was speechless. This *boroom saret* was vicious indeed. Ousmane Sow let his anger build up inside him before he declared, sounding like a man who has a few bones to pick with the rest of the world, "Why then should I not be allowed to call my horse Tumaini in this lousy country where even the wrestlers step into the arena with their torsos draped in the American flag? Why?"

I'm glad that rebels like Ousmane Sow exist; they push us face down into the morass of our lies. I had no choice but to admit defeat. Trying to hide my embarrassment, I said with a nervous chuckle, "You're quite right, Ousmane, Niarela is the only place on earth where horses are neighing at sunrise in the most delicious Swahili!"

The fellow did not seem to find my joke very funny. To Hell with you, Ousmane Sow! He is always out of sorts, this cart driver from Niarela, because nothing happens the way he wants it to happen in our country, and probably also in the rest of the world. As a result, he wants to fire at everything that moves. And yet, I am deeply fond of Ousmane, I have to say.

And now we will let him drive his horse through the streets of Dakar, wishing him lots of clients. Let's turn our attention to another house in Niarela now, that of *Monsieur* and *Madame* Soumaré, which is how this couple of perfect cretins wishes to be addressed. Every time I hear screaming and yelling in the neighborhood around the time of the prayer of *tàkkusaan*, I know they're at it again. Then things start heating up in their place and true to their claim that they do nothing like the rest of us poor devils in Niarela—they only insult each other in French, by the way—it's you bloody son-of-a-bitch, you're full of shit and goodness knows what else, while the woman is threatening, horror of horrors, to fuck her husband's father, and this can go on for hours on end. Benches are being smashed against window panes, the television gets knocked off its pedestal, and then you suddenly hear the woman yelling for help; in brief, it makes you think things are really serious. Niarela is a place where we don't just stand by and listen while our neighbors are busy beating each other up, you know. Unlike those whites in a black skin that you find in the more affluent areas of Dakar, we do what we can to separate them and restore peace. If something like that happens next door to us, we don't close our windows, complaining about the noise, and we most definitely do not call the police. That's why I took it upon myself one day to go and reason with *Monsieur* and *Madame* Soumaré. I am not an anxious person by nature, I think, but when I recall the afternoon I spent in the company of those two nutters, it still sends shivers down my spine. I was convinced I wouldn't make it out of their house alive! The husband started showering me with obscenities spiked with those foreign words they love so much, but then, all of a sudden, the two of them seemed to have forgotten about their quarrel and were in perfect agreement that they should gouge out my eyes and cut off my tongue.

For as long as I can remember, I have never come across anybody in Niarela even remotely like this couple. What an arrogant twit, this Mr. Soumaré! And so conceited, for no reason at all! He thinks he can impress us with his gold-rimmed glasses, his suits and his stripy ties! You should see him when he gets out of his pathetic, dusty little frog of a car, straightening his jacket and strutting to his front door, with his chest all puffed up and bundles of files clasped under his arm. He would never dream of saying hello or even just looking at the people he walks past. He makes me laugh, this moron, and let me tell you why! He can swagger and strut in front of anyone he wants, but I do not understand why Mr. Soumaré makes this huge effort pretending he's so terribly important. How stupid does he think we are? Here in Dakar it's common knowledge that the people who matter live in Les Almadies and Fann-Résidence, taking it easy in their opulent mansions complete with swimming pools and every other imaginable luxury. But if you're reduced to having to rent one of our miserable shacks in Niarela, there's really no need to go to the trouble of putting on such a pompous performance. Having said that, his wife, Madame Soumaré as she's known, is quite magnificent, yes, she's hot, as you youngsters would say. Tall, slim and refined, with sublime black skin, she is one of those women who only have to sway their bodies to make respectable family men lose their composure and curse Cheytan the Tempter.

So that's Niarela for you.

Ousmane Sow, the cart driver, plus *Monsieur* and *Madame* Soumaré . . .

Is that all? No, of course not. I could tell you the story of each one of my little jesters here and might even do so from time to time in these *Notebooks*, depending on whom I've just bumped into. Why not? It is bound to be amusing to take a peek behind the scenes and surprise the shadow puppeteer at work. All he has to do is pull on his strings, and faint silhouettes start milling about on the wall. These are the inhabitants of Niarela, those puppets on the string, and yet they claim in all sincerity that they're made of flesh and blood. In their naivety—or should we say conceit?—they believe they are completely free in their movements. But the day is not far off when one of them is squirming with pain, vomits a bit of blood, and dies. Nobody has had time to understand why. His parents lay him gently in his grave, as though they're afraid of waking him up, and after that, tears keep flowing all night long. The next day, a newborn utters his first cry in a neighboring house, and everyone shouts for joy. One of God's-bits-of-wood leaves, and another takes its place; the factory is running at full capacity, even if nobody understands how it all works. What more can we expect? It's the same in the bush where a hundred-year-old kapok tree dries up, sheds all its leaves and is knocked over by the slightest gust of wind. Almost immediately, in the same spot, a sturdy shrub with robust green foliage begins to grow, proudly reaching up into the sky. And that's it. Let me tell you, Badou, all things considered, almost nothing new ever happens between the cradle and the grave. Supposing the dead were to wake up and return to earth tomorrow, they would find the streets in this town looking pretty much the same as when they were still living here.

Yes, it's not a simple matter, but since it is the will of the One and Only God who created heaven and earth, we have no choice but to accept it.

.　■　.

This morning, I woke up with the first rays of sunshine. I spent more than an hour just calmly and quietly walking up and down the courtyard, and I felt better for it. At that same instant, when I heard Imam Keita's voice rising up to heaven, I could sense your shadow near me. You were taking your time paging through these *Notebooks*. I couldn't actually see you, of course, but I most definitely heard you complaining. I didn't take it personally, so don't worry, but your comments on my long-winded yarns struck me as rather sarcastic. If I heard you right, you were mumbling that if the rest of my story was like this, I might be going to a lot of trouble in vain.

The harshness of your voice surprised me. You never used to talk like that before. It's the exile, I guess. Exile makes you tense and edgy.

■ ■ ■

A few days ago, I asked your mother Bigué Samb, "How old was Badou when his father, Assane Tall, got on the plane and left for Marseille?"

"Eight months and five days," she said, without a moment's hesitation.

I was surprised by her precision, but I shouldn't have been. If you want to understand what really happened, the first thing you need to know is that for Bigué Samb time has stood still since the day when—with you strapped to her back—she said good-bye to your father at Dakar airport.

Having answered my question, she added, as if talking to herself: "Yes. Badou Tall was only eight months and five days old. Not long after that, he got the measles."

She stopped talking for a moment, shaking her head. "I remember how afraid I was my little boy might not recover."

THE BOOK OF THE WINDS

IT WAS ON A THURSDAY, JUST BEFORE NIGHTFALL, WHEN I WENT WITH A group of friends to collect Assane Tall's mortal remains. When we reached Ngalla Diop Street, the last junction before the airport, we found ourselves stuck in the middle of a huge crowd. There were thousands of people there, mostly youngsters—some on motorbikes, others crammed into overcrowded mini-buses, shaking their fists, but the majority were on foot, running around aimlessly in all directions. All were in a state of great excitement, shouting and clapping their hands or drumming on car bonnets: "Moo-dou Cissé! Moo-dou Cissé! Long live Modou! Long live Modou!" Loudspeakers were turned up to the max, blasting music, and we repeatedly saw pedestrians stopping briefly, tapping the ground with their feet and performing a quick little dance, twirling around four or five times before they vanished again into the seething cauldron of the streets of Dakar.

The name they were shouting—Modou Cissé—is very common in our country. Hundreds of thousands of our fellow citizens are called that. I guessed immediately that all this cheering had to be addressed to our famous singer, since he alone is capable of attracting such an exuberant crowd. His admirers worship him like a god, claiming he has the most beautiful voice in the world, something that is a bit of an exaggeration, if you ask me. To tell you the truth, this whole circus exasperates me. While those kids are screaming their lungs out, shouting the name of their idol in unison, cynics are ruthlessly enriching themselves at their expense.

Modou Cissé had just returned from abroad after receiving an important international award. That at least is what I was told afterward. It was obvious that this was causing great excitement across the whole country, and the singer's triumphant return to Senegal completely dominated the radio and television news. At a press conference, while performing some grotesque dance steps worthy of the clown that he is, President Daour Diagne had announced he would be at the airport himself. The poor imbecile even went so far as to describe himself as Modou Cissé's "Number One Fan."

It was a most unfortunate coincidence that all this happened just after we had heard about Assane Tall's death in Marseille and while we were trying to scrape together the money that was needed to repatriate the body. As you can imagine, we were definitely not in a mood for reveling just then. And yet, Badou, it was as though tens of thousands of the inhabitants of Dakar had congregated in high spirits to celebrate your father's death. It was a complete surprise to us all, and alas, it meant that the homecoming of Assane Tall did not take place in a suitably solemn atmosphere. Our cortege had great trouble trying to forge a path through the huge crowd, even before we were suddenly blocked at an intersection by a group of sinister-looking, angry young men. What was causing their anger, we didn't know. They had heard that the crafty Modou Cissé, who remained invisible to all, was hiding in the hearse. We swore that wasn't true and suggested they should go and look for their great singer somewhere else, but they weren't convinced, and a few of them gave our van a couple of violent knocks. Luckily, one of their comrades was more reasonable and managed to calm them down. All of a sudden they seemed to regret their behavior and allowed us to pass, with gestures so theatrical they almost made us laugh. A few of them even started saying prayers for Assane Tall.

■   ■   ■

Someone came to tell me a woman by the name of Yacine Ndiaye was on the phone from abroad.

I remember our conversation.

"I would like to speak to Nguirane Faye Tall, the father of Assane," she said after the initial salutations.

"Assane Tall?"

"Yes. His other name was Assane Faye. He was a football player here in Marseille."

"That's my son. And you, who are you?"

"My name is Yacine Ndiaye, but I don't think you know me."

"Tell me about your family here in Senegal?"

"I am calling from Marseille."

"I know. But what family do you belong to here in Senegal?"

This first exchange with Yacine Ndiaye should have been enough to make me realize we would never get along and that she would bring nothing but bad luck to our home in Niarela. Why didn't she just say to me, "I am a member of the Ndiaye family from such and such a place in Senegal" to give me even the vaguest idea about the person I was talking to? It seems utterly trivial, Badou, but I assure you, these small little details do ease the conversation. Later on I understood that Yacine Ndiaye was under a lot of pressure at the time and that she literally had no time to lose. But that does not change the fact that for me this phone call was very unpleasant and distressing.

Even over the phone, you can often sense what's going on in a person's head. She clearly found my long-winded salutations superfluous, but trying her best to remain polite she said, "I'm sorry, but this is a long-distance call, and I have to be brief."

That's when I became aware of my heartbeat hammering inside my skull. I asked, " Is something the matter with Assane?"

Since there was no reply, I tried again, "Is Assane sick?"

Yacine Ndiaye's voice was calm but grave when she said, "Assane was sick for a long time, and now he has succumbed to his illness."

"And when did this happen?"

"Assane died last night."

Assane died last night.

It took me a while to grasp the meaning of that sentence.

Why did this woman, about whom I knew absolutely nothing, make me feel so ill at ease? Looking back, and in light of the terrible events that have shaken Niarela since then, I could quite easily claim today that I had a hunch something wasn't quite right from that very moment. But that would be a lie. I was just deeply distraught. I cannot deny that she talked about Assane's death with a certain sorrowful restraint, and I have no reason to believe she wasn't genuinely upset. But considering the harshness with which she announced the news, I still feel she lacked tact, and quite possibly manners as well. It was her silences that were more disturbing to me than anything else. Every time she stopped talking, the tension in the air became more palpable, and I couldn't help thinking there must be something specific she expected from me without wanting, or being able, to ask for it. But finally she couldn't hold back any longer, and she burst out, "So how are we going to do it then?"

"What are you trying to say?"

Thank God this was the first time I had lost a close family member in a foreign country, and in my state of anguish, I wasn't really thinking about the practical details. That is why I didn't immediately understand that Yacine Ndiaye was alluding to the transfer of Assane Tall's mortal remains from Marseille to Dakar. She eventually overcame her embarrassment and explained the situation. "Assane's body is at the morgue; here, the hospitals charge by the day and it mounts up very quickly. I have enough to buy tickets for myself and the children, but you, his relatives in Niarela, need to take care of the rest."

It was only then that it occurred to me to enquire about the exact nature of the relationship between her and Assane Tall.

"I am Assane Tall's widow and I am coming to Niarela with our two children, Mbissine and Mbissane."

"Mbissine and Mbissane?" I mumbled. "You are Assane's widow . . . Your two children . . . ?"

At that point in the conversation she seemed to get very irritated and she said, "I really think it's best if I talk to someone who understands French. When you have managed to find enough money over there in Niarela to cover the costs of the repatriation of Assane's body, you can have them call me back."

Who was this Yacine Ndiaye? What was she doing in France? I had absolutely no idea. Just one thing was overwhelmingly obvious, and that was the fact that to her, Assane's death was *our* problem and not hers. Did the marriage to your father prove a disappointment? She certainly didn't appear to feel any love or even respect for him anymore. I'm sure you remember I let you speak to her on the phone. She repeated her morgue story to you, this time in French, and you reported back to me that she kept saying: "The bill is going to get bigger every day." It was like an obsession for her. That was, for you as well as for me, our very first contact with Yacine Ndiaye. True to your nature, you kept your reserve during your conversation with her, and it was difficult for me to work out what you thought of her.

At any rate, you didn't seem too deeply affected by the loss of a father you only ever knew by name.

For me, on the other hand, the death of Assane Tall was a story that nearly drove me out of my mind.

Abandoning one's family for more than twenty years, that simply cannot be right. We had no idea what kind of life Assane had been leading in Marseille. Was he happy there, by and large, or was he more often miserable? We simply had no idea. Decades later, there was only one thing left for us to do, and that was to shoulder the burden of his death. The worst part was his behavior toward your mother, Bigué Samb, but that is an understatement. In my opinion, what he did to her was a shameful betrayal.

Later on, when Niarela fell on hard times, we realized she had never forgiven him. For years, Bigué Samb kept her yearning for revenge to herself. We were all taken by surprise when she started to strike. She had a heavy hand, and there was absolutely nothing anyone could do to stop her.

■   ■   ■

I welcomed Yacine Ndiaye to my house with open arms. She was my son's widow, and in some way it was as if my son had returned to be at my side again after abandoning me for nearly a quarter of a century. I was desperate to find out what had happened to him during all those years he had spent living so far away from us. What on earth could have made him decide we no longer existed—not just me but also the rest of the people in Niarela, the place where he was born and grew up? The story behind all this could not be a simple one, nor could it be a story that was easy to tell. I had hoped Yacine Ndiaye could gradually be persuaded to open up a bit, or that there might be a few fleeting moments when she would get carried away with her memories and give me a more detailed description of Assane's life in Marseille. I know you will object, asking what use it can possibly be to hark back to the past.

I have asked myself that question several times without being able to answer it. Perhaps it was because I simply didn't want to die with that empty feeling in my heart, caused by my son's excessively long absence. I have to admit that

I only became aware of this wound at the moment when Assane was being prepared for burial, but it was—and it still remains to this day—very deep. Yacine Ndiaye was the only person who could have healed it.

But that was an illusion I had to give up very quickly.

It is now nearly two years since she took up residence in the left wing of our house, and to this day, she refuses to talk to anybody about anything, and especially about Assane Tall. It's quite simple: for Yacine Ndiaye, I, Nguirane Faye, am just a useless object, no different from the rest of the furniture in this house. Like a forgotten bench in the corner, or the canary under the mango tree. Anything except a human being.

On top of that, she has managed to turn everyone in the whole neighborhood against her. She and her two children not only consider themselves as strangers in Niarela, but to them, this is not their country. I don't believe they are trying to behave like *Toubabs* on purpose. It comes quite naturally to them.

In order to punish her for her condescending attitude, Niarela has started telling all sorts of horror stories about Yacine Ndiaye. I have heard people say it was her fault if Assane Tall at some point started going off the rails.

"At the beginning, Assane was determined to lead an orderly life. He had married a woman called Nathalie."

"Yes, Nathalie Cousturier."

"That's it. A decent little nurse."

"And then this person by the name of Yacine Ndiaye came on the scene and destroyed their marriage."

"One day, she beat poor Nathalie Cousturier black and blue. That's when Nathalie decided she'd rather be safe than sorry and left Assane to her."

"A slut with an attitude problem!"

"Just picture this: apparently she used to parade up and down the Rue des Dominicaines in her pink boots, her wig, and with her naked thighs exposed to the freezing cold on winter evenings. *Revolting, if you ask me!*"

"No need to go all the way to Marseille to find out what goes on there! She doesn't know Niarela, that one!"

"My cousin Ndeye Sarr has told me everything. This woman, if only you knew! Cocaine, whiskey and pastis. Nothing escapes us. What on earth is she thinking?"

"And as if all that hadn't been enough, she infected Assane with the evil sickness."

These are some of the things people say; the trouble is, that's not all . . . we've heard other things that are even more vile. Impossible to tell which of these rumors are true and which are false.

The remarkable thing is that to this day, no one has ever heard your mother Bigué Samb uttering a single bad word about Yacine Ndiaye.

PLAYING IN THE DARK

"Where are you, Badou? I have been searching everywhere for you."

"Here I am, Nguirane."

"It's time for our three little glasses of mint tea."

"Let me prepare it."

"What! . . . You, Badou, making tea? Wouldn't it be better if you left that to young Birame Sène . . . ?"

"I just bumped into Birame Sène under the arcades, not far from the Calypso night club. He was on his way to the stadium; you know as well as I do that he never misses a match when Niarela is playing."

"You're right . . . Does that really mean you, Badou . . . are going to make our *àttaaya*? I don't want to upset you, but . . ."

"Tonight, Nguirane, I am going to serve you the most delicious mint tea you have ever tasted!"

"Let's see about that. But tell me, Badou . . . ?"

"Yes."

"Do you actually listen to the stories I tell you?"

"Do not doubt that for a single second, Nguirane."

"All right then, the time has come for me to entertain you with my most enigmatic stories."

"I see shadows fluttering around you."

"From so far away?"

"Yes indeed, Nguirane."

"Of course, Badou. I have no reason to doubt you . . ."

■   ■   ■

The narrow, winding path in the middle of the forest seems to go on forever and ever. It is pitch-dark. My eyes are glued to the tiny strip of yellow earth that I can make out in the darkness. It resembles a feeble ray of light. I must not stray from it, for if I do, I'm lost.

After all, this is the only way I can get to you.

The twittering of the birds in the treetops has suddenly stopped.

Thousands of wild animals are following closely in my tracks on velvet paws; it's so quiet you would think they're holding their breath. Now and again, I see their eyes glimmering through the undergrowth and the tall grass.

The young panther is getting impatient and says in a low voice, "He's quite reckless, that one. What are we waiting for then, why aren't we leaping at his throat?"

His mother admonishes him gently: "Beware of the Son of Man, my child. What a strange creature he is: he walks on only two paws and never stops devising new ways to hunt us down. This solitary walker may be intent on setting us a trap. Man is a creature that loves to kill. We don't know why, nor does he himself."

And now, Badou, here I am by your side, safe and sound.

We are sitting on a mat in the middle of the courtyard, talking about everything and nothing and enjoying our *cere baasi*. Try as you like to hide it from me, I can sense that your nerves are on edge. We are sipping our mint tea in silence, and I want to test your self-restraint. The suspense is getting too much for you, you are on tenterhooks, and yet, you are too proud to go down on your knees, begging me to talk.

You know that I am doing all this mainly to keep myself amused—but seeing you, who are normally so calm and laid back, in this state of inner turmoil, moves me greatly.

After the third glass you finally can't take it anymore, and you plead with me to tell you everything I know. I must confess—not entirely without a certain sense of glee—that in reality, I neither saw nor heard a single thing when I was trudging all alone through the heart of the forest. Your answer comes like a shot, with such determination that I am quite taken aback: "That doesn't matter. Tell me anyhow."

"Tell you what, Badou?"

"All the things you have neither seen nor heard in that place. And, Nguirane, if the words weigh too heavily on your tongue, give them wings, turn them into birds like the ones that glide through the air."

Hearing you talk like that, I nod my head, with a smile in my heart. Now I know you are no longer a child.

■ ■ ■

The mirror covers the entire surface of the wall.

It's the biggest mirror the man has ever seen in his life. Instead of his own image, it throws back at him an entangled mass of bodies, twisted and intertwined like the gnarled branches of a baobab. The figures are warped, their faces hideously blurred, grimacing, and seemingly attached to the wrong bodies. They strike him as familiar and strange at the same time. He can't be sure, of course, but the one with the grey hair and thick glasses at the very bottom of the picture could quite easily be him. Next, he notices an old woman sitting on the doorstep of one of the houses in the HLM district. She looks serious, preoccupied, with her eyes glued to the *layu* of rice she is holding in her lap. Painstakingly, she is picking bits of dirt out of it—tiny little black things—that get tossed into an iron pot. And yes, this time there can be no doubt, it's the Mother. Mother Soukeyna Sall. But Mirror, why can't you leave her in peace down there? Does your heartlessness really have to go that far? And over there, a few years earlier, one of the streets in the Medina. Number 5, I think it says, where it intersects with one of the big avenues. The sky is still overcast after the thunderstorm the night before, and rainwater has formed small puddles that come right up to the bottom of the rickety shacks. Buuba Këriñ, the charcoal seller with that shady, vacant look in his eyes is busy covering up his merchandise with a large sheet of thick, blue plastic. How strange, he should have done that before it started raining, it's quite useless now. He remembers how they used to steal charcoal from Buuba Këriñ when they wanted to roast cashew nuts or make tea. His whole childhood comes alive right here, in this little street. Every time the weather was cloudy like today, they brought out their rubber soccer ball and laid out two opposing sides between the ramshackle houses. There was left-handed Babacar Mbow, who later became known as the giant of Ndem-Maïssa, and also his cousin, the tall, slender Alassane Niang, alias Joe, who died in some dormitory town in a foreign country—God rest his soul! And let's not forget the two boys from the Bèye family, Assane Preira and Ben Diogaye . . . Suddenly he can see them all, right there, flat against the wall! His heart is pounding. All this has stirred up his memory so much that he has become very agitated and starts cursing the mirror for bringing the dead and the adolescent back to life so quickly. Slow down Mirror, not so fast!

On hearing his lamentations, the mirror cannot hide its irritation. "He who can satisfy you has yet to be born, Sons of the Earth! You can cope with almost anything except the solitude of the grave, and nothing in the world terrifies you as much as death. So why are you complaining about these flashes of eternity I am offering you? I have unraveled time in the opposite direction and turned you into the cherished child again, frolicking and gamboling about on the banks of this majestic river, shouting for joy in the rain. Now do tell me please—what more do you want to make you happy? I advise you to take heed and not to provoke my displeasure! If I shatter into a million pieces, you won't just be plunged into death and desolation, but into something infinitely worse: nothingness and everlasting silence. Surely that's not what you want?"

This fills him with fright: "No, I don't want that. I want to dream. Please let me visit the place where time can neither go forward nor back!"

.   ■   ■

"Badou, tonight we will set off in search of Mame Ngor."

"Mame Ngor? That name means nothing to me, Nguirane . . ."

"Mame Ngor is the founder of our lineage."

■   ■   ■

Sitting under the mango tree in the middle of the courtyard, opposite the zinc entrance gate, I contemplate the first rays of the rising sun on the horizon.

Niarela is still fast asleep, and I am counting my prayer beads. Every now and again, the silence is broken by the raucous cry of a bird. It's our neighbors' parrot, telling us noisily how much he detests the bars of his cage.

I empathize with him, since I am not at peace either. It's a mystery to me why it is almost always around this time of day that my mind takes great leaps into the past, reviving long forgotten memories or images of my nearest and dearest. Whenever Ndambaw, your grandmother, comes back to me like that, my heart feels heavy and I say a silent prayer for her. Yes, Ndambaw, that good woman, she wasn't only my wife but also my best friend.

I hear a sound on my left. Someone is turning a key. The door leading to Yacine's living quarters opens and she appears, accompanied by a man. It's always the same one, a certain Tamsir Bâ. Since the day he was introduced to me under that name, he has barely spoken to me again.

He frequently spends the night with Yacine Ndiaye, who is supposed to be mourning Assane Tall's death. The whole of Niarela knows he is her lover. They walk straight past me. Perhaps they think I am still in bed.

In his sermon, Imam Keita launches a blistering attack against moral depravity, reminding us of the dreadful punishments set aside for widows who misbehave during their mourning period. Although he doesn't name names, it's not difficult to guess who he is targeting this morning.

After prayers, I go to exchange greetings with my neighbors. I enter each one of the houses, and everywhere I repeat the same question: "Did you spend the night in peace?"

Everywhere, without exception, the answer is yes, and then I am asked: "And you, Nguirane, did you spend the night in peace?"

This has been the start to my days in Niarela for almost forty years.

Afterward, I go back home and sit down under my mango tree.

Soon it will be seven o'clock in the morning, and the house is waking up. Every sound, every movement is intimately familiar to me. I see the faces without really having to look at them, and I am only half-conscious of the voices I hear. Thioro Thiam, always in the same old wrapper with its pattern of red-and-black butterflies, tied above her breasts, is crouching in front of the stove. She is one of my tenants, and at the same time every day, in that same corner of the courtyard, just beneath her window, she cooks millet porridge for her husband Lamine's breakfast. Lamine, meanwhile, is listening to the daily news in his bedroom. He is a factory worker with a keen interest in politics, and morning after morning the voices of the country's top young journalists can be heard coming from his radio. The fast-paced, staccato speech of these reporters often makes me think there must have been some dreadful disaster during the night, something like the sinking of the *Joola*, for example, or an attempt on President Daour Diagne's life.

The taxi that arrives every morning to pick up my neighbor Oulimata Mané's children, Gnima and Daouda, has just stopped outside the front gate, hooting twice. Before leaving for school, all neatly dressed and kitted out, they both come to greet me, and little Gnima makes a respectful curtsy. To tease her a bit, I say, "What a scatterbrain you are, my darling spouse! You mustn't go to the market again without first asking me to give you today's spending money. Look, here you are." What an astonishingly precocious young lady she is, Gnima! She bursts into laughter, takes the twenty-five franc coin I am holding out to her, and says with her high-pitched little voice: "Don't worry, my dear husband, tonight I am going to prepare the most delicious *daxin* with mutton tripe for you that you have ever tasted in your life!"

As soon as the two children have left, Lamine emerges from his room and walks up to me. It's obvious the day has got off to a bad start for him. Try as he might to hide his anger, he cannot control the shakiness in his voice when he says to me, "Old Nguirane, excuse my choice of words, but our politicians are no better than a pack of rabid dogs! They loot our country, and once they've ruined it, they go and live a life of luxury on the Côte d'Azur or some similar place. This is simply not acceptable! If they think we are no better than a herd of cattle they can lead to slaughter, they are mistaken!"

As I listen to him, I say to myself that if there has ever been a day in Lamine's life when he has truly wanted to wring someone's neck, it must be today, on this Friday morning. It's always the same story: a group of youngsters in their prime hear a report on the radio that makes them cross, and at the first opportunity, they smash everything to pieces. In the heat of the moment, it happens that they even cause bloodshed. But what exactly put Lamine into such a state? He is so furious, he forgets to tell me.

I could have asked him, but I am lost in old memories. Lamine reminds me of my own youth. Mind you, I had a lot more fire in my belly than he does. In my folly, I was convinced that "to die for the Cause" was the most desirable thing that could possibly happen to me. Unfortunately, I was just an ordinary unskilled worker and unaware of the fact that I was dealing with devious politicians. True cynics, they were. For intellectuals like them, the Revolution and all the rest of it was nothing but a big joke. They could see I took it all very seriously, and they used me. Today I feel embarrassed when I remember how naive I was in those days. I am often tempted to ask Lamine to take things a bit more lightly. The day is not far off when he will discover the bitter truth, but by then it'll be too late. He can't see through those villains who's strategy it is to make him do all the hard work while they go on feathering their nests, leaving him stuck in this miserable hovel for the rest of his life, waiting for Thioro Thiam to bring him his bowl of early morning *fonde*. If I tell him that, he'll just laugh at me. He will say: "Here goes another one of these old fuddy-duddies who doesn't understand that times have changed!" No Lamine, times never change. There he is, walking away with his swaying sailor's gait, his blue overalls under his arm. He gets as far as the front door, but then turns round and comes back again. I ask him if he has forgotten something.

"No," he says.

I see him hesitate. Lamine is visibly perturbed, and that worries me. I can tell this has nothing to do with politics.

I repeat my question: "What's the matter with you, Lamine?"

That's when he starts talking to me about you, Badou: "Last night, I saw Badou Tall in my dream, old Nguirane. I don't remember what we said to each other . . . That's all . . . I just wanted you to know that . . . After the prayer of *tisbaar*, it would perhaps be a good idea if you call in the children from the neighborhood to give them alms, biscuits, sweets or some rice cakes. It will be good for Badou."

"I will do it, Lamine."

Lamine has suddenly become very emotional. It may be because of his dream or simply because we have just mentioned your name for the first time since you left Niarela. Emphatically, he declares, "Old Nguirane, I never met a better fellow than Badou Tall in my entire life. No matter where he is on this earth, God will watch over him, don't ever doubt that."

At that point I tell Lamine I am practically certain I won't see you again and that the mere thought of it makes me very sad at times.

He shoots back, "Don't mention bad luck, please, old Nguirane!"

Just after you left, the whole of Niarela kept asking: "Badou Tall—where can he possibly be?" But that doesn't prevent Lamine from asking me the same question all over again: "Can it be true that even you, old Nguirane, aren't sure of Badou's whereabouts?"

Clearly, Lamine wasn't entirely convinced. It was as though he was saying to me: "You can hide the truth from the rest of the people here in Niarela, old Nguirane, but I live next door to you, almost like your own son, so why aren't you telling me where he is?" Lamine was not the only person to think like that in Niarela. I heard him muttering to himself that I wasn't telling him the truth. So I had to swear yet again he was wrong, and that I was expecting a letter from you any day.

Lamine seemed to believe me, and suddenly he was lost in his thoughts, slowly shaking his head. "If you, old Nguirane, don't know where Badou is right now, then who can? You were everything to him."

"Badou was everything to me, too," I said.

Then Lamine left, and all was quiet again in the courtyard.

As sometimes happens, inexplicably, I felt I was being watched. For several minutes already, there was this strong physical sensation somewhere in the nape of my neck. When I looked up, there was a cat sitting on top of the wall that surrounds the compound. We looked at each other. The glint in its eyes suddenly made everything seem unreal and vaguely unsettling. Without taking its gaze off me, the cat meowed, first once, and then again, before taking a supple leap and vanishing into the neighboring courtyard.

I never saw the animal again. And yet, not a single day has passed since then without my thinking about it. And when I do, I get the strangely uncomfortable feeling that it wanted to settle some old score with me.

Slowly but surely—and that's what I find so surprising—it made me ask myself questions I had never asked before.

Your name is Nguirane Faye. But who are you really, you, the man by the name Nguirane Faye? Don't you think that by now, close to the end of your life, you should at least be able to state clearly who you are?

Suddenly and for no obvious reason, I remembered the night you fell ill. It was an acute attack of cerebral malaria at two or three o'clock in the morning. Not a single bus or taxi in sight at that hour. Your mother, Bigué Samb, did not hesitate for a second. She tied you to her back, and the three of us set off across the deserted city.

When we got to the main city hospital, the doctor on duty examined you. He sounded terribly aloof when he said, "If you hadn't brought this boy now, he would have been dead by sunrise."

Another meow.

I turned round and looked at the wall again, but the cat was gone. Where could it possibly be?

. . .

As quick as a flash, I see myself bending over the lake. The water is clear, the surface perfectly smooth.

You call yourself Nguirane Faye, but who are you?

My alter ego seems amused by my bewilderment, but I am keen to take up the challenge. I want him to realize that he has no right to taunt me, and that I actually do know a thing or two about myself. Less than a year after I was born, my mother Khemes Sène fled from Mbering-Saaj in the Sine Delta, and somehow we ended up here in Niarela. And now I am in my eighties. My skin is on the light side, I am quite tall, and despite my age, I still manage to hold myself upright. What else? My father's name was Dibocor Faye. Yes, all these small, seemingly insignificant details make up a human life, and they have helped me find my bearings here on earth. It would definitely be wrong to accuse me of just standing by passively in the face of injustice. During my time as an employee at the Air Liquide factory, I led some very tough strikes there. Although I was tortured and imprisoned more than once, I always came out more determined than before to fight for my ideas and make them prevail in the end. I belonged to a group of patriots actively opposed to the submission of our country to foreign rule. I even went to Accra with my comrades, where President Kwame Nkrumah gave us a handsome sum of money and promised us guns.

I am saying all this in the full knowledge that it's not the correct answer to such a seemingly straightforward question: *Your name is Nguirane Faye, but who are you?* After so many lost battles and faded hopes, here I am now, at the mercy of the passage of time, like a hollow gourd swept away by the waves. You will understand when you read my *Notebooks* that mine was not what one would call a happy and fulfilling life. I have spent years literally just staggering around in the dark. No doubt it would have been better if I had steered clear of all those dreams and grandiose ideas. To spell out the brutal truth: my social status is nil, and not a single soul remembers me now. One day passes, then another and another. Each comes with its tribulations and its little sorrows. If we put them all in a row, one sunrise after another, that, apparently, is what we call time. Or a human life. Is it really that simple? No matter—each passing day brings us a bit closer to the one that blots out all the others under a thin layer of sand.

I may be talking to you about this only tonight, but I remember very clearly the first time I had this feeling of having been born in vain. The cat with eyes like glowing embers turned everything upside down for me.

On that day, I thought, "The God who made this and every other universe created us all, my name is Nguirane Faye and I am a descendant of Mame Ngor Faye. And yet, how can I claim to know myself if I don't even know who my ancestor's father and mother were? How many thousands of years ago did I set off on this journey that has taken me, Nguirane Faye and none other, all the way to the tree under which I am now sitting, in the courtyard of this house in Niarela, right here, and nowhere else in the world?"

You may well think all this is strange, Badou. And yet, sooner or later, every single one of us must set off and revisit his most distant past, asking himself when this whole story *really* started for him, and by that I mean his life among the rest of humanity. To accept that we don't know anything about all these things is like resigning ourselves to dying before we have even been born. But he who is courageous enough to travel back in time will eventually find who he was looking for: his deceased ancestors. Day and night, he'll have to listen to their pathetic weeping and wailing. He will hear the dead imploring God to take them back to their loved-ones because they are sick and tired of being shut up in their graves. As for you, Badou, never forget, please, that the present lives in the heart of the past. If you don't want time to run away from you again, be sure to catch them both in the palm of your hand and remember to close your fingers very tightly around them.

The sudden appearance of this cat, its meowing, and the vague sense of anxiety this kind of animal tends to inspire at times, all that has been troubling me for several days now.

It's as though a voice kept on saying to me, "Get up, Nguirane, go and say at least one prayer at Mame Ngor Faye's grave. There are still a few people left in Mbering-Saaj who remember the ancestor and who can tell you about him. Don't you want to know who you are and where you originally came from?"

■　■　■

And so it was, Badou, that I closed my bedroom door behind me one morning and set off to the Colobane bus station. Our Toyota minibus drove out of Dakar, past Rufisque and Bargny, and after the exit at Diamniado we continued straight down toward the Sine Delta. That's when scenes of my childhood started coming back to me. In my mind's eye, I saw a group of men sitting on the ground in a big inner courtyard covered with fine, yellow sand. Where was that? I can't remember. All I can say is that it was quite far away from Mbering-Saaj. About a dozen villagers were sitting in a circle, and there was one particular name that they repeated again and again. The way they spoke about Mame Ngor Faye, the ancestor who came from a small town in the Sine Delta, was imbued with respect and even, it seems to me, a certain amount of fear. His name fascinated me, and I wanted to ask all sorts of questions about him. But I was only a child and afraid that all I would get for an answer was a slap in the face. I imagined the adults putting me in my place with indignant remarks like "Who gave you permission to meddle in the affairs of the grown-ups?"

"This is simply unheard of!"

"One must wonder what the world is coming to, really!"

"Leave me in peace, cheeky little brat!"

All this seems to have happened in another lifetime, Badou. But time itself has never slowed down its pace and a few years later, having become a grown up myself, I took a wife and came back to live right here in Niarela with my family. And to this day, the name Mame Ngor Faye has never stopped going round and round in my head. I may never have met him, but that doesn't stop this ancestor from following me virtually everywhere. His soothing shadow is by my side night and day. He has been waiting patiently for centuries. And, you know, Badou, I sometimes tease him a bit. Then he rises up from the dead, pulls himself up to his full height and says to me, "Let those people talk, Nguirane. Just be aware that every single word that comes out of their mouth is a lie. The truth is this: if I am your ancestor, it is because you yourself have given birth to me."

With longing I look up at the stars, hoping they will send me a sign, but the stars are mute. Only the wind—yes, the wind still carries Mame Ngor Faye's breath.

Badou Tall, don't you want to know what the grown-ups in the sandy courtyard were talking about? Ask me, and I, Nguirane Faye, will tell you.

"I am asking you, Nguirane."

All right then, listen.

One of them started singing the praises of the ancestor's vast erudition and soon the others joined in in unison: "Even the royal families entrusted their children to him."

"No matter whether you were the child of a king or a pauper, he treated everyone the same. He was a righteous man, and princes with all their haughtiness didn't impress him."

"All right, I grant you that, but what about that terribly short temper of his?"

"Yes, his fits of rage were notorious!"

"He made you shake like a leaf in his presence."

"We can all pretend to have forgotten his outbursts, except you, Malick!"

When Malick heard his name, he looked up. With a nervous flicker of a smile, he agreed. "It's true, he never forgave me a single mistake. I remember the day when he chained me to a wooden post inside his sheep enclosure, where I was forced to spend the night sleeping with the animals. The following morning, at the crack of dawn, I got woken up with bowls of ice cold water and his lashes left me bruised and bleeding!"

Toward the end of his life, Mame Ngor Faye moved from there to Rufisque, where he settled down and married Bintou Diarra. But since they were both already quite old, the marriage was a sham. And now, Badou, just to tease me, you probably want to ask, "And the ancestress? What did they say about her?" Well, as odd as that may seem to you, nobody has ever mentioned her in my presence. So about the woman who gave birth to my father's father, I know nothing, not even her name.

You wanted to know what people were saying about Mame Ngor Faye. I have faithfully told you all I can remember. If I add a single word to this, it will be pure invention. Oh well, why shouldn't one invent a few things every now and again? Surely it's better to do that than to leave the portrait unfinished. Mame Ngor Faye was very dark skinned and a man of enormous physical strength. He was also extremely tall, almost a colossus. And, based on numerous eyewitness reports, I think I can state with confidence that he was an irascible figure whose murky eyes struck fear in people's minds. I always picture him crouching on a sheep skin with a cluster of young disciples at his feet; spellbound by the depth of his knowledge of the Divine, they are listening to his teachings of the One and Only.

How long ago was it when all of this happened? Just look at my white hair and my wrinkled skin and you will know that if it wasn't two whole centuries ago, it can't have been far off.

■ ■ ■

Mbering-Saaj is a small town about two hundred kilometers east of our capital. I got there in late morning. I climbed out of the Toyota minibus and wandered around for a long time without encountering a single living soul. In the past, a newcomer arriving in a place as deserted as Mbering-Saaj on that morning would have known instantly that everyone had gone to work in the fields. But times have changed and I was deeply perplexed by the dead silence in this town, which, at so early an hour, was already stifled by the heat of the sun. I continued walking haphazardly up and down the bumpy streets, hoping I might meet someone I could talk to. The few houses that weren't locked up seemed uninhabited.

Eventually I noticed a man all by himself, who was leaning against the bamboo fence of one of the homesteads.

I went up to him. We exchanged greetings, and he didn't take his eyes off me. He was probably asking himself, *Who is this stranger? What is he doing in our town?* I wanted to reply to his unspoken questions, but could I tell the very first person I came across why I had decided to go on such a long journey? It would have been a bit difficult to say to him, just like that, *I heard a cat meowing in Niarela very early one morning, and so I came here to find out more about the ancestor.*

Surely he would have thought I was mad. But this also I have to say, Badou: that fellow leaning against the fence didn't strike me as completely normal. His skin was covered in a rash that must have been terribly itchy. He kept scratching himself while simultaneously making soft little clucking noises, and all this was punctuated by a lot of twitching and grimacing that distorted his face horribly.

This is how I introduced myself to him: "My name is Nguirane Faye. Nobody knows me around here, but Mbering-Saaj is my home, since this is where I was born. You and I must be related, because my father Dibocor Faye was Mame Ngor Faye's grandson."

He looked up. "Did you say Mame Ngor Faye, stranger?"

As I had secretly anticipated, his facial expression changed.

Full of hope, I replied, "Yes, they called him Mame Ngor, but his real name was Birane Faye."

The man frowned and shook his head slowly and absentmindedly. "And you, stranger, you are trying to tell me you are his son?"

"No, that's not what I said. I said I am his great-grandson!"

"How can it be that you are the grandson of Mame Ngor Faye?"

"You're not listening to me! I am not his grandson, but his great-grandson!"

"Oh well, that's the first time I hear that Mame Ngor Faye was anybody's father or grandfather. Since when have you been his son, stranger?"

The fellow was obviously pulling my leg. I was fast losing my temper and replied sharply, "You seem to be playing the fool, my friend. What I told you is perfectly clear."

It was as though he had been waiting for his chance to fight this out with me. Having spat a large glob of phlegm directly at my feet, he took a few steps toward me, shaking with rage. His eyes were bulging, and his yelling must have boomed right across town, "Do you know who you are talking to, stranger? Oh, to Hell with it! Just like everyone else, you obviously think I'm crazy!"

Hearing this convinced me that the man must be deranged, and I started backing off to get away from him.

You remember Wolof Njaay's words, don't you, Badou: *If you want to embark on a boat to get to the other side of the river and the man at the helm is not quite in control of his senses, stay on the bank and let him leave without you.*

To be on the safe side, I was trying to get out of his way when a voice coming from behind said very quietly, "Stay calm, stranger, and don't, whatever you do, attempt to run away from him, because he would catch up with you in a flash and wring your neck as if you were a chicken. Just take a look at him, this fellow has superhuman strength."

I turned round and saw a very old man, much older than myself. With his pipe in his mouth, he gazed at me for a long time. His face had a mischievous expression and in a conniving tone of voice, he said, "My ears managed to steal a few patches of your conversation, stranger."

Unsure of myself, I replied, "Why did he want to attack me? I assure you, I have come here with the best intentions in the world."

The old man smiled at me, and the skin around his little eyes became even more creased than before.

He said, " I remember the name of a certain Birane Faye from my childhood. He died in Rufisque. It's him you are looking for, right?"

"Yes. Most people knew him by the name of Mame Ngor."

"In that case, we are talking about the same person." After a brief silence, he said, still looking at me, "And now stranger, I want you to explain to me in your own words why you have come all the way to Mbering-Saaj."

"I am here to visit my ancestor's grave and say a prayer for him."

"Say a prayer for Mame Ngor . . . that's certainly the first time I have heard such a thing. Here in Mbering-Saaj, nobody remembers ever having seen a relative of Mame Ngor Faye coming from far away to visit his grave."

His voice, which suddenly sounded hoarse and tense, intrigued me. Was he accusing me of having abandoned my ancestor, or did he mean the ancestor did not actually deserve a visitor to come and pray for him?

I felt slightly lost, but on the spur of the moment, I said: "For me, there is nothing strange about the fact that I haven't visited the ancestor before now. I live in Milan, and this is the first time in years I'm back in Senegal."

His response was scornful and sarcastic: "So you live in Milan, do you?"

"Yes. And there . . ."

The old man cut me short with two words, which he pronounced slowly, one after the other: "You lie." He sounded cold and heartless.

He paused, and then he said, "Nguirane Faye, you are lying. You don't even know where the city you are talking about is. Furthermore, I want to inform you that I know you much better than you know yourself. I can tell you the exact place from where you left the capital early this morning to travel to Mbering-Saaj. Without moving from this spot, I have watched you climb into a minibus at the bus station in Colobane. You took a seat at the back and handed the conductor a ten thousand CFA franc note. I heard you say you wanted to go to Mbering-Saaj. And you should also know that if it had pleased me, that Toyota would have rolled over going round the first bend, and you would never have made it as far as Mbering-Saaj. For someone like me it's really nothing to make their damned minibuses topple over on the road. I've caused the bodies of dozens of passengers to be crushed and scattered across the ravines more than once before. When you got here, you wandered around aimlessly for a long time, without encountering a single living soul in this town. And yet, from the moment you arrived in Mbering-Saaj, hundreds of pairs of eyes followed your every move. Yes, with great amazement, we all watched you as you were gingerly putting first one foot down on the soil of Mbering-Saaj, and then the other. You couldn't see any of us, but we were all able to see you. Wherever you went, you were being watched, and people were saying to each other under their breath, 'Indeed it looks as though this stranger is a genuine descendant of Mame Ngor Faye. What is he doing here? How can it be that this man has the audacity to come from so far away to challenge us?' That's the truth, Nguirane. And if you dare tell me any more lies about the city of Milan, that'll be the end of you."

I wanted to reply to that, but the words, like tiny bubbles of air, simply burst at the back of my throat and died there. So I decided to observe him all the more carefully. I was almost disappointed in the end that I couldn't discover anything unusual about him. He looked like skin and bones in his grey *sabadoor*. His white slippers were covered in a layer of dust, and there was nothing special about the *tengaade* planted on his head. That was the kind of headgear worn by peasants for protection against the sun since time immemorial. The old man seemed normal in every way, and that may have been the very reason his words were so disturbing to me.

At any rate, nothing was going according to plan, and I was beginning to think of this trip to Mbering-Saaj as pointless and downright dangerous.

The old fellow started talking again, in an icy, supercilious manner, and without taking his eyes off me: "I have called you a liar, Nguirane. How do you react to that?"

All I was able to muster was a pathetic mumble: "I implore you to be lenient with me. It's all I can do."

"Lenience or pity is not what this is all about. I want to know the truth, and nothing but the truth. Why have you come here, and what are you doing here among us? You don't seem to realize that this is a matter of life and death."

A matter of life and death . . .

My heart was pounding: yes, I had got myself into a fine mess. I couldn't help thinking of my early morning encounter with that cat in Niarela. I actually thought I could hear it meowing again. The old man kept looking at me intently, while thoughtfully sucking his pipe. What was I going to tell him? There are words that no Son of the Earth can utter without coming across as mentally deranged.

I thought, "I can never, ever, let him know that this whole story started with a meowing cat in Niarela and that it was that very cat whose meowing brought me here to Mbering-Saaj because I want to find out who I really am, and from which corner of His heaven God has plunged me, Nguirane Faye, into the maelstrom of time and the chaos that makes up this world. I am sure that if I tell him such utter nonsense, he will think I'm teasing him, and that could be very bad for me."

To change the subject, I asked him, "And you, who are you, then, old man? What is your name?"

"Nguirane, this is the beginning of the end," he said, after eyeing me disdainfully for several seconds. "Here in Mbering-Saaj even those who never set eyes on your ancestor know how much damage he did to us. I want you to be very clear about this: for us, Mame Ngor Faye was the worst of men."

These words struck me as so outrageous that I instantly forgot about my fear. "My friend, I was just asking for your name, and instead of answering me, you heap insults on my family . . ."

He looked me up and down again and said sharply, "I am going to repeat once more what I have just told you: Mame Ngor Faye, your ancestor, was the worst of men."

"What did you just say? Have I heard you correctly?"

"Yes, you have heard me correctly. Here in Mbering-Saaj, we remember Mame Ngor Faye's cruelty very, very clearly. Even the newborn infants are scared in Mbering-Saaj when someone mentions his name."

I am quite certain, Badou, that I never felt quite so inadequate at dealing with a situation as I did then. With bitter clarity, I said to myself, "One can barely imagine how atrociously the ancestor must have behaved toward the inhabitants of Mbering-Saaj if their hatred for him has lasted so many years."

My mind was on fire, although I had no idea what this was all about. Why all this shutting of doors when I arrived in this town, one after the other?

I tried to prod him a little bit. "There is no minibus going to Dakar until tomorrow. That means I am going to have to spend the night in Mbering-Saaj."

The old man pretended he hadn't heard me and asked the same question for the third time, "Why did you come here, stranger? I know you have answered me already, but I want to hear you say it again."

In the face of so much arrogance, cold rage suddenly gripped me, leaving no room for any other emotion.

I had no choice but to confront this, at the risk that it might cost me my life.

At this point in my story, I must tell you about a conversation I had in my youth with a man who was famous for his profound knowledge and wisdom. I was faced with a particularly difficult decision, and having listened to me patiently, he said, "My son, every time someone wants to trample on your dignity, remember the saying by Wolof Njaay. If you want to know which saying I am talking about, ask me, my son, and I will tell you."

"I am asking you."

"There goes a saying by Wolof Njaay: *If you insist on playing the drum with an ax, you will only be able to obtain one single sound from it, no matter whether it is sweet or unpleasant to your ears.*"

Badou Tall, there are days when we have to be strong enough to remember the simple fact that we will not die twice, but that death is an event just as unique and ludicrous as the sound of this drum. You can be afraid of it, of course, but not to the point of allowing just anybody to humiliate you.

That gave me the strength to answer him in a voice that was firm and clear, "If I have come all the way to Mbering-Saaj, it is for one reason, and one reason only: I want to know who this Son of the Earth by the name of Nguirane Faye really is."

Clearly intrigued by my manner of speaking he frowned. "Which Nguirane are you talking about? Is there another one apart from you?"

"I mean the Nguirane Faye who is standing right here in front of you. I am talking to you about myself and I want you to listen very closely to what I am about to say to you, old man. A few days ago, a cat looked deeply into my eyes and then it meowed twice. On that day, I lost my peace of mind, and it was then that I at last decided to find out who I am. A man who doesn't know where he comes from is like a leaf torn off a tree by the wind. It ends up whirling around in empty space. Just like this leaf, he is condemned to a life of idleness."

The piercing gaze of the old man reminded me of the cat in Niarela. First, he slowly shook his head, and then he pointed to a tree, entirely devoid of foliage, with a dry, grayish trunk that was covered with thin black cracks. "Do you see the *kàdd* over there?"

"The one that seems to be leaning toward the setting sun?"

"Yes. They are talking to each other, those two."

"Talking to each other . . . What can they possibly be saying?"

"Oh, nothing in particular. It's the hour when they usually bid each other farewell."

I was completely bewildered. "Bid each other farewell? Who is saying farewell to whom?"

"The setting sun to the *kàdd*."

"I want to know the hidden meaning behind those words."

"There is no hidden meaning. Every day at this hour, they bow in sync to bid each other farewell."

All this made very little sense.

"But . . . Wait a moment . . ."

No sooner had I calmed down a bit than his voice became harsh and menacing again: "You should mind your own business, stranger! You'd better leave now. When you get to the *kàdd,* turn left. After a few hundred meters, you will see the graveyard where your ancestor is buried."

I tried my luck with irony, "Well, well, well! The whole world should come and take lessons in hospitality from Mbering-Saaj!" I knew perfectly well, of course, that my cocky little remark was just a pretense intended to gloss over my abiding fear of the old man.

Clearly it was better not to provoke him.

Oh Badou Tall, what a story! What an incredible story! Just think of me there, with all my hopes and expectations of a royal welcome in Mbering-Saaj! I had really and truly expected my close and distant relatives from the neighboring villages to drop everything and come running at once, and I had imagined that, while we were paying each other our mutual respects, all the collective emotion and nostalgia would inevitably lead to a great deal of sobbing and shedding of tears. I had the strong sense that I had lived through all these scenes before and had seen all those people coming up to me and saying, in mock disbelief, "God Almighty! So the great Mame Ngor's very own flesh and blood is with us again. The stranger we see before us is called Nguirane Faye, a genuine great grandson of the chief who was the best and most righteous one we ever had."

I had even worried that in the course of their quarrels they might come to blows about who deserved the privilege of inviting me to his home, and that, because I didn't want to offend anybody, I would end up having to stay on a lot longer in Mbering-Saaj than originally planned. Every time I announced I was going back to Niarela, they wouldn't hear of it and repeated their tales of the exploits of my glorious ancestor, the intrepid conqueror who was also a great visionary and builder, all at the same time.

"A man of God like there are only a handful in an entire century!"

"At the time when he came to live in Mbering-Saaj, the pagan warriors were slaughtering innocent people, pillaging our villages and raping our women. With the Holy Book in one hand and his sword in the other, he alone dared oppose them."

"Ah, those despicable Unbelievers! It's best not even to talk about them.

Veritable hyenas, they were. They didn't care that he was trying to extricate their children from the clutches of idolatry, far from it. First they got drunk, gulping down countless bowls of palm wine, then they humiliated Mame Ngor Faye, kicking him and pissing on his head."

"But the truth of the heart never fails to triumph over brute force. Who still talks about those dissolute savages who were unable to restrain their morbid desires? Who among us would not be ashamed to admit today that he is descended from those pagans?"

"The poet Serigne Mbaye Diakhaté has left us his description of the senselessness of what was happening during that time. Nobody could have said it better!"

"Let's listen to a bit of what the great Serigne Mbaye Diakhaté had to say, my friend!"

And then, solemnly and with great dignity, one of them started chanting in a deep, sonorous voice:

Those who never stopped quarrelling
And thrusting their daggers in each other's bellies,
Those who did nothing but drink from sunrise to sunset,
Who can say today where they are now, the vile miscreants?
There surely cannot be a more heinous crime
Than to violate God's commandments.
He who is oblivious to this
Is bound to meet with a bad end.
Nobody knows
What has become of all those dissolute
Princes and ordinary men of the people you have all been
Swallowed up by the earth.
You, who were great once upon a time,
And you, the paupers of long ago,
Let me ask you: who knows today
What's become of you?

After this poetic interlude, the conversation started up again, in an even more animated fashion than before. "Mame Ngor Faye! A learned man of a new breed such as we have never seen here before!"

"True, he was a difficult character, but that's always the case with people of great integrity in this world so corrupted by lies."

Badou Tall, had I heard those perfectly plain words while I was down there, I would be a changed man today. "Nguirane Faye, a descendant of the ancestor who saved the souls of the pagans, Nguirane Faye, a descendant of the Master of Mbering-Saaj."

That's the vantage point from which I would like to see the world around me. A horizon very unlike my own interior landscape, which has always been far too narrow. It's a world that is much more open, where the air is pure and alive with the aura of Mame Ngor Faye. He founded a new nation down there in the Sine, where at every sunrise you can still hear the whinnying and neighing of his thoroughbreds galloping around the blazing huts. Screams of terror fill the air, and thousands of innocent people are dying. It certainly is not pleasant to watch. But isn't that how time has always given birth to itself?

At Mbering-Saaj, among the snake worshippers, Mame Ngor covered himself in glory by braving a thousand dangers.

When the battle is over, he leaves. Can you see him, Badou, at the very moment when I am talking to you about him? He walks in silence, apart from his men. They follow him at a respectful distance, because he wants to be the one leading the way. All the birds of creation are fluttering and twittering above his head, and further afield, the tall trees are leaning toward him as if offering him their shade, since the sun is already sweltering hot. He is lost in his thoughts, and barely aware of what is going on around him.

■　　■　　■

The old man stood in front of me and seemed to be reading my thoughts—at least that is how I interpreted the sneering look on his face. I couldn't really face the prospect of having to endure the chill and the damp out here for an entire night.

While trying hard to keep my composure, I said, "There is no way I am staying outdoors until morning."

"Well, then you should go back home before nightfall."

"I made a long journey to track down Mame Ngor's grave."

"So what?"

"Well, surely there must be someone who can lend me a room until tomorrow."

He made no reply.

I added, "I am prepared to pay."

With a scornful glint in his eye he said, "Like you, your ancestor was very stubborn; he never gave up. But that did not help him, I'm afraid. We forced him to his knees in the end."

Despite all that, I had the feeling he harbored a certain affection and secret admiration for Mame Ngor's strength of character.

"Surely you won't refuse me your hospitality," I said.

"We don't want you here, stranger."

It was as though we were no longer ourselves, he and I. It seemed as if our words, formed in the long forgotten past, had come and settled on our lips of their own accord.

He insisted, and this time he did so in a peremptory tone, "Be gone. Consider yourself lucky to be able to return to Niarela alive after treading on the soil of Mbering-Saaj."

Without a word, I started walking toward the graveyard. I could feel the weight of his gaze in the nape of my neck, and my steps were faltering.

■   ■   ■

There is another eye. We don't know it, and we cannot see it, because it is buried deep inside us. And yet, this inner eye alone gives access to the most secret places, places where none of us will ever set foot.

Far away, almost in line with the horizon, I could see a row of *kàdd* with fissured, grayish trunks; they had no leaves, but they were tall and slender. Interspersed between their roots were mounds of sand, most of them two to three meters apart. They were the graves, or rather what was left of them. Except for the occasional twittering of a few birds, there was total silence in the cemetery.

I had been wandering around for hours, increasingly oblivious to any lurking dangers. I simply couldn't have made such a long journey just to let fear get the better of me. I was walking up and down between the graves at a leisurely pace, taking my time to read and reread each inscription. Sometimes I had to brush away the sand that was covering the small nameplates, and if I found a name even vaguely reminiscent of Mame Ngor Faye, I felt eager to continue my search. And yet, something told me that this couldn't be the place where Mame

Ngor's body was buried. Certain signs, or rather vague inklings, convinced me of that more and more as I was trudging around in between the *kàdd*.

Today, back in Niarela, I understand that I basically lacked the courage to confront the awful truth: there was nobody down there for me to look for.

I was probably reluctant to put an end to my search, purely because I couldn't face the idea that the moment would come when everything was over, forcing me to leave the town without knowing where to go next.

But after a while, I realized I had no choice but to accept things as they were. Night was falling. Standing at the entrance of the cemetery, I noticed the few scattered lights of Mbering-Saaj toward the West. The town seemed even farther away now than a few hours ago. I felt like I was on an island encircled by a fringe of lights in the middle of a sea of darkness. The moment I turned my head the other way, total obscurity blotted out everything. It was as if I was suddenly both blind and unable to breathe. And yet—I guess in an extreme situation you adapt quickly—it didn't take long before I was almost at ease in this graveyard. My sense of pride told me to stop shaking like a leaf in front of people who would remain forever invisible to me. This was where my ancestor had covered himself in glory and I owed it to myself to remain worthy of him. And anyway, *if your enemy prays that you should starve to death, burp loudly every time he walks past you.* This proverb came back to me at the very time when I felt utterly overcome by my hatred for this enigmatic town.

I had no choice but to wait it out until the morning when I would be able to go and catch a minibus on the main road. Armed with a stick made of *kel*, I sat down, and, leaning against a large rock, I started piling up a heap of pebbles in front of me.

Although the wood of the *kel* is well known for its hardness, it was a laughable protection against snakes, jackals, and, last but not least, the inhabitants of Mbering-Saaj. I was determined of course, to sell my skin at the highest possible price, but it was obvious I wouldn't be able to defend myself very well with that stick.

Soon the little town was totally immersed in the dark. It was fascinating to watch the lights going out one after the other.

I was probably dozing when I heard footsteps crunching the grass nearby. The profound silence meant every sound was very distinct. I was just about to open my mouth when a voice said softly, "No need to be afraid, it's me."

I was on edge and prepared for anything.

"Who are you?"

The man was trying to sound like someone who is aggrieved because his friend has forgotten him after a period of separation. Only, it didn't ring true.

"So you already don't recognize me anymore, Nguirane Faye?"

There was something quite unique—but what? How I wish I knew how to describe it!—in the way he was pronouncing my name. Nothing but my fear prevented me from recognizing him sooner. It was the old man with the *tengaade* and his pipe.

He sat down on the ground opposite me and came straight to the point. "So have you found what you were looking for, Nguirane Faye?"

I was quite taken aback by his way of addressing me so naturally, without the slightest hostility in either his words or his gestures. I even thought I could detect a tinge of weariness in his voice. It's of course possible that my memory was playing tricks on me, but I definitely felt that away from the prying eyes of his people, he was relieved to be able to just be himself. This fleeting impression was quickly replaced by another, much more unpleasant one. I suspected this man was mocking me. I was on my guard and wanted to remain aloof, so I said, "It was you who chased me out of town like a mangy dog, wasn't it?"

"You shouldn't be so vindictive, Nguirane. Forget that incident."

Hearing him speak so calmly infuriated me.

"What's your name, old man?" I asked with the brazenness of someone who has nothing to lose.

"No reason to be so bad tempered, my son. In Mbering-Saaj they call me . . ."

He told me his name, but I cannot recall it, however hard I try. If one day I should remember it, I will write it down here in these *Notebooks* for you. For the first time since my arrival in Mbering-Saaj, I felt as though I had gained the upper hand over the person I was talking to. Barely able to conceal my anger, I said, "You have finally told me your name. But that's not enough."

"What else do you want to know, Nguirane Faye?"

"I want you to tell me why you are playing with me like this. I want to know what kind of game it is you're playing. I won't let you leave here until you have told me."

Although it was pitch-dark, I could sense that this gave him a start, and I quickly understood that I had overestimated myself.

"Don't speak to me like this, please," he said, in a voice that had suddenly turned icy again.

Those words were enough. A few furtive gestures told me he was armed—probably with a dagger—and that he was ready to use it.

One might say my hour of truth had arrived. Never have I felt the cold breath of death so close to my skin as I did then, nor have I ever been so afraid. And since I vowed never to lie to you, Badou, I have to admit that my conduct on that occasion wasn't exactly courageous. I very quickly forgot all my aspirations to heroism, and not a single one of Wolof Njaay's proverbs came to my rescue. All I could do was beg this stranger to have pity on me, while trying to avoid total shipwreck in a last-ditch attempt at preserving my dignity.

"If—entirely unintentionally—I have hurt you, I want to ask your forgiveness," I said.

"I am glad you have come to your senses at last," said the old man. "It's better like that for you."

He paused, as if trying to control his anger, and mumbled something. I was relieved. I knew then that the danger had passed. Another spell of silence followed, and finally he said calmly, but perfectly aware that I was at his mercy, "Let me repeat my question one more time: have you found what you were looking for, Nguirane Faye?"

I responded in a tone so neutral that I myself was surprised: "Despite walking around the cemetery several times and stopping in front of each grave, I have been unable to find even the slightest trace of the ancestor. Tomorrow morning at first light I am going back to Niarela."

Again, I was tempted at that point to drop a sarcastic little remark about the unforgettable hospitality proffered by the people of Mbering-Saaj, but was too much of a coward to actually do it. He did not respond, and I expressed my disappointment by saying, more to myself than to the old man: "I should never have left there."

"You shouldn't talk like that," he replied. "I assure you that you will not leave this town empty-handed."

I looked at him. Although my eyes were a bit more used to the darkness by now, I could barely make out his silhouette. But, due to the sheer intensity of the moment, this hardly mattered.

"Yes," he said, "I am here to give you something as a gift from Mbering-Saaj."

"A gift from Mbering-Saaj?"

"Yes."

That was all he said, visibly keen to remain shrouded in mystery. All this was beginning to get too much for me.

"I have literally bent over backward to avoid being difficult," I said. "Don't you think you should rather leave me alone in this place where you are forcing me to spend the night?"

I was perfectly calm when I said this, hoping that my tone of voice would make him aware there was a certain line that nobody must overstep.

He was surprisingly conciliatory. "I understand your bewilderment, Nguirane. The gift I have brought you from Mbering-Saaj is neither palm wine nor dried fish nor baskets of mangoes or papayas."

"Well, what is it then?"

"It is neither cassava nor any of the things one usually offers to a visitor before he leaves."

"What is it, then?"

I made no attempt to hide my growing curiosity.

"Nothing that would weigh heavily upon your shoulders, Nguirane. I have come to bring you some words."

"Words?"

"Yes, Nguirane. I am bringing you some words from Mbering-Saaj."

There was yet another silence. Neither of us said anything, for different reasons, I guess. He was taking his time, getting ready to carry out a mission that was clearly of the utmost importance to him. I, on the other hand, was utterly dumbfounded. Despite the gravity of the moment, I couldn't suppress a wry little smile, since the unusual ways of the inhabitants of Mbering-Saaj amused me. Funny birds they were, these people. Quite complicated, in fact. And then I had a surprising reaction: I burst out laughing. To this very day, I cannot say whether I did it on purpose or whether it happened spontaneously. Most probably it was just a release of the tension building up inside me while I was waiting. The old man seemed neither angry nor keen to call me to order. Once I had regained my composure, he simply said, "Now listen to me carefully, Nguirane. Here is what I have come to tell you on behalf of Mbering-Saaj."

For the first time since opening these *Notebooks*, Badou, someone other than I will speak to you. I am passing his words on to you exactly as they came out of his mouth. I have neither left out nor added a single one. For that reason alone, I wish I could remember the old man's name. However, that may be a lot less important than we think it is.

. . .

How often in the course of your lifetime do you see your own face in the mirror, Nguirane? Probably not very often, just like the rest of us. No human being, unless he is somehow deranged, will stand in front of a mirror for hours on end, looking at himself. It is in the nature of our reflection to be fleeting.

Joy. Anger. Sadness. All this comes upon us without warning and is gone in a flash. There is never enough time to examine the traces left behind on a person's face. But there is another mirror that gives you the chance to read your soul. Do you want me to tell you what that is? It is the eyes of the others. The eyes of the people close to you, or even the eyes of a passing stranger of whom you only catch a glimpse in a narrow little lane downtown; someone you will see once, in other words, and never again. You would be surprised how much the stillborn glance from those eyes can tell you about yourself.

You are me.

I am you. This is as true for the members of a group as for each human being on his own.

But the day inevitably comes when a nation is afflicted by adversity. Things lose their proper shape; they become blurred and indistinct. The wise man says, "Alas, what has happened to the path leading us to our Truth? Suddenly our feet, instead of being planted firmly on the ground, are floating in empty space. Trickery and lies have gained the upper hand, and all at once, we are cut off from the signs and signals that used to guide us. He who has done this to us, who is he, and where did he come from?" A handful of courageous men rise up above the multitude, exclaiming, "Why should we sell our souls for next to nothing? Let's rebel against foreign rule."

They are treated like cranks.

People tell all sorts of nonsense to pacify them. "Haven't you heard it yet? The new wind will purify the air."

People taunt them. "Can't you stop talking about your boring old ancestor? He was defeated and humiliated. Why would you want us to join him on his interminable, aimless wanderings?"

Think of the mango leaf, Nguirane. Full to bursting of the waters of heaven, breathing the air with all the vigor of its lungs, green and intensely alive, it is the essence of life itself, and myriad different species of butterfly are weaving a crown of many colors above its head. When birds come to tickle it, it quivers with pleasure.

However, one day that same leaf becomes unrecognizable. Little by little, it starts to decay. First a few small, yellowish patches appear along the edge. Then you see a hole, followed by more and more gaping holes. It gets creased, gradually loses its sap and before long the leaf has become like an old man whose rotten teeth are falling out one by one. One evening, a solitary walker treads on it, and it turns to dust.

Here in Mbering-Saaj, it has always been our custom to be very hospitable. Far and wide, Mbering-Saaj was known as a haven of peace. Back in the days when our neighboring kingdoms were embroiled in ferocious wars against each other and when honor and fortune were measured by the number of enemies killed on the battlefield—that is to say when madness and hatred ruled supreme—everyone knew that once a fugitive had crossed the border and managed to reach Mbering-Saaj he was safe.

And now, Nguirane Faye, I will tell you something that I have kept secret from you up to now: it was us who sent you the cat you heard meowing the other morning in the courtyard of your house in Niarela. We called you, you came, and now you will hear what we have to say to you about your ancestor Mame Ngor.

First of all, Mame Ngor didn't even belong here. Like a lost soul, he just arrived one day from Ndiorène, the land of his birth. He'd been presumptuous enough to think he could turn the minds of its people inside out, so he was chased away from there. After spending a long time listening to his prophecies without having the slightest idea what he was talking about, his relatives in Ndiorène quite simply told him, "Mame Ngor, leave us in peace, please. We want you to go somewhere far away from here."

Afterward of course, like so many other nations, Ndiorène succumbed to the giddy ideas of the Nameless One and ended up adopting the doctrines Mame Ngor had tried to impose on them. I am telling you this just by the way, Nguirane, but the fact is that the people of Ndiorène have only themselves to blame for being so feeble-minded. When they look back on their most distant past today, they cannot understand why the dates and places that make up their history don't speak the same language. Here in Mbering-Saaj, on the other hand, we have remained faithful to the path our Ancestor traced for us. For centuries, we have had to deal with strangers coming here from every corner of the planet. Without exception, they all tried to break us—just into two pieces, mind you, not more. Please take careful note of that. We managed to get rid of them all in the end. We aren't stupid, Nguirane, we know how the world works. And we know exactly what a disgraceful state of indignity other nations have sunk into, for one reason and one reason only, and that is their inability to remain themselves. Being ashamed of oneself can have extremely tragic consequences. We have seen it with our own eyes, since it has happened to our neighbors. We, on the other hand, refuse to be like the dead leaf that is trodden on and reduced to dust by a passerby who is not even aware of it. No, the sap in our veins is nourished by the rain and the wind, and bold enough to lick the face of the heavens.

That's who we are.

We've always known it.

Mame Ngor, alas, didn't know it.

He was the most arrogant individual we ever set eyes upon in Mbering-Saaj. It was our custom never to refuse strangers who came here anything, and Mame Ngor was welcomed with open arms. He wanted land, so we gave him land. He wanted to marry one of our young women, and nobody found the words to oppose him. When he told us about his travels to other countries, we were enthralled, since we weren't used to having strangers living with us here in Mbering-Saaj who had visited such mysterious, far-away lands. We saw him as someone with great knowledge, and so he quite naturally became one of the most highly respected men in Mbering-Saaj. But he misread our generosity for weakness and said to himself, "These people in Mbering-Saaj are ignorant of the Truth, that's why they don't resemble me. I am going to turn them into human beings worthy of that name."

He, like so many others, thought he could fill our heads with a lot of hot air about exotic places with outlandish names.

One day, we were utterly bewildered when we heard him scream, "I am offering you Truth as vast as the entire universe, and you want to talk to me about the way things are done in your godforsaken little corner of the planet! How much longer are you going to obey that ancestor of yours? Don't you see, blockheads that you are, that he was not infallible?"

On that day, Nguirane, we understood that the moment had come to give Mame Ngor a clear answer.

This is what we said to him: "The Ancestor is still alive in us, and we know he is infallible. He has never misled us. Why do you want to make us exchange him for another?"

Instead of calming him down, as we had hoped, our words only intensified Mame Ngor's rage. In response, he roared that we were more akin to wild beasts than human beings.

Have you ever heard anything more insulting, Nguirane Faye? Today, more than a century after they were spoken, these words are still ringing in our ears.

On the verge of madness, Mame Ngor was not content with the sacrilege he had already committed. Eager to impress us, he declared, "Tonight, something exceptional will happen in Mbering-Saaj. Each one of you will see it with his own eyes, and that will be the end of any doubts you may have wanted to cast on the unique Truth."

At the appointed hour, we followed him deep into the forest. There, in a clearing, we waited for his miracle, but it never happened. All that mumbo jumbo, the oscillations, the rolling of eyes and the incantations came to naught. Believe me, we nearly killed ourselves making fun of him behind his back. But it was a terrible setback for Mame Ngor and seemed to make him more hysterical than ever. He started telling us far-fetched stories about the birth of the universe, the composition of matter and the movements of the stars. Nothing he told us bore any resemblance to what we knew! How could a man who claimed to have traveled around the world be so wrong? And furthermore, he never uttered a single sentence without more or less openly accusing our Ancestor of being a liar.

The whole thing was a scandal, and the moment had come to put an end to it.

And now, Nguirane, my father, my very own father will take over and speak to you. The words he addressed to your ancestor all those many years ago have been passed down by the chroniclers through the generations, and they are as follows: "Mame Ngor! Mame Ngor! Mame Ngor, you came to us as a stranger, and we received you with kindness. Why don't you stay where you belong? The sky above our heads is made up of billions of stars. Believe me, Mame Ngor, we can tell you everything about each one of those stars, we can tell you how it was born and when it will die. Mame Ngor! Mame Ngor! Mame Ngor . . . stay where you belong!"

These powerful words were spoken by my father in the midst of a long spell of silence; they put Mame Ngor into a state of violent agitation. Looking wild-eyed and furious, he cupped his hands around his mouth and yelled, "Are you pretending you can count the stars in the sky, people of Mbering-Saaj? Do you realize what that means? I do not know your Ancestor, and I don't want to know anything about him, but I am telling you that he has purely and simply deceived you! Oh, if only you knew what's in store for you!"

What impudence! The crowd started to show signs of irritation, and someone called out in disbelief, "Is it really our Ancestor you are talking about in those terms, Mame Ngor?"

But to remain truthful, I have to admit that Mame Ngor, your ancestor, was a man of great courage. No doubt his fearlessness saved his life on that fateful day, as it had done so often before. Although his life was at risk, he remained firm. "People of Mbering-Saaj, I urge you to distance yourselves from the man you call your Ancestor. He has already lost you, and he will lose your children as well. That man knows nothing about the sun and the moon, and he is a fool. Do not put your faith in his lies!"

Not one of us was prepared to believe that a normal human being could possibly say something so outrageous, in broad daylight, in a public square in Mbering-Saaj without being struck dead by lightning that very instant. A few admitted later on they first started having doubts at that moment.

One person asked him, "If our Ancestor is lying to us, who will tell us the Truth?"

Mame Ngor was a stubborn man, clearly unable to let go of his idée fixe. "Your Ancestor is a fool," he replied.

"Well, we are listening, Mame Ngor. Talk to us, since you alone know the Truth."

As I told you before, Nguirane, many of us were appalled by Mame Ngor's brazenness. If we let him speak, it wasn't just to confuse him, but because we were genuinely eager to hear what a man like him had to say to us. We think we have always been open to the outside world here in Mbering-Saaj and on that day, your ancestor almost succeeded in converting us to his ideas. We formed a circle around him so we could listen to him undisturbed. It wasn't long, though, and we gazed at each other, aghast. Before us was a deplorable sight; first his muscles started twitching, then his entire body was racked by convulsions and his face turned into a hideous grimace—that's the state Mame Ngor was in when he addressed us in a language we had never heard him speak before. We didn't understand a single syllable of what he was saying.

It occurred to us afterward that we may have been wrong in thinking he was talking to us and that he was actually embroiled in a huge quarrel with invisible beings. We could see he was fully absorbed in battling the forces of darkness, but at the same time he seemed terribly lonely.

This appalling spectacle took away our last remaining doubts. The sages of Mbering-Saaj said, "This man deserves our pity, for only a madman would behave like that. It is our duty to cure him."

It was decided to entrust him to the Master who often in the past had wanted to draw our attention to Mame Ngor's case. But, outraged at the idea of being taken in hand by one of us, he showered the Master with insults and accusations and put up such a violent struggle that we feared for your ancestor's life.

We were tired of fighting by then and proposed a sort of truce: "Mame Ngor, maybe the path you have chosen is the best one for the whole of mankind. That's not impossible. Here in Mbering-Saaj, we don't claim to know who on this earth is right and who is wrong, but no outsider has the right to interfere with our decisions. We are telling you to stick to your convictions and let us stick to ours; it's the only way we can live together in peace. Since we have never chased a stranger away from Mbering-Saaj, we won't force you to move very far from here. All we ask is that you settle down somewhere close to the border of our territory so that we can all live in peace."

Mame Ngor did not object.

For several years, he kept to himself. We thought he had recovered his senses. How wrong we were. Mame Ngor was a crank on the brink of insanity, prepared to go to any lengths in order to impose his mad ideas on other people. No, he hadn't given up on his plan to subject us to his rules; all that had changed was his way of doing it. He was patiently weaving his web, secretly planting his newfangled ideas in the heads of our children and sowing discord among the most powerful families to secure political support. He even managed to conduct himself like a great sage when settling quarrels he himself had furtively instigated.

One day, he started speaking his strange language again, but that wasn't all.

Armed with a piece of wood, he drew some signs in the sand: "The signs you see here," he said, "indicate the Way, the only one that is viable for all human beings."

So Mame Ngor was back at it again, peddling his harebrained ideas. This time, however, we were trapped. He now had support from many of the influential personalities in Mbering-Saaj, either because they'd been won over by his nebulous promises or because they wanted to take revenge on others for cheating them. One morning, we noticed a triumphant sparkle in his eyes and he finally looked more relaxed. According to the chroniclers, this was the one and only time he ever attempted to smile.

He declared, "From now on, I alone will be the ruler of this land."

We all paid allegiance to him. Only the proudest and most prescient among us chose to leave and go into exile that very night.

Mame Ngor's reign was brutal and barbaric. His men often seemed to pillage, torture and kill more for their own amusement than out of political necessity. In the beginning, the shock was so great that no one had the courage to oppose Mame Ngor. The streets of Mbering-Saaj were deserted immediately after sunset, and before long, neighbors stopped standing in the doorways for their usual friendly chats. Everyone was terrified of being denounced to Mame Ngor's henchmen. Only our women dared resist, albeit not openly. They did this by composing songs with a double meaning—in a slightly altered form, we still hear them today—mocking the cowardice of their brothers and husbands in the fight against the Lion of Mbering-Saaj. Surreptitiously and with great cunning, they also ridiculed the tyrant himself while pretending to extol his courage and integrity. Oh, those were dark years, Nguirane! If only you knew how much we suffered! Allow me to take you on a brief excursion into our tormented past.

Mame Ngor has taken it upon himself to dispense justice in the public Meeting Square of Mbering-Saaj. The sessions are open to the public. Not content with having his opponents assassinated, he insists on openly humiliating them, too. One of the chroniclers describes how he used to lie stretched out in his hammock, with our most beautiful young girls, all of noble birth, massaging and fanning him. A long line of ordinary citizens are waiting to pay tribute to him with bowls of sour milk or other food items—you may be interested to know, Nguirane, that your ancestor had a passion for *ñeleŋ* and Birane Diop mangoes.

Occasionally he looks up, chewing a mouthful of food. He runs his eyes over the crowd. All of a sudden he asks, "Where is so-and-so today? We haven't seen each other for a while. Ha! Could it be that so-and-so is hiding from me?"

This is a terrifying question, because everyone knows that so-and-so will be dead by nightfall. He emerges from the crowd and kneels down in front of Mame Ngor. The latter, after a lengthy silence, points an accusing finger at him. "My friends here in Mbering-Saaj, I am calling on you as my witnesses. I have been told that behind my back, this man tells absurd lies about the human anatomy and the origin of the salt in seawater. I bid him to repeat his clandestine words here and now, in front of everyone."

The unlucky fellow starts to whimper like a child and swears, shaking with fear, that he has always been faithful to Mame Ngor's teachings. "I have never done anything bad! My benevolent king, it's my enemies that are slandering me."

The crowd sneers at the accused, they spit in his face and they insult him.

Mame Ngor smiles: "Are you also denying that you have disregarded the food prohibitions I decreed?"

The accused remains silent. Now he is trapped. He knows that his moment of truth has arrived.

This time, Mame Ngor's words sound more solemn: "You all know I am not a good judge since I tend to listen to my heart. I would rather let you decide this man's fate, people of Mbering-Saaj."

Immediately loud voices are heard, coming from the crowd. "Let's condemn him to death, the drunkard! The drinker of palm-wine must be put to death!"

Mame Ngor makes a fleeting, perfunctory gesture and immediately a bunch of burly young men overpower the poor wretch and drag him away into the bush. As soon as it is dark, his family will hear the sinister growling of the hyenas, gorging themselves on his flesh.

But, Nguirane, no matter how long or how dark the night, the day will come when the sun appears again on the horizon. A few brave men awakened us from our slumber. They decided to attack Mame Ngor's troops, refusing to give in. The battle was ferocious and continued for several months, but finally, Mame Ngor ordered his army to retreat. This is how he was finally beaten; the scene has remained etched in the memory of all who witnessed it for the rest of their life, and we, the people of Mbering-Saaj, have inherited that miraculous moment as our legacy. Mounted on their snow-white steeds, one and all, with their swords held high, Mame Ngor and his horsemen circled Mbering-Saaj seven times, uttering war cries in their weird, incomprehensible language. The neighing of the horses grew louder and more vehement all the time. Before turning his back on us for the final time, defeated and with fury in his heart, Mame Ngor cursed Mbering-Saaj. What a short memory he had, your ancestor! Had he forgotten already that our people have always taken revenge, blow for blow? When he cursed us, threatening to make us perish in an abyss filled with white-hot embers, we cursed him back even more forcefully. If only you could have seen our Ancestor on the battlefield, astride a leopard! As he pounced on the enemy, his mount was sucking the stars out of the sky with his breath, whereupon the fish, in terror, huddled up against the rocks at the bottom of the sea. It's amazing to think that we are descended from this giant, we, the people of Mbering-Saaj. I don't want to upset you, Nguirane, but your ancestor's thoroughbreds nearly made us laugh with their little circus number! A few weeks later, he came back and tried to overpower us in the dead of night. But we were expecting him, and we were prepared. We definitely don't count ourselves among those nations that succumb to a surprise enemy attack twice. Mame Ngor and his men hardly had enough time to set a few huts ablaze when we were already there, beating them back. We made mincemeat out of them and—let disgrace and misery be heaped upon them a thousandfold!—Mame Ngor and the other two survivors of his army owed their lives to a cowardly escape.

I would like to leave you with this final message, Nguirane Faye: we have been assaulted by far more powerful foreigners than Mame Ngor in the past. There were times when they came from the east, and there were times when they came from the west. They never spoke a language we could understand, but all of them, with equal determination, wished our Ancestor dead. And they were mad enough to want to make us his murderers! They thought of themselves as eagles and regarded us as the kind of prey that would be easy to devour! Well, we were forced to disillusion them very, very quickly. Nguirane, we may be cut off from the outside world here in this desolate spot, but the turmoil so many of our neighbors are in tells us that we were right. They feel sorry for us, it seems, but here in Mbering-Saaj, we don't envy them. And always remember this, Nguirane Faye: I am not talking on behalf of millions of human beings. What I am saying is meant for the few thousand inhabitants of Mbering-Saaj who are happier here than anywhere else on earth.

And as for you, I realize it's uncomfortable for you to be leaning against this rock while your body is slowly getting drenched with dew. However, the sheer fact that you are sitting at the entrance of this graveyard shows you are still alive. By chasing you away from Mbering-Saaj today, we have done exactly the same thing to you that we did to Mame Ngor a century and a half ago, with the sole difference that in those days we were armed. I told you that no one has ever come here to pray at Mame Ngor's grave. That should have helped to convince you that your ancestor is not buried here. Go and look for him elsewhere. And how can you possibly imagine you were born here? That really is the height of madness.

I wish you a peaceful night, Nguirane. Nothing will happen to you this time: we called you, you came, and we have told you what you needed to know. But if between now and the end of time any descendant of Mame Ngor dares to set foot in Mbering-Saaj again, he will pay for it with his dear life.

THE TALE OF THE ASHES

I CAN SEE HOW BAFFLED YOU ARE AFTER HEARING THE STORY ABOUT MY trip to Mbering-Saaj. Lost in your thoughts, you have been sitting there for a long while, leafing through these pages. I hear you murmuring, "For once, I really disagree with Nguirane . . ."

Slowly, I straighten myself up. I am surprised. "What do you mean, Badou?"

You recognize my voice, and you look around, but you cannot see me.

I reassure you, "I am at your side, Badou. I will be with you on your life's journey until the very end, even though you won't be able to see me."

Now, at last, you are prepared to speak your mind. "The night you spent in Mbering-Saaj has not been in vain, Nguirane."

"I was dead beat when I got back home . . ."

"I know. But you learned a lot down there, didn't you?"

I just about have the strength to snigger. "I would have preferred to remain completely ignorant of Mame Ngor's pathetic exploits on the battlefield!"

You think I am trying to make fun of you, and you nearly lose your temper with me. "Stop pulling my leg, Nguirane. You may be peacefully asleep down there, but your memory is wide awake. Never in your life have you learned so much about yourself as you did during that night in Mbering-Saaj."

"I'm not sure I understand what you mean . . ."

"Nguirane, you love talking to me about mirrors all the time. Now it's my turn to tell you that Mbering-Saaj has held up a mirror to you."

We continue chatting about Mame Ngor for a little longer, and I say to you, "The grave I searched for in vain in Mbering-Saaj is somewhere else. When you are back in Niarela, I want you to go and find the place where the ancestor was laid to rest. That will be the starting point of our family history."

This seems to give you a fright. "What you are asking of me is beyond my strength."

"Don't get me wrong. Remember that time is circular and the ancestor is not yet born. It's you yourself who have to give birth to him."

.　■　■

It is Friday, the day of your father's funeral.

Large numbers of relatives and friends are flooding in from everywhere, since after the prayer of *tisbaar*, it will be time to go to the cemetery. Together with some of the other young men from the neighborhood you are busy putting up the big tent right here where I am sitting now. Next, you start arranging the rows of chairs inside. The early afternoon heat is almost unbearable.

Obviously, for me, this is not just a normal day like any other. I have to supervise everything. But in reality I am mainly concerned about Mbissane and his sister Mbissine, the two children Yacine Ndiaye brought back with her from Marseille. They simply don't fit in with the other children in Niarela. They do everything differently, and I am worried they might misbehave toward the many mourners who will be at the funeral. No matter where they go, I will never let Mbissine and Mbissane out of my sight, ready to intervene the moment they put a foot wrong.

Ngoné Thioune, one of our neighbors, has hobbled over from her place and is shouting at the top of her voice, "Mbissane! Where on earth are you, Mbissane? Come here!"

Someone jokes, "Ah, our two little *Toubabs*!"

"They can't be far," says another, "I saw them around here just a moment ago."

Ngoné Thioune starts yelling again, "Mbissane! Mbissine!"

The boy comes sauntering round the back of the house and stops dead right in front of Ngoné Thioune. He haughtily looks her up and down and stamps his foot on the ground. With an irritated gesture, he rattles off something very fast in French.

What insolence! Mbissane is in trouble because Ngoné Thioune is not the kind of person who will let a naughty little boy be rude to her without teaching him a lesson. She grabs one of his ears between her index finger and thumb, and, giving him a harsh look, more to scare him than out of anger, she scolds him, "Stop talking to me like that, little brat! If you ever do that again, I will make you pay for it very dearly. And don't you dare move so much as an inch from here!"

After that, Ngoné Thioune resumes her shouting, "Where is the other one? Mbissine! Where are you, Mbissine?"

Mbissane looks puzzled and tells her something for the second time. Ngoné stops a young man who is walking past. "What did he just say?"

The young man smiles. "I heard it, but he talks too fast, the little chap, I can't understand a word he's saying."

Then he turns to the boy. "Your auntie Ngoné wants you to repeat what you just said!"

"My sister is deaf, so there's no point in calling her name. This is all just so silly!"

The young man does his best to translate for Ngoné Thioune. "He says that Mbissine is deaf."

At that point Ngoné called you, Badou Tall, "Go and fetch Mbissane's little sister for me. I want to talk to both of them."

You don't have time to reply to her. Mbissine, who was probably hiding not far from here, is coming up to you.

While I look at her, my mind turns back to her father's time in Marseille. A whole chapter of Assane Tall's life, the most important one in fact, will remain a mystery to me forever. Mbissane was born as a result of it, as well as this little eight-year-old girl, Mbissine, for whom her mother—may God forgive me for thinking this!—is an extremely bad role model. That at least is what people are whispering in Niarela. The other thing they say is that Assane Tall's widow has been slightly unhinged for several years now.

There you are, walking past, just as Imam Keita and I are finalizing some of the details about the funeral. After prayers, the mourners will want to pay Assane their last respects. It's a delicate situation: we have to avoid letting the ceremony drag on for too long without offending anybody. I see you walking up to your mother, Bigué Samb, and while you are talking to each other I suddenly realize the shocking finality of it all, the fact that it's all over for Assane and that by the end of the day he will have been laid to rest for all eternity under a few inches of sand.

Now you are standing next to Mbissane. He is telling you something, and I see you nodding your head. A moment later, his sister Mbissine joins you. She, too, is saying something to you and gesticulating vividly with her little hands.

Ngoné Thioune, who is watching the three of you from a distance, rests her chin in her hand and exclaims, "These two little *Toubabs*! Their presence in Niarela is not a good omen! I, Ngoné Thioune, am telling you right now that this story is bound to end badly!"

"You are not the only one to think that, Ngoné!" echoes another voice.

I can assure you that none of us here in Niarela has ever come across a woman who behaved like Yacine Ndiaye. She spent her entire mourning period crouching on a mat on the floor, with half her face hidden behind a scarf. When members of our family came to pay their respects, she held out her hand to them while keeping her eyes averted, then abruptly pulled it back. Initially, a few of us thought her conduct was due to the depth of her sorrow. But in reality, it was her way of letting us know that she didn't want anyone to come near her. That, incidentally, was what made people hate her so much, right from the start. And that is also why, without ever mentioning her name, people welcomed every opportunity to denigrate her. "It's no secret how she was earning her living in Marseille!"

"Uglier than a she-monkey!"

"I am not surprised that she hides her face!"

"A widow who invites a drunkard into her bed! This is unheard of in Niarela!"

I know these last words concern none other than Tamsir Bâ, Yacine Ndiaye's lover. Never will I forget the day I dared to broach that subject with her. "Tamsir is my cousin," she replied crisply.

"A cousin who comes and spends the night with you?"

"Yes," she said, seemingly unfazed, "he comes and keeps me company."

Yacine Ndiaye didn't even attempt to tell a decent lie. I could sense that she was furious with me, and I expected her to explode at any moment, shouting, "Stay out of this, Nguirane, this is none of your business!"

So I just said to her, very firmly, "I don't care whether he's your cousin or not, but I do not want to see this young man in my house again."

Despite the fact that no one found out about it, and there was no shouting and screaming or anything like that, what happened next was simply awful.

Without raising her voice, Yacine Ndiaye told me straight to my face, "How dare you speak to me like this, Nguirane Faye, are you trying to give me orders, me, Yacine Ndiaye? Take a look at this . . . Yes, open your eyes wide, Nguirane Faye, and see what I have to show you."

I looked at her. Nothing could have prepared me for what she had in store for me. She was standing in front of me, with her legs spread apart, and her loincloth open. Her index finger was pointing at her vagina, and in her usual icy, provocative tone of voice, she said, "Can you see this, Nguirane Faye? Can you see it clearly? It's mine and I offer it to anybody I like."

That day, my ears heard forbidden words and my eyes saw what they should never have had to see: the courtyard of the house suddenly became pitch-black. I implored God to pardon me, because such things only happen to those who have deeply offended Him in some way. I was convinced my last hour had come.

When I regained consciousness, the whole of Niarela had gathered around me.

"What happened, old Nguirane?"

"Nothing."

"What do you mean, nothing? Without Dr. Fall, it would have been the end of you. Your screaming terrified us, Nguirane, and now you pretend it was nothing!"

They made me swallow the syrup Dr. Fall had prescribed and kept on asking me questions. I refused to answer them.

This is the very first time I have told this story to anyone. Am I doing this because I have sworn to keep nothing hidden from you? No doubt. But I also have the feeling it is easier to unburden oneself by means of the pen than through the spoken word.

■　　■　　■

For the family of the deceased, the ceremony at the end of the widow's mourning period is supposed to be a second time dedicated to prayer and meditation. Yacine Ndiaye turned hers into an occasion for unbridled revelry. You had already left Niarela by then, and so you were spared the spectacle of seeing her friends and relatives invade our neighborhood when they started arriving from I-don't-know-where. They turned the music right up and danced for three days in a row. In between two songs by the famous Modou Cissé—they could be heard all the way across the entire district, meaning several hundred meters away—the griots gave some of their riotous praise-singing performances in honor of Yacine Ndiaye. Her female friends were tossing banknotes into the air, which the griots snatched up in midair and pinned to their richly embroidered robes.

The inhabitants of Niarela, including me, were all utterly shocked and at a loss as to what should be done. To everyone's surprise, your aunt Diabou went up to the group of women Yacine Ndiaye was with and scolded the dead Assane Tall in front of everybody present, "Assane Tall, can you hear me? Only God Almighty knows where you are right now! You should know nevertheless it's your fault that these wretched people have had the insolence to come and disrupt our lives here in Niarela!"

As usual, Yacine Ndiaye pretended she had heard nothing.

I took Diabou aside. "Diabou, if you really feel you have to say this sort of thing, please don't do it now . . ."

That was exactly what she'd been waiting for to unleash her fury on me. "You, Nguirane Faye, should keep your mouth shut! You will never dare to speak up because you have always relied on your family's support! It's an open secret—we all know about it! What's going on in this house isn't normal, and someone has to speak up. Wherever you are, Assane Tall, I want you to be aware that you are to blame for everything that's happening here today! What have you made of your life, Assane Tall? You went to Marseille because you wanted to have fun, and every time we invited you to come back home, your reply was: 'Just let me be—I am a man who is hard at work. I am busy piling up the money I want to bring back to Senegal!' Well, Assane, the fruits of your labors are right here in front of our eyes: two kids about whom nobody can say whether they are fish or fowl, not to mention all your other little bastards that we haven't seen yet! But what bothers me most of all is this, Assane: you have your peace and quiet now, wherever you are, having had a ball in Marseille, while we have to put up with all the suffering and humiliation that's the result!"

Somebody said to her, "What on earth are you thinking, Diabou? Didn't

Nguirane Faye make it clear to you that this is the wrong time to say these things? Surely it's not your responsibility to lecture people who think it's better to throw parties than to glorify God through songs and prayers for Assane. We will each one of us have to justify our actions on Judgment Day."

I took Diabou's hand again and said very quietly, "Diabou . . ."

She looked at me as though she'd never seen me before; then she burst into tears and apologized, "Excuse me, Nguirane, I shouldn't have talked like that."

"It's all right, I know how you must feel, but please get a grip."

At that moment, Ngoné Thioune came to tell me there was a problem with your mother, Bigué Samb, "What do you mean, Ngoné? "

"Follow me, Nguirane," she kept repeating urgently, while pulling me by the hand.

One of the local Niarela women sitting in the tent saw us walking past. Pressing her hands against her temples in despair, she shouted, "Out of the whole lot of us, you, Bigué Samb, are the best! If any of us women are your enemies, they have good reason to be afraid! The punishment God has in store for them will be terrible!"

When I got to Bigué, she was rolling around on the floor like a woman possessed. She had ripped her clothes to shreds and covered herself with sand, and she kept on clawing and scraping her face and her flanks with her fingernails. Several sturdy young men were doing their best trying to subdue her.

I bent down to her: "Do you have any faith in divine justice, Bigué? If you do, you have no right to behave like this."

All she could muster was a pathetic little whimper. She was in such a state that there was no way she could have replied to me.

To see her in this near-demented condition took me straight back to the past. What a contrast between this scene and the one of her bidding farewell to Assane at the airport all those years ago. The occasion was simultaneously heartbreaking and endowed with all the hopes of two young people on the threshold of life. The harsh truth is, though, that we are nothing but paltry playthings in the hands of destiny—it could drive you insane when you stop and think about it. Yes, Bigué Samb and Assane Tall, there's a tale to keep you awake at night! Just think, it is your very own father and mother we are talking about. I am not planning to tell you everything I know about this story—not even in *The Book of Secrets*—and I suppose you don't want to know it all, anyway. They started making an exhibition of themselves when they were both still extremely young. We found it touching and amusing back then to see them so glued to each other all the time, in such a hurry to live out their precocious passion so fully. More than once, Assane let himself get beaten up by young fellows who were stronger than him, just to protect Bigué. Then he left for Marseille, and after a while, their love began to cool down more and more. During the first few months, Assane wrote long love letters to Bigué. In these letters, he gave her pretty little names like "Flame of My Heart" and such like, which were probably not of his own invention, but pinched from books, and she, who had barely been to school, proudly repeated them back to everyone. The letters either contained detailed descriptions of Assane's daily life over there, or he would tell her about his extended late-night strolls in the Vieux-Port area, always with the same group of friends.

From time to time, he would send her cuttings from the local newspapers referring to him, Assane, as one of the greatest soccer players the local team had ever known. The two lovers had plans, of course. Assane said he was looking for a house so that you and your mother could join him in France. Bigué's female friends had started working on the wedding preparations, when, quite suddenly, the letters became less frequent. After a few months, Bigué no longer dared put the question to the postman on his daily rounds in Niarela. That's when we all noticed her growing hatred for Assane, a hatred no human language can possibly convey. We were dumbfounded, but what were we to do?

All that resurfaced in my memory while the others were splashing cold water over Bigué Samb to revive her.

Someone turned up the sound and "Mbëggeel," one of Modou Cissé's most famous songs literally exploded in the air. First separately, and then all together, Yacine Ndiaye and her female friends started dancing in the alleyway, rapturously clapping their hands and tapping their feet.

Never have I felt such a profound aversion for Modou Cissé's music—or perhaps for just any music whatsoever—as I did on that day.

■　　■　　■

Living under the same roof with Yacine Ndiaye certainly isn't easy.

Yesterday, while I was performing my prayers, little Mbissane came and peed right in front of me, nearly wetting my carpet. I call him little, but a ten-year-old is really no longer a child. When I told him that it's not nice to do that, he stuck his tongue out at me. I then asked Arame, Yacine Ndiaye's maid, to inform her mistress about the incident. Her response was that I should come and see her if I needed her. Well, I don't consider it appropriate at my age to add fuel to the fire, so I went to see Yacine Ndiaye and said very calmly, "Yacine, you are letting my grandchildren run wild, it seems to me . . ."

"What have they done?"

When she asked this question, her tone of voice was so belligerent that I almost wanted to leave it at that.

"Whenever he sees me praying, Mbissane comes and either throws stones at me or he pees on my carpet," I replied.

"That's not a nice thing to do, but don't you know that all children behave like that? And now would you excuse me please, old Nguirane. I am busy. If you insist on discussing these things further, I can send for you later on."

That was simply too much for me and I totally lost my self-control. "So my coming to see you in person still isn't enough, Yacine? Are you going to go so far as to kick me out of this apartment?" I asked her.

Her response was to curl up her lips in disdain. I was beside myself by now and I screamed, "Since you seem incapable of teaching your children manners, I will take care of that from now on."

Without warning, Yacine Ndiaye leapt to her feet and stood in the middle of the room: "The day your hand touches Mbissine or Mbissane, I will have you arrested!"

I very nearly slapped her face, but held back just in time, worried that this might stir up the whole of Niarela. Since the entire neighborhood was waiting for a chance to teach her a lesson, I imagined all the young men would immediately come running and possibly flog her to death.

So I tried to reason with her. "Don't you think, Yacine Ndiaye, that we should make an effort to live in peace in this small house? After all, Assane—"

She interrupted me before I could finish my sentence. "Do you have to talk about Assane Tall all the time? For me, that chapter is finished!" This was the first time since all this trouble started that I had heard her attacking Assane directly.

"What reproaches do you have against my son?" I wanted to know.

"That's completely beside the point. It is my life we are talking about here, and let me tell you something else, old Nguirane: if you don't stop bothering me, I am going to kick you out of this very house!"

"You're going to kick me, Nguirane Faye, out of this house? Is that what I have just heard you say or did I get you wrong?"

"That's precisely what I said."

At that point I finally understood that very serious things were happening here that had previously escaped my notice. I wanted to give myself time to put my ideas in order and started walking toward the door with the words: "All right then, Yacine."

As I was leaving Yacine Ndiaye's apartment, I bumped head-on into Tamsir Bâ, her supposed cousin. When I looked at his hair and intensely bloodshot eyes, I thought to myself: "This young fellow must be ill. No one in good health can possibly have such a bizarre hair and eye color." He looked like a real monster.

NINKI-NANKA, A FICTION

LET ME PUT THE QUESTION TO YOU ONCE MORE, BADOU TALL: WHICH SUN-rays caress your eyelids when you wake up in the morning?

All I know is that you must be somewhere far from our country, which is in a very bad way. Nearly all the young men your age are condemned to exile. And in the places where our children end up, they get treated like modern day slaves. I do hope that's not the case with you.

Never lose courage! Not a single day goes by without my prayers for you rising up to heaven.

■   ■   ■

The *Notebook* you are holding in your hand is unusual in that it is the only one I wrote with a single stroke of my pen. I have called it *Ninki-Nanka, a Fiction* be-cause I wanted to amuse myself a little. The main reason for this title is, though, that nothing you read about here has actually happened. Why do you think it was that on the corner of one of those narrow little lanes in Niarela I suddenly wanted to part company with you and go and lose myself in a world with which I am no longer very familiar? The answer is quite simple and straightforward:

while I was narrating my little stories about Yacine Ndiaye and her two children to you, President Daour Diagne was hard at work pushing our country to the very edge of the precipice. His persistence and single-mindedness in this can only be described as diabolical. I consider it my duty to talk about the dark clouds I see gathering above our heads, and it's out of deep concern for you that I want to tell you about my fear of impending disaster.

I sometimes have the impression President Daour Diagne secretly hates us. Does he think it's our fault that he is old and nearly impotent, despite all his efforts to convince us of the opposite? If that's the case, his enemies are quite right in claiming that his fear of death is eating away at his soul and messing up his brain. Are there any misdeeds or offenses he is trying to punish us for? I have absolutely no idea. All I know is that I am not the only one who worries about the future. The people we should always listen to are undoubtedly our poets. A few days ago, I heard one of them broach this topic on the radio with his "Eulogy to Daour Diagne." Do not be taken in by that title! While pretending to praise his qualities as Father of the Nation, this poet actually annihilated the president with his savage diatribes, which is how our nation has always taken revenge on its despotic leaders. "But of course, Daour, he said to him, you are a giant. The wind is scared of you, you see, and no longer dares to blow anywhere near us." The poet was also amazed that Daour Diagne had apparently "Managed to imprison the waves behind the walls of a dungeon, since he couldn't bear to hear them singing the song of our freedom."

Having said that, I doubt nevertheless that Daour Diagne and the pathetic little thugs who make up his inner circle deserve such intricate figures of speech. For my part, I have decided to keep it simple and describe the chaos toward which these people are pushing us in the manner of the authors of the realist school. So please don't be surprised if the figments of my imagination bear a close resemblance to a great many scumbags whose names and pictures you regularly come across in the newspaper. Even a child would understand very quickly that Dibi-Dibi, for instance, is a carbon copy of President Daour Diagne.

And, Badou, I'm sure you know our popular saying that a wise man is not someone who stands in the middle of a heap of burning ruins, exclaiming, "I knew this would happen!" The true sage forewarns us about an imminent disaster in order to prevent it from happening, either through the medium of speech or with a modest work of fiction like the one you're about to read here.

■ ■ ■

For almost three years now, Atou Seck has been listening to the crackling sound of machine guns and watching columns of black smoke rise into the sky from all over town.

When the civil war started, it looked as though the government soldiers—all neatly shaven and kitted out in their shiny boots and smart uniforms—had the situation under control. A few army units took control of the main intersections, and their tanks made sporadic forays into the inner city. The street children, always excited when there's a commotion, immediately formed a circle around the soldiers who were busy speaking into their walkie-talkies. Their faces were grave, but in fact they seemed calm rather than concerned.

Casting his mind back on the civil war when he is alone in his derelict house, Atou Seck has the feeling it has crept up on them without warning, as furtively and stealthily as a predator holding its breath in order to escape the notice of its prey.

Right at the beginning, it was small, nimble detachments, and occasionally even snipers, that were harassing the government troops. After launching an attack, they would immediately disappear again under cover of darkness. The curfew President Dibi-Dibi was forced to impose, which gradually extended over the entire country, failed to have any effect. Within six months, the government troops had suffered thirty-seven casualties. In retaliation, the army massacred a few hundred people and laid waste to several large buildings.

Afterward, a quarrel broke out among Dibi-Dibi's generals, and today, nobody knows exactly how many armed factions are attacking each other or who is fighting whom. To make things worse, the insurrection bears the hallmark of a certain squadron leader Zero, who is normally invisible. When he is giving press conferences, all you see is his AK-47 and his piercing, suspicious eyes peeking out from behind a beige balaclava.

One hears people say: "It's amazing to think that all this started as a simple student protest."

"Yes, it's incredible, isn't it?"

"With a less lily-livered president than Dibi-Dibi, it would never have come to this."

"He started to panic when he learned that certain young officers among his entourage . . ."

"It's very easy, dear friends, to blame Dibi-Dibi for all our troubles. Don't forget that you voted for this Dibi-Dibi of yours in a democratic election!"

And so on and so forth.

Atou Seck was perplexed by all this, but it began to dawn on him, too, that a seemingly trivial little thing can ruin an entire country.

In the republic of Diafouné, this seemingly trivial little thing was a brief period of unrest among the female traders of Kimintang—the largest street market in the capital, and thus in the entire country. It was an everyday occurrence. The women were fed up with exorbitant taxes and corrupt officials, and so one morning, they called a meeting. Their leading lady addressed them, "President Dibi-Dibi is our brother, and he is a man with a big heart. His ministers are hiding the truth from him, but if we march to the palace, he will listen to us, for we are his beloved sisters."

The march, which has since become known as "The March of the Women of Kimintang," was organized with feverish excitement. On the appointed day, an exceptionally bright and colorful procession made up of flute players, acrobats and drummers set off in the direction of Dibi-Dibi's palace.

The students found out about this and said to the women, "You are our mothers and our sisters. We will help you make yourselves heard. Dibi-Dibi knows all about us."

The women traders of Kimintang accepted their offer and the students joined them among great cries of jubilation. But they also shouted out insults that decency prohibits me from recording in this book. The truth is that this civil war started in a perfectly fraternal manner: the market women wanted to draw their brother Dibi-Dibi's attention to their hardships, while the students were keen to lend their sisters in Kimintang a helping hand, with a pinch of revolutionary zeal thrown in for good measure.

As was his habit, President Dibi-Dibi suspected that his enemies were up to mischief. He said to himself, *We'll soon see who is going to bugger whom.* To gain time, he allowed the demonstrators to camp in the palace grounds. Political rabble rousers—but also quite a few petty criminals—used the opportunity to join the demonstration. They were doubtless the first to throw stones at the palace facade. Mirtaa, Dibi-Dibi's daughter, was walking up and down her balcony when one of the projectiles hit her forehead. Seeing Mirtaa covered in blood and crying her heart out made Dibi-Dibi mad with fury. He called in his army chiefs and told them, pointing at the crowd: "See for yourselves what they've done to my daughter."

The following day, newspapers and television channels all around the globe were showing pictures of the one hundred and thirty-seven victims of the carnage which followed. And here are just a few of the headlines that appeared on the front pages of the major international daily papers:

BLOODBATH IN THE REPUBLIC OF DIAFOUNÉ . . . DIAFOUNÉ: 137 DEM-ONSTRATORS KILLED BY THE ARMY . . . YET ANOTHER AFRICAN COUNTRY IN TURMOIL!

That's how the civil war really began.

Slowly but surely, Diafouné got used to the bad news. There were many people with grievances, all of them eager to make their voices heard. Dibi-Dibi, on the other hand, only started to worry when his soldiers staged a mutiny because they hadn't received their wages for several months. In a televised speech, he described them as traitors, whereupon the very same soldiers broke into the defense minister's office, tied the poor man up and cut him into neat little squares and triangles. When they were finished, everything was carefully loaded into a wheelbarrow and pushed through the streets, accompanied by the familiar rhythms of patriotic songs.

One year after these hostilities broke out, it transpired that tens of thousands of peasants had left their villages and small towns and were heading for the capital city en masse. At nightfall, they camped wherever they could. Their nightly festivities were always very lively, and there was always plenty of food, because several animals were slaughtered every day. After seeing everyone singing, dancing and getting drunk on beer, many of the young men in the towns they were passing through joined the cheerful procession the following morning.

The army was ready and waiting for them as they were approaching the outskirts of the capital. Thousands of casualties were the result. And since it never occurred to anybody to remove them, the dead bodies just stayed there, rotting under the sun of Diafouné from that day onward.

■　　■　　■

The man is standing on the seashore. He has spent the last few minutes waiting for the voice of Imam Dione, a voice intimately familiar to him. He checks his watch, murmuring: "The hour of the prayer of *tàkkusaan* has passed. Why has Imam Dione remained silent?" The man knows the answer perfectly well, but it is too distressing for him to confront the truth.

He, Atou Seck, is the last remaining inhabitant of Gouye-Guewel who hasn't fled.

Atou Seck clearly remembers the day when thousands of his neighbors and friends, for fear of being caught in the crossfire, decided to leave and seek refuge elsewhere. But where exactly? Nobody knew. Staying put would have been tantamount to sitting back and waiting for certain death. So they thought it would be better to go where their legs could carry them, no matter where, a bit like when we instinctively fight back if we're attacked, even though we know it's pointless, but without being able to stop ourselves from doing it.

Cooking pots, armchairs, household appliances, and even old television sets are piled up on top of trucks and carts. Days of uncertainty lie ahead and everyone is stocking up on drinking water, dried meat, millet and rice. Those who thought of all the eventualities are even packing a small First Aid kit containing Nivaquine, alcohol etc. The crowd is huge, thousands of people are running around like ants, but Atou Seck has the feeling he is watching some sort of shadow dance.

From time to time, shots ring out somewhere down south. That means an attack on Gouye-Guewel could be imminent. But who is the assailant? The insurgents or the official army, referred to on the radio as the loyalists? Nobody knows.

Within a few minutes, the column of refugees has shrunk to a dot on the horizon. Atou Seck is wrapped up in his thoughts as he watches them move farther and farther into the distance. Right next to him, the crashing of the waves. The ocean is angry. Atou Seck wonders whether the sea is upset with the inhabitants of Gouye-Guewel for having entrusted their destiny to Dibi-Dibi, a half-demented freak who never stops talking, or whether it is perhaps telling them to stay and defend their houses instead of running away like cowards.

At his back, Atou Seck can hear footsteps. He turns round. One of his neighbors, a young man called Omar Diaw, is walking toward him. So at least he is not totally alone in Gouye-Guewel. But he soon finds out that Omar Diaw and his family are leaving as well. They are just a bit late.

Omar Diaw says to him, "Atou, what are you doing here all alone? Don't you know what's going on?"

"I do know," he says calmly.

With vivid gestures, Atou Seck starts talking to him about the way scavengers fight for the carcass of their prey. Omar Diaw, who remembers him as a more moderate man, wonders whether he hasn't suddenly lost his reason, like so many others in Gouye-Guewel.

"Which carcass are you talking about, Atou?"

"I am talking about the politicians of this wretched country," he says, looking around in disgust.

"You're right, old Atou, but this is not a good time to talk politics. We have to think of getting you to safety. Armed men are marching toward Gouye-Guewel."

"Who are they?" Atou suddenly wants to know.

Atou Seck can tell from the unmistakable shakiness of his own voice that he is much more worried than he dares to admit.

"Nobody knows anything about them," Omar Diaw says hastily.

He pauses, looking straight into Atou Seck's eyes, and adds, "Atou, the fighting in Gouye-Guewel will be very fierce. They say that he who succeeds in taking Gouye-Guewel is practically assured of gaining control of the capital and of the whole of Diafouné. Come with us, old Atou."

Atou Seck has already stopped listening to him. He is thinking of his own family. Where is Lalla, and where are their grandchildren?

He puts that question to Omar, who looks at him without saying anything. Atou Seck reads sadness and confusion in his eyes and insists. "Omar, I have the right to know. This is about my family. Tell me the truth."

Omar Diaw lowers his head.

"I have the right to know," Atou repeats.

Omar Diaw is stammering something about reprisals against civilians. A terrible massacre. He gets carried away and starts describing details.

Atou Seck exclaims, "And my family? Lalla and our grandchildren . . . ?"

For two or three seconds, Omar Diaw has the peculiar feeling that old Atou Seck is suspecting him of having killed his family.

He mutters, "God never makes mistakes, Atou. He always does what's best for us."

Atou calms down a bit and asks, in a broken voice, "Did they have to suffer?"

Omar Diaw is almost relieved to be able to tell him that the first casualties fell in a salvo fired by the attackers: "It was only afterward that all hell broke loose. They had lost some of their men in that same place a few days earlier. So they took revenge."

It is not the first time that Atou has felt sympathy for the victims of catastrophes like this one who don't even get the chance to find out *who is coming to kill them* or *for what reason exactly* they have to go through such excruciating suffering and die.

Omar Diaw has the impression that Atou Seck is experiencing a flashback of his entire life, but it's time to go. He cannot leave him alone in Gouye-Guewel.

"Atou, let's go back to your house. I will help you get your things together. You must come with us."

"Where do you want me to go, Omar?"

"We are all leaving, as you can see, Atou, but not a single one of us knows where we are going. We will start walking along the road straight ahead of us, and that's that."

Atou shakes his head. "I still cannot believe that such horrors have been perpetrated here in this country. It all started in such a brutal way. Isn't it incredible, Omar?"

"It's atrocious," Omar answers hurriedly, since he definitely doesn't want to embark on an interminable discussion. Time is running out. Atou can see that Omar is only interested in one thing right now, and that's to save his own skin. His lips are dry, his gestures clumsy, and his gaunt eyes speak of his palpable fear. For days on end now, Omar has had constant visions of himself dying a horribly painful death. All this is unbearable to him. Although he feels sorry for Omar, Atou Seck cannot suppress a fleeting internal smile. He used to be such a bigmouth, Omar. As a worker at the Air Liquide factory, he had been renting a small room in Atou's house, together with his wife Nabou Sarr. Atou Seck remembers his keen interest in politics. Having started out as a reluctant Dibi-Dibi supporter, over the years, he turned into a keen champion of his regime. A few weeks ago, after listening to the news early one morning he went to find Atou Seck under his acacia tree. He gave free rein to his rage. "Old Atou, excuse my choice of words, but our politicians are no better than a pack of rabid dogs! They loot our country, and once they've ruined it, they go and live a life of luxury on the Côte d'Azur or some similar place. This is simply not acceptable! If they think we are just a herd of cattle they can lead to slaughter, they are mistaken!"

Right now, however, as things are heating up, Omar, the firebrand, only has one single idea in his head, and that is to leave Gouye-Guewel and go as far away as possible.

So Atou Seck says to him, "And now our paths will separate, Omar. I am going to pray for you."

Hesitantly, Omar Diaw joins both his palms together and holds them out to him. Atou Seck murmurs a few short verses from the Koran, putting his hand on Omar's shoulder with the words: "Farewell, Omar. We will not see each other again. My whole life is here at Gouye-Guewel and this is where I want to stay while I am waiting to die. May God the Almighty protect you all, your family and you yourself."

Omar Diaw takes leave from him in great haste. After a few minutes, he turns round, but his wife and children call out to him, asking him to hurry up. He starts to run and catches up with them.

Atou Seck does not take his eyes off them until they turn round a street corner and disappear.

He calmly continues on his way back to his house.

■   ■   ■

For several days now, he has eaten nothing but stale bread. He still has enough *kenkelibaa* tea, but the charcoal is almost finished. Soon he will no longer be able to cook any food or have a hot drink.

In the early afternoon, he was wandering up and down his courtyard for almost an hour. He is surprised to discover that being alone makes him much more alert to certain details. This is practically the first time he has ever taken note of the rather basic architectural features of his house. The zinc entrance gate is on the left, and on the same side there is a row of small rooms under a pink tile roof. Omar Diaw had been renting two of those.

Atou Seck tries to make his transistor radio work. When he turns it on, it makes a few hissing noises and stops. Then it starts up again before dying out completely. "The batteries must be finished," he thinks. It's too bad; all the shopkeepers in Gouye-Guewel have left with their merchandise piled high on their carts.

He hears a muffled sound. A bomb. A few seconds later, a machine gun salvo from quite far away. For some days now, he's had the impression the fighting is getting closer and more threatening.

■   ■   ■

A mouse brushes against his ankle and slips into a hole under the fence.

All sorts of creepy-crawlies are running around everywhere, in search of crumbs and leftovers. And as for birds, there must be tens of thousands in Gouye-Guewel. Atou Seck loves listening to their high-pitched chirping and the flapping of their wings. When he looks up at the sky, he is amazed to see all these birds fluttering and twittering above his head. It's as if they had appeared out of nowhere to keep him company.

Not far from him, there are a few kitchen utensils—mortars, calabashes and pots—covered in a fine layer of dust. His gaze is fixed on a grain of red dust as it whirls around in empty space and is taking its time to settle on a bowl. Another grain of dust has just got stuck to it. One might call it a fine rain, with each drop falling separately from the others. A graceful little dance, and a welcome distraction for him. Within the short span of a few minutes, the foliage of the acacia tree has acquired a reddish coat.

■   ■   ■

The days come and go.

He often talks to himself, just to hear his own voice. Sometimes it seems as though the combatants are on the verge of entering Gouye-Guewel. But then, a few hours later, silence reigns again.

This war is a mystery to him.

■   ■   ■

Roukhou-Djinné. Satan's Den, in other words. Before the war, this used to be the sleaziest part of Gouye-Guewel. Atou Seck still can't believe that he can now wander around Roukhou-Djinné without seeing drunkards emerging from the brothels on the opposite side and staggering around among the street-sellers' stalls with their kebabs and fritters. The upturned wooden tables and chairs lying scattered all over the narrow little lane—so narrow, in fact, that *in the old days*, only cyclists and pedestrians could use it—are a reminder of the haste with which the fugitives abandoned the area.

Roukhou-Djinné, its bars and its two-penny prostitutes. And let's not forget the way it settles its scores. At sunrise every morning almost without fail, there was a body drenched in its own blood under a streetlight. The most commonly used weapons were knives and broken bottles. The police would arrive to take a statement, with sirens blaring and their beautiful blue lights flashing. But in Roukhou-Djinné, nobody sees the need to talk to the cops. It's a point of honor and besides, why get mixed up in any of this? It's common knowledge that the policemen couldn't care less. A couple of tramps disemboweling each other in Roukhou-Djinné has about the same level of importance as a lizard basking in the sun in the savanna.

Atou Seck has entered a small square and stops in front of Diallo's shop. The whole district used to come here and lean on Diallo's counter to buy—or more likely, to borrow—some oil, a few kilos of rice or a piece of soap. He tries to remember: when was it again that Diallo came and settled in Gouye-Guewel? The images inside his head are a blur. The truth is that nobody ever really knew very much about this crafty shopkeeper. Early one morning, people saw him getting off one of those trucks coming from Conakry, carrying a small bundle of clothes. He said he was originally from Koundara. A Fulani from Fouta-Djallon. That's why everyone decided to call him Diallo. He himself clearly wasn't too keen on going around telling people his life story. He spent all day every day sitting at a low wooden table, selling a bit of everything in tiny little bags: powdered milk, tobacco, Chinese green tea, and a candy made from baobab fruit called "monkey bread." The Guinean had the habit of serving his clients while sucking very hard on his pipe—he loved blowing up his cheeks like a set of bellows—and teasing the young girls of Gouye-Guewel. After three years, he had saved enough to buy himself quite a large house. In front of this house was a signpost with two enigmatic words painted in black: "Duggal seet," or "Come and see." A near perfect code name, considering Diallo had rigged up a clandestine bar in his backyard and some rooms for rent by the hour.

When Diallo died, his son, Ibnou, an earnest, well-mannered boy, kept the shop, but decided to close the family brothel. This could have been done quietly and discreetly, only Ibnou Diallo did the exact opposite by blowing up those rooms with dynamite—in his opinion, they had been under the diabolical control of Cheytan for too long. The explosion made a lot of noise, thick black smoke rose high into the sky, and Ibnou Diallo was hailed by the notables of the district.

Atou Seck ventures a look inside Ibnou Diallo's shop. It's empty. Next, the empty field where as young boys they used to play their noisy soccer matches. Just like the other landmarks in Gouye-Guewel, such as the public fountain and the street junctions, it seems too big and expansive for what was a relatively modest number of people. Kitchen utensils and small household objects have been dropped here by the inhabitants during their flight, reluctantly, one might say, due to the lack of space on their small trucks and carts.

His walk takes him to the Palace cinema. A giant poster with the words "Apache Fury" shows some Indians wearing brightly colored feather head-dresses and fighting American soldiers at the foot of a hill. Their horses are rearing and trampling on the dozens of bodies that are lying scattered on the ground. This was the last movie the inhabitants of Gouye-Guewel had the chance to watch before the war catapulted them out onto the road and turned them into refugees. "Where on earth can they possibly be now?" Atou Seck wonders with a tender little smile.

As he is walking past a public rubbish dump, amid all the garbage, he spots a piece of stale bread. He considers picking it up. He might need it soon. But he leaves it and walks on. He will not stoop so low.

Even if you are dying of thirst, never drink water from the sewers. The day will come when rain will fall in abundance from the sky and then you won't be proud of yourself.

He does not really care for most of Wolof Njaay's proverbs, since most of them are a bit too cynical for his taste. This one is an exception.

■   ■   ■

For over two hours, he has been trying to get up onto his feet and go for his daily walk in the courtyard, but in vain. The repeated attempts have made him dizzy, and he feels like he is about to pass out. A voice coming from deep inside him says that if he gives up now, even for a single second, it will be the end of him, for good. The rats, lurking in the shadows, are waiting impatiently for the moment when they can nibble his flesh. They know hunger and thirst have sapped his strength. They can see death prowling around him. They themselves are death. Soon his body will be cold, and out of their holes they will come, one after the other, with their sinister little squeaking noises.

. ▪ ▪

The radio has started up again. A journalist is bellowing into his microphone. Atou Seck notices his voice getting louder, more jerky. Talking himself into a frenzy, he predicts the defeat of Dibi-Dibi's opponents, calling them "insurgents" and then announces that President Dibi-Dibi is going to deliver a speech to the people of Diafouné.

Atou Seck can barely believe it: the radio has started working again all by itself . . .

▪ ▪ ▪

In the middle of the night, he is woken up by a nightmare. He jumps up from the mat where he had been asleep and walks to the entrance gate. Facing the street, he shouts at the top of his voice, "Shame on you, Dibi-Dibi! I, Atou Seck, herewith declare that I hate you, Dibi-Dibi! You have plunged us into fear and despair!"

After that, he lies down again and goes peacefully back to sleep.

▪ ▪ ▪

Let's face it: It wasn't Dibi-Dibi's lot to move into the presidential palace by walking over tens of thousands of dead bodies. Nor did he stage a coup, occupying the radio stations, closing the airport, condemning corruption and announcing the beginning of a new era. The reality is that the elections that brought him to power were free and fair. After he had been punching the air of Diafouné with his fist for a quarter of a century many of his fellow citizens were saying to themselves, out of sheer desperation, Why not vote for him, a man so energetic and full of resolve? He may be old, but he is bound to get things going. And besides, it doesn't cost anything to try.

But here is the catch: a nation's destiny is not a garment you try on in a hurry while doing your shopping at the supermarket.

For Dibi-Dibi's opponents, many of whom started off as his most fervent supporters, this is one of those home truths they find harder to swallow than *tulukuna*. They would love to spit it out again if they could. Well, they have missed their chance. They can't even argue that Dibi-Dibi didn't openly show who he really was while making his bid for power. No, he had been talking utter nonsense for decades and made it crystal clear to everybody that, if he was ever in his right mind for a single day, that day must have been a very long time ago. After all, hasn't every single one of us seen that little glimmer of madness dancing in Dibi-Dibi's eyes? Year after year, in meeting after meeting, in the big cities as well as in the remotest villages, he used to repeat: "I know about all your problems and there isn't a single one that I cannot solve." This sentence, which became famous, was immediately followed by an even more famous gesture: Dibi-Dibi, looking down on the crowd and waving a key in the air, the key of change that is supposed to open the door to prosperity even for the poorest of the poor.

That was all that was needed to drive the crowd into frenzy. One day, he told a group of young supporters who had come to listen to him near the market place of Kimintang, "Those of you who are without a job, raise your hand, raise it high in the air!"

Immediately, thousands of hands went up and Dibi-Dibi shouted, "You will all have jobs if you vote for me! If I don't give each one of you a job, you can go and tell the whole world that I am the biggest liar on earth!"

According to the reports, Dibi-Dibi himself felt he had taken things a bit too far that day. When he got into his car, he asked his chief adviser and confidant, "Do you think they believed me when I said I was going to give them all jobs? Perhaps that was pushing it a little bit, don't you think?"

This adviser was not a boot licker. On the contrary, he was one of the few people Dibi-Dibi respected. He shook his head and said calmly, like a man who has seen this kind of thing before, "No, Dib. Not a single one of them believed you."

That threw Dibi-Dibi into a panic. It was only a few days until the elections, and he started talking about wanting to fix his mistake. So the adviser said, cunningly, "It's best to do nothing, my friend."

"But you told me yourself that they didn't take me seriously! I need to know . . ."

The adviser smiled. "That's exactly why they're going to vote for you."

After a moment's reflection, he added, "If you ruin these young peoples' dreams, they'll make you pay for it. You must never forget that they have been told so many lies that the best way to plunge them into despair is to tell them the truth."

Dibi-Dibi's face lit up. "It's not the first time I have heard that bullshit . . ."

"Correct. It comes from your old enemy. The honest politician. The indomitable one. He who has never had to recant. One might call him the politician who doesn't like politicking! He repeats his little spiel at every single meeting and he claims that he tells his supporters some very hard truths. This is the result."

"You're right, he gets hammered at every election, that guy!" sniggered Dibi-Dibi with malice, letting himself sink deeper into his seat.

Dibi-Dibi hated this opponent's guts, because that man wanted to be seen as a scientist—an even greater scientist than the great Dibi-Dibi? Impossible!—and was trying to change the rules of the game. There was nothing he, Dibi-Dibi, wouldn't do to win votes. Playing the clown had never been a problem for him; in fact, his pathetic antics were probably an expression of his true nature. His political gatherings were veritable fun fairs. Dibi-Dibi loved mingling with the dancers so much that he regularly ended up rolling around on the floor, with the public calling out to his opponents, "Be afraid, monkeys, the Lion is on his way!"

"Monkeys, be afraid! Here comes Dibi-Dibi the Lion!"

"Truly, God has endowed this man with every talent!"

"He will bring so many billions to this country, we won't know what to do with all the money!"

"We have no room in our hearts except for you, Dibi-Dibi! This is God's will, and there is nothing the slanderers and those driven by envy can do to change it!"

From time to time, one of his party leaders shouted into the microphone: "Dibi-Dibi?"

And the crowd responded: "Long live Dibi-Dibi!"

This reminded Atou Seck of his conversations with Omar Diaw. At the time, Omar was one of those fanatical Dibi-Dibi supporters who could be found in large numbers in a popular district like Gouye-Guewel. He never missed an opportunity to praise Dibi-Dibi's exceptional qualities. One day, Atou Seck got so irritated by this that he said to him, "Omar, it's possible that your hero is an unusual human being, but I, Atou Seck, have just one small problem with him."

"And what's that?" asked Omar Diaw.

"The way he walks, Omar. Have you ever really seen how Dibi-Dibi walks?"

"I'm not sure I understand what you mean, old Atou Seck."

"Dibi-Dibi waddles exactly like a duck, Omar. Do you really think it's wise to entrust our people to a man who walks like that?"

Omar Diaw burst into laughter and turned to the crowd. "Hey, good people of Gouye-Guewel, please take care of our old uncle Atou Seck. He's losing his marbles!"

The most notorious gossip- and scandalmongers of the district were there like a shot, forming a circle around them.

Atou Seck reassured them, "It's nothing, you know what we're like, Omar and I, we enjoy teasing each other a little bit."

Two days later, he confided to Omar Diaw, "Omar, since you are almost like a son to me, I think I will probably vote for your Dibi-Dibi. I'll do it for you. If so many people in this country believe in him, why shouldn't I give him a chance, even if I don't like him?"

Omar Diaw had no time for Atou Seck's pedantic quibbles. He had just won another vote for Dibi-Dibi, and that was really all that mattered to him. Pleased and relieved, he exclaimed, "I wouldn't have expected anything less of you, Atou! Having spent your whole life fighting for worthy causes, surely you wouldn't want to deprive your grandchildren of the good fortune they have at their fingertips!"

"What kind of good fortune are you talking about, Omar?"

"If Dibi-Dibi gets elected, all the jobless young people will find work. That means you won't see a single one of them loitering in the streets anymore!"

Atou Seck looked at him for a long time before asking him with incredulity, "Do tell me, Omar, if it's so easy to provide everyone with jobs, why haven't Dibi-Dibi's opponents already done it? Are you suggesting they let our children starve to death out of pure malice?"

With the most serious expression he could muster, Omar Diaw replied, "You know, Atou, there are scientists who can explain the secrets of matter and the movements of the planets. We don't understand what they're saying, but we still know they are right. Politics, too, is a science, and Dibi-Dibi is one of those exceptional creatures who can make things happen that you and I would think impossible. And don't forget that Dibi-Dibi has learned this science at the greatest school of the world."

"What are you telling me there, Omar? Where is that school?"

"It's in the country of the *Toubabs*!" Omar said triumphantly. "Dibi-Dibi and his opponents were all in the same class. But make no mistake, he was always miles ahead of them!"

Now, Atou Seck couldn't help himself anymore and he burst into laughter. "So you're saying that all our politicians went to the country of the *Toubabs* in order to learn how to deal with my problems here in Gouye-Guewel? Does that make sense to you, Omar?"

"The earth doesn't stand still, Atou!"

Atou Seck shook his head with a treacherous little smile. "I have a confession to make to you, Omar: I am very worried about Diafouné and its future."

Omar Diaw's face clouded over. "And why would that be?"

"Because of the countries all around us. I'm sure they are just waiting for the first opportunity to steal Dibi-Dibi from us. It makes a lot of sense, doesn't it? Why should they have to die of hunger while the solution to all their troubles is right on their doorstep?"

Omar Diaw brightened up. Playing along with the banter, he said cheerfully, "Is that all, Atou? Then there's no need to worry; we are not going to let anyone steal Dibi-Dibi from us!"

He paused for a moment, then he looked at Atou Seck and said in a low voice, "The real problem, Atou, are not our neighbors but the big countries like Canada and America. Those whites who have always taken away all our riches won't let us keep Dibi-Dibi unless they are sure we are prepared to make absolutely any sacrifice to keep him!"

When he heard these words, Atou Seck understood once and for all that he was dealing with a crank. He reassured him, "They will never have any reason to doubt it. On the day when these people arrive here to kidnap Dibi-Dibi, I myself, Atou Seck, will be the first to lie down on the runway at the airport to prevent the plane from taking off!"

Omar Diaw realized that Atou Seck was pulling his leg, but he didn't mind. What he wanted was a vote for Dibi-Dibi, and he got it.

Atou Seck watched him walking away and mumbled, "I have no choice but to wait for that fellow under my acacia tree. He'll be back soon, and then he will sing a very different tune!"

And indeed the day arrived when Omar Diaw came to find Atou Seck under the acacia and said to him, "I owe you an apology, Atou . . . You tried to warn me, but I was both deaf and blind. This Dibi-Dibi and his gang behave like greedy scavengers!"

Atou Seck pretended he didn't understand. "What on earth has happened, Omar? You're always so full of anger—that's not good, Omar."

"Dibi-Dibi and his clan are busy destroying this country, Atou! For them, Diafouné is a cake, and each one of them just wants to grab his slice."

"That's exactly what I told you, my dear Omar. A nation should not entrust its destiny to a man who can't even walk straight."

■　■　■

During the first few months of his reign, Dibi-Dibi put on a good show. But it wasn't long before it dawned on people that he had no idea where he was leading the country.

■　■　■

As the years went by, Dibi-Dibi's dementia became more and more evident. Locked up inside his palace with its enormous mirrors on the walls, he did nothing but stare at the only image he was able to tolerate: his own.

On one occasion at least, it looked as though he had come to his senses again. A short-lived bout of humility caused him to publicly reproach himself for his tedious, interminable television appearances. But then he made a rambling ten-hour speech to apologize for this.

Another time, when he announced to the nation that he was planning to make a speech, political observers tried to predict what the subject might be. There were innuendos of a crisis in top government circles, possibly even involving strategy changes. The appointed hour arrived, and Diafouné played its national anthem. But Dibi-Dibi, as it turned out, just wanted to ask his fellow citizens one question: what had happened to the ducks he remembered from his childhood? In the past, these feathery birds were waddling around everywhere, he was sure of that, and he simply couldn't understand why they had since disappeared from the towns and villages of Diafouné. He even became quite poetic when he started reminiscing about the mother ducks and that rasping, unmistakable sound they made, almost like a groan. It wasn't very melodious, he admitted, but their ducklings, those soft little balls of yellow fluff, used to bring tears to his eyes, the eyes of one of the most eminent ecologists of all time! No, it really didn't make sense that there wasn't a single duck left in Diafouné. Having to govern such a peculiar country, a duckless country, or, more precisely, a country where all the ducks had dissolved into thin air literally overnight, well, that was simply too much for him! He was deeply grateful to his beloved people for placing their trust in him, but, as far as the ducks were concerned, there was absolutely no way he could compromise. It was a matter of principle for him, meaning he was prepared to resign and give the green light for early elections.

Nobody will be too surprised to hear that Dibi-Dibi had the basement below his palace converted into a dungeon. It is rumored that this is where he makes lepers rape the wives of his enemies. The latter are put in leg irons and forced to watch the spectacle. Dibi-Dibi, meanwhile, frantically struts up and down the torture chamber, mopping his brow and spurting a string of expletives. He calls the women bloody whores and eggs on the lepers, referring to them as his valiant warriors. Go on, fire at that enemy vagina and wreak havoc on all those stinking what's-their-names for me!

And who could forget the meeting he held in February-the-16th Square? That was the day when, without warning, he interrupted his speech saying he had to take an urgent phone call. Then, in full view of everybody, he took off his right shoe, lifted it to his ear and shouted, "Hello! Hello!" He listened to the person at the other end with a grave and thoughtful expression, slowly moving his head up and down and constantly promising to do his best. When he had finished, he explained to the crowd that Tony Blair had just consulted him about his problems over there in England, and that he, Dibi-Dibi, simply couldn't leave his old mate in the lurch, since that wasn't his way of doing things. Yes, he said, Tony Blair was faced with a difficult decision, and he thought there was only one person on this earth wise and intelligent enough to give him sound advice, and this person was none other than his good self, Dibi-Dibi. This was nothing new, he added, asking his advisers, all nodding eagerly, to confirm this. All those heads of state with their solemn faces and their nuclear warheads, well, without his modest insights, they would have blown the planet to smithereens a long time ago!

■   ■   ■

The ancients, so intimately familiar with the history of Diafouné, could still recall Daaw Demba, the ruler of the Cayor between 1640 and 1647. His power went to his head, and for seven long years, Daaw Demba unleashed a reign of terror where the most ordinary gestures of everyday life became grounds for the death penalty. His subjects were forbidden to consume both fresh and salted meat, and a newly married man was prohibited from deflowering his own bride—obligingly, Daaw Demba himself took on that task throughout his entire kingdom. His secret agents crisscrossed the Cayor in the most deceptive disguises, and if two of the king's subjects were spotted holding an intimate conversation, or if they were heard laughing out loud, they had their heads cut off on the spot, since that, too, had been officially banned by Daaw Demba.

■　　■　　■

In the end, however, the Cayor did not find it very hard to rid itself of Daaw Demba. All the conspirators had to do to get rid of the tyrant was to wait for him to fall into the trap of his own vanity. Forced into exile, he died a miserable death, far away from home and forgotten by all.

And as for Dibi-Dibi, his hour of truth is not as far off as he likes to think. Since he was betrayed by his generals, he's been hiding in his palace where he alternates between bouts of dejection and exaltation. His fits of rage are apparently so extreme that he injures himself occasionally by hurling everything he can lay his hands on at the mirrors. His fear of being poisoned, we are told, has pushed him to the brink of starvation.

■　　■　　■

In New York, they are talking about dispatching a contingent of soldiers to Diafouné. The United Nations has decreed that to restore peace, military intervention is needed.

Commander Zero's message is clear, however: "Foreign soldiers will not be allowed onto the sacred soil of our country. Should the UN decide to send troops, we have no option but to fight them."

■　　■　　■

The night has been quiet.

Atou Seck blinks, and then slowly opens his eyes a little to the first rays of dawn. In all his life, he has never felt closer to the earth and the trees that surround him.

He has always been able to tell upon waking, purely based on those subtle, barely perceptible variations of light, whether it's closer to six or seven o'clock in the morning. One or two little sunrays more or less? Perhaps. But why that is, he doesn't know. The voice of Imam Dione is echoing inside his head. He is grateful to still have the strength to get up and perform his ablutions. During prayers, it seems as though he is no longer alone in the house. Someone is secretly observing him; he can feel it more and more clearly. He listens more intently, but all he can hear is the sighing of the wind in the foliage, followed by the gurgling of his intestines.

A few moments later he hears barking coming from the river banks, or perhaps even from the sea, to the west of Gouye-Guewel.

"Stray dogs," he mutters to himself.

■　　■　　■

The first explosion makes the doors and windows shake. The ones that follow are equally deafening. With raucous cries, thousands of birds emerge from the trees and start circling above the courtyard until, suddenly, they change direction all together and fly north. Atou Seck does not budge from his mat. He has remained calm throughout. He is just curious to find out what will happen next.

A few minutes later the sound of whistling bullets fills the air. A noise he only knows from the cinema. He tries to imagine Gouye-Guewel after the battle: a lunar landscape, with smoke rising up from piles of rubble and hundreds of dead bodies being devoured by vultures. Dozens of craters, dug out by the bombs.

After three hours of fighting, the shooting ceases toward midday.

He can hear human voices coming from the little alleyway.

Soldiers, no doubt.

"There is no one here," one of them says.

"Indeed, that appears to be the case."

They stopped in front of Atou Seck's house, and the first voice is heard once more, "But you never know."

"That's true, my boy. You never know."

They must be thinking of landmines. Or an ambush. They are quite right to be taking precautions, Atou thinks. There it is again, the rattling noise of machine gunfire. One of the two soldiers utters a horrific scream. The detonations, punctuated by more screams, increase very briefly, and then Gouye-Guewel is quiet again.

.   ■   ■

It suddenly occurs to Atou Seck to go and look for the soldiers in order to give himself up. But as soon as he tries to stand, he gets dizzy and has to sit down again. He feels as though he is suffocating. His heart is racing and he gasps for air.

.   ■   ■

Atou Seck looks up, and there she is in front of him, leaning against a large grey and black stone with her two front paws suspended in the air. Her gaze is fearful and sad at the same time. "I have never seen anything like this before," Atou Seck murmurs, "I can't remember ever coming across a human being with such a hairy body before . . . And her tail! It's so long!"

It is a female monkey.

"She must have been hiding in the dark, watching me all this time," Atou Seck thinks to himself. And now she has lost her fear and has come out into the open. That must mean that his end is nigh and this monkey knows it. She is here, waiting for the moment when she can pounce on him and quench her thirst with his blood. This is the first time he feels any regret for not listening to Omar Diaw's advice. He should have left with the others. Having one's death pangs sullied by the loathsome howls of a monkey, that's humiliating. He doesn't deserve that.

Her eyes. She talks to him with her eyes. But that doesn't mean Atou Seck understands what she wants from him. She is as motionless as a rock. Her gaze is sending out silent words that hover in the air for a moment, then vanish. Atou Seck imagines himself chasing those words like a child running after soap bubbles on a rainy day. When the little one stretches out its hands trying to touch them, the bubbles burst without a sound, and the child shrieks with joy.

It's beginning to dawn on him that the presence of this monkey cannot be a coincidence. Everything around them seems to have been waiting for this animal to appear. She has taken her place in this setting in the same way as a creature of flesh and blood slots into a picture to fill an empty space.

The arrival of this monkey, so silent and yet so alert, has changed everything.

The grey and black stone that serves as her armrest.

The clothes line that cuts across the courtyard, with its red and white plastic pegs swinging softly in the wind.

The long wooden bench. That was where Atou Seck's friends used to sit during their lively games of checkers. They were so hooked on the game that they often spent the whole day there, pushing the pieces around the board. But now the wooden bench is upside down. For him, that spells solitude and exodus.

A sudden gust of wind rattles the front gate. The monkey flinches, turns round, and quickly swivels her head from side to side. Atou Seck is surprised to see her suddenly getting so nervous.

But she calms down very quickly. That doesn't bode well for Atou Seck. She disappears behind the house and when she returns, she positions herself directly in front of him, transfixing him with her suspicious gaze.

She obviously thinks he is planning to trick her. He wants to tell her this is not true, but he can't open his mouth.

His lips are parched.

■   ■   ■

Two days later, without warning, he sees the monkey leaping out of the tree and planting herself right in front of him again. She seems even more agitated than during her previous visit, but in a different way. This time, she has a very clear idea in her head. She moves behind the checkers players' bench, then back toward Atou Seck. The noises she makes as she returns to her original spot are almost human. "Any moment now she'll grab my hand and show me what she's hiding over there," Atou Seck thinks, vaguely amused by her antics. She is growing palpably impatient with Atou Seck's reticence.

He gets up and follows her. You never know. When a wild animal suddenly appears out of nowhere, one has to be careful.

The two babies are huddled up under the bench. They peer at him with dark and fearful eyes.

■   ■   ■

On that same day, she left them with him in the courtyard. Before he even had the chance to figure out what was happening, she was gone.

■   ■   ■

But Atou Seck was in good spirits. He adopted them without a moment's hesitation. Playing leapfrog with them and even talking to them from time to time slowly brought him back to life. They may not have been able to answer him, but he pretended not to notice. He was fed up with hearing nothing but the echo of his own voice. Right from the start, Atou Seck was convinced they were there purely to cheer him up. He thanked his lucky stars for sending him two grandchildren.

One morning, at around ten o'clock, they were all dozing together on his mat. Barely conscious of what was happening to him, Atou Seck could feel a rope being wound around his body. They were chuckling happily as they bustled about, and he thought they had invented a new game. In reality they had tied him so tightly to his acacia tree that from one minute to the next, he had become their prisoner, incapable of the slightest movement.

■   ■   ■

At least once a day, they go out and leave him alone. As far as he can work out, they go rummaging around in the garbage heaps and investigate the kitchens in the abandoned houses of Gouye-Guewel. They might bring back a few small chunks of cassava, a piece of banana peel, or some peanuts, and on a lucky day even some large cashews.

They put his food on the mat, making sure he is able to reach it with his mouth. It is demeaning, but he has no choice. How distressing to have to contort oneself like that in order to eat, but when he manages to snatch a crust of bread, he quickly takes it between his teeth and starts chewing it slowly. After a few days he has perfected the technique and not a single crumb of his meager rations is lost. The two little monkeys sit there, observing him and accompanying his meals with their malicious chuckles.

If they are unhappy with Atou Seck—and that happens almost all the time—they whack him with a stick and say things he doesn't understand. They can get so furious that he is afraid they might kill him on the spot.

■　　■　　■

Sometimes, usually in midafternoon, Atou Seck watches as they groom themselves. They shave, take long showers, and then each put on smartly tailored light blue suits. They always wear exactly the same clothes: white shirt, brown hat, big dark sunglasses and a red tie. Whenever he sees them getting dressed up like that, Atou Seck knows they are about to take him on one of their little strolls around Gouye-Guewel. They loosen the rope around his neck and drag him along the streets of the neighborhood. They never fail to stop at the drinking trough near the public park. He hesitates every time before drinking its greasy, greenish looking water, but he has to do it. Without further ado, he crouches down and lowers his lips into the trough to quench his thirst.

Atou Seck obediently does their bidding. But he still hasn't stopped wondering why they treat him like this. Occasionally, he even jokes with them as if nothing had happened. But that's something they cannot stand. He has the impression that the mere sound of his voice puts them into a state of shock. Are they perhaps amazed—you simply never know—that humans are able to speak as well? They look at each other in disbelief and their dramatic gestures convey their exasperation. He receives a few lashes with the whip, and they pull harder on the rope.

■　　■　　■

Every now and then, the mother returns.

They go and meet her on top of the enclosure. They hug each other, she delouses them, and they purr with delight. Seeing the three of them so happy together gives Atou Seck high hopes every time that she will take them with her when she leaves again. But the female monkey's departure is always as sudden as her arrival.

■　　■　　■

Atou Seck has found names for them. "You, the little male, will be Ninki. And you, his younger sister, are going to be called Nanka." Atou Seck mutters to himself, "Ninki-Nanka."

. ∎ ∎

Ninki-Nanka—they are all the company he has in the world. Although they detest him, it is reassuring for him to have them around. It would all be fine if he could only talk to them. He misses nothing so much as the warmth of a voice. It's strange, but *before*, he had the reputation of being taciturn, very stingy with words. And now, his favorite pastime is listening to the conversations the two monkeys are always so absorbed in. What can they possibly be talking about? Atou Seck thinks they may even be using a real human language. Human, but at the same time perhaps unknown to all humans. So he tries to listen intently, hoping to catch just one word of what they are saying. Just a single word. But his hopes are always dashed. They talk too fast, these little monkeys. Each sound crashes so violently into the next that it almost makes his skull hurt.

Ninki goes up to his little sister and whispers something into her ear. She listens to him, frowns and slowly nods her head.

That's enough to give Atou Seck a huge fright. Monkeys whispering secrets to each other, surely that's one of the scariest things in the entire world! Monkeys don't whisper. That, at least, he is certain about.

∎ ∎ ∎

"Oh well, the war between Dibi-Dibi and Commander Zero is clearly not preventing my two little monkeys from living like royalty!" Atou Seck says to himself with a snicker. Each one of their meals is a veritable feast. A few evenings ago, they started having dinner outside in the courtyard. Seated at opposite ends of a long table, they help themselves to thinly sliced roast beef or grilled grouper. Oysters and prawns frequently feature on their menu. Those are the times when they are rather less talkative than normal. They lift their fork to their mouth with an elegant flourish and then chew their food with great relish. They seem to like fruit, but not nearly as much as he would have expected from this species of animal. Little Nanka definitely adores persimmons. She puts them in the freezer overnight, and the next morning they have ripened in the cold. She then takes them out, cuts them into paper thin slices, bright orange in color, and drops them into a bowl of yoghurt. Atou Seck has never seen them drink wine except at mealtimes, but they clearly cannot tolerate much alcohol. One glass is enough to make them tipsy, and more than once, Ninki has come and pissed on his prayer mat in his inebriated state, giving him an insolent look.

■   ■   ■

"Listen to me, abominable creature! I sacrifice my life for you, and instead of thanks, all I get is your ingratitude!"

Unable to understand the reasons for this unexpected outburst of rage, Ninki and Nanka stare at each other in surprise. But no sooner have they turned their menacing gaze on him than he is begging for mercy. "It's not you who are making me so angry, my adorable little grandchildren! My enemies are on their way from the hereafter to attack the earth. I can hear the clattering of their footsteps in the sky! They have seen how much you are spoiling me—me, your grandfather—and that makes them jealous! We must be vigilant, for soon they'll be right here in the courtyard of this house! They are cannibals, they want to devour our guts, but we won't let them do that to us!"

When he stops talking, Ninki walks up to him with a banana in his hand. He waves it in front of Atou Seck's face, who tries to grab it with his teeth, but Ninki suddenly throws the fruit far away. Then he opens his mouth wide and starts beating his chest and uttering incomprehensible grunts. Atou Seck hangs his head. Quickly and discreetly, Ninki gives his sister a signal at which Nanka jumps over the wall and returns with a stick that she passes to Ninki.

Atou Seck is huddled up against the tree trunk in anticipation of his lashes. The little monkey lifts his hand as if to hit him, then drops it with an expression of utter contempt on his face. He walks back to the house, without so much as having touched him.

■   ■   ■

All three of them looked up at the sky at the same time. It was the first time since the beginning of the war that they noticed the small fighter planes above Gouye-Guewel. After several flybys, the planes, which were now flying at a lower altitude, started dropping their bombs onto targets they had no doubt identified in advance. All of them were located near the zoo. Atou Seck wondered what had happened to the animals—panthers, giraffes, and hyenas—that the children used to come and see every Sunday from all over the town. They were probably abandoned by their keepers and died from starvation a long time ago. They must have been so dirty and malnourished that they could never have survived in captivity. Maybe the war was a kind of salvation for them. It dawned on Atou Seck that that was where Ninki and Nanka must have escaped from. He put the question to them, but they didn't hear it because the entire area was shaking from explosions that were probably causing a lot of damage much farther afield. The hostilities in Gouye-Guewel had started up again, amid all the devastation and the buildings that were already in flames. Watching their tanks revving up like frightened horses could have been almost comical, had the battle for the zoo between insurgents and the national army not been so ferocious.

It looked as though the clashes of Gouye-Guewel might turn into the decisive battle.

When all was quiet again, he heard a political commentator make the following statement on air: "It will be easier to seize Gouye-Guewel than to control it." He found it hard to believe that Gouye-Guewel, this ghetto of down-and-outs, should be a place of such strategic importance. After all, it was not the only area that was wedged between the river and the sea. Atou Seck was convinced its inhabitants would be chased out of their houses after the war. It was unheard of for ordinary people to be taking it easy on the beach instead of toiling away from morning till night. Having the sea breeze gently tickling their nostrils just like that must be a random little error, and would be rectified when the time was right, no matter whether Dibi-Dibi or Commander Zero carried off the final victory.

■   ■   ■

"Ha! My two little bastards! Nobody except you shrieks like that, nor would anybody else make such a deafening noise in the living room. So they're still busy creating a complete shambles in there!"

Having managed to loosen his rope a bit, Atou Seck has crawled right up to the living room door. He positions himself near the window from where he can observe them without being seen. There they are, lazing about on the sofa and watching television. Atou Seck can hardly believe his eyes. Since when has the TV been working again? "Monkeys who fix televisions! Whatever's next in Dibi-Dibi-Land?" he mutters.

He is holding his breath. If they discover Atou Seck is spying on them, he's dead meat. Ninki, the boy, is a real sadist. Making people suffer clearly gives him pleasure.

On the screen, a young *Toubab* woman is pacing up and down, talking very fast into a microphone. The words coming out of her mouth sound like the rat-a-tat noise of an old moped that doesn't want to start. "One wonders how she manages to breathe!" Atou Seck thinks. After several minutes, she finally stops talking and with a sweeping gesture, she points to six small steps covered with a red carpet. The next moment, first one singer appears in front of the rapturous audience, and then four or five more are lining up on the stage. All are dressed in fluorescent suits, shouting at the top of their voices and gesticulating wildly. Since their eyes are bulging and their mouths are so horribly distorted, they must be singing love songs, Atou Seck thinks to himself. Most of them are pressing their hands on their heart and are grimacing dreadfully. He manages a wry little smile when he sees all these young artists dancing like a troop of monkeys. Now he can understand Ninki and Nanka's new love for the television much better. More and more often, he sees them glued to the screen for hours on end. It is like an addiction for them.

Frequently at night, music wafts across to him—muffled sounds, as if coming from another planet.

■　　■　　■

After that, it's as though he has been completely forgotten. They will just briefly abandon the screen to make themselves an espresso in the kitchen, and then they're back on the sofa again. Atou Seck's new pastime is to secretly watch Ninki and Nanka watching television. At times he has trouble understanding what is going on. Nanka comes rushing into the living room and starts mimicking the female singer on the podium. Then she suddenly stops dead, holding out her hand to her brother. He walks up to her, grips her waist and they start dancing, going round and round in circles and lifting their feet up very high in front of them. There are moments when Atou Seck has to admit that their tango is not entirely devoid of grace. He wonders whether these two little monkeys aren't themselves just images from the TV.

Atou Seck can feel death drawing stealthily closer, ready to strangle him by gradually tightening its grip. But he is not going to let that happen to him.

He must be strong. In his state of distress, he is beginning to think the animals are planning to wipe out the entire human race. "They want to kill us all, one after the other; that's what they want to do. They're going to take as long as they want to achieve this, without even being aware of it, because time doesn't exist for them. The worst of all wars is when you don't even know where the battlefield is anymore."

. . .

A ceasefire agreement has been signed. Or at least that's what the voice is saying on the radio.

Since yesterday, Gouye-Guewel has been completely calm. Dibi-Dibi's army seems close to victory. The news plunges Atou Seck into despair. He simply cannot take the fact that this madman will go on governing the country.

. . .

In a special newsflash on the official radio channel, Commander Zero's death has been announced. The reporter admits that it has yet to be confirmed, but he sounds optimistic.

Commander Zero, the rebel leader, the man with his beige balaclava and the machine gun barrel pointing up into the air. Atou Seck doesn't like him either. But no matter what, he wants Dibi-Dibi's troops to get beaten. It has to happen. One way or another, the country must let Dibi-Dibi know it's over and that his hour of truth has arrived. That will be Atou Seck's very own, personal revenge. Ninki and Nanka will be in deep trouble when that happens. They will beg him to spare their lives, but he will be merciless. In preparation of his fight against the forces of Evil he decides to gather whatever information he can find about the enemy.

No stone will be left unturned.

The development over hundreds of millions of years of a species that tolerates heat better than cold. In captivity, in the zoos, they perform their acrobatics and pull funny faces to avoid having to starve to death. Granted, children throw them peanuts and biscuits, but what a way to live! A race of pathetic creatures that survives on garbage and whose disappearance would do humanity as a whole a great deal of good. While in one country—he seems to remember it's in India—killing this animal is against the law, elsewhere, it gets turned into a delicious roast. Yes, those are his kind of people, that is what he calls a civilized country. He would love to have a nice spider monkey roast for supper, seasoned with garlic and plenty of chili. The true connoisseurs say spider monkey is juicy and tender. It makes him salivate just to think of it.

■　■　■

On the Rock of Gibraltar, a baboon, with his hands in his pockets, walks into a little grocer's shop on Cannon Lane—one of several streets that intersect with Main Street. He knows Rodrigo Mancera, the proprietor, very well. Actually, Rodrigo is one of his closest buddies. When it's his turn, he hands him a pack of Marlboros. It is the end of the day, and the shop is about to close. Rodrigo takes two bottles of beer from the minibar and offers one to Baboon. They drink and they talk about nothing in particular. But tonight, they at least have a small scandal to gossip about. Artemio Vargas, the shadiest and most notorious cop in Gibraltar, got caught at last. Drug trafficking and illegal immigration. He was in cahoots with one of the ferrymen. "These ferrymen are the biggest scourge in town," complains Rodrigo Mancera, who always has something to moan about. Baboon concurs by blowing puffs of smoke into the air. "This time they've managed to collar him," he says, sounding pleased. "At the very moment when the guy was about to hand over the dosh. A double crime—caught in the act. There's nothing he can do, old Artemio." Rodrigo is not so sure about that. He has realized that politicians aren't terribly bothered about the law, and has become disillusioned. They're all the same, rotten to the core, that's what he thinks of them. "This is Gibraltar," he says calmly. "Just wait and see." Then he questions Baboon about his life in the jungle. That's always how it starts between the two of them, with these trivial little questions that you ask a friend to fill an awkward gap in the conversation. "How do you make love?" asks Rodrigo, who has read, or perhaps only heard, that the male and the female shag each other while swinging in the air, just holding on to tropical jungle vines. The grocer finds that incredibly romantic, but it's still rather bizarre, he thinks. It seems to Baboon that Rodrigo Mancera, who is utterly intrigued by the whole thing, wants to try it out for himself, as it were. Obviously, Baboon quite likes him to think of his people as possessing an unusual sexual creativity, but there is simply no truth in it. It makes him smile, and he categorically denies all their bullshit about what goes on in bed when actually there isn't even a bed. "There is absolutely no reason why we should get laid in such a dangerous way, Rodrigo. I bet you've never seen anyone making love with his tail wrapped around a branch, my brother!" After a pause, which allows him to revel in Rodrigo Mancera's disappointment and irritation, he concludes: "We do it on the ground, just like everyone else. What makes you think we're so complicated, man?"

Later on, during their pub crawl in town, Rodrigo wants to know how they choose their leader, what their favorite fruits are and whether it's really true that they turn their young into succulent meatballs that they marinade in lemon juice before consuming them with relish? And what about their music, yes, especially their music! You know there are people who say they have tiny droplets of mambo, rumba, jazz and blues in their veins—what do you think of that? And all those many different species of baboons, I mean really, what's that all about? The place is crawling with them, they are absolutely everywhere! How many of them are there all in all do you think? We basically have no idea and the scandalmongers claim that that's why they're constantly bashing each other on the head with machetes . . . Rodrigo Mancera himself doesn't believe a word of it, of course. Everybody knows he's not a racist, and besides one mustn't forget that Baboon is his best mate. In fact he thinks he has heard that an absolutely phenomenal monkey was only recently discovered in the Forest of the Bees in Gabon, on the banks of the Efuwé River. Apparently the tip of his tail is so dazzlingly white that it blinds all those who stare at it! This story has made a big impression on Rodrigo Mancera as well—just imagine, you're a bit too nosy, you're looking at a tail from too close by and hey presto, you get punished for your sins right there and then! I was gobsmacked! Things are certainly different over there, in the Forest of the Bees, very different from home indeed . . . And in order to really squeeze it dry, this topic that seems so endlessly fascinating to Rodrigo, he wants to know what Baboon is doing here, so far from the forest, it's not as if he is keen to chase him away from Gibraltar, but a foggy rock in the middle of the deep blue sea, that's not exactly the jungle, is it, the trees are missing, the dark green foliage, the lianas, the wild berries and all the rest of it, Rodrigo Mancera finds it hard to believe that he has left all that natural splendor behind just to come and drink beer in this gray hellhole; it's simply such a hideous place, Gibraltar. Baboon feels like telling him that his questions are utterly preposterous, that he should rather go there and see for himself that there are trees in that forest that almost touch the sky, what is he thinking, we, too, know how to scrape the sky, but the truth is that all this stuff bores him stiff, he just wanted to go out and have a quiet pint with his mate without turning the whole thing into some bloody lecture—he's not an intellectual, after all. But, Baboon is quite aware of the fact that Rodrigo is essentially a decent fellow who is just talking nonsense because of what he sees on television every night and he doesn't want to disappoint him. After their fourth outing, he has grown exceptionally fond of Rodrigo Mancera and is perfectly prepared to take him to the most far-flung corners of the jungle, yes really, why shouldn't he? It must be conducive to the progress of mankind if the Sons of the Earth get to know each other better. Baboon recites the great epic of his people and tears well up in his eyes. Soon his feelings of sadness will cause him to shed floods of tears. Down there, the old people never tire of telling the younger generation these stories, he says ecstatically, and Rodrigo Mancera can see it in his friend's eyes how much he is missing the forest all those many miles away on the other side of the ocean.

One day, he tells Rodrigo, the Monkey Army decides to put an end to Lion's arrogant and despotic behavior. The way they do this is very simple: several hundreds of thousands of them start pursuing him everywhere, filling the air with their deafening shrieks, a noise that is so peculiarly shrill and becoming shriller and shriller all the time. To start with, Lion quite likes the Monkey Army's suicidal tactics, since it means he no longer needs to go hunting; he can just grab them like fruit that's fallen off a tree, and he always has more fresh meat than he can eat. He devours so much of it that he has to take a good long siesta to digest all that meat. But hold on, that doesn't work, because the members of the Monkey Army continue to make an intolerable racket with their piercing screams. He gets up, roaring like thunder, and starts massacring them again by the thousands, this time not to eat them but to clear a path for himself. But the more he kills, the more of them he sees crowding in on him. The monkeys, far from being intimidated, simply leap across their brothers' bodies and continue to torment him. Every time the wild beast stands still and gets ready to attack them, the Monkey Army reads shock and horror in his face. While some of them are pelting his head with all sorts of projectiles, others are daring enough to cling to his mane. In a final burst of indignation, he attempts the most regal and spectacular roar of his life, but he is exhausted, and the sound that comes out is barely more intimidating than the meowing of a cat. And that is all that is necessary to unleash a veritable frenzy of jubilation among the Monkey Army. Finally, as he lifts up his paw in order to fight off some of his most insolent assailants, Lion topples over and collapses to the ground.

At that point, something astonishing happens. Hanging on to the branches of a tree, or squatting on the ground right next to him, one million monkeys are so quiet you could hear a pin drop as they watch him die a slow death.

The moment their enemy has stopped breathing, they scatter and disappear into the forest and carry on bickering exactly as before.

It's not the first time Baboon told Rodrigo Mancera this story, but he still finds it fascinating. For the little grocer from Gibraltar who is also a great admirer of Che Guevara, this is proof that a united people will never be defeated.

At about two o'clock in the morning, their pub crawl around the bars of Gibraltar still isn't over. Rodrigo Mancera starts teasing him, hey Baboon, if only you could see yourself, you're totally pissed, man, you're a weakling, a wimp, after two whiskies and a few beers all you can do is talk gibberish. This is a serious insult and Baboon decides to prove him wrong, even if it should cost him his life. Without a word, he walks out into the traffic on Calle Comedias. Standing in the middle of the road, he waits for the cars to approach him, one after the other, and just at the very moment when he is about to be run over, he nimbly leaps out of the way, not without lifting his cap and saluting the driver by taking a deep, elaborate bow in the manner of the Spanish bull fighters. He then asks Rodrigo Mancera to do the same, go on my boy, we'll soon know which one of us is more sloshed. Rodrigo Mancera rises to the challenge and in the end they both congratulate each other on their bravery and for the thousandth time that night they pledge eternal friendship between their nations. But Baboon doesn't hold his liquor well and when he is in that state, he just goes on and on about the complicated history of his people. It all comes bubbling up to the surface and starts to file past them: the Spanish *conquista* in Mexico and Guatemala, the massacre at Wounded Knee, the Algerian War and the Voulet-Chanoine Mission, all Rodrigo Mancera's dirty tricks, we haven't forgotten any of them, you see, and it seems a little bit too easy now that everybody's dead and our treasures have been carried off, to come and say, OK, Baboon, those horror stories of the past, they're over now, that's ancient history; let's make a new start, let there be nothing but peace and harmony between us from now on and let's all behave like civilized people. No really, that's just a bit too clever, my friend. Yes, he says, I like you a lot, we're brothers and I'm prepared to die with you if your life is in danger that's all fine Rodrigo, but I don't have a short memory, you know, so don't take me for a fool please. Rodrigo abandoned him a few million years ago, and that still torments him. To be completely honest, he, Baboon, feels quite traumatized by that betrayal even now. They were romping around in the trees up there, near the clouds, feeding on succulent mangoes, berries and green leaves. And then, one day, when he wanted to chat to Rodrigo on the branch next to him, he was gone. "Since that day you have been looking down on me!" Baboon screams furiously, almost prepared to fight it out with Rodrigo Mancera there and then. And besides, Rodrigo's children, should they really be allowed to call him Baboon-with-Scalded-Buttocks, and how about Consuelo, his wife, who avoids him while she's pregnant, because, horror of horrors, the baby might be born looking like a baboon? He has a good mind to tell Rodrigo in no uncertain terms that he finds his arrogance hard to comprehend!

And on he goes in the same acerbic vein, "You are no longer one of us, Rodrigo Mancera, *Homo sapiens* and *Homo sapiens*. Or something like that. Finally, many generations and several million years later, this species reaches its pinnacle in the form of a little grocer in Gibraltar who isn't even a genuine *guevaristo*! Bravo, what an achievement, young man! Just between you and me, Rodrigo, there's no reason to be so stuck-up—when someone falls off a tree, we call that a fall, don't we? Every day, your destiny is closing in on you a bit more. You are totally ignorant of the mess you're in, and you haven't the foggiest idea where the paths you have marked out for yourself are going to lead. Swallow your pride and come back home, Rodrigo Mancera. We may not be smart enough to build airplanes, but we are a lot less stupid than you, that's for sure. Ah, I nearly forgot that little thing you've invented that is so brilliant. Money. You love it so passionately that you have lots of affectionate nicknames for it: Dosh. Dough. Moolah. Green. Loot. And that's probably not all. We laugh about it so much here that it makes the baobabs and tamarinds quiver all night long. Bits of paper with mysterious scribbles on them. Nothing more. And yet, be on your guard if you haven't got any of them. Every disease known to man will be lying in wait for you, together with hunger and thirst, basically all the most terrible afflictions imaginable, and they will kill you in the end. My brother, am I right in thinking that you only betrayed me so you can totter around in a haze of lunacy, full of bitterness and hatred?"

Rodrigo Mancera bursts out in a fit of laughter and gives Atou Seck such a powerful slap that he wakes up with a start, drenched with sweat. He jumps up from his mat and tries to run straight ahead. But that is a bad idea because it tightens the rope around his wrists even more and he lets out a long scream. Nanka sees him writhing in pain and goes back into the house to call her brother. He emerges from the living room, scolds Atou Seck and ties him more securely to his tree.

▪   ▪   ▪

It's a cloudless night in the middle of September. The sky is so clear that when the man looks up, he has the sensation of being in direct contact with the most radiant stars, just as it sometimes happens with the clouds, when quite out of the blue, for no particular reason, they take on the shape of a polar bear or a cruise ship. For several days now, the same wind, cool and gentle, has been blowing on Gouye-Guewel, but it is not strong enough to get rid of the swarms of nocturnal insects. The mosquitoes clearly know that Atou Seck's hands are tied behind his back since they are attacking his face in small clusters, creating a constant buzz in his ears. He has grown weary of constantly having to shake his head to chase them away—unsuccessfully, of course—so he covers himself with his blanket.

At this precise moment, the objects around him start moving. He sits down again, waiting for the explosion. A streak of light shoots up above the trees and then drops down into the sea with a muffled hissing sound.

Then there are footsteps and he thinks, "They're here." He wonders whether it is Dibi-Dibi's army or Commander Zero's insurgents, but almost immediately decides that it actually makes no difference.

The sound of footsteps is getting fainter.

All of a sudden, Atou Seck can no longer control his anger toward Ninki and Nanka. "You little good-for-nothings! Just you wait until I get a chance to deal with you once and for all! That'll be the end of you lounging around on the sofa all day long, watching television! Lazybones!"

Atou Seck manages to drag himself to the door again. The TV is on, and a soccer match is showing. The referee is holding up a red card in front of one of the players. With his hands folded on his head, he is begging not to be sent off the pitch. The player who got hurt by him is flat on his back, squirming with pain and clasping his right ankle. That means there are still countries where people play soccer. A different world, so to speak. Ninki and Nanka are blissfully oblivious to all this. They are fast asleep on the couch, cozily snuggled up to each other. Atou Seck looks at his watch: "Three o'clock in the morning . . . I'll at last be able to get some sleep."

■   ■   ■

He is waiting.

For what? He doesn't know. He is not afraid of dying. That happens to everybody all the time.

More gunshots. This time they have nothing to do with the war. The sound of shooting comes from the living room.

"Not that blasted television again!" he growls.

The gunfire is coming from all directions, and on top of that, tanks are taking aim at fugitives who are running for cover in the woods. Soldiers are falling like flies, dozens of them. There are bodies rolling around in the dust all over the place; they are piling up in a narrow, dried up riverbed.

A few minutes later, the shots have died down to a faint echo and the combatants' voices are fading into the distance. At that moment, the lens zooms in on one of the soldiers—he looks very young. He is stretched out on the green grass; his eyes are turned inwards and he is staring into the void. There is a blood-red hole in his chest. He is dying. Gradually, the colors on the television screen are becoming brighter and more vivid, and it is obvious that the film is running backward. The young soldier and his fiancée are on top of a hill. They are laughing and chasing each other. They are madly in love. She puts her finger on the soldier's nose as if to say: "I breathe through this," and her eyes sparkle with boundless happiness. The young soldier pulls her close to him, without saying a word. The fiancée is one of those ravishing, slender actresses who drive people crazy, although nobody has any idea what makes them so irresistible and so much more enchanting and alluring than other women who look almost identical to them. She has exquisite, delicate features, long, jet-black hair, and the gentle curves of her body make her look sensual and fragile at the same time. Again and again they embrace each other and then they part, murmuring words Atou Seck can't understand.

The young soldier bids her a solemn farewell, and Atou Seck has no trouble guessing what he is saying to her. The words have remained the same, of course, ever since the birth of Man and ever since he set boldly forth to stain the earth with his blood: "Marguerite, I have to go and defend our country. I have told you that you are the one and only love of my life, and when I return, we will get married." Words to that effect.

Marguerite is in floods of tears. Her fiancé tries to comfort her and then, suddenly, something unexpected happens: Marguerite starts taking her clothes off and frantically throwing them all around her. It's clear that she is losing her mind. Her eyes and every one of her gestures betray a fierce determination, an unspeakable recklessness. She has decided to give herself to him before he walks into that infernal carnage, and nobody can stop her. But the young soldier blushes and, while squeezing her tightly against his body, tries to make her comprehend that he wants to protect her honor.

At this point in the movie, Atou Seck notices that Ninki and Nanka have become very agitated. They are literally beside themselves. On seeing the young woman in the nude—her near-perfect, truly sublime shape—they start jumping up and down in the living room, slapping each other on the back with glee. Oh la-la! What a grand spectacle we have there right in front of our eyes! But when the soldier refuses to play along, they are furious, calling him impotent. To Atou Seck, it looks as though they doubt that an individual who backs away from the body of a woman will have the courage to defend his country. That must be why the two little monkeys start hitting the screen as if trying to beat up this fake soldier.

"It seems that these two little scoundrels understand this language that I myself have never heard before . . . Could they have picked it up by watching TV? With those two, anything is possible."

He returns to his mat, and there, with his eyes half closed, he pretends to be fast asleep.

■   ■   ■

"What day is it?" Atou Seck wants to know. Monday? Tuesday? Wednesday? He has no idea. At Gouye-Guewel, the days go round and round in a circle. They are all exactly the same, like blindfolded children playing hide-and-seek. Each one pulls the mask off the next one, and so it goes on, forever and ever. For several weeks now, Atou Seck has been unable to distinguish dawn from dusk.

■   ■   ■

He has finally managed to undo the rope. For the first time since their arrival at the house, he can move around freely. As the only person in the deserted streets, he is in control of Gouye-Guewel. He feels well. His lungs are drawing in the sea air and the breeze is caressing his face. He feels invigorated, cleansed somehow, of every impurity.

But near the zoological garden, he spots a number of giant vultures sinking their powerful beaks into rotting corpses. As he is approaching them, they let go of their prey, lazily flap their wings a few times and come to rest on the roof of a house or on the power lines. As soon as he gets out of their sight, they return to the carcass and carry on ripping it to shreds.

He is lucky enough not to come across any guerrillas.

He could escape from Gouye-Guewel if he wanted to. But the thought doesn't even cross his mind. There is no way a couple of monkeys are going to make him run away; after all, he is Atou Seck, the son of Fara Birame Seck and great grandson of Sangoné-Penda Seck, who heroically sacrificed his life at the Battle of Somb! He will go back and sit under his acacia tree. There, he will wait patiently for the hour of his revenge. Under no circumstances is he going to turn his back on the enemy swords!

When Ninki and Nanka hear him opening the zinc gate, they pounce on him with fury. Atou Seck pretends he has no idea what they mean and says innocently, "Ah! Here you are again, my dear little chaps! Grandpa went out to stretch his legs! Why didn't you come along to keep me company? I am upset with you, I can't deny it!" His contrived cheerfulness makes them even angrier. They are clobbering their chests, stamping their feet, and finally they leap on top of him. They shower him with insults, and Atou Seck realizes that they are speaking the same language as the young soldier and his fiancée Marguerite.

Ninki ties a piece of cloth over Atou's eyes and mouth, leaving only a tiny slit under his nose to let him breathe. While the lashes are raining down on him, he remains completely rigid. Even when blood starts dripping from his wounds, he does nothing to defend himself. Now Nanka goes to the kitchen and comes back with some ground pepper that she sprinkles on his open wounds. Atou Seck hears himself uttering screams that sound almost inhuman, and he begs them for a coup de grâce to finish him off.

In response, the two monkeys slap their thighs, roaring with laughter.

. ■ ■

What a strange creature you are, Son of the Earth! So many feelings you have mixed up inside you, but no idea where they come from.

Suddenly, words start singing all by themselves inside his head. He knows this tune very well—it sends shivers down his spine. Is that a real song, he wonders, or are these just random words, stirred up by the wind, whirling around in the air and following Atou Seck step by step on his last journey?

Man ràkkaaju naa! Waaw, man ràkkaaju naa!

He feels entranced. It's the words that are singing and he is accompanying them. He is, and that must be made clear to everybody, the griot of the wind. His voice has faded to a murmur.

Man ràkkaaju naa! Waaw, man ràkkaaju naa!

He tries to remember the words of the song and the place where he heard them long ago . . . so long ago. It was such a long time ago . . .

Man ràkkaaju naa! Waaw, man ràkkaaju naa!

He is thinking of those old *bàkk*. Names of wrestlers come back to him. Youssou Diène. Mame Gorgui Ndiaye.

Where are you, Ninki? And you, too, Nanka, where are you? Come and untie my hands, so that I can at last give the wind his freedom again!

If only he could remember . . .

Man ràkkaaju naa! Waaw, man ràkkaaju naa!

If only he could catch hold of the meaning of these words at the last moment . . .

Gaynde Njaay, mbarawàcc!

Nobody will ever know why, but whoever hears these three words in Diafouné becomes invincible.

■ ■ ■

In the blink of an eye, the house has started filling up with soldiers. They seem to be coming from all directions. Their uniforms mean they must be Dibi-Dibi's men. Terror grips Atou Seck and he wants to flee, but his tethers lacerate and burn his body as soon as he tries to move. All he can think of doing to save his skin is to shout, "Long live Dibi-Dibi! Long live Dibi-Dibi!"

But even that he is forbidden to do; he cannot open his mouth. His scream gets stuck in his throat, where chunks of sentences collide with each other. Chaos. Panic. The turmoil of the battlefield.

There is no time to think, since everything is suddenly happening too fast. Shouts and whistle blows are echoing from everywhere, an officer is bellowing orders and his men position themselves in front of every door, ready to open fire. A few seconds later, shouts are heard coming from the trees and more soldiers—this time *Toubabs*, all of them—are jumping down into the courtyard in small units of two or three. They, too, start fanning out in all directions, machine gun at the ready. They seem nervous. Their captain is talking to the commander of Dibi-Dibi's soldiers, and calm returns to the house.

"Since when have these *Toubabs* been actively involved in the battles of Diafouné?" he wonders. He has never once heard that being mentioned on the radio. So they hid the truth from him all along!

He gets up, determined to find out what is actually going on. After all, whether there is a civil war or not, this is his house. About twenty more *Toubab* soldiers push their way through the front gate and are coming toward him. They look aggressive. What a story! How extraordinary to think that these young men were hiding in the trees all this time, observing his every move and gesture, while he was convinced he was completely alone in Gouye-Guewel!

Ninki and Nanka emerge from the living room, accompanied by one of the foreign soldiers. The latter turns to his boss, saluting and clicking his heels. Then he bows, with a respectful nod to Ninki and Nanka. The officer turns to the two monkeys, eyeing them with interest, and then greets each of them with an energetic handshake. It's the first time Atou Seck has noticed a fleeting smile on the face of the foreign general. He is taken aback by the general's courteous behavior toward Ninki and Nanka, but he can't control himself anymore, and bursts into laughter. "This is what the end of the world must be like! You dirty little beasts, Monkeys-with-Scalded-Buttocks, do you want to drive me mad? Who can explain to me what's going on in Diafouné?"

There is no answer. And maybe he didn't actually say anything.

The monkey takes one leap over the fence, and there she is, standing in front of him. Suddenly the courtyard is deserted again. Just like the morning fog evaporates with the first rays of sunshine, the soldiers have disappeared without a trace. Even Ninki and Nanka are no longer there. He and the she-monkey are alone. They gaze at each other in silence.

She pulls out a revolver from under her loincloth and calmly takes aim at Atou Seck's forehead.

One last time Atou Seck feels the wind caressing his face.

Man ràkkaaju naa! Waaw, man ràkkaaju naa!

BRIEF ESCAPADES

THESE DAYS, BADOU, THE WALLS OF BUILDINGS ALL OVER THE CITY ARE plastered with huge posters of our two top wrestling champions of the moment. In the evenings, in front of the television, or sitting around sipping our customary three cups of tea, at street junctions, in taxis, or on the radio, there's only one topic of conversation, and that is the upcoming contest next Sunday. It's an exaggeration of course, but some people like to refer to it as the "Fight of the Century." Basically, the entire country is holding its breath, and according to the newspapers, the sixty thousand seats of the Léopold Sédar Senghor stadium are already sold out. I know how fond you were of this sport and that's why I am talking to you about it here in this *Notebook*. You must be dearly missing the wrestling matches at the Iba Mar Diop stadium, right next to the Medina. You started going there as a small boy, and when you turned eight, you announced you wanted to become a champion as famous as Mbaye Guèye, Toubabou Dior or Manga II. How you used to pester me with your endless questions about Abdourahmane Ndiaye Falang, Mbaye Dia Diop, Fodé Doussouba, Pathé Diop and Landing Diamé! But I enjoyed talking to you about those famous names, because it took me back to my own childhood. And even now, they are still very fresh in my mind, since, quite apart from their sheer physical strength and courage, those wrestlers were also true poets.

Each one of them conjures up certain tunes in my memory, each one brings back a gesture, a *voice*, a harmony, both perfect and unique in the world. I can't even begin to describe so much beauty to you. By contrast, and I hope you don't mind my saying so, I cannot really get excited about our monsters of today who do nothing except bash the hell out of their opponents. If, like everybody else, I am planning to watch the fight on TV next Sunday, I guess it's only so that I can report back to you. I already know in advance that the *bàkk* are going to be a letdown and that, once the show is over, people will only be interested in the millions these wrestlers are pocketing, and not in their talent. You can call me churlish and accuse me of being too quick in cutting the gods of our stadiums down to size, but that's what tends to happen with people my age. When you get close to the end, you always think everything was better in the past. Is that a trick which helps us convince ourselves that we can leave this earth without regret? Quite possibly.

But I hope you won't be disappointed when you read these lines one day. I know they made you dream, these champions of ours. Draped in their brightly colored loincloths, they made the arena come alive with their singing and dancing. I will never forget how it fascinated and amused you to watch them pouring bowls of sour milk over their naked torsos, cracking eggs, or watching their opponent through a hole in their sandal before hundreds of white pigeons were released into the air above the arena of the Iba Mar Diop stadium. Then, just before sunset, Khar Mbaye Madiaga's voice could be heard, drowning out everyone else. Her songs made a mockery of those burly fellows with their big muscles who seemed so scared of each other:

> *Wrestling is strictly for real men!*
> *You look terrified!*
> *Shame on you . . .*
> *Even your sisters and your wives*
> *Would show more courage in the contest*
> *Than you!*

All this is highly charged with emotion, Badou. Nobody remains indifferent to it, neither you nor any other son of our nation. If, one day, you remember this in the foreign country where you are now, you will probably think: "Soccer is definitely very popular where I come from, but wrestling, in the old style as well as the new, is the most apt reflection of the soul of our people. We have practiced it since time immemorial and it is to our nation what sumo is to the Japanese." In the same breath, you will say to yourself that it's quite normal for journalists from all corners of the world to come and take pictures of these fights only to announce later, on their television channels back home, "What you are about to see here is called Senegalese wrestling. These champions' ancestors invented it over three thousand years ago, and today it's their national sport."

Well, I'm going to have to disappoint you for the second time, Badou, because this is simply not true. We owe Senegalese wrestling as we know it today to a French adventurer by the name of Maurice Jacquin.

Let me tell you how it came about.

Having tried his hand at all sorts of odd jobs, this *Toubab* decided to open a carpentry workshop near where he was living, on Sandiniéry Street. When the other *Toubabs* in Dakar started ordering their furniture from him, he became a bit more successful. But he wasn't the most peace-loving individual, our Maurice Jacquin, nor was he particularly interested in spending countless hours behind the counter, dropping the pennies he had earned into the till, and doing that day after day for the rest of his life. He was a warrior at heart, in actual fact, a man with a hankering for adventure who despised people prepared to put up with the poor hand destiny had dealt them, office workers with an inflated ego, for example, or potbellied bureaucrats content with their dull, humdrum daily grind.

That's when he came up with the idea of organizing wrestling matches with a difference, as you will see a little later in this *Notebook*.

Grand Makhou, as we called him, one of our senior mates in Niarela, was among his very first apprentices. He was an unrepentant rabble rouser in his own right, who liked to introduce himself as Makhou-the-Lion, hitting his chest with pride.

One day—I remember it as if it were yesterday—he took me by the hand and said, "Come on little Nguirane, let's go and pay that crook Maurice Jacquin a visit."

I can't have been much older than six or seven, but the way he said this told me that Grand Makhou wasn't just planning a simple courtesy visit. The steely look in his eyes and his clenched jaws were unmistakable signs that he was planning to beat someone up.

And as for Maurice Jacquin, I can still see his angular, haggard face, his hooked nose and the covetous expression in his devious eyes. He was tall, but his shoulders were bent, and I even seem to remember—although I am not completely sure on this point—that he was slightly hunchbacked. His khaki pants were a bit too short for his spindly legs and on that day, oddly enough, he had a yellow pencil stuck behind each ear. As the only *Toubab* in the entire workshop, he was also the boss. When we arrived, he was moving from one group of workers to the next, barking his orders in a few curt, brusque sentences.

I soon understood why Grand Makhou had looked so distressed when he asked me to accompany him to Maurice Jacquin's workshop. The *Toubab* owed him money and he wanted to be paid right there and then.

I was one of the Niarela street kids back then, and Grand Makhou was a living legend to us. Whenever a grown-up had given us a thrashing, we went straight to Grand Makhou and complained, whereupon he immediately beat up the perpetrator. He invariably obliged without asking questions, as a matter of principle as it were. Principle number one of Grand Makhou the Avenger was that children are sacrosanct: you never hit a child. He was a tough guy who was not in the habit of bowing to authority or of putting up with anything he considered unjust. Even if I don't really know how to explain it to you, it's a fact: although Grand Makhou hated any kind of histrionics, he ended up hitting and punching from morning to night, usually to protect the underdog. I guess that's what tends to happen when you decide to stick up for other people.

Instead of telling Maurice Jacquin straight what the purpose of his visit was, Grand Makhou embarked on a long litany of salutations, which he repeated incessantly. He did this because he wanted to avoid humiliating his debtor in public.

Maurice Jacquin, who was busy sawing a piece of wood, had the brazenness to say to him: "Listen, Makhou, don't pester me with your *salamalecs*, OK? As you can see, we're working!"

Well, well, well! Nobody talks like that to Makhou the Lion! This puny runt of a *Toubab* must be mad, I said to myself.

Grand Makhou couldn't believe his ears. "D'you really think you can get away with talking to me like this, Mister White Guy? You know what? I'll fuck your mother right here till she keels over in front of everybody!"

He lost no time and started walking up to Maurice Jacquin, perfectly in step with the menacing clicking sounds of his thumb and middle finger. "I want my cash and I want it fast! So hurry up or I'll—"

Suddenly, there was total silence in the workshop. For a few moments,

Grand Makhou and Maurice Jacquin were facing each other like two rams about to lock horns. The workers all pretended to be busy, but I could tell they were on tenterhooks.

Now it was Maurice Jacquin's turn to yell. "You're threatening me, eh? You must have some nerve! Me, Maurice Jacquin! Go on, get out of my space! Fuck off before I kick your arse!"

I have told you already, Badou, Grand Makhou was one of those fellows who wasn't afraid of nothing. And he most definitely didn't allow anyone to be rude to him in public. He took two or three steps backward, pulled something out of his belt and started walking toward the *Toubab* again. Maurice Jacquin saw a blade flashing in Grand Makhou's right hand and started to retreat a bit. But Grand Makhou kept advancing, twirling his mini-dagger between his fingers, clearly determined to make use of it.

One of Maurice Jacquin's workers—he struck me as the most senior—said to Grand Makhou, without taking his eyes off his work, "Makhou, are you aware of what you're doing?"

"I couldn't care less what happens to me," Grand Makhou growled, shaking with rage. "Either this *Toubab* hands over my money, or I'll make mincemeat out of his bloody guts."

The *Toubab* he was talking about was a pitiful sight to see.

And Grand Makhou added, vehemently, "Yes, that's what I'm going to do, I, Makhou-the-Lion, and then I will go and spend the night in prison."

In the same quiet, sincere voice as before, the old carpenter said, "There's no need to lose your temper, Makhou. If you play it more coolly, you can take your money and go home without a fuss. These people are not to be trusted, Makhou, they won't allow an African to stand up to them. How much does he owe you?"

"I found nine wrestlers for him last month. He knows how much that comes to."

Maurice Jacquin was a tough cookie himself, but he knew that Grand Makhou was a hothead, and he certainly didn't feel like being eviscerated by him. He regained his composure and pretended he had just been joking: "Makhou he lova money too much! Me pay money!"

Grand Makhou still looked tense and edgy while Maurice Jacquin paid him what he owed him, and we left the workshop having won the battle, in full view of the baffled employees.

Back in Niarela, he handed me a few coins and said: "Young lad, do you know Tina Delgado, my Cape Verdean girlfriend? Go and give her this hundred-franc note and tell her I want a *kacuupa* from Hell tonight. I'll bring the beer and the gin. We're eating at her place tonight, my gang of *ceddo* and I!"

Grand Makhou, you old devil!

As soon as I come across him in some remote corner of my memory, I instantly get very emotional. He was a real man, that fellow. He was neither rich nor famous, but he knew how to command respect, and he got it. Looking back on it now at my age, Badou, I realize we had a lot of people like that here, people just as proud as Grand Makhou. Cheikh Anta Diop. Amilcar Cabral. Mongo Beti. Samory Touré. Thomas Sankara. Lumumba. You know all those names. Each one of them was a Man of Defiance in his own right, and for that reason and for that reason alone, the white colonizer killed them or at least reduced them to silence. But I still can't understand why, everywhere on this continent, but also outside it, Grand Makhou has always ended up being beaten, and why, despite his bravery, he was always eventually brought to his knees. We were able to say *no*, but that clearly wasn't enough. There was something else that we lacked. I still don't know exactly what that is. Don't be shocked if I mention those giants of our history in the same breath as a man as ordinary as Grand Makhou. That was just a little aside I wanted to add so I could share my concerns with you.

I have given you a description of the fight between Maurice Jacquin and Grand Makhou. The *Toubab* behaved badly on that occasion, there's no doubt. But deep down, he was quite a decent fellow. To us, he had nothing in common with the rest of the *Toubabs* at that time; he didn't hide himself away in a posh villa in the Plateau district, and we always saw him as one of us, right from the start. His passion was sport of any kind, and he quickly became fascinated by the *mbapat*, which he never missed.

I'm sure he had been hatching this idea for a while, when one sunny morning we found out that Maurice Jacquin had opened his own wrestling arena in Niayes-Thioker, not far from where we lived. The news caused a stir in Niarela, and we listened to our leading local personalities openly expressing their amazement: "A wrestling arena, did I hear you correctly my dear fellow?"

"Yes, absolutely. It's basically like a large room where wrestling matches are held."

"Since when have wrestling matches taken place indoors?"

"I know it's odd, but that's how it is—"

"I'll have to go and see that for myself!"

"I want to come too! Let's go! *An egg bouncing from one rock to the other!* Wolof Njaay always said that was impossible!"

"All right then, let's all go and see how such a marvel can become reality!"

Maurice Jacquin's hall was just behind the El Malick cinema. When the inhabitants of Niarela arrived there, a huge, fierce-looking fellow was blocking the entrance. They looked at each other incredulously. What a great start. Did that mean one now had to pay to be able to watch a wrestling match?

They asked the doorkeeper, "So it's no longer just a simple game? Is that what you're saying, my friend?"

"Yes, it is," replied the doorkeeper, "but it's different from our kind of wrestling."

"What do you mean?"

"Here, the wrestlers also throw punches at each other."

"What do you mean, throw punches?"

"They punch each other real hard," said the doorkeeper who suddenly looked a lot less intimidating.

It was obvious he enjoyed talking to the new arrivals about a subject he had probably never had the courage to discuss before.

Shaking his head with a mixture of repugnance and bewilderment he added, "These fights are extremely brutal. I have to clean the floor after each encounter, and there's blood everywhere, I assure you."

"And that's what you call wrestling? The same as our kind of wrestling?"

The doorkeeper pulled a long face. He looked doubtful. "All I know is that Monsieur Jacquin calls them wrestling matches . . ."

The doorkeeper seemed just as unsure about the whole thing as the spectators, who ended up paying for their tickets and then took their seats around the arena. Most of the wrestlers were beefy young domestic servants, usually in the employ of the *Toubabs* in the Plateau district.

That was the day Maurice Jacquin and Grand Makhou met for the first time. The latter caused a sensation, I have to say. It was beyond Grand Makhou's power of self-control to just sit back and watch while there was a fight going on. One of the wrestlers was literally wiping out his opponents, one after the other, with a few well-placed uppercuts.

When Grand Makhou stepped into the arena, he knocked over his *ndënd* with one single, ruthless kick. His fight with the champion of Niayes-Thioker was long and grueling. After an hour, their faces were bloodied and they were close to collapse from exhaustion. They staggered around the arena, punching the air with their fists. To the surprise of those who didn't know him, Grand Makhou won his very first victory. Maurice Jacquin grabbed his hand and lifted it up triumphantly, then he draped him in the blue-white-and-red flag and handed him a small sum of money.

When he got back to Niarela, the reception he received turned into a riotous spectacle. Grand Makhou, who by then already saw himself as the greatest champion of all times, improvised a number of unforgettable *bàkk*. One thing is clear, Badou, Grand Makhou was invincible, he was our demigod, but his singing was terrible! His voice was about as harmonious as a barrel of oil that's being poured out over a pile of rubble.

This was the beginning of the most glorious chapter in Grand Makhou's life. For eight years, his back didn't touch the ground once, and that made him a national hero. When he ran out of suitable opponents, he decided to become Maurice Jacquin's right-hand man. They started traveling to all the *mbapat* together during the rainy season, recruiting the most talented wrestlers and inviting them to participate in combats. The winners were not well paid, but that didn't stop the rumor from spreading in the popular districts that if you were young and strong, you could earn a bit of money by hitting the living daylights out of another young fellow in a hall in Niayes-Thioker.

So this, Badou, was the strange idea that began to take root in everybody's mind. Soon you could see all the ruffians in town queueing up outside Maurice Jacquin's wrestling arena. And why should anybody be surprised by this? These strapping lads were beating each other up all the time anyway, just for fun. So now, at least, they had a good reason to do it: money.

This is how our so-called national sport was born in 1930, in the Niayes-Thioker district.

Maurice Jacquin was so stupendously successful that the wrestlers from the countryside started to converge on Dakar en masse. Crushing an opponent's jaw, gouging out one of his eyes or biting off his ear became a pastime and a profession. Maurice Jacquin eventually gave up carpentry and hired some touts. At this point of my story I must admit that certain revelations I have to make to you are causing me quite a bit of embarrassment. I think it's best to reserve the juiciest details for my *Book of Secrets*. For the moment, let it suffice if I tell you that I know of at least three of the great Niarela families who acquired their millions through the despicable business of touting. Today their descendants are sitting on that immense fortune, looking down on the rest of the world with disdain. But we, who know the whole story, secretly joke about it. They grew rich because their fathers were cretins who used to spend their days loitering around Dakar harbor. When they spotted a fellow with an athletic build, especially among the dockers, they accosted him: "Hey my boy, do you know there's money waiting for you somewhere?"

"What do you mean, money?"

"Well, my friend, you've obviously never heard of Maurice Jacquin, the *Toubab* of Niayes-Thioker. He's opened up a wrestling hall over there."

"A wrestling hall?"

"Yes. And he pays well, he is a generous man."

"But I've never done any wrestling in my life!"

"That doesn't matter! With the kind of biceps you've got, you will be able to floor just about any opponent with a single punch of your fist!"

They carried on talking like this and finally a deal was struck. "OK. I'll be there on Sunday."

Maurice Jacquin's touts also went to Casamance, to Salum, to Futa, to Kedugu, and to the Cayor. They suggested to their young recruits that they should follow them to Dakar. If they showed any hesitation they were cruelly mocked. "Are you trying to tell me you actually enjoy your miserable life here, in the middle of nowhere? This backbreaking drudgery under the scorching sun, scraping the ground with your pathetic little hoe, is that the sort of life you want? You could earn a lot of money and have a lovely time in Dakar! Do you hear me? A really lovely time! Dakar is a great city, it has everything you could possibly wish for, and all the beautiful girls will be at your feet! How can one be so young and at the same time so reluctant to live life?"

And what's your story, Maurice Jacquin? They say you ended up here by accident. Apparently you were en route to America when your boat cast anchor in Dakar harbor, and you just stayed on. Our girls were just so incredibly hot. Rumor has it, by the way, that you left lots of little bastards in your wake. But that's another story. You didn't have two pennies to rub together, so the other *Toubabs* helped you out. Out of generosity? Perhaps, but I personally believe they didn't want the blacks to witness the embarrassing spectacle of a white guy fallen on hard times. That would have made quite a lot of theories go up in smoke.

So here you are, Badou, now you know why freestyle wrestling only exists in Dakar. You won't find it anywhere else in the world, not even elsewhere in Senegal. So if we continue thinking of it as our ancestral sport, that turns us all into descendants of Maurice Jacquin. Then there is nothing strange about the fact that our wrestlers now drape themselves in the American flag instead of the sumptuous loincloths they used to wear in the past, and that our good old *bàkk* have been replaced by dances from nowhere, which absolutely nobody can understand, least of all the dancers themselves. And you will also find that the wrestlers no longer have names like Dame Soughère or Boy Bambara, but call themselves whatever they fancy.

I am perfectly aware, Badou, that turning one's back on the outside world is tantamount to the kiss of death. It's bound to be a good thing if a nation lets the winds that are blowing from all corners of the globe expand its chest, but not unless we do what we can to preserve the crucible destined to receive its breath when they are blowing. Life, after all, is not born out of the void.

▪   ▪   ▪

At sunset yesterday, a lone traveler came to town. He thought he had managed to blend in with the crowd, but we noticed straight away he was a stranger. He kept stopping to read the signs on the shop fronts or to check house numbers, and, since he didn't know which way to go, he repeatedly turned round and walked back the way he came. It was the end of the day, the traders of Niarela were starting to lower their blinds, and the streets were nearly empty. The stranger found himself in a public square, where he put his bag down on the ground and settled down under a lamppost.

Vigilant citizens were watching him from the houses nearby. A few of us went outside and walked around him in circles, pretending to be preoccupied with our everyday chores. The man seemed completely oblivious to our clandestine maneuvers. He took a grapefruit and a penknife out of his satchel, cut the fruit down the middle in one go and started sucking each half with obvious relish, like someone who has all the time in the world. When he had finished, he wiped his hands with paper tissues and soon he was fast asleep.

It's possible that while he slept, a lot of people came and crowded around him. This part of town is becoming more and more dangerous, and one can never be too careful. It wasn't long before the police started taking an interest in the stranger as well. But I know nothing about all that. What I can say, and what is beyond doubt, because we all witnessed it with amazement, is that when he woke up the next morning, he walked to the public fountain of Niarela and washed his face. Then he tossed his Kleenex and his grapefruit peels into a dustbin, and with supple, careful and measured steps, he started walking toward the outskirts of the town. That was the last we saw of him, and he was never mentioned again. Later, we heard that he apparently stopped for breakfast at Diéwo Bâ's *tangana* near the bus station, but nobody was prepared to confirm this with absolute certainty. The question whether or not the man ordered a café au lait and Diéwo Bâ's famously delicious *pain-beurre-chocolat* at the *tangana* aroused such heated arguments that on at least one occasion this very nearly ended in a fist fight. All this happened for no reason whatsoever. A person—anybody, in fact—ought to be entitled to sleep under a lamppost in an unfamiliar place without giving an excuse or an explanation.

It also occurred to me that during that particular night, the wind—or the singing of the birds or whatever else, even a barking dog for that matter—might have relayed to this stranger the most powerful message he had ever heard in his life. Who knows? Maybe the otherworldly sound of a voice, familiar, yet distant, was ringing in his ears as he slept. It's possible—yet again, how are we to know?—that his brief sojourn in our town changed his life forever.

After all, mine was never the same again after the day I witnessed, completely by accident, one of Cheikh Anta Diop's rallies in Niarela.

■　　■　　■

As is my habit on such occasions, I stood at the very back of the audience. I didn't like them, those politicians who kept pitching up in Niarela, telling us the same old twaddle, so I always made sure I was in a spot that allowed me to leave discreetly the moment I had enough. I have never managed to listen to a single one of them right to the very end.

From where I was, I could see a tall man with an emaciated face addressing the crowd. He wore a gray, unlined jacket with short sleeves, and behind the thick glasses, his eyes looked alert and anxious at the same time. He looked tired and must have had a difficult day. That's maybe why it suddenly struck me that the parlous state our country was in must be making him really miserable, causing him great pain, and that he wasn't just in Niarela to win our votes.

Every election was rigged in those days, and he knew perfectly well he had no chance of winning this one. While he was addressing the crowd, I did more than just listen to him, I *watched* him, without being able to detect the slightest trace of dishonesty or insincerity in him, you know what I mean, don't you; that specific way our politicians have of revealing their duplicity through their facial expression, it's like a secretive little wink, meaning "Yes, yes, I'm talking, I'm talking all day long, but you know perfectly well I'm just bullshitting, I am an old hand at this and it's OK to vote for me because you and I are the same, sly and devious!" It isn't often that you feel you can trust someone instantly, the first time you meet him. Of course I expected to hear him promise to build us schools and hospitals, and I think he did in fact mention it briefly, like everybody else, but it was obvious his true aim was to change people's attitude, to profoundly reshape our way of looking at the world. To put it in a nutshell for you, Badou, for once I had the feeling that here was a human being who didn't just want to use my problems to further his pathetic little career. He was talking to me about my personal destiny and about what I was doing here on earth. I actually had the impression we were looking straight into each other's eyes and that he was talking to me alone, from man to man, as it were. I was enthralled by the magic of that moment. Cheikh Anta Diop seemed so fragile to me that, strangely enough, I felt more desperate to protect and to shield him than to be saved by him myself.

Normally, these are not the things you are supposed to think of when you have a man in front of you whose job it is, technically speaking, to convince you that he can improve your life. But I am convinced, Badou, that we can gain access to the true essence of another being in the most unexpected ways. The mere possibility of a purely human relationship with Cheikh Anta Diop meant I was sold on his vision of Africa from the moment of our first encounter that day.

Later on, I have tried to understand more fully what it was that made this man stand literally head and shoulders above the rest. I quickly realized that my instinct hadn't deceived me. If in a poor country a political leader is genuinely disinterested in money and prestige, that counts for more than any of his ideas. Anybody can have ideas, or pretend to have them. Think for example of our very own Daour Diagne. Forget about all his jabbering for a second and observe him carefully. What do you see? A vain, avaricious and petty old man on whom one would rather not waste one's time.

Cheikh Anta Diop, on the other hand, has always walked a path that was completely straight. His supporters found it hard at times to live with that degree of moral rectitude, and that's when he used to say to them, "There is never a valid reason to lie to those who have put their trust in us. The truth may hurt them, or even plunge them into despair, but at the end of the day it makes us all stronger."

More often than not he had to forge ahead completely alone, but that didn't mean he ever allowed anybody to stand in his way. Basically, everything he has done, said and written in the course of his life can be summed up as follows: the time that elapses between a man's birth and his death is as brief as a flash of lightning in the sky, and it is usually entirely devoid of truly important events. Therefore, if one doesn't even have time to live, one ought not to spend it telling lies, neither to oneself nor to anybody else.

Let the example this man has set inspire you, Badou. If you do, none of God's creatures will ever be able to influence you against your will.

Cheikh Anta Diop was laid to rest in Thieytou in his sixty-third year. He died quite young, considering the prodigious body of work he left behind for us to ponder about.

On every single God-given day, I include him in my prayers.

■   ■   ■

I am sitting in front of my house.

Two men are walking past. They are not from Niarela. I have never seen them before.

I catch a shred of their conversation: "Well, my friend, what's the news in the country?"

"Heavens! The country . . . We're in big trouble, you and I. Move over and make way for the young, as they say!"

I imagine a mischievous smile lighting up his companion's face as he replies, "I know you, old fellow. Whenever you talk like that, you're trying to hide something from me."

"Oh, it's nothing serious," says the other one, "it's just that your younger sister is giving me a bit of trouble."

"Who do you mean? Kiné?"

"Yes of course, who else?"

The first speaker says in a voice that sounds affectionate and slightly sad at the same time, "Kiné and you . . . don't you think it's time you came to an understanding once and for all or break up?"

Now they've disappeared around the corner, and the street is quiet again. But it won't be long before two different, anonymous voices fill the void. Their sentences will hover in the air until the wind sweeps them up, high into the sky, maybe even all the way to the word cemetery. And immediately afterward it is as though those words had never been heard anywhere on earth.

■   ■   ■

Last night I thought of my father again. I'm not sure whether I can claim to have known him any better than the ancestor Mame Ngor.

A childhood memory, nevertheless.

He must have found out that I had done something very, very naughty. And now I see Father again, his whip at the ready. I bend over, my hands clasped on top of my head, waiting for the lashes.

Nothing happens.

When I lift my head a little to look at him, Father is standing right in front of me. Never before have I seen so much contempt emanating from the countenance of a human being.

He drops his rod and walks away without a word.

■   ■   ■

It was after the prayer of *tàkkusaan* and I was out on my daily walk when I noticed a group of people crowded together in the middle of the street. I approached them. Two taxi drivers were embroiled in a violent argument. The younger one, practically still a boy, was threatening to strike the other one with a wrench, while both hurled insults at each other and the crowd had a hard time trying to separate them. To my great surprise, their bosses—the owners of the taxis in question—instead of joining in the fight, as often happens in these cases, were not fanning the fire but did what they could to calm their apprentices down by telling them there was no point in causing bloodshed for the sake of a few passengers.

Right next to me, a cola nut seller solemnly declared: "When it comes to clients, God either gives them to a taxi or he doesn't, just as it pleases Him! Beating each other up does not make the slightest difference!"

There were loud murmurs of approval from the crowd, and a few minutes later all was quiet again. It won't be very long before the next quarrel, of course. That time, it might be between a young woman and those gangs of pickpockets that operate in and around the Niarela market. Although several of them have been badly beaten up over the past few months, their number is growing and they are getting more reckless all the time.

After that, I managed with difficulty to clear a path for myself between the stalls, the small artisans' workshops and the garages of the mechanics. The hardest part was trying to get out of the way fast enough to avoid being splashed by water from the puddles that hit the curb every time a car drove through them. And as if that hadn't been enough, it was impossible to take even a dozen steps without being pounced on by hordes of little *talibés* or stumbling over heaps of scrap metal and garbage.

You get the picture: it was anything but a relaxing little afternoon stroll.

With its decrepit old shacks and that heady mix of smells originating from beer, urine and cannabis, Niarela certainly doesn't strike you as the greatest place on earth. The moment it rains, all the drains are blocked, and we can barely leave our houses because they are under water. Niarela sometimes reminds me of those alcoholics who've been wrecked by drink but whose impeccable attire is a pathetic attempt to hide their state of internal decay.

Almost every time I get swallowed up in that chaos I suddenly ask myself what has become of the old Niarela as it used to be. Vague memories of its past glory are all we have left of it today. The fact is that in the days of the *Toubabs*, Niarela was the residential district for Africans. Many of our greatest artists and most famous sportsmen, like your father Assane Tall, for example, were born here. That means that within the century and a half of its existence, our district—one of the oldest in Dakar—has gone sadly downhill.

I still remember the time when the forest with its little bit of wildlife—a few snakes, jackals and squirrels—started just beyond the outskirts of Niarela.

Maybe the reason why we have always led the way, not only in the capital city, but also in the entire country—my apologies to those who resent this!—is that nothing has ever entered Senegal without passing through Niarela first.

Is there anybody in this city who doesn't remember Fara Mbodj, the first Senegalese who owned a car? Well, he came from here!

To be sitting behind the steering wheel of his very own "Versailles" during the thirties was simply a feat of grandiose proportions for a son of this country. This is why Fara Mbodj decided to organize a feast fit to match that exceptional event. How much his beautiful black "Versailles" had cost him? That we didn't know, but we were pretty certain that he must have spent almost the same again on the naming ceremony of his beloved toy. Marabouts came and sprinkled holy water on the "Versailles," Fara Mbodj's female cousins served hundreds of calabashes of *laax* and the griots stood to attention, evoking the heroic exploits of Fara Mbodj's forebears—that they were all gloriously successful goes without saying. The celebrated warriors rode around the battlefields of the Waalo on their fiery steeds, and so it was only to be expected that one day the neighing of their descendant's magnificent "Versailles" would be heard echoing up and down the streets of Dakar. Fara Mbodj tossed bundles of banknotes at the praise singers, while the witchdoctors, who were supposed to protect his car against the evil eye and vipers' tongues, received their remuneration afterward, in private.

And as if that were not enough, Niarela was also the first place in Senegal where you could see a proper razor in action. I'm sure this will make you smile, Badou. I won't be surprised, in fact, if you are wondering whether Grandpa Nguirane Faye just talks a lot of nonsense in this *Notebook*. A razor in action? Yes, Badou, a razor. Nowadays we have thousands of barbers in the country hailing from Sao Vincente, from Sal, from Praïa, or another one of the Cape Verde islands. There was a time when these immigrants were really needed here. They were the ones who introduced us to razors, and I can tell you, too, that it all started with a man by the name of Toy Delgado. And where do you think this innovator decided to set up shop? You're spot on: in Niarela. Let me also just mention in passing that in my *Brief Escapades*—the very book you are reading right now—Grand Makhou asks his girlfriend, a certain Tina Delgado, to cook him a *kacuupa* from Hell. Tina was Toy Delgado's granddaughter, you see. Let's not be ashamed to admit it, but until Toy, who famously pioneered the safety razor, arrived in our town, we were shaving our heads with bits of broken glass. The inhabitants of Niarela were so baffled by this novelty that their daily gossip soon turned Toy's razor, which seemed to move all by itself, into a contraption dreamed up by the indefatigable Cheytan. The most inquisitive among them were so awestruck by the subtle and mysterious workings of Toy Delgado's razor on the skulls of his clients, they say, that they ended up hanging around in his hairdressing "salon," all day, and this "salon" wasn't much more than a sheet of canvas, of course. Every time a tuft of hair fell to the ground, dozens of young lads pounced on it, jostling, scrambling and shouting at the top of their voices. It was pandemonium, and what they did with all the hair they collected remains a mystery.

The *Toubabs* were already in control of our lives by then. You know the sort of people they are, don't you: prepared to do anything to keep the gentle sea breeze to themselves. And since they wanted to build their villas, offices and factories in the Plateau district, they started pushing us out toward the south of Dakar.

However, they couldn't drive us too far away, since they still needed us to cook and clean for them and see to all the menial tasks in their offices and factories. For lack of a better way to put it, I feel Niarela was basically the backyard of the Plateau district. One way or another, we were all at the beck and call of the *Toubabs*. The maids and the boys lived in close vicinity to the foreigners, and that meant they got involved in all sorts of wheeling and dealing. Due to their proximity with the whites, they often became—can you believe it?—pretty influential and respected personalities.

You should have seen us on our way into the city center after the prayer of *tisbaar*. I am talking about a time, Badou, when the horse-drawn carriage was a means of transport reserved for the privileged few. Picture them looking down on us from their seats up there, like royalty, while we, the riffraff, were trailing along behind or next to the horses, forming a kind of guard-of-honor for those fake whites, without even being aware of it. I still see them in my mind's eye, my *évolués*: shipping clerks, bookkeepers, the black elite, if you like. They used to go to their offices in jacket and tie, wearing pith helmets. Some of them were reciting verses by Lamartine or Victor Hugo from their lofty position, while those too shy and reserved for that simply kept their faces buried in *Paris-Dakar*, the only daily paper available to us in those days.

As for me, I was a worker at Air Liquide, the gas factory near Kayes-Findiw. I'm sure I became a militant member of the Parti Africain de l'Indépendance out of contempt for those conceited idiots who were so proud of being slaves. I remember how we kept asking ourselves the same, admittedly rather odd, question over and over again: are we *too* communist or *not* communist enough?

If I became a card carrying party member, I certainly didn't expect that to help me find answers to riddles like this one. I was clearly a bit misguided to begin with, but I firmly believe we did what we could to help bring about the liberation of our country. It wasn't easy, believe me. Our fellow citizens thought we were cynical and pretentious, and at Gouye-Mariama, a police superintendent by the name of André Castorel used to torture our comrades with abject cruelty.

And today, the country is in the hands of Daour Diagne. I believe that can only mean one thing: we have failed. Still, I have no regrets.

THE TALE OF THE ASHES

I HAVE SOME GOOD NEWS FOR YOU FROM NIARELA. BAÏDY SALL'S WIFE HAS given birth to one of God's-bits-of-wood, and he carries your name. I myself only heard the news on the day of the eighth day ceremony, which was very moving for me. Our neighbors all remembered how close you used to be to Baïdy. And, as always, everybody praised your appetite for hard work and your discretion. You are sorely missed here, Badou.

But you also know how wary we all are of words and their potential destructiveness. Someone said, "You should stop talking like that about Nguirane's grandson. It will bring bad luck upon Badou Tall, wherever he may be."

Baïdy Sall has behaved as a true friend in making you godfather to his son. When you were small, you were both very attached to me; I remember it perfectly. That's why I was so surprised to learn that this is the fourth child Baïdy has had since he got married. How quickly time passes! I give thanks to the Creator for granting me the happiness of seeing the children of my grandchildren with my own eyes.

That also means that the end is not far off. My body sends me that message every single day. On the way home after Baïdy's naming ceremony, I fainted near the National Lottery kiosk. A neighbor who happened to be passing by took me home in his car. When I came round, I recognized my savior's face. I could hardly believe my eyes—it was Mr. Soumaré. Elsewhere in *Tale of the Ashes*, the *Notebook* you are reading right now, I made savage fun of him and his wife. Maybe I shouldn't have. The truth is that the very same Mr. Soumaré has been extremely kind to me. He called Dr. Jibril Fall, who prescribed some medicines, and then he immediately went and bought them for me at the pharmacy. These small incidents are quite sufficient to make us realize that, underneath their hard outer shell, people are often much better than we think.

But be that as it may, I knew I had to take things a little bit more easy from then on. And yet, as soon as I felt better, I started skipping from one *Notebook* to the other again. I still don't sleep well. I get excruciating migraines from time to time. It feels as though thousands of ants are crawling all over my skull. But I love talking to you. And anyhow, it's better not to think about our last hour—it always comes too soon, and we never know by which door it will enter the house.

∎　∎　∎

A storyteller lacking in strength of character may find himself drawn to obscure places where all the doors are firmly locked. If the last word of the fable refuses to drown itself in the sea, not a single child with eyes full of wonder will hasten to breathe in its fragrance, hoping to enter Paradise.

The path gives way under my feet and every so often, I feel a bit lost.

But you would be wrong to assume I have forgotten about Yacine Ndiaye.

∎　∎　∎

Her comings and goings in our neighborhood had been continuing for months, without her ever so much as making eye contact with a single one of us. This must have made Yacine Ndiaye think she didn't exist for us. In reality, however, she never made a move that we didn't secretly observe, analyze and comment upon.

That's what we are like here in Niarela. Maybe one shouldn't spell these things out so clearly nowadays, but it's the truth nevertheless: being a stranger in our midst is very easy. For us, the outside world starts just beyond the walls of the last houses of the district, and in our eyes, everything repeats itself endlessly, from generation to generation, and has done so since time immemorial. The same families are at each other's throats over a patch of land or a seat on the town council, the same sanctimonious and stilted old dignitaries—they make us laugh, to be honest—strut around with carefully measured steps, looking grim and suspicious, and the greasy trickle of water that runs from our house to Captain Baye Ndéné's with all its twigs, plastic bags and household garbage floating in it, is also still the same. And every time a girl and a boy from Niarela embark on a clandestine little love affair, we oldies cannot suppress an affectionate smile about the way nothing ever changes from one century to the next.

I have said it already, haven't I: Yacine Ndiaye pretends we don't exist. I am one of the few people she deigns to greet once or twice a day. But she does so in her own, inimitable manner, without ever bothering to look at me or to open her mouth.

In the whole district, your mother, Bigué Samb, is the only person who seems to have managed to get close to her. We have no idea how she did it. Quite by accident, I discovered one day that they had become friends. Initially, I found it hard to believe, but now, I actually feel happy about it. After all, their three children have one and the same father: Assane Tall.

■ ■ ■

He had one great passion, your father Assane Tall, and that was soccer. As an adolescent, he used to spend hours juggling those multicolored little rubber balls called "Casaflex" that were so popular back then, but which are no longer to be found in the shops nowadays. At night he would quickly wolf down his plate of *mbuum* before carrying on with his exercise routines under the streetlights on the main road. His mates, who were probably studying for their arithmetic or geography lessons, used to ask him to go and play elsewhere, but he refused and kept his eyes firmly fixed on the little ball, making it roll around on top of his head and passing it from one shoulder to the other. "Hey, Nguirane," my friends used to tease me, "what kind of potion did you give this boy to drink on the day of his naming ceremony? His obsession with balls is really quite extraordinary!" I sometimes scolded him about it myself, but to no avail; he was determined to do what he wanted. I have to admit that it made me immensely proud to witness his rise to stardom in the Niarela soccer team before he had his brief hour of glory as champion of our Senegalese national team. He was a local celebrity for quite a while before he left for Marseille, which was a sort of climax. No one can deny that it was thanks to him that Niarela was always in the papers. So in the end, I felt that he was right to follow his path rather than listen to my paternal advice. Going to France, to play for a team like the one in Marseille, that was quite an achievement. The greedy ones among us said Assane Tall went there to earn *cartloads of money*, as the saying goes in this country, and everyone was secretly looking forward to getting their share.

But as you know, the only thing we ever got back from our famous soccer champion was his corpse at the airport.

■　■　■

The morning didn't end well for Yacine Ndiaye. First, I heard a terrifying scream, and then I saw her. There she was, writhing and thrashing on the ground, with her face horribly contorted and saliva drooling from her mouth. Nearby, Mbissine and Mbissane flinched and huddled up to each other, trying to squeeze into one of the recesses in the wall. Their eyes, which spoke of nothing but emptiness and fear, broke my heart. Surely these two children, who had never done anybody any harm, didn't deserve this. When I got closer, doing my best to comfort them, they pressed their waiflike little bodies still more tightly against the wall, and the convulsive shaking of their shoulders signaled to me that they didn't want to be touched. It was as if they wanted the earth to split open and swallow them up once and for all.

When I went back to their mother, she still hadn't stopped groaning and thrashing around on the floor. Afterward we learned that far beyond Niarela, hundreds of people from the surrounding areas had heard her ear piercing screams.

We were all pleased about what was happening to Yacine Ndiaye and—to be frank—not one of us made any attempt to come to her aid.

In her delirious state, she was talking in several languages at the same time and her words were so muddled that each one of us heard something different. According to some, in between her groans she claimed she was a *Toubab*. Whether that was actually true is difficult to say. All I know for sure is that she repeated a specific name over and over again, a name so complicated that no one could remember it. Was she crazy enough to believe this would be her new name from now on? Her fiercest enemies just couldn't let such a perfect opportunity to poke fun at her pass. "What a weird name for a woman from this country!"

"She'd be well advised to go back to the place where people can at least pronounce those barbaric syllables!"

I don't pretend to be any better than the rest of us, but I felt embarrassed when I realized that my heart was quite simply overflowing with hatred. I was convinced this was our chance to defuse that diabolical contraption before it blew up in our faces one day. The trouble was that every time I wanted to reason with the people of Niarela, the same image came back to me again. Looking straight into my eyes, Yacine Ndiaye lifts up her wrap and opens her legs, pointing her index finger at her vagina. She has the insolence to tell me—me, the father of her late husband!—hey there, old Nguirane, take a good look at my flesh! Who gets to taste it is my decision. Since the day when my eyes had to see that and my ears heard those words, I have been unsure whether my body has closed down for good or whether it is rather in the process of detaching itself from me bit by bit.

If I ever had any feelings of sympathy for this woman, I have definitely lost them now. As far as I am concerned, she can perish like a mangy bitch, she doesn't deserve any better.

Please forgive me for telling you that story the other day. It wasn't easy. My hand wanted to pull back, but I hadn't forgotten my oath. I owe you all the truths, even the harshest ones.

■　　■　　■

A morning like any other in the life of Yacine Ndiaye in Niarela. She must suddenly have felt the urge to go out for a stroll in the main street, which is where you see us all sitting around in small groups near our workshops or outside our houses, playing checkers or listening to the radio, and where we are, very discreetly of course, constantly on the lookout for the slightest incident in the area, all those juicy little scandals that make a good story and easily lend themselves to a bit of embroidery.

Yacine Ndiaye is wearing her smartest outfit, complete with perfume and makeup. One of the apprentices from Pape Kandji's garage is walking right behind her, fooling around and copying her every movement. The moment she looks like she's about to turn round, the boy quickly falls back into the stride of a normal pedestrian. We find his clownery hilarious.

"That's her," says somebody.

"You're right."

"The foreign lady."

"Ugly as a she-monkey. Makes me wonder how Assane Tall could have married her."

"Do you actually believe it? That they were married, I mean?"

"They were living together under the same roof."

"That means they were living in sin."

"Yes, the kind of sin God never forgives!" another one adds triumphantly.

"Do you know what Wolof Njaay used to say?"

"*A* Toubab *in a black skin is always a* Toubab *and a half.*"

"I think Wolof Njaay is right, as always!"

Yacine Ndiaye all on her own could be described as a foreign invading army, while Niarela is a small defenseless country. Does she have any idea how much we hate her? It seems unthinkable to me that she doesn't even have an inkling. Her arrogance toward us, the pompous way she walks, her conceited demeanor and stony facial expression—all that is her own choice.

And yet, this morning, she stops for a little chat with Thierno, the newspaper seller.

"A magazine called *Marie Claire*?" asks Thierno, scratching his head. "I'm sorry, but I don't know that one."

After a moment's reflection, he adds, "I'll ask my friends if they have it, and I will bring it to your house."

"Thanks, but that's not necessary," replies Yacine Ndiaye.

"*Marie Claire . . . Marie Claire?*" Thierno repeats, suddenly conscious of having been the focal point of the whole of Niarela for the past two or three minutes.

"It's my favorite magazine," says Yacine Ndiaye. "I used to read it in France."

Thierno's cleverness means he has understood that this is his one and only chance to find out a bit more about the foreign lady and he grabs it: "So does that mean you used to live in France?" he asks, in an admiring tone of voice.

"I still live there," Yacine Ndiaye corrects him proudly. "I came to Dakar just to sort out a few problems, but soon I'm going to go back home."

"You're really going back there?" Thierno asks with fake incredulity.

"I've packed all my bags and am ready to go!" Yacine Ndiaye replies.

"They say it's lovely over there. The day before yesterday, one of my friends told me something about the country of the *Toubabs*."

Yacine Ndiaye sounds interested. "What did he say?"

"A tourist offered me a fat banknote after buying several of my newspapers."

"And then?"

"I was pleased and said to the tourist, 'I hope God will send you to Paradise!' After that, my friend started mocking me, saying the *Toubab* would be bored there."

"Oh really?" says Yacine Ndiaye, slightly confused.

"Well, it's because the *Toubab* has already experienced all the pleasures of Paradise on earth, which means he's not going to discover anything new up there!"

Yacine Ndiaye smiles and says, "Yes, it's a wonderful country. You want for nothing in France."

After a brief pause, and without taking her eyes off Thierno, she adds with a teasing little smile, "I bet you would like to go there too, wouldn't you?"

"Of course I would, like everyone else in this country. I dream of flying away with the bird . . ."

Yacine Ndiaye frowns. "Flying away with the bird? Which bird?"

Thierno stretches out his arms, moving them up and down like the wings of a sparrow hawk, and starts spinning round and round while making a loud humming noise.

Yacine Ndiaye realizes he is pretending to be an airplane and bursts out laughing. This is the first time we've seen her laugh in public.

Inevitably, following this conversation with the foreign lady, Thierno was inundated with questions for days on end. His reply was always the same: "This woman is mad. I have observed her very carefully, and I swear to you she's mad."

He fell silent for a moment, and then he started nodding, with an alarmed look on his face, and said, more to himself than to the rest of the world: "By tomorrow, everyone will know she is stark raving mad. But don't forget that it was me, Thierno, who said it first in front of everybody, right here in Niarela."

■　　■　　■

Seemingly oblivious to the many pairs of eyes that are secretly devouring her without ever focusing on her directly, she is wandering around the stalls piled high with papayas and soursops, but stops now and again to look at a fillet of sea bream or some red mullet, and finally turns into one of the narrow alleyways stacked with bags of rice and millet. You might have said she was a ghost. In the hustle and bustle of the market, a tiny bubble of silence forms in her wake. Everyone is thinking about Thierno's words a few days earlier.

Not just ugly. Bonkers, as well.

. ▪ .

Roughly a week later, I saw your mother, Bigué, leaving Yacine Ndiaye's apartment. "Since when has Bigué been in the house?" I was wondering. She never crossed my threshold without first coming to greet me, even in my bedroom if need be. It was our long-established ritual to spend a bit of time discussing neighborhood and family news before she would facetiously call me her penniless old husband and get on with her chores. On that particular afternoon, she had chosen to go and visit her new friend right away. In actual fact, it was a jolly little party that was walking toward me. Tamsir Bâ, the man with the bright red eyes and hair, Yacine Ndiaye's lover, was holding her two children by the hand. Yacine Ndiaye greeted me in passing. Mbissane pulled his hand away from the red-haired man and stuck his tongue out at me, only the way he did it was slightly less insolent this time, it seemed to me.

Bigué Samb detached herself from the group to come and chat with me for a bit.

"I had no idea you were in the house," I said to her.

I couldn't hide my sense of irritation from her and, above all, my sadness. As if it was the most natural thing in the world, Bigué Samb told me she had helped Yacine Ndiaye with her shopping.

Again, I wondered to myself, "What an odd friendship this is. What does it mean?" It was absolutely extraordinary to witness the proud Bigué Samb acting like Yacine Ndiaye's dogsbody. Something must have escaped my notice, but what? I had no idea. I had no choice but to accept things as they were.

As always, it didn't take long before Bigué Samb started talking about you.

"Grandfather Nguirane, have you had any news from my son?"

"Badou Tall?"

"Yes, Badou. I'm sure on the day when he finally decides to write, his first letter will be addressed to you."

There was a brief silence. We looked at each other but did not speak. We suddenly both remembered the same incident. It was so many years ago. Bigué Samb and Assane Tall bidding each other farewell in the departure lounge at the airport. Looking back on it now, and considering everything that has happened since, this farewell scene seems even more moving than it must have been at the time. In my memory, it has something surreal about it. Bigué Samb. Assane Tall. I see them both before me, close to tears. When we get back to Niarela, Bigué Samb is still crying and her friends try to comfort her. "Don't cry Bigué, you know very well, our men always end up going far away. It's their destiny."

These are words we have all heard a thousand times. They make exile seem heroic and try to soothe the pain it inflicts.

I said, "Badou is a man. It's a man's destiny to go far away, Bigué."

I immediately realized that I had just reopened an old wound for Bigué Samb. I didn't do it on purpose. There are times when echoes settle on our lips and then just slip away of their own accord. And forever afterward, they remain as elusive to us as the batting of nocturnal insects' wings.

■　■　■

One day, there was talk in Niarela that Yacine Ndiaye had decided to return to Marseille. Where did this news come from? None of us had the faintest idea. With this woman, nothing ever happened in a way that could be described as normal. She and I were living in the same house, and she was, after all, my daughter-in-law. And yet, I wasn't informed about her impending departure until the last moment. This certainly surprised me, but deep down, I was more relieved than upset.

The day before her trip, she and Bigué went to the Sandaga market to buy some everyday necessities. When she came to say good-bye, she seemed slightly feverish but otherwise in good spirits. To my great surprise, she even held out three banknotes of five thousand francs each to me.

I said to her: "That's a lot of money you are offering me there, Yacine."

You know very well, Badou, don't you, that every nation on this earth has its own way of doing things. I was expecting her to reply by saying: "Oh no it's not, old Nguirane, I just can't give you any more right now. But as soon as I get to Marseille, I will be in touch." That, at any rate, is the sort of thing we are supposed to say in a similar situation to put the recipient at ease. She, however, just stood there gaping, and without any idea how to react to my simple words. I also think she felt I was being too sanctimonious and shouldn't make such a fuss.

Wanting to ease the tension in the atmosphere a bit, I wished her a safe trip and added, "You mustn't forget to write to my grandchildren once you're back in France."

"Which grandchildren?" she asked, gesticulating with both hands.

She didn't understand that I was talking about her two little ones.

"Mbissine and Mbissane," I replied in the most serious tone of voice I could muster. "Didn't you know they are staying in Niarela with me?"

Suddenly, there was an expression of unspeakable horror and indignation on her face. I smiled. Then she realized that I was teasing her, and she smiled back.

·   ■   ■

The next day, well before the time Yacine Ndiaye was supposed to leave for the airport, I sat down under my mango tree as I always did. I couldn't help feeling pleased, because her presence in the house had become stifling. Soon, a taxi would arrive and we would be saying our good-byes to each other, with pleasant words and benedictions. Appearances would be kept up, and I would at last regain my peace of mind.

Toward midday, Yacine Ndiaye walked past me with an enormous red suitcase, but, instead of putting it down in the middle of the courtyard and going to fetch the rest, she did something utterly astounding. She sat down on a chair and started emptying the entire suitcase. She was much less relaxed than the day before; she was quite nervous, in actual fact. I watched her picking up every single garment, unfolding it, patting it with a mystified expression, and then dropping it at her feet. After that, she went back to her apartment, muttering to herself, and brought out a second suitcase which she inspected just as scrupulously. Gradually, Yacine Ndiaye got more and more worked up and let slip some rather vulgar swearwords that she repeated over and over while hitting her thighs at the same time.

I felt very intrigued by all this, but since I had promised myself to stay out of her business, I didn't ask any questions.

A little later, a taxi pulled up outside the house, and I could hear a car door being slammed shut. It was Bigué Samb, who had come to accompany Yacine Ndiaye into town. When she saw the clothes scattered all over the ground, she covered her mouth with her hand in shock and exclaimed, "What's going on, Yacine?"

Sweating and frantic, incapable of uttering a single word, Yacine Ndiaye gave your mother a blank stare. Her lips were trembling.

Bigué Samb continued, "Weren't we supposed to call on Sinkoun Camara before I take you to the airport tonight?"

Sinkoun Tiguidé Camara. There's a name you'll do well to remember, Badou. This servant of Cheytan is someone you will soon come across again in my *Notebooks*.

"I can find neither my passport nor any of my other papers," Yacine Ndiaye said in an utterly pathetic voice.

"Your passport?"

"I can't find any of my papers. Neither my passport nor anything else. Nothing."

In her state of distress, she seemed to be relying entirely on Bigué Samb for help, almost begging her to perform a miracle.

Bigué Samb started checking the suitcases all over again but gave up very quickly.

Yacine Ndiaye, still profoundly dejected, turned ever so slightly in my direction as she declared, "I'm sure my thief is right here in this house."

Did this mean she suspected me, Nguirane Faye, of having something to do with this? That was so absurd I didn't waste any time on it.

Bigué Samb sounded warm and affectionate when she said, "That's my girl. Always ready for a fight, my Yacine!"

"Take a good look at me, Bigué," Yacine Ndiaye said with despair. She pointed at her left forearm. "Can't you see that with this black skin and without my papers I cannot prove who I am? I don't know what to do, Bigué."

After a brief silence, she burst into sobs.

"Don't worry," Bigué Samb said with resolve. "Just follow me."

Yacine Ndiaye stood up. They climbed into the taxi and I realized then that Bigué Samb hadn't even seen me. But I knew exactly why I was suddenly so unimportant to her: she was far too busy homing in on her prey.

She was behind the mysterious disappearance of Yacine Ndiaye's passport. I didn't have the slightest doubt about that.

. ■ ■

It was the moment just before prayers at sunrise.

We could hear the growling of the royal drum in the distance.

Suddenly there was a voice drowning out the call of the muezzin. "I am the Messenger and I have come to wake you up with my words of peace, people of Niarela! Old and young, men and women, your prince commands you to leave your beds and go and wait for him in the Meeting Square! People of Niarela, listen to my words of peace."

In less than a quarter of an hour, the Meeting Square was packed with people.

The wait had begun.

Initially, the crowd was calm and quiet. The inhabitants of Niarela were still a bit sleepy and asking each other what was going on. Some thought they had heard the prince was coming from the East, and all eyes were turned in that direction. Minutes passed, then hours.

The waiting was becoming more and more tedious and intolerable.

For a while, a few live wires managed to cheer up the anxious ones, but soon a growing, general sense of impatience and irritation began to take hold.

"Where is he?"

"Who are you talking about?"

"I am talking about the one who told us to assemble here. Where is he?"

"You're right, we have been waiting a long time for him."

Ousmane Sow, the cart driver, the most vociferous of all, could no longer contain his anger. "We should all be ashamed of ourselves! A man we don't even know talks to us about some prince, and the next thing you know we're standing here in the middle of Niarela from sunrise to sunset!"

Ousmane Sow's words were followed by intense hissing and murmuring that swept from one group to the next, getting louder and louder as time went on. Once again, Ousmane Sow had managed to spell out loud and clear what others didn't even dare to think.

"Let's go home and stop this stupid nonsense!" shouted some of the people.

But the very moment when the crowd was about to disperse, a voice boomed across Niarela, so forceful it made not only trees but even brick walls tremble. It seemed to be coming from everywhere at once, from the sky, from the depths of the earth and from the houses nearby.

"Of course you can leave! Just go! May the wind speed up your steps! But if that's because you don't want to hear me anymore, let me tell you it will be in vain. No matter how far away you go, my voice will fill your hearts with shame. Oh inhabitants of Niarela, how could you think of me as a mere mortal? I told you I would be back. And here I am."

On hearing those words, the whole of Niarela became very worried. With fear in their eyes, people started looking around in all directions.

He was back again.

The syllables of his name were rustling in the silence, and yet, nobody dared to pronounce it.

Ali Kaboye . . .

Ali Kaboye was back in Niarela.

．　　．　　．

Ali Kaboye, that doesn't sound like a name from these parts. No one in Niarela knows what it means. It's true that our three cinemas, the Empire, the Roxy and the Agora, show Westerns all the time and perhaps the man enjoyed them so much that his childhood dream was to be a cowboy, massacring the Sioux and the Cherokees.

He may well be claiming this is his name, but we have no idea where he is from originally. I think I was one of the few who noticed the first sightings in Niarela of a tall stranger dressed in rags, with a massive face of a dull black complexion and a totally bald head. His pestilential smell, his festering sores, and especially his openly exposed private parts, which he was in the habit of scratching frequently and vigorously, made us all think he must be one of those vagrant lunatics of whom there were unfortunately quite a number in town. You will instantly recognize Ali Kaboye by the way he walks —looking up at the clouds, he throws his right foot forward, puts it down on the ground, and then waits for the other foot to follow. This is why he always gives the impression of being in a great hurry to get to a specific place, and at the same time he appears to be in a state of extreme mental agitation. This is rather bewildering for us, and the more cowardly people here in Niarela are so nervous about this, I think, that they stay out of his way if they possibly can. On the other hand, even lunatics can't all be expected to walk the same way. So there was really no reason to make such a fuss.

One nice morning we woke up to the discovery that he had made himself at home in a shack, and there really is no other way to describe this assemblage of tomato boxes, old newspapers, wooden planks, and milk cartons propped up against a wall under a streetlight. Initially, there were a few, admittedly rather feeble, complaints about his continued presence in the area, but that didn't go on for long. Very soon, the neighbors left him in peace in the assumption that just as he had suddenly arrived out of nowhere, he would one day quietly vanish into thin air again. The lunatics in this city have always behaved like that. It was impossible to know why they never felt at home anywhere; they had never found it necessary to give any explanations in this regard, and nobody gave a damn, to be honest. He kept bellowing, either at himself or at the demons of his past, which must have been stubborn and difficult, "I, Ali Kaboye!" So that was his name. Ali Kaboye. The more inquisitive souls among us found out that the man had lost his reason during his military service at the Dakar-Bango boot camp. Apparently he was on guard duty in the bush one day, and, in broad daylight, he witnessed a scene humans are not supposed to see—djinns having sex, or something of that sort. We all know that certain hours of the day and the night are reserved for these supernatural beings. Even a sentry armed to the teeth ignores such a taboo at his peril! It's just not a good idea to strut around anywhere you please, pretending you're walking down a little street in your native village. The djinns are scared of neither an AK-47 nor a MAS-36. And to make things worse, they are extremely touchy.

Soon after he had "moved" to Niarela—if this is indeed an apt expression—Ali Kaboye started manifesting a tendency for violent behavior. When the children on their way home from Clémenceau Primary School teased him, he regularly pelted them with pebbles and showered them with insults. The language he used was so crude that I cannot possibly repeat it here. He even ended up injuring some of them. One of his favorite tricks was to hide in the recess of a wall near Koussoum beach. From there, he would suddenly leap out in front of solitary walkers holding out his hand to them in a threatening way, without saying a word. People attempted to get away from him, but he had this dreadful knack of cornering you in silence, which was actually far more terrifying than any clamoring or shouting. If a person tried to tiptoe around him, Ali Kaboye would block their passage, always with his hand held out and with that strangely absent look in his eyes. He never uttered a single word, or even a grunt, but his whole demeanor seemed to be sending out a very clear message: "You know I'm mad, don't you, and all this might end badly, since your life is in my hands right now." Having made sure no one was watching, the walker would hastily drop a coin into his hand. There really was no other way of extricating oneself from this calamitous situation. Ali Kaboye would then let the imprudent victim pass who made a solemn vow never, ever, to go near this godforsaken place again under any circumstances.

One day, however, Ali Kaboye committed a fatal mistake. It all started with Bolchoï, a dog whose name, it is safe to say, was just as bizarre as Ali Kaboye's. Bolchoï could not stand Ali Kaboye. Generally, the animal could be described as rather docile, or even slightly timid. And to the best of our knowledge, he had never borne a particular grudge against lunatics in general. Before Ali Kaboye's arrival, there had been quite a number of them living in Niarela for either a few months or even several years, and, just like the rest of us, Bolchoï had never objected to their presence in the area. But in Ali Kaboye's case, things were totally different. I am not sure whether it's appropriate to use the word "hatred" to describe the feelings of a dog, but it definitely seems as if Bolchoï hated Ali Kaboye with every fiber of his being. It was almost like a personal vendetta between the two of them. The moment the animal laid eyes upon the vagrant lunatic, he would start barking and attacking him, trying to bite his calves. If his intention was to terrify Ali Kaboye, he succeeded admirably. We saw him taking to his heels on more than one occasion, with Bolchoï in hot pursuit. At times, the dog even gave the impression he wanted to sink his fangs into his throat. It really was incredibly funny, especially for the children, to watch this colossal figure of a man jumping over hedges and the small puddles in Niarela, calling for his mummy to come to his rescue.

And then, one morning, Ali Kaboye managed to bewitch Bolchoï with some sort of magic formula. Bolchoï came and lay down at his feet, wagging his tail, full of trust, serene and looking positively ecstatic. This was to be the poor creature's final gesture of friendship. Ali Kaboye, an old army hand, as I've mentioned to you before, decapitated him with one clean blow of his dagger. But that wasn't the end of it. Clearly intoxicated by all the blood, he walked around Niarela brandishing Bolchoï's head and uttering long, incomprehensible war cries.

Now, the owner of this dog was none other than Captain Baye Ndéné. This officer and seasoned alcoholic was an important personality in Niarela, and we were actually quite proud of him, since he was one of Daour Diagne's army commanders. At the time when all this happened—and I am talking about the shocking slaughter of Bolchoï—the president had just put him in charge of the entire military detachment at his palace. If we want to give credence to the intimate revelations of his drinking companions, this mustachioed giant with his huge beer belly—a daredevil at heart—was bored to death in that position. Captain Baye Ndéné preferred the brothels in the seediest parts of town to the presidency with its elegant drawing rooms. He liked the kind of places where, instead of bowing and scraping, people assault each other with obscenities and broken beer bottles. As a soldier, he was of the pugilist variety, and he detested the chiefs-of-staff with their maps, their cautious, painstaking maneuvering of enemy positions, and their endless strategic planning. In a nutshell, he detested anything that delays total onslaught. And yet, Captain Baye Ndéné undoubtedly had a sense of honor. He loved an honest battle, a good punch-up, as it were. His only problem was his readiness to use just about any pretext to provoke this kind of altercation. One evening, after overdosing on the old *bunukabu*, he even went so far as to fire shots into the air, wreaking havoc in a bar that belonged to his old buddy Mapenda. There was definitely cause for serious concern at that point, but no one did anything about it in the end.

When he received the news that Bolchoï had been murdered, Captain Baye Ndéné was slumped in his own vomit and excrement after a monumental boozing session. It barely seemed to affect him. Despite the fact that he was basically comatose, a few bystanders who witnessed this scene were surprised by his reaction, since everybody knew how attached Baye Ndéné was to his little dog.

But a few days later, he staged a meticulously planned ambush aimed at Ali Kaboye.

It was late that evening, and I was passing the colonnaded office block that houses the Crédit Foncier, when I heard screams.

As I got closer, I saw Captain Baye Ndéné teaching Ali Kaboye a lesson that he wouldn't easily forget. Not even remotely thinking of defending himself, the poor devil implored Baye Ndéné to spare his life and swore he would never kill Bolchoï again. Captain Baye Ndéné, who had just smashed a bottle of Heineken, took one of the shards and planted it on Ali Kaboye's naked skull with a single-mindedness that can only be described as cold and sinister. Ali Kaboye's face was all bloodied up, and his groans were gradually turning into whimpers. I was quite convinced that that would be the end of him. Who exactly had alerted the police I don't know, but they arrived and seemed to find it extremely difficult to establish the actual sequence of events. Who was the madman who had been described to them? Judging by the appalling spectacle they were witnessing, it could have been either one of the two men.

Immediately after this incident, Ali Kaboye disappeared from Niarela, and we thought we had gotten rid of him forever. All of a sudden, the district seemed less filthy and the air cleaner. Everyone was relieved. Baye Ndéné did the right thing, everyone said approvingly. Having an army officer living in our midst certainly had its uses. People were full of contempt for Ali Kaboye's cowardice and his screams of terror would certainly be remembered for a long time to come. Being mad is not a good enough reason to provoke Captain Baye Ndéné! Yes, yes, our Baye Ndéné was far too powerful for that faceless man with no past who had suddenly appeared one day out of thin air. For an ex-squaddie from the Dakar-Bango bootcamp to brazenly challenge one of the most brilliant officers in our national army, that's pure folly indeed!

■　　■　　■

Several months later, Ali Kaboye returned to Niarela. Barely anything had changed, but it was immediately obvious that he wasn't quite the same man as before. Eager to escape our attention, he rushed straight back to his shack with large strides. There he fell into a deep sleep, snoring loudly for four days and four nights.

By sunrise on the fifth day, he was gone.

Two years passed.

Then, one evening in July, the town was hit by a thunderstorm. Unusually, for a time like this, the power had not been cut, and everyone was at home, drinking tea and watching television.

Just before midnight, as I was getting ready for bed, voices could be heard in the street. Someone seemed to be calling for help. "Thugs, no doubt, who still haven't stopped beating each other up in the rain," I said to myself. Getting mixed up in their rows could be dangerous, so we always did our best to stay away from them.

Just like all the other inhabitants of Niarela, I found out later on that this racket had in fact been caused by one and the same individual. But his singing was so out of tune that no one was able to identify his voice.

Would it have occurred to any of us, after that fatal night during the rainy season, to think of Ali Kaboye? I doubt it, since the man hadn't started terrorizing us yet in the way that I will describe to you later on. One might even say, at the risk of shocking certain sensitive individuals with a highly developed sense of morality, that to us, Ali Kaboye was not actually a true human being. In our eyes, he was a lunatic just like the rest of them, an ordinary lunatic, an individual who was just "normally mad," as it were. Three days after his disappearance, we had forgotten all about him. Maybe we even thought he was no longer of this world. I presume you will find what I am about to tell you harsh and cynical, but it's a fact: we thought he was dead, since people like Ali Kaboye usually die at an early age. Everyone knows that these vagrant lunatics are not entitled to medical treatment when they get sick—which they often do—and that, since they scavenge for their daily rations on public rubbish dumps, they literally stuff themselves with dangerous bacteria. If they are lucky enough to survive all the microbes, they unfortunately have every chance of being wiped out by one of those reckless drivers who don't even find it necessary to stop. And heavens, if people out for a Sunday walk stumble across one of their mangled bodies by the side of the road, it hardly feels like the end of the world. You understand what I'm trying to say, don't you. If Ali Kaboye gets run over by a train or a taxi tomorrow, nobody is in danger of losing any sleep over the salvation of his soul, and it's highly unlikely that anyone will make a heartrending, melodramatic scene claiming that something essentially Human or whatever has just died in him. Well, we obviously all agree that Ali Kaboye is not an animal, but that still doesn't make him much more than a rough draft of a human being. A creature suspended in the void. Floating, as it were. And yet, that doesn't necessarily mean his death would leave us totally indifferent. In fact, those whose task it is to uphold law and order would probably be extremely upset by it, and no doubt they'd immediately treat us to a very moving demonstration of their patriotism. What matters most to these people is the hygiene of our beloved nation. They object to dead bodies obstructing our roads and, they grumble, it just doesn't make sense, those vagrant lunatics who do nothing but wander around, they're making honest citizens live in fear, they spread loads of germs, microbes and viruses, and that's putting it politely because what we're actually talking about is shit—shit that not only stinks, but is also extremely contagious. What, if anything, are our authorities doing about it? And with this very searching question in mind, everyone goes home and then it's business as usual again. Why get all worked up about it, why go to the trouble of taking the decomposing body to the morgue and bother the undertakers? Surely the municipality will deal with it sooner or later. The poor wretch has neither a family nor an address, so he won't object if we throw him into the communal ditch.

This, just between you and me, is the short version of what could have happened to Ali Kaboye.

Alas, we quickly realized we'd got the wrong end of the stick entirely and that the Ali Kaboye saga was not over yet. The man who had been singing so out of tune in the rain was none other than him.

During that night, after two or three hours of silence, he came back and his shrill, inimitable voice brutally roused us from our sleep. "People of Niarela, I am back. I am here to ask you a very simple question: why, with the exception of good old Nguirane Faye, did nobody come to my aid when Baye Ndéné was trying to kill me? Please don't tell me you can't remember, abominable bunch of hypocrites! Now listen to what I, Ali Kaboye, want to tell you. I returned to Ndimboye, my native village. Oh my goodness, I can see the astonished looks on your faces, while you're tucked up in your nice cozy beds. Are you amazed to learn that I, too, was born somewhere, and that just like you, I have a father and mother? My relatives have sent me back to Niarela with the words: 'Ali, you must never hurt anybody again.' So there will be no more attacks on your children as they walk to Clémenceau Primary School, and I promise never to rip off your wives' and daughters' loincloths again on their way home from the market. Furthermore, I solemnly pledge to leave the solitary walkers in peace from now on. I am a man of peace now. But be aware that you will always hear my voice; every single day I will talk to you, from sunrise till sunset. And, people of Niarela, expect to be woken up by Ali Kaboye's voice in the middle of the night!" The inhabitants of Niarela had been holding their breath listening to him, and when he was finished, there was a general sigh of relief. There was no serious cause for concern—it was all just a lot of hot air, one might say. The worst threat Ali Kaboye could make was to announce he would turn into a peaceful lunatic, which is what you would normally call an idiot. All right then, you can be our village idiot. Why not? That might even be quite amusing.

As it turned out, it certainly wasn't amusing for everybody.

Ali Kaboye's initial forays were reserved for Baye Ndéné, his deadliest enemy. The surprise effect made them all the more vicious and brutal. Every time the proud captain was on his way home from the presidential palace, Ali Kaboye was there, pretending it was a coincidence. Then he started crooning a song about a Warrior who had trouble with his gut because it was bloated and dilated by the sheer weight of his own shit. The Warrior, Ali said with a snicker, let off very noisy farts, and it stank across a radius of several kilometers, but nobody dared to hold their nose because the Warrior was also a drunkard who was known to get violent and aggressive. So, Ali Kaboye went on singing, for fear of having their skulls lacerated with broken bottles, people pretended that the gas that had escaped from the Warrior's gigantic anus smelled very good, really so exceptionally good and that their nostrils had never inhaled a more subtle and delicate scent.

Initially, Baye Ndéné chose to ignore Ali Kaboye. He had, in the meantime, got married to the daughter of Gora Mbaye, a rather stern and uptight dignitary from Niarela, and so it wasn't really proper for him anymore to get embroiled in fisticuffs in broad daylight with such a nonentity. He was nevertheless convinced he would be able to bring Ali Kaboye to book one day. He was biding his time, and there he was, strutting up and down the little lanes of Niarela, trying to look the part as supreme commander of the presidential guard. But we knew Baye Ndéné well enough to be able to tell from his churlish expression that he felt deeply humiliated by Ali Kaboye's assaults. We were secretly pleased, of course, to see our arrogant military leader so helplessly exposed to the taunts of a vagrant lunatic. After a while, the boldest among us started to mock the officer in public. If Ali Kaboye imitated the sound of thunder in a subtle allusion to the Warrior's bloated gut, the young people pretended to be completely enraptured. "Oh la-la! What a divine whiff of incense! It really smells too delicious around here!" We all know that children love absolutely any opportunity to start a quarrel. The moment they spotted Baye Ndéné's gleaming silver Simca 606, they would run and call Ali Kaboye. Like clockwork, he was there with his party piece, the kids singing the refrain and clapping their hands. Baye Ndéné was so exasperated by this that from then on, he started driving home very late at night, but that didn't help: without fail, Ali Kaboye would pop up at some street corner, and make the unfortunate Captain's intestines give off the most breathtaking sounds.

Baye Ndéné's exasperation was painful to watch. This officer with the rough chin, who was normally so self-confident and cocksure, was but a shadow of his former self. At one point, we heard it being said that he and his new wife were leaving Niarela and moving to the Paul-Morel Barracks, the official quarters reserved for high-ranking army officers.

But that was just a rumor.

Ali Kaboye, a madman? He may well have been. But there was method in his madness—his actions always came across as premeditated and carefully planned. Having won us all over to his side against Captain Baye Ndéné, he started sowing discord among us.

This is how he did it.

He would stand in the center of Niarela, staring at the palm of his right hand. He had a booming, powerful voice, and the words he used were as follows: "Here is my mirror. I can see them all in the mirror, every single one of them."

His whole demeanor indicated he had some rather harsh revelations in store for us, but hesitated to spell them out. The reason for this was that he felt he didn't have the right to expose the individuals concerned to the wrath of their neighbors, despicable though they were. In places like Niarela family feuds often go on smoldering for generations. So it was quite natural that some of us could hardly wait for the moment when Ali Kaboye would finally make up his mind to malign our arch-enemies. We didn't exactly form a circle around Ali Kaboye in order to listen to him, no, but when he was playing those little games with his fake mirror we were never very far away, under the pretense that we just happened to be in the area, totally by chance. We tried to prick up our ears, but Ali Kaboye seemed to have enormous fun testing our patience. Standing at Niarela's busiest intersections, and with a mischievous glint in his eye, he always bellowed the same mysterious phrases with great verve: "Here is my mirror. I can see them all in the mirror, every single one of them."

When was he going to speak out at last? He seemed to change his mind at the last moment every single time, just when we thought we could already see the words we were waiting for so desperately, fluttering around his mouth.

But one day he flew into a rage, and it didn't take long before the whole of Niarela was crowding around him.

"Poor little girl . . . One night, you went to bed, pure and innocent. When you woke up, your vagina had been ripped to shreds, your vagina was covered in blood. Since that day, you have not been able to hold your head up straight. You know your mother knows. You both live in fear. Shame on those who ruin a childhood like a pack of baboons ruin a crop of cassava! Here is the mirror. I, Ali Kaboye, see everything."

There was a leaden silence. Every single face had the same bewildered expression and seemed to say: *I told you so* . . . That same evening, people dropped a few gentle hints about a number of incidents that everybody thought had been forgotten for a long time. Over the next few days, people kept repeating Ali Kaboye's words over and over again. They even started mentioning names, including those of certain prominent personalities whose reputation was seemingly beyond reproach.

Before long, living in Niarela had become quite risky. Gone were the days when you could cheat on your wife or your husband without being in danger of becoming the target of Ali Kaboye's vitriolic remarks. One of us had been put in charge of the money we had painstakingly collected to build a new mosque. He used it to go on a pilgrimage to Mecca. This made Ali Kaboye so furious that he composed a song about impostors and religious hypocrites. We were able to identify the culprit without any trouble, and I think I can say that Ali Kaboye genuinely hated this person.

As one might expect, people were soon whispering that Ali Kaboye was one of those supernatural creatures, one of those beings inhabited by the Divine. Our children were forbidden to tease him and it soon became customary to solicit his advice if someone was planning to get married or to emigrate—secretly, of course—to Lampedusa or Barcelona. His answer to these enquiries was always the same: there is no mirror in the world that can show us these events before they have happened. "Marry anybody you like, get in your boat and go to Spain or wherever else, I wish you luck, but my mirror has nothing to say about that," he added, visibly irritated to have to make such an obvious statement.

I don't know why, but I was the only person in Niarela for whom Ali Kaboye showed even a modicum of respect. More than once, he refrained from spouting obscenities in my presence. When I think back on all that, I am pretty sure Ali Kaboye was perfectly sane and making fun of us.

But at the same time, I see the other Ali Kaboye in my mind's eye, the one who used to go completely berserk every now and again and left us in no doubt whatsoever that he was stark raving mad. I remember the week for example, when, like a teacher in front of his students, he delivered a learned lecture about the origins of the kiss in Senegal, or rather about the fact that one fine day we started kissing each other on the mouth the way lovers do at the cinema or on the platform of a train station. Yes, that was quite something, wasn't it!

Based on the idea that it must be possible to trace this back to its beginnings by examining the course of our national history, Ali Kaboye said angrily he was sure he could identify the man and the woman who were the first after the arrival of the *Toubabs* to mingle their tongues and their lips, their saliva and all the rest.

This made us laugh, of course, but he didn't mind. He treated us like dimwits, neither worthy of his rage nor of his superior scholarship, contenting himself with the observation that this was a lot more important than we might think.

Thanks to Ali Kaboye we also got used to the following: he told the same stories for several days in a row, with identical words and gestures, like an actor on stage plays the same part night after night. Soon the whole of Niarela knew his tirades by heart. The younger ones among us took great pleasure in copying Ali Kaboye's intonation and his unmistakable way of gazing at his mirror.

If, just before all this was happening—and this includes the even more serious events that were to follow—somebody had told us that one day a madman would come and camp right under our noses, we would simply have laughed it off. But at the same time nobody could explain why Ali Kaboye, the man whose body was covered in festering sores, who used to roam around the streets of Niarela stark naked, and who was continually being harassed by swarms of flies, had captivated not only our minds but also our innermost thoughts to the point where we had literally become obsessed with him.

Not surprisingly, our politicians were the first to grasp how Ali Kaboye's notoriety might be exploited. His growing influence on public opinion turned him into a direct but disloyal competitor for them, if one can put it like that.

And those whose memory hasn't let them down will surely remember the year when nine people, including a six-year-old child, lost their lives during the mayoral election campaign in Niarela. The father had been foolhardy enough to bring him along to one of the rallies at a critical time, when the battle was unusually harsh and both parties used their dirty tricks wherever possible. Each camp had hired tried and tested slanderers, and never before had Niarela seen such a display of gall and venom on the occasion of an ordinary local election. Its outcome, it must be added, was completely unpredictable.

It went like this.

A few nights before the election, at an hour when the whole of Niarela was fast asleep, you could see furtive shadows sneaking through the deserted, silent lanes of the district.

Ali Kaboye was a light sleeper. He sat up, listening to the noises outside his shack. A voice he had never heard before greeted him, and his reply proved that he was in a foul temper: "What do you want from me? Go back where you came from. I don't want to know who you are and I don't want to talk to you."

The visitors, who had probably anticipated this rude reception, didn't take it personally. The one who seemed to be their boss said calmly, "You wouldn't talk like this if you knew what we have got for you, Ali."

"What is it?" Ali Kaboye asked.

"Money," said the voice.

"Money?"

"That's it, Ali, bags and bags of money."

"Well, in that case, I'm interested," said Ali, smiling to himself.

"It's a gift for you," said the person in the same unflustered tone of voice.

"A gift . . ." said Ali Kaboye. "A gift in exchange for what?"

The visitors looked at each other, slightly lost for words. One of them cleared his throat and said, "It's got to do with the election, Ali. There's a very bad man who wants to become our mayor."

"No need to mention his name," Ali Kaboye said drily, "I know who you're talking about."

"Well, there you are. That man is a liar and a thief, he'll never build any hospitals or schools for our children."

"Are you trying to say he is one of those blasted demagogues? Son of a bitch and enemy of the people? What do you want from me?"

"The man is a liability for Niarela. He must not be allowed to become our mayor."

"I see what you want," said Ali Kaboye, gravely nodding his head. "You're looking for somebody who'll publicly slander him for you."

"That's about it."

"Then you're going to have to shell out lots of money," said Ali Kaboye.

They showed him the bags again: "This is only the first installment. Above all, don't forget to tell the public everything this impostor is hiding, Ali. The people deserve to know the truth!"

Ali Kaboye took his time counting the banknotes, and then he said: "It's a deal. Dish me all the dirt you've got about the man. Make sure you don't leave anything out—the devil is in the detail, as they so rightly say. Make up a few malicious stories if you like, but watch out and don't exaggerate, my friends, for if you want to be good liars, you should always stick very closely to the truth."

At the end of this encounter, Ali Kaboye showed his visitors how he was planning to ridicule their enemy by pulling all sorts of funny faces. They found this very amusing and as they left, they congratulated him on his good citizenship and his talents as a comedian.

The next day, more shadows were silently sneaking along the narrow streets of Niarela. They were the opponents of the visitors from the night before. They were looking for Ali Kaboye. He said to them, "I was expecting you."

They looked at each other in surprise and asked him all sorts of questions. This was his simple answer: "I am Ali Kaboye. Here is the mirror. I can see you all in the mirror. I can see every one of you."

After a pause, he added, "No need to name names."

They showed him bags full of money.

"We don't want to buy you, we know you're not open to bribery, Ali."

"You're quite right," he sniggered, "in this country, only the fools are honest."

"That's it, Ali, we have brought you a gift."

For the first time in years, Ali Kaboye wanted to burst out laughing. These guys were really quite incredible.

"What do I have to do in return for this gift?" he asked.

They nodded and looked at each other as if to say, He's not such a fool after all, our Ali, . he understands perfectly what's going on. Ali thought these people were more fanatical and more dangerous than the previous lot. One of them described the leader of their rival party as a hyena with stinking breath and its supporters as a bunch of rabid jackals. Then they told him what they wanted from him.

"I got it, you want me to insult him in public?"

"Exactly. You are the only person in Niarela whose voice really counts, Ali."

"All right, I'm listening. Dish me all the dirt that you know about him."

He gave them his little lesson about the art of lying, which is so much harder than it looks, and they slandered the other camp with great gusto. They, too, said good-bye to Ali Kaboye with joy in their hearts.

I'm sure you are wondering, Badou, how I found out about those two clandestine meetings. Nothing could be simpler: everything we know about them, we owe to a certain Ali Kaboye from our glorious past! Elsewhere in the city people had television and radio. We were lucky enough to have Ali Kaboye as well. With his infallible memory and natural talent for narration worthy of our greatest storytellers, he amazed us when he started disclosing all the details of his nightly meetings with high-ranking politicians in Niarela. The facts he presented to us were true and difficult to believe at the same time. One thing I found particularly amazing was the fact that Ali Kaboye's description was a great deal more elegant and sophisticated than one would expect under the circumstances. I really do not quite know how to express the feelings I experienced then. It was a sensation of elusive beauty all the more difficult to describe since it was born out of such a hideous story, a truly disgraceful story that left no room for anything except hatred and destruction. Was that because, for reasons best known to himself, Ali had chosen to tell us the story in images? He said, for instance, that his nightly visitors came to see him under a veil of secrecy, adding, "The silence was so profound that you could hear every single dewdrop falling on the sand." I found that very evocative.

As far as our two mayoral candidates were concerned, they appreciated those stylistic niceties a lot less, since Ali Kaboye was cheerfully setting about to ruin them. "I, Ali Kaboye, never break a promise," he shouted. "I promised them to talk, and that is what I will do. They came to see me in the middle of the night, and they said, 'We want to buy a bit of your venom, here are bags and bags of money!' People of Niarela, who was it who told them that I, Ali Kaboye, son of my father and my mother in Ndimboye, am a viper or a green mamba? Who told them that?"

After giving us time to revel in his words, he announced, in a voice tinged with equal amounts of irony and rage, "I know everything and I will tell everything. I promise you, I am not going to be shy, hehe!"

The truth is that he was so forthright that Niarela came within an inch of sinking into chaos. Violent fights erupted, and Molotov cocktails and tear gas grenades exploded above our heads while the police had a hard time trying to reestablish order in the district.

■　　■　　■

From time to time, Ali Kaboye barricaded himself in his shack for days on end. His silence troubled us. Life continued as before, but we were on tenterhooks.

Our hearts didn't beat as briskly, the faces were anxious, and the sky seemed to hang lower than before. It was as if a void had opened up somewhere in Niarela.

■   ■   ■

But that's how it is: even the most beautiful fables come to an end, and the end of Ali Kaboye, alas, was not a happy one.

In a nutshell, he had overplayed his hand and that led to his downfall. I'm sure you know the story about the madman who is congratulated by his friends for having managed to point out the moon in the sky and who proudly shouts, "And here you can see the second moon, just slightly to the left!" I think the same thing happened to Ali Kaboye. He had so much power over us that it went to his head and caused him to lose any sense of proportion. That was undoubtedly the reason why he committed his second big mistake after murdering Bolchoï, Captain Ndéné's dog.

One day, we heard him shooting his poisoned arrows at those he liked to call the "men without color." What did he mean by that? It was the first time he had used this expression and each one of us came up with a possible answer to this riddle. After a while, it became clear that this was Ali Kaboye's name for the *Toubabs*, who, according to him, were running our country from so far away that it was impossible to see them with the naked eye. He alone, of course, was able to clearly distinguish each one of these "men without color" in his famous mirror. That was new. And dangerous. Very dangerous. It had nothing to do with our petty local quarrels. Ali Kaboye's invectives against those unspecified invisible creatures alarmed our authorities greatly, since their number one priority was to stay on good terms with President Daour Diagne.

The notables of Niarela held a secret meeting and said, "Now Ali Kaboye has really crossed the line."

This was tantamount to a death sentence.

Soon afterward, it was executed.

Only those in Niarela who were naive or cynical didn't know who had razed Ali Kaboye's shack to the ground and why we neither saw nor heard from him anymore.

But, as always, the truth was bound to come to light.

And the truth was as follows: Just off the beach of Koussoum, some men in balaclavas had slit Ali Kaboye's throat and thrown his body to the sharks. Who were those villains? People were whispering certain names, but nobody dared to spell them out loud and clear.

Ali Kaboye's assassination plunged us into sorrow and anguish. He assumed the aura of a martyr for freedom and a man of great spirituality with a pure and noble heart.

His posthumous glory was such that we ended up having false Ali Kaboyes just like there are false prophets. But the man was definitely unique, and the swindlers were all exposed and in some cases severely punished. An adventurer appeared in Niarela who wanted to be addressed as the Commander of Dreams and who told the crowd that had come to listen to him, "In actual fact, let me tell you that the man named Ali Kaboye never existed! You have all dreamed him up in broad daylight, since in this day and age, where vice has gained the upper hand, entire nations can lose their sense of reality!"

He also said we were lucky, since if he hadn't come to wake us up, Niarela would have been swallowed up by the sea of Koussoum.

Some youngsters shouted abuse at him, telling him to go and spout his nonsense somewhere else, and so he dropped his false beard, his walking stick, and all the other paraphernalia impostors tend to have on the spot and fled.

Ali Kaboye's life had not been in vain; it became a source of inspiration for our younger generations.

He resurfaced in our memory as an utterly free spirit of luminous serenity. It became customary in Niarela to quote his lucid and inspirational sayings all the time. The fact is that even from his grave, Ali Kaboye remained alive, unlike those of us who are slumped in front of the television night and day.

Badou Tall, everything I know about life, I owe to two men: Cheikh Anta Diop and Ali Kaboye. You would do well to follow in their footsteps yourself.

■　　■　　■

The emerald is buried under the seas, and the skin of the sky is tight as a drum. A single blow of his ax makes the sky spew the glittering light of myriad stars. The path will be arduous. Blood is dripping from hands lacerated by thorns and Death, like a famished beast, is forever prowling around the Just.

That was how Ali Kaboye used to talk not long before he died. We didn't know that this was his way of bidding us farewell.

■　　■　　■

Shadow or ghost? The way he walked wasn't the same as before. Completely out of the blue, he would appear at street corners in Niarela. He looked as if he were walking on water; there was no tinkling from the little bells he wore around his neck and if he wanted to speak, his vocal cords made no sound.

When he started rebuilding his shack, his hammer-blows on wood, or even on iron, were inaudible. His eyes didn't see us, and we wondered whether the light reaching his eyes came from faraway celestial bodies.

On his way home after a working day at the palace, Captain Baye Ndéné stopped outside the shack. He spent a short time observing the scene, murmuring words that must have been an expression of wounded pride and hatred. He was at a loss to understand this world where you could choose to refuse death just because it's better to be alive. Of course it is better to be alive than dead. But if that was the case, then why had he spent the best years of his life as a soldier, learning how to slaughter his fellow men?

He wasn't going to stand around and do nothing.

■　　■　　■

As soon as I heard the screaming—even before I was sure it was Ali Kaboye's voice—I thought of him.

My blankets were warm and cozy, and I had no desire to get out of them. And although this is harder to admit, there may have been another reason why I hesitated. When a man calls for help in the middle of the night, there is always that little goblin whispering in our ear: *Stay out of it, just pretend you haven't heard anything; saving people's lives is a worthy thing to do, but there's no need to play the hero, why be the only one to risk your life?*

I didn't hear it, that little voice, because once I had emerged from my state of semiconsciousness, I realized that Ali Kaboye's screams were addressed to me, Nguirane Faye, and to me alone. His killers had him in their clutches and he must have known that this time, Captain Baye Ndéné wouldn't give him another chance.

I got dressed in a hurry and left the house with a pounding heart. What could I possibly do, all by myself, against Ali Kaboye's attackers?

The screams seemed to be coming from several directions at once, and after wandering around aimlessly for half an hour, I still hadn't come across a single living soul in Niarela. Not far from Diédhiou's house, in a place known as Hawkers' Corner, I stopped, trying to decide which way to go. As I was about to turn into a narrow, sandy lane, a stone came flying and knocked my fez off my head. I didn't have time to hit back, but I recognized the massive silhouette of Captain Baye Ndéné.

For a few seconds I stood there, and then, not knowing what to do and probably also afraid of suffering the same fate as Ali Kaboye, I decided to go back home. As I was passing the workshop of Demba Thiam, the goldsmith, right next to the Empire cinema, I changed my mind. This spot, dark and well concealed, was an ideal vantage point. I positioned myself there in order to see what would happen next.

Tumaini, Ousmane Sow's horse, neighed twice, and a dog responded from far away. Otherwise, the district was perfectly quiet. All I could hear was the gentle rustling of the leaves in the wind. I was sure Captain Baye Ndéné and his henchmen must have dealt with Ali Kaboye and finished him off.

After waiting in vain for a long time, I returned home and went to bed.

At sunrise, on the way to the mosque, somebody asked, "Did you hear what I heard at about two o'clock in the morning?"

"You mean the man calling for help?"

"Yes . . ."

"He was a scoundrel. Our youngsters taught him a nice lesson."

"So there is someone we're not going to see again for a while in Niarela!"

I kept my mouth shut. There was no point in adding to their falsehoods. They knew. They knew everything. The prayers I said for Ali Kaboye that morning came from the bottom of my heart.

■　　■　　■

One day, when he saw us sitting near Ali Kaboye's shack, Captain Baye Ndéné grimaced in disgust and said, "Don't you think it's time we finally got rid of *that*?"

He meant to sound lighthearted and chummy, but this was an order, so much was obvious. Since Ali Kaboye's second death, Baye Ndéné had started behaving like an army commander just back from a victorious campaign. You could tell from certain little gestures so typical of people who wield a lot of power that he was becoming increasingly intoxicated with his own importance. We no longer saw him getting drunk in public, and, instead of chatting to us as a neighbor or childhood friend about the mundane happenings in our district, Captain Baye Ndéné was now displaying the mannerisms of the so-called benevolent politician who condescends to listen to the grievances, petty problems, and anxieties of the man-in-the-street. With his arms crossed and a thoughtful look on his face, he allowed each one of us just a glimmer of hope that, thanks to his inordinate kindness, he would put a word in on our behalf with President Daour Diagne "at our daily briefing," a turn of phrase he never neglected to slip casually into the conversation at an opportune moment.

He was so powerful now that it was impossible to refuse this man anything he asked for. That's why nobody made the slightest objection when his right forefinger pointed at Ali Kaboye's shack with disdain. I hasten to add that slowly but surely the shack of the late Ali Kaboye had collapsed and was not much more than a pile of rubble with an oily, blackish liquid oozing out of it. The roof had been partly blown off by the wind, and its sheer presence in this spot made the landscape seem a bit eerie.

One of us drove the point home with particular relish: "The Captain is right, two or three days ago, I saw a huge rat coming out of there."

Mada Diop, who was tasked with the demolition of the remnants of the shack, was a young man with a sturdy body and a simple mind. For a few coins, he was prepared to take on the most unpalatable jobs: unclogging latrines, filling up ponds with water, or fixing a roof.

At that point, the whole situation took an unexpected turn. No sooner had Mada Diop administered the first hammer-blow than we heard a piercing scream. He was bent double and shaking his hands in pain—they were in flames . . .

After the poor wretch was buried, the notables of Niarela reproached themselves once more for having underestimated Ali Kaboye.

Now Talla Ndiaye, the carpenter, was called in. Talla may have been a little less muscular than Mada Diop, but like so many taciturn individuals, he had the reputation of being able to tame the forces of darkness. Unfortunately for him, he could not even get to Ali Kaboye's shack. About twenty meters away from there, he suffered an attack of vertigo, sat down under a lemon tree, started vomiting blood and, without so much as a whimper, gave up the ghost a few minutes later.

Talla Ndiaye had been a modest man, honest and with a big heart. His death affected me very badly. It was a sign that the hour of truth had arrived for Niarela. There we were, standing in a semicircle around Talla Ndiaye's body, gazing at each other anxiously. We were all thinking the same thing: "Ali Kaboye is inside this shack, he can hear us and he can see us this very moment."

When something extremely serious happens, the resulting fear doesn't necessarily provoke screams and general panic. On that particular day, a number of Niarela's inhabitants reacted with hypocrisy. Since they valued their peace and quiet above all else, they uttered vociferous complaints about Captain Baye Ndéné without ever pronouncing his name. Why treat one of God's innocent creatures with so much brute force? That's what they wanted to know. After all, Ali Kaboye had never done anybody any harm in Niarela! Regarding Ali Kaboye's second death, they were sure the deed was premeditated, and that the assassin would soon be apprehended, since *What's the point in hiding to gulp down one bottle of whiskey after another; the day will come when we will see you staggering across the town square, blind drunk, and then your secret is out in the open!*

Veritable salvoes of Wolof proverbs were flitting through the air. There was the one about the camel's fart, which, as we all know, is positioned as high up as the anus from which it escaped, while the noise it makes is not very discreet and will eventually be heard by absolutely everybody. And then there is the one about the murderer who should not be too surprised that his hands are stained red from the blood of his victims. If, in Ali Kaboye's case, the killers thought they could escape justice, everyone else knew they were very naive.

You can steal my drum my friend, but that's not enough—you also need to be able to play it without my finding out about it, and I'm not deaf, ha-ha!

"That's what happens when you judge a man by his outward appearance," observed Ousmane Sow, the cart driver. We should mention at this point that he had become one of Ali Kaboye's most fervent partisans.

"God punishes the proud," someone else said approvingly.

From that day onward, nobody dared to go near Ali Kaboye's shack anymore.

.   .   .

The man was of medium height, but the *tengaade* on his head made him look slightly taller. Quite apart from affording him protection against the sun, it actually seemed to be an integral part of him. He probably never took it off except in bed. His walking stick and his long white beard indicated that he must be very old. In fact he was like one of those storybook characters who, we are told, are a hundred and fifty or two hundred years old, but for the narrator this is just a figure of speech, of course. Despite his great age, an air of vitality emanated from his entire being. He came across as so distinguished and self-assured that we instantly took him for a Master of the Initiates.

He modestly introduced himself to us as a beggar, reciting a few verses from the Book in return for a bowl of rice, some biscuits or a handful of dates. Everybody who approached him to give alms was struck by the intensity of his gaze, which somehow did not seem to fit with the rest of his face.

People were whispering that he was a fake beggar and a true saint. When this rumor reached the ears of Gora Mbaye, Captain Baye Ndéné's father-in-law, he called one of his servants: "Go and tell this old beggar the whole world is talking about that I, Gora Mbaye, Captain Baye Ndéné's father-in-law, am ordering him to come and see me this instant! Make it very clear to him that Gora Mbaye, one of the dignitaries of Niarela, doesn't like to be kept waiting!"

It didn't take the domestic servant long to track down the beggar. With the typical haughtiness of an underling who is proud to be serving his powerful master, he went up to him and said, "Gora Mbaye, my master, commands you to follow me without delay. He wishes me to inform you that he hates being kept waiting by miserable paupers like you!"

Even before the old man had opened his mouth, his piercing eyes filled the servant with terror. "Tell that man to come and kneel in front of me before I step across the boundary of Niarela. If he doesn't, I suggest that his relatives go quickly and buy seven meters of percale!"

He paused, then he took a handful of sand, blew on it and said calmly, "Just as it is true that these grains of sand have dispersed toward the south, the destruction of the man named Gora Mbaye is assured."

Gora Mbaye was so overbearing and arrogant that everybody in Niarela expected him to react with indignation. We were looking forward to playing the supporting role in a battle of giants between the proud Gora Mbaye and this unusual beggar.

The battle never took place, Badou.

On the contrary, it ended up being the craziest day in Gora Mbaye's life! His servant must have been pretty convincing, because our man was absolutely terrified and instantly set off to search for the old beggar. With bare feet and a frantic look on his face, he went randomly from street to street, harassing everybody he came across with questions about a beggar wearing a *tengaade*. Without waiting for an answer, he would then go rushing down yet another street. It was incredibly funny to see Gora Mbaye in such a state, but he scoffed at our laughter. He just didn't want to die, that's all.

He eventually found the beggar who was not nearly as harsh as anticipated when he told him, "So here you are at last, Gora Mbaye. It's better like that for you."

Still shocked at the thought that he had cheated death by a hair's breadth, Goya Mbaye was lost for words.

The old beggar, who seemed to find him quite pathetic, even showed a certain compassion and sympathy for him and genuinely tried to help: "Listen to me carefully, Gora Mbaye. For a long time now, Niarela has been trying in vain to demolish Ali Kaboye's shack. Here is what you need to know if you want to find a solution to this problem; there is only one man who can get rid of it for you, and his name is Isma Ndoye."

He was quiet for a moment and then started again, clutching the handle of his walking stick with both hands, in a pose that must have been typical of him, "Nobody else will be able to do it. Isma Ndoye is the only person in the world who can get the job done."

Gora Mbaye was still sweating and hadn't quite recovered from his fright. With a confused look on his face, he mumbled, "Who is this man?"

"He comes from the village of Mbao."

"Do I have to go and find him?"

"No. He will come to Niarela by himself. But you need to understand something else, Gora Mbaye: nobody can prevent Ali Kaboye from coming back."

"Ali Kaboye is coming back to Niarela?" exclaimed Gora Mbaye.

"Yes," the beggar said simply.

"Can't you help us?"

The old man gently shook his head. "There are many of us in the Seven Heavens, and yet, so far, we have failed to bring Ali Kaboye to his knees. He's invincible, that man, because he knows how to shift the signs. We don't know what to do about it. We have never come across such strength of purpose in one solitary Son of the Earth. Does what I am saying make sense to you, Gora?"

"No, all this sounds like gobbledygook to me," said Gora Mbaye, totally beside himself. "I haven't understood a single thing."

"But it's really very simple."

Gora Mbaye was completely and utterly fed up with celestial metaphysics and signs that certain people assume the right to disturb, just like that, without any reason. Rather than listening to the beggar's explanations, he clung to the idea he was obsessed with. "Is there nothing you can do for us? We don't want Ali Kaboye to come back to Niarela. Believe me, old man, nobody wants him here!"

Gora Mbaye found it unfair that Ali Kaboye was, in a way, the only creature on earth who couldn't be killed off once and for all.

This made the beggar smile for the first time—he found Gora Mbaye's dismay almost touching. "What is it you want, Gora Mbaye? Captain Baye Ndéné and you have killed Ali Kaboye and let his body, weighed down by a big rock, sink to the bottom of the sea. What more can you possibly want? Do you think I can transform his remains into sea shells? Do you want shells to decorate your living room, is that what you would like?"

Gora Mbaye, who had just, more or less in public, been accused of having murdered Ali Kaboye, looked around with a worried expression. But he still had enough presence of mind to ask the old man, "Does that mean Ali Kaboye is definitely coming back . . . ?"

"That's right," the beggar interrupted.

"If that's the case, why should we pay Isma Ndoye to demolish his shack?"

"What you are saying makes sense, Gora, but you are saying it out of ignorance."

"Oh really?" said Gora Mbaye.

"Without Isma Ndoye's help, Ali Kaboye will torment you until the end of time."

"I understand what you mean," said Gora Mbaye, although he hadn't understood anything. "How much do I owe you right now?"

"Nothing," the beggar replied tersely, visibly irritated. "Save your money for Isma Ndoye. He charges a lot, believe me. Good-bye, Gora Mbaye."

And just as loud and clear as the camel's fart that is very high up and destined, in the long run, to be heard by absolutely everybody, all sorts of far-fetched rumors started to circulate about Ali Kaboye. People out on a nocturnal stroll claimed they had seen a ball of flames emerging from the sea of Koussoum that was floating upwards and setting the sky on fire. The next day, on the coast near Melilla, a group of emigrants with excellent eyesight were scanning the sky and spotted one of our compatriots perched on the clouds, daydreaming. Having observed him carefully through their telescope, they noticed that he looked infinitely sad, with his eyes fixed on a particular area in our city that, according to very complex and learned calculations of probability, had to be Niarela. This forced even the greatest skeptics to admit that Ali Kaboye would never let his killers sleep in peace. Claims were also made that he had a habit of transforming himself into a mosquito at night. Under that guise he started buzzing vengeful words, accompanied by lots of giggling, into the ears of certain people who kept tapping their temples in vain, trying to chase away the nasty little beast. All this was reported with gentle irony.

Several months passed.

One day, a big, strong fellow appeared in Niarela saying his name was Isma Ndoye.

"Where are you from?" people asked.

"From Mbao," he replied tersely.

Right from the start, this young man struck us as an aggressive, irascible individual who was also exceptionally rude. But we needed him. Niarela had been waiting for him for months without having the courage to admit it, and now he was here. Within a few minutes, the entire district had crowded around him.

"I, Isma Ndoye, can liberate you from Ali Kaboye," he said as he took off his *anango*.

"Is it the old beggar who sent you here?"

This question may have been somewhat superfluous, but it certainly wasn't offensive. And yet, it made Isma Ndoye absolutely furious and to distract him, Gora Mbaye asked, "How much are you asking to be paid, stranger? We have heard your fees are very high."

Isma Ndoye bent down to Gora Mbaye's ear and whispered an amount. Gora Mbaye's face immediately clouded over. Looking at him in dismay he exclaimed, "What you are asking is more money than has flowed into Niarela since the day it was founded!"

Afraid that he might have offended him—and probably also in order to avoid getting embroiled in the whole business of the Seven Skies, he added, in a more conciliatory tone, "We are prepared to pay, but you have to be reasonable."

Isma Ndoye—he certainly was a nasty piece of work, that guy—was still so angry that he didn't even deem us worthy of a reply and picked up his *anango*. When we saw he was getting dressed again, we begged him, "Are you really going to abandon us, your brothers in faith, into the clutches of Cheytan just like that?"

He let his eyes wander over the crowd and said with contempt, "What faith are you talking about, bunch of hypocrites! At the moment you snuffed out the life of that Son of the Earth, you should have paid heed to the eagle that was gliding in the air above the waves of Koussoum! He saw everything. He saw every single one of you. Do you want to hear the tale of Ali Kaboye's second death?"

No one dared to say a word.

Captain Baye Ndéné, who had only just arrived, forced his way through the crowd and said, as he was walking toward Isma Ndoye, "Who do you think you are, stranger, to demand more money from us than this whole country has ever seen? I, Captain Baye Ndéné, don't like that kind of mockery, is that clear?"

Baye Ndéné was coming straight from the brothel, reeking strongly of *bunukabu*. I forgot to tell you that due to Ali Kaboye's stubbornness and refusal to die once and for all, the man was down in the dumps again and had started drinking like never before.

Gora Mbaye tried to save the situation: "We are grateful to you for coming all this way to assist us," he said to Isma Ndoye. "The problem is that we don't have enough money to pay you."

"All right then, that means I'm going back to Mbao," Isma Ndao replied coldly.

Just then, as the crowd started to disperse, I sensed that someone was looking at me. I turned round, and there was Captain Baye Ndéné with bloodshot eyes from all the alcohol, barely able to stand up straight. Nevertheless, when he spoke to me, his voice sounded almost normal. With that peculiar lucidity of the drunkard that can be so terrifying at times, he said, "What's the matter with you today, Nguirane?"

I immediately got the gist of his question but pretended I hadn't understood what he meant. "Why are you asking me that?"

"You didn't open your mouth while we were talking to that stranger. And by the way, you seem more and more withdrawn these days, Nguirane . . . What's the matter with you?"

Keeping my cool, I said: "What is the matter with me is called fear, Baye Ndéné."

He frowned: "Fear . . . ?"

About a dozen people had gathered around us and some others had even come back again. Everybody was staring at me.

I started again: "Did you really listen to that man who claims to be from Mbao? While he was talking, I closed my eyes, and I heard Ali Kaboye's voice."

"Which one? Do you mean our Ali Kaboye?"

"Yes, our Ali Kaboye."

There was a great hullabaloo.

Suddenly, everybody looked apprehensive. One of our most respected dignitaries—forgive me for not divulging his name—was so badly let down by his intestines that his *caaya* nearly dropped to the ground.

We felt that we had no choice but to put renewed pressure on the authorities to get rid of Ali Kaboye's shack. But our petition just made them laugh. Didn't we realize the government had more important things to do, for goodness' sake?

PLAYING IN THE DARK

I HOPE MY SHUTTLING BACK AND FORTH BETWEEN PAST AND PRESENT isn't making you dizzy. But before I move on, you need to know that the story that follows goes back several decades and has nothing whatsoever to do with Yacine Ndiaye or Ali Kaboye.

As far as Yacine Ndiaye is concerned, just be patient; one of these days I will reopen her *Notebook*, just for you.

This morning, I want to talk to you about another woman. A woman I have loved. Faat Kiné. She played an important role in my life.

Picture this: I am an employee at Air Liquide and I have just turned thirty-two. Almost every night, we meet up in her modest two-room flat in Colobane, which as you know, was a pretty sleepy backwater in those days. Even today, in fact, as soon as you get a bit farther away from its main focal points at nightfall—the roundabout, the market that's trying so hard to compete with Sandaga, and the houses and public buildings around there—certain corners of Colobane can be extremely quiet. In Faat Kiné's little courtyard, we almost feel like we are alone in the world, and this is helped by the fact that the old couple next door is so discreet. When the sky is clear, we lie on a mat for hours on end, gazing at the stars. Television doesn't exist yet, and so we listen to the radio, sipping our mint tea. Faat Kiné is not very talkative and our conversations are always interspersed with long silences. These silences don't bother us. The truth is that just to be lying there, next to one another, enjoying the balmy night air together, means happiness for us. We avoid great verbal outpourings because we want to preserve the secret dignity of that happiness. Our love, which is solid, can do without them. Instead of working out the details of our future life together in advance—the name of the first baby, how to furnish our new house, and whether or not it would be a good idea if Faat Kiné, a social worker, started looking for a job somewhere near my factory—we discuss the small little things that happen in everyday life. In fact, we spend most of our time talking about our families and friends and I have to admit that we often end up saying nasty things about people we don't like. *This is the first time I've told anybody, but such-and-such—you would never have guessed it, I expect—is hiding a dark family secret.* Things like that, which are maybe a tad unwholesome. But that only brought us even closer together, this feeling of having the others—all the others, in fact—against us.

But don't forget, it's the fifties. Faat Kiné and I are young, our blood is still fresh, and we know it. The desire comes almost all by itself. Our two bodies know each other well, one has to say. Had we been able to dissolve into each other, we certainly would have done, but as it is, we emerge from our embraces exhausted and drained, staring into empty space.

Yes—those were our evenings in Colobane.

But one of those evenings was—how can I put it?—so special that it continues to haunt me even now, after so many years. I remember it down to the tiniest detail, and it still troubles me a bit as I write these lines.

I have to tell you about it.

We're lying wrapped in each other's arms, in silence. The sky is clear, and, as so often, we have the feeling that words would only disturb the soft vibrations of the night. We are like two children lost in an inhospitable place, a forest or an unfamiliar city, somewhere like that. Are we going to find our way in this total darkness? Perhaps it's due to this vague fear of danger that we are caressing each other with such unusual tenderness. When I penetrate her, she receives me like never before, with the most extraordinary delicacy. Only, the pleasure is tinged with a hint of bitterness. At that strange moment we all dread when we find ourselves outside the other person's body, naked and alone, somber thoughts overwhelm me. With my eyes closed, I see two little black ants trying in vain to get to the top of a hill. We are in our prime, we have our whole lives ahead of us and yet, at this moment, our very youth strikes me as absurd and disagreeable. Everything seems to be telling me we're already old, worn out and jaded.

Back in the living room, she sits down on the floor with her legs crossed, while I am on the sofa. My fingers are playing with her breasts, before letting go of them and moving further down to that furry place that's still hot and moist.

Our conversation turns to Mame Ngor. As so often before, Faat Kiné wants me to talk to her about my ancestor. I tell her what I have picked up here and there. Not a great deal, in fact.

She thinks it's pointless for us to have come into the world one day, only to disappear again the same way and leaving behind no trace in anyone's memory.

Faat Kiné tended to be a very serious and thoughtful person at the best of times, but that night, she seemed more preoccupied than usual.

I am concerned. "What's the matter, Fatou?"

After a brief silence, she calmly replies, "The truth is, Nguirane, that I feel like I have never had either a father or a mother."

After she was born, her mother took her into the bush in order to kill her. But someone surprised her while she was digging a hole near a shrub and she fled, leaving the newborn behind.

For a long time, Faat Kiné believed she was the daughter of the people who had taken her in, but they eventually thought they should tell her the truth about her own history.

I then start asking her if her mother got arrested, but I don't finish my sentence. The whole thing is so stupid it makes me totally confused. Faat Kiné senses my unease and pulls me gently toward her until I join her on the carpet.

I was asleep, and I had a dream that I am going to describe to you now. I don't want you to miss even the minutest detail.

I am alone outside Faat Kiné's house, waiting for a taxi. It's completely dark. From the edge of the embankment, I see hundreds, perhaps even thousands of identical little cars driving past. They are not all one compact mass, but they rush past at a mind-numbing speed, one after the other, with all their lights shining. I'm beginning to think that there is perhaps just one car going back and forth so fast that at every moment it fills my entire field of vision. And for hours on end, all I hear is the same metallic noise: "Beep! Beep! Beep!"

Is it possible to ask oneself, in the middle of a dream, whether one is really dreaming? At any rate, that is exactly what's happening to me. The road is like a tunnel, stretching toward infinity. It's strange that the tunnel is so dark despite all the cars with their dazzling headlights. I feel like I am standing under a brightly lit vault. Maybe I thought I had somehow been locked up in my own grave.

"Beep! Beep! Beep!"

Soon it is no longer a question of finding a taxi to get back to Niarela. I just want to get away from here as quickly as possible. The way I am gesticulating at these car drivers is becoming increasingly frantic and distraught, but not one of them looks like he is inclined to stop. To be honest, I'm just assuming that these little machines are actually driven by human beings like you and me, because try as I might, I haven't been able to make out a single one of them behind the wheel. How can a normal person possibly drive this fast in a tunnel that is both so dark and so immensely bright, and why do all those cars have the same black color and the same curved shape?

Don't forget what I told you at the beginning of my story: I had just turned thirty-two. That means I had this dream in 1954. This detail, or rather this date, has its own importance and you will soon understand why.

The next day, I woke up feeling mildly anxious. Oddly enough, that's what always happens if I have had a vivid dream the night before—the following morning, I usually can't shake it off for a long time. They strike me as a foretaste of death, these nocturnal plunges into a world that is surreal and perfectly plausible at the same time. I would almost say I prefer nightmares. They are so chaotic and crazy that they actually end up being more reassuring.

More than forty years have passed.

How many nights and how many sunrises have been swallowed up by the void, taking with them our ludicrous hopes and aspirations? What have I got left of my nights in Colobane with Faat Kiné? Believe it or not, but neither of us knows today whether the other one is alive or dead. We have walked totally separate paths. It's not easy to explain exactly how a being that was once more important to us than any other got lost along the way. I have seen lovers spend more time and energy on their separation than on their actual relationship. In our case that process was gradual and painless, I suppose, right up to the moment when further encounters, whether in Colobane or elsewhere, would have been pointless and embarrassing. But the truth is that this morning, as I sit here, bent over this *Notebook*, I can see Faat Kiné all around me. Almost half a century later, the sound of her languorous, slightly melancholic voice still resonates inside my head and her body hasn't stopped stirring inside mine.

And now, another dream I had last night, has turned me into a vigorous young man again. I am sure you will find this equally hard to believe: forty years later, I relived that entire night in Colobane in a dream.

Everything came back to me, Badou, exactly how it happened. We made love in silence, with the same expansive, precise and measured gestures as always. Our mouths pronounced the exact same words. I talked to her about Mame Ngor, the illustrious ancestor, and she told me all over again how her mother tried to kill her shortly after she was born. I recognized Faat Kiné's voice without any shadow of doubt, I assure you.

The oddest and most bewildering thing however was—and telling you this unsettles me a bit—that while I was dreaming this, I also dreamed I was back in a dark tunnel flooded with light and thousands of small black cars of the same curved shape were coming toward me. They couldn't stop and were chasing each other at such a mind-blowing speed that they appeared to be standing still. "Beep! Beep! Beep!"

It's all there, Badou.

The things that took place, the things I really experienced all those years ago, side by side with things that never happened. The waters of those two rivers mingling, that's death. When the night has become bright as day, there can no longer be any doubt that the end is nigh. Madness is on the prowl, too. Madness. Death. They sneak up on us on velvet paws, those two nasty bitches. And yet, when you dream you're dreaming, doesn't that mean living your whole life backward, from beginning to end? It can make you dizzy. You prick up your ears to ensure that at least you're not deaf when your final hour approaches. For it is then that the Master of the Worlds, in His infinite grace and benevolence, offers you a second life on earth. On your deathbed, you hear His voice: "Get up and live your life again, Nguirane Faye. From now on, you will grow one year younger with every year that passes. You are eighty years old now. In seventy-nine years, you will have become a twelve-month-old infant again. I, the Almighty, grant you this favor. Unlike the first one, your second life shall be a time of happiness. See, Nguirane, how merrily it's moving toward its elder brother, all smiles and arms wide open. You'll know everything that's going to happen beforehand, even the exact day and hour of your death. And so one morning, your family members will wake up and say, 'The moment of the birth—and thus the death—of our dear Nguirane is approaching. It's time to prepare his funeral.'"

. . .

Badou, when you start paging through some of these *Notebooks* after your return, I'm sure you will say to yourself: "What an old chatterbox he was, my grandfather Nguirane Faye!"

But you will quickly realize that I don't actually deserve to be judged so harshly. I'm not one of those old geezers who do nothing but talk drivel all day long. I am giving you advice, and what you do with it is up to you. I consider it my duty to protect you against the Evil One, without wanting to force anything upon you.

Yes, that's right, I'm talking about the Evil One. Cheytan.

You know perfectly well how enterprising and energetic he is, that fellow. You can accuse him of virtually anything except of not knowing what he wants. And to achieve his aims, he never tires of dreaming up new disguises, masks, and tricks. He deserves the most loathsome names but is entirely lacking in scruples and doubts. In addition, he looks perfectly nondescript. Although his knobby, misshapen body looks like it was patched together in a hurry, it has energy in abundance. His ideas are simple, and his thinking is torpid. And yet, when he wants to sow discord, destroy friendship and love, or even cause great nations to drown in their own blood, he comes up with endless tricks and he never gives up! When you think about it, it's really not very surprising that so many world leaders secretly admire him. As soon as someone wants to wreak havoc, no matter where on this planet, the Evil One is there to lend him a helping hand.

Each and every day, he is up with the first rays of the sun and out hunting. With his evil eye and a heart overflowing with malice, he discreetly mingles with the crowd and eavesdrops on all their conversations undetected. If he hears anything good being said about a person—Yes, of course! Such-and-such! How decent, knowledgeable and generous he is!—he immediately vows to destroy him. Somewhere in town Such-and-Such, so ingenious and talented a person that he's been nicknamed The Truth-Teller, or better still, the Miracle-Maker, is busy leading lost souls back onto the right path. Apparently he is speaking tonight, somewhere between Grand-Yoff and Niarela. Nothing upsets the Evil One more than to think of him winning over the crowd with his mellifluous words. He takes note of the exact address, and with large strides, he rushes to the venue.

Whatever you do, Badou, make sure you don't lose track of him. The predator has located his prey. He won't let go of it again. In anticipation of tonight, a tent has been pitched in the middle of a public square. The Miracle-Maker excels with his perfectly honed metaphors, parables and proverbs. His voice is mellow yet forceful, his gestures are dignified and full of restraint. A true magician, this Miracle-Maker. He permits himself a few digressions here and there, all of them relevant and to the point. He has mastered the art of false modesty and comes across as extremely humble; each one of his gestures, on the other hand, tells you that he thinks he is Truth personified.

Everyone listens respectfully to his magisterial exegesis about Good and Evil. He makes the audience laugh by ridiculing the one called Lie, the favorite weapon of the Evil One and the bane of modern societies.

And yet, on this particular night, the orator suddenly seems slightly less at ease than usual. He twists and turns and he grimaces; he searches for a word, and, having found it, he immediately makes a mistake again. Many want to blame his nervousness on exhaustion. Only a few of the listeners can sense there is something more serious going on, without being able to say exactly what. Nobody has seen him, but Lie has just slipped into the Truth-Teller's clothes—admittedly, they're slightly too large—and now he is tickling and scratching him, calling him a liar, a pleasure-seeking intellectual and a devious scoundrel. He only stops when he has confused the Miracle-Maker totally. While all this is going on, the Miracle-Maker has not lost his composure. He tightens his jaws, certain that this is just a challenging moment he has to live through. But he has underestimated the Evil One, who is tenacity itself. After doing his utmost to physically torment his victim, he suddenly emerges from his hiding place and positions himself in the middle of the circle. He looks around nervously, panting and quite out of breath, like a man who has been running for a long time. Everybody is bewildered and wondering, "Where has he come from, this ruffian? How dirty and unkempt he looks! Is he perhaps a criminal who has escaped from Rebeuss prison?"

But he has already started tormenting the Truth-Teller. "Are you really the Truth?" he asks him in an insolent tone of voice.

The other one stays calm and replies, "Yes. Some people call me that."

"Answer my question! I don't care about the nonsense others are talking. I want to know if you yourself think you are the Truth."

The Miracle-Maker keeps his composure since he is a man with a great deal of experience and insight. He says to the intruder, "Whoever you are, please go away. This is a place where we cherish peace with all our hearts—we disapprove of pointless quarrelling."

That is exactly what the Evil One has been waiting for in order to turn up the heat. "Miracle-Maker, my foot! Which particular truth is this you're talking about? You can hoodwink those idiots who lap up every word you say, but I know all about you and impostors of your ilk. Given half a chance, I'll beat them to a pulp!"

The looks he is getting from the baffled crowd tell the Miracle-Maker his honor is at stake. He cannot allow this Nobody to insult him without fighting back. Yes, he needs to do something, but what? He is at a loss because—and you would do well to remember this—Truth is neither used to public embarrassment, nor to hardship or any kind of setback, in fact. That's what you might call his weak point. Everybody is impressed with Truth, because he is always right and admired by all and sundry. Even if they can't understand his pretentious gibberish, people praise the depth of his thinking, his wise judgments and mind-blowing dialectical skill. Truth also wreaks havoc in the hearts of beautiful women with his attractive, delicately embroidered and neatly pressed garments. Make no mistake, with his perfectly trimmed mustache underlining the regularity of his features and with those gold-rimmed spectacles that frame his sparkling, sensual eyes—the eyes of someone who loves the pleasures of life—Truth is very seductive. And Truth always succeeds; there aren't many who dare oppose him, and hardly anyone would attempt to humiliate Truth in public. That is why he can't defend himself against Lie, that vile bandit too boorish to hold his own in the sort of verbal skirmish where Truth excels. Within a few minutes, the Miracle-Maker has straightened himself up, finally determined to face the enemy. But he is in for a nasty shock: the Evil One, despised by all but hardened by his deprivations and a much tougher and more savage way of life, is much stronger than he is. In his fury, the Evil One strikes him with brutal force, tears his clothes to shreds, yanks out his teeth and tosses them to the crowd. And now our Truth-Teller, with blood dripping from his mouth and eyes bruised and swollen, is reduced to begging the audience to come to his rescue, and suddenly, he sounds quite different. When the carnage is finally over, the unfortunate Miracle-Maker really isn't very nice to look at. Lie and Truth are busy hurling harsh accusations at each other. "You are not the Truth!" shouts the one. "You are the Lie," stammers the other.

After that, nothing is as it was before. The Evil One takes advantage of the chaos and goes on the prowl again. No one feels like listening to the Miracle-Maker's mumbo jumbo anymore.

People denigrate him by saying things like: "All this pontificating about Good and Evil . . ."

"Nothing but smoke and mirrors, my friend! Smoke and mirrors!"

"It's all very well to pretend you are learned and wise, but what is much more important is to win respect!"

"A man who does not know how to fight for his ideas shouldn't be allowed to speak!"

"That was the last time I left home to go and listen to those impostors."

That's what our compatriots are like, Badou. They never know whether to love or hate those who have, in one way or another, managed to rise above them. Although they are clearly in awe of the Miracle-Maker, they secretly dislike the excessive power of the Truth he embodies. But what they dislike most about Truth is his total, almost obscene lack of imagination.

FAREWELL, BADOU!

HE MADE THE ROYAL DRUM ROLL AGAIN.

"It's our sovereign's command," he says, "that we should go and wait for him in the Meeting Square."

Yes, it's true, Badou Tall: early that morning, the words I was waiting for rang out all over Niarela.

Ali Kaboye is back. That means I can leave now, with peace in my heart.

■   ■   ■

The following day, a large crowd has gathered in the Meeting Square. This monarch presides over a reign of terror. He is bloodthirsty. Only a madman would be foolhardy enough to defy him.

After several hours have passed the people are getting impatient: "Where is he?"

Voices can be heard from everywhere, saying, "What, if anything, do we know about the Son of the Earth we are waiting for in this scorching heat?"

"He appears to be our king."

"That's not true," someone says boldly, "our kings have all been dead a long time."

And then a passionate supporter of the modern Republic with its parades and its voting booths triumphantly reminds everybody that kings are a thing of the past, thank God, those autocrats whose madness lasted for centuries.

He speaks the truth, that fellow.

Noisily, the crowd shows its approval. "You are spot on! They used to do exactly as they pleased, our little Negro kings. You remember Daaw Demba? Mad as a hatter. And brutal he was, too. That was a long time ago, but he definitely wasn't the kind of fellow who would have allowed his subjects in the Cayor to go and vote once every five years on a sunny Sunday! Let's be honest, we've seen some really fantastic progress thanks to democracy, whether the perennial naysayers like it or not!"

And then a third one really wants to get to the crux of the matter. "Has Daour Diagne ever ordered drum rolls when he wants to address us?"

"You're quite right, my friend; he usually speaks to us through his beloved television, our President Diagne."

The centuries are locking horns like angry rams. Niarela is at a loss as to which lessons it needs to learn from its own history, and the people are in distress.

While all this talking is going on, the town crier suddenly appears from the west and yells, "Good people of Niarela, the Commander of the two River Banks is here!"

The crowd splits to let him pass.

He is tall and his garments are stitched with gold and silver thread. An indomitable being, he radiates strength and absolute freedom. He is completely motionless, not facing the dumbstruck crowd head-on, but at an oblique angle. Like a hurricane, he is alone with himself. His eyes are riveted upon everyone, yet seeing no one, and he appears to be dancing while keeping his body perfectly still. After letting his gaze wander back and forth over the crowd for a long time, he turns to the four corners of the horizon, one after the other, holding his hands stretched out toward the sun. Then, having lowered his right knee to the ground, he takes a handful of sand and brings it up to his mouth, standing up at the same time.

His lips are moving slowly, almost imperceptibly.

When he has finished his incantations, he lifts his head, surveying the crowd once more. He walks up to an old woman and leads her into the middle of the circle. Opening his fist, he says to her, "Take this, Mama. I am giving it to you with a pure heart. Bad luck will never enter your house again. None of your family and friends will ever suffer hunger or thirst again."

■　　■　　■

That's how Ali Kaboye appeared to us, one Monday in midmorning. It was a day unlike any other.

We heard someone say, in amazement, "There can be no doubt. God is the Greatest!"

This last story, Badou, is not an eyewitness report. I wasn't part of the crowd that was waiting for Ali Kaboye. I did not see the town crier broadcasting his message up and down the streets of Niarela. Nor did I hear the sarcastic comments made by nameless voices about Daaw Demba, the cruel Damel of Cayor.

I was flat on my back with a fever when Ali Kaboye returned to take possession of Niarela once more.

Farewell, Badou.

No story is ever entirely finished. And what I also believe is that no human life ever ends at the right time. I entrust you to Ali Kaboye. He will take better care of you than anyone else in the world.

PART 2

I, ALI KABOYE

Shame on the nation that is deaf to its own madness.

Am barke àggul ci di def lu ñu dul wax
Defkat bu dee def waxkat it ma ngay wax.
Oh my Master, there is a limit to your power and that's my liberty!
If you want me to keep my mouth shut, be righteous.
Do nothing that I might want to denounce.

—*Seriñ Musaa Ka*

NGUIRANE FAYE TOLD YOU THIS BEFORE HE LEFT US: NO STORY IS EVER finished. That's how it will be with the war between Niarela and myself, Ali Kaboye.

Yesterday, I transformed myself into an ant, and I clung to the ankle of a man who was walking down the street. He was with a friend, and I heard him complaining about his wife, a certain Ndoumbé. "Ah! Ndoumbé and you!" said his companion.

"Women! If only I could understand them!" said the first one. "Ndoumbé wants us to move far away from Niarela. She's afraid, she says."

"Afraid? What is she afraid of, Tidiane?"

Tidiane, as he was called, hesitated briefly—he may have been embarrassed to let such a shocking thing escape from his mouth—and then he explained: "She says Ali Kaboye is coming back . . ."

At that point, the other one started laughing out loud. "Are you out of your mind, Tidiane? You must be just about the only inhabitant of Niarela who hasn't heard about the imminent return of Ali Kaboye!"

"Does that mean it's true?"

"As true, Tidiane, as the day is born and then dies immediately after the sun has set! One day, they say, the town crier will beat his drum, and a man will appear."

"It will be him . . ."

"It'll be Ali Kaboye."

"God Almighty!"

"They also say that by then, he will have lived among us for years in secret."

"What's that you are telling me there?"

"I am only telling you what I have heard, Tidiane."

Then Tidiane exclaimed, as if talking to despair itself, "And I was so sure that Ali Kaboye story was finally over!"

"It is written that Niarela will never be finished with Ali Kaboye."

There you have a man who has understood everything, Badou.

As far as you are concerned, good and generous Nguirane Faye, may you rest in peace. You have never known what it means to tell a lie. And here in Niarela, you were alone in that.

Each and every day, my prayers will rise up to heaven for you.

■   ■   ■

What a spectacle I witnessed today, as I was walking round a narrow street corner, Badou! I am still shaken by it. I encountered a group of proud and joyful young men who had their hair braided in the traditional style and were wearing long beaded necklaces and copper bracelets. Everything about them radiated vigor. Their gait was supple and resolute, reminiscent of the *ceddo* of old going to war. And I, Ali Kaboye, stared at them in amazement, since the gestures and the gaze of each one of them said to me, *I am African, I am black, and, no matter what anybody might say, that's the most marvelous thing in the world.*

Yes, it was Cheikh Anta Diop who taught us to look at ourselves in the mirror without shame. And, people of Niarela, I was certainly deeply touched by so much energy in motion, but I have to confess that something in this story troubled me very deeply. If you want to know what that was, ask me, people of Niarela, and I will tell you.

"We are asking you, Ali. What was it that troubled you?"

Seeing those young black men having to imitate themselves in order to avoid being confused with anybody else. Isn't it terrible, this fear that forces us to reproduce the same thing over and over again? Do we really have to agree to die before we can have a hope of survival?

Oh, all you scholars with your endless colloquiums and conferences, please ask those young men I came across just now these very simple questions: "What are you afraid of, my sons? Why all this mimicry, why are you copying yourselves?"

■　　■　　■

Patrice Lumumba.

This isn't the way you put a Li'l king in his place. After a century under the whip, what do we say, Patrice? *Yes Saah. No Saah.* We've cut off their heads. Their hands. Torn out guts. And their testicles were lying scattered all over the banks of the Congo. In terms of importance one might say it was roughly comparable to a few fish bones floating on the water. And you have the insolence to insult our king under the pretext of independence. That'll cost you. I'm sure you know that photograph of Lumumba with his hands tied behind his back, Badou, you see it everywhere. One soldier has grabbed him by the hair, two or three others are kicking him and some more are shouting abuse at him. His white shirt is in shreds, and he looks so terribly fragile. Yes, that's him, literally tossed to the dogs in the street. One should always look at this picture together with its counterpart: the Li'l king listening to the unauthorized speech of the Congolese prime minister. Baudouin's pale face side by side with the face of the Insolent One who is being tortured in broad daylight in an army van. Neither of these two pictures makes sense without the other one: the crime of lèse-majesté and its punishment. The point here is not to humiliate the Congolese prime minister but to settle the score on behalf of the Belgian king. Wiping out Lumumba at some discreet location by lodging two bullets in the back of his neck would have been pretty much standard procedure in those days, but that simply wasn't enough. An example had to be set that would make the whole world sit up and take note. So the man is sliced in half, right down the middle they say, but that's still fiercely debated even now—some of our historians support the view that, alas, it was a far less methodical kind of butchery. Then the body is cut up into smaller pieces. And even smaller ones after that. All of this gets dropped into a barrel of sulfuric acid and for several hours, the Belgian police commissioner Gérard Soete and his brother keep watch. They are perched on the rim of the barrel, their eyes riveted on the seething flesh. They go and have a smoke in the garden, they return, exasperated at how long this cooking process takes, damn it to hell, this big black body's takin' its bloody time to dissolve into nothingness, wouldn't you say?

Oh, and before I forget: Gérard Soete made sure he dislodged two teeth from Patrice Lumumba's carcass, wrapped them carefully in his handkerchief and pushed the whole thing deep into his pocket. His grandchildren back in Bruges had the right to find out one day how those blacks in the Congo were taught manners.

Your Highness, your revenge was terrible.

■　　■　　■

That just happened yesterday, Badou Tall, on January 17, 1961, to be precise, in the Republic of Congo. Every radio station I have listened to this morning talks about it. But the news stories of the world never reach Niarela, and so its inhabitants don't know what's going on. I always knew they were wimps, but not to this extent. Don't they make you feel sorry for them? Well then, let me tell them this story, and none of them will be able to say anymore that they didn't know.

■　　■　　■

The puppet on duty is called Joseph-Désiré Mobutu. They say he is a CIA operative. He never let Lumumba out of his sight for a single second, since the Americans were out to get him as well. The poor man really had absolutely no chance of escaping his fate. A communist in a country that's bankrupt, that may still pass. But with all those diamonds, the cobalt, those tons and tons of copper and uranium, it simply wasn't a good idea to be in the wrong camp. And besides, Sir, there was the little question of manners. You do not speak to our king without his permission. We'll kill you with our very own hands if you do, and in addition we'll make sure you lose your right to a cozy little grave. I'm terribly sorry about all of this, but you have been asking for it. A captive who has barely been released from his shackles should not be so cocky.

It was ritual murder, Badou, that's what it was.

And now Joseph-Désiré Mobutu is waiting for his reward. He will be generous toward his benefactors. They'll have everything they could possibly wish for as long as he can step out of the clouds on TV every night, carrying his diamond-studded walking stick and wearing his trademark leopard-skin cap.

Cries of rage fill the air from Conakry to Belgrade.

People of Niarela, I want you to know that the city of Dakar is doing its bit. I am just back from the university. Thousands of demonstrators were marching past me on the Ouakam road, brandishing the Congolese flag and huge photographs of Lumumba. What are you waiting for, why aren't you joining them, people of Niarela? I know, I know—you are telling yourselves that all he had to do was to keep his mouth shut, Lumumba, since this is what happens to a black man who oversteps the mark.

You are spitting your venom.

He was just playing the hero, you think. Too bad for him.

That's what happens when an egg bashes its head against an iron door!

That's how Wolof Njaay puts it. And then there are all those demagogues who never stop talking about the cruelty of white people. The thing is that actually they are no more evil than a lot of other people, these whites. But how could anybody be so ill-mannered? It's really an unfortunate breach of etiquette, or of protocol, if you like, this Lumumba affair. That's all it is, at the end of the day. In my opinion, our hero missed a brilliant chance there to sort out his own personal affairs. It's so seldom that you have the opportunity to rub shoulders with these monarchs with plenty of diamonds stuck to their skulls. So when you do, why not make the most of it, there's no need to be ashamed. I personally would have been quite straightforward with my request, at any rate. *Baudouin, Your Highness, I love Agatha, I want to marry her, the problem is just I'm totally broke, so could you perhaps help me out a little bit, yes I know, Your Majesty, she'll be my third wife, that means it's not very Catholic, this whole story, but don't forget, please, we're Muslims here in Niarela.* He would have smiled discreetly, the king, because it's quite funny—don't you think?—to go and talk to him just like that about Agatha, my fiancée, and the religious strife around here, on the very day of our independence.

People of Niarela, does he who has spoken these words deserve to be called a human being?

Badou, they are tied to their shackles on the edge of a precipice. They are trapped inside a ring of fire. They are afraid of being reduced to ashes, and they are afraid of making the slightest move to escape from the flames. So they just stay sitting where they are, with death staring them in the face from every direction, mesmerized and waiting to get swallowed up by the abyss.

The reason they hate Lumumba: they had to get off the fence and take sides in all this madness.

■   ■   ■

Guns for you. Guns for your enemies. At my third whistle-blow, Fire! Let the best man win. But this one will never lose. He is a bit stingy, and you beg him to give you a little something extra, let's say a dozen mirrors or three pearl necklaces. After a bit of haggling, you always manage to strike a deal in the end. Your people are swallowed up into the belly of an ancient ship and then your land is gone too, leaving nothing but a cloud of black smoke above the sea.

Wow, the night was hot, my friends. I screwed the lot of them, whether or not they were virgins, ripe or still green, I didn't give a damn.

When you wake up, noble Prince, you won't be drunk anymore, you'll just have a hangover. Your latrines stink of pork liver pâté and heaven knows what kind of brandy.

It's hard to believe how you're just shitting and pissing away the centuries that make up our destiny.

■   ■   ■

I fell asleep a bit earlier than normal. Toward eleven o'clock, I felt someone tapping me on the shoulder. I blinked. Somebody was bending over me, murmuring in an almost inaudible voice:

"Ali . . . Ali . . ."

The man was visibly afraid of being seen, even by a perfectly harmless nightwalker, for example.

"Who are you?" I asked.

"Are you trying to say you don't recognize me anymore, Ali?"

"No, I don't," I replied. "What do you want from me?"

I'd had a difficult day and was not in a very conciliatory mood.

"It's me, Daour," said the stranger.

"Daour? Which Daour?"

"President Daour Diagne, your friend."

I wasn't fully awake yet, but I noticed a whiff of disappointment in his voice. With a harshness I myself found surprising, I replied, "I don't have any friends! Leave me in peace! I, Ali Kaboye, have neither friends nor family. Leave me in peace."

These words were followed by an oppressive silence. He went outside to wait for me by the entrance of the shack. I had upset him, and there was tension in the air, believe me. I suddenly feared for my life, and that made me feel wide awake. I got up, more out of caution than out of hospitality.

When I pushed the curtain aside, I saw Daour Diagne standing under the streetlight. It wasn't the first time he had woken me up like this in the middle of the night. For a few seconds, he looked at me gravely. There was no need for him to try quite so hard to make me change my mind. I have to confess that I was beginning to get worried. How could I so easily forget that Daour Diagne was the president of the Republic, meaning that I, together with all the other citizens of our country, was at his mercy? He was perfectly at liberty to lodge a couple of bullets in my head that very instant if he felt like it and calmly continue on his evening promenade as if nothing had happened. And then there was another thing that I was very sure about: unlike Captain Baye Ndéné and all my other assassins, Daour Diagne and his ilk never miss their target. It's people like them who really put the fear of God into us vagrant lunatics.

No use pretending that nothing stops us in our tracks, it's not true. You will never see us loitering near a house that is guarded by a pack of dogs.

Yes, yes, Wolof Njaay—who is not very fond of us, by the way—often talks a lot of nonsense. But in this particular instance I agree with him wholeheartedly: no matter where we are in the world, we lunatics always have to be wary of the president of the country. It may well happen that we are walking past the presidential palace one day, thinking—with legitimate pride—of the one person from our midst who showed himself to be very deserving, so deserving in fact, that he is now exercising the highest office, as they call it. You cannot imagine, in fact, how hard it is for the likes of us to be recognized for who we really are! A lunatic, no matter how intelligent, has to overcome a number of stubborn prejudices if he wants to persuade an entire nation that he is their most able son. And yet, it does happen, it even happens quite often, and that's why, thank the Lord, the world often manages to avoid being ruled by those who think they are gifted with reason. Observe them carefully, one after the other, our current Masters of the Universe. They're almost always slightly deranged. You can see it in their eyes: that deep sense of loneliness combined with a glint of madness.

"I am coming, Daour!" I said, still slightly confused.

"Don't keep me waiting," he replied curtly.

The president's voice suddenly sounded a lot less benevolent and chummy.

What a strange life I was leading! If we were schoolboys in a playground, I would say you can call me President Daour Diagne's whipping boy! Does he really think someone in my situation should be denied every bit of rest? He loves dragging me out of bed in the middle of the night to give me the same lecture over and over again. "Ali, I'm lost. As you know, I have had to fight fierce battles for many years to get to the top of this country. I was the one who kicked out the whites, our oppressors! My people trusted me, but look at me now: I am completely lost. I would never have thought this could be so difficult. I really, really need your help. What should I do, Ali? Tell me, and I will follow your advice."

At times like that, I feel sorry for Daour Diagne, and I am very frank with him. "Listen Daour, the entire country can see we're drifting like a rudderless ship on the open sea. Sometimes it even looks dangerously lopsided. You have no idea where you are taking us, Daour, and we are going to end up in deep trouble. This is what you should do: make an appearance on television and tell our people you underestimated the problems you're facing and that you have decided to resign, because you are not able to help any of us lead happier lives. Do the honest thing and say to the people: thank you for electing me, I have tried my best, but heavens it's hard! Daour Diagne, call the journalists and tell them that! I know it's not easy, but the fate that awaits us otherwise is a lot worse."

This kind of advice is bound to get him rattled. It brings out the wild beast in him, and he erupts, "Aa-li! Aa-li Kaboye! It's obvious you are stark raving mad! Do you want my guys to kill me, is that what you want?"

Now and again he stops his tirade, eyes me suspiciously, and pretends he is joking. "Do you perhaps want me dead, like the rest of them?"

"No I don't, but you asked my advice, and I have given it to you, as a friend."

That helps to calm him down. "Yes, you're the only one who doesn't lie to me, Ali, and that's why I like talking to you. But please understand: I'm lost. During the day, I am proudly at the helm of the ship, scanning the horizon with my binoculars, and I see airports, broad-gauge railways and all the rest coming to me. I galvanize this nation of idlers into action, I make them move forward. Do you think I can ever allow myself a moment's hesitation? If I did, this country would go to rack and ruin literally overnight!"

"Do not speak of bad luck, Daour! This country of yours is of no use to me, but I don't want to see it collapse. May God prevent that from happening! Right now, Daour Diagne, my friend, you should go and rest; you have a long, hard day ahead of you tomorrow. Return to your palace and let me go back to sleep."

"Sleep? Surely you're not thinking of sleep, Ali!"

"What do you mean, Daour?"

"I am trying to find the right path to follow, Ali. I need you to guide my steps. I am surrounded by people who are incompetent, depraved and corrupt. They're pigs and I cannot prevent them from wallowing in the mud. Please don't let me down, Ali . . . I trust your wisdom."

When Daour talks to me like that, I can read his innermost thoughts. I can almost hear the words bounce off the inside of his skull. He says to himself, "Those lunatics, they're the only ones who know *the* way." That's not true, of course, and we have a good laugh about it when we meet up among ourselves, by the way. If we did know the way, we wouldn't be wandering aimlessly around the city all the time, don't you see. But we let them talk, it flatters our vanity a bit. We're also human, after all, we have our little foibles.

This, in brief, is what my impromptu late-night audiences with President Diagne are normally like.

Tonight, though, everything is different: for once, Daour Diagne hasn't come to solicit my advice. He seems excited and in a very good mood. I think he is even a little bit tipsy. We get into his unmarked Volvo 240 and go for a drive, and he doesn't stop waffling and talking utter nonsense, good old Daour.

After a quick tour around the sleeping city, he makes a sweeping gesture with his right hand, pointing at what lies before him, and says in a peculiar way, "Take a good look around you, Ali. Do you see that tarred road over there, those trees, these houses, and the pieces of paper you see fluttering in the wind? Can you see all that, Ali?"

"Yes, Daour. Why do you ask me that?"

"Listen to me carefully now, Ali. Everything I have just mentioned, but also the ships on the sea, the football stadiums and the hotels, all this belongs to me, since this entire country is mine."

When he says this, his voice sounds calm and full of wonder, but I can sense his agitation. A cat came out of a house and tried to cross the road. Daour

Diagne could easily have avoided it, but he pushed it against the edge of the pavement and shouted, as he was running it over: "Meow! That's the end of you, little motherfucker of a pussycat!" I looked at Daour out of the corner of my eye, thinking that things were clearly getting worse, but I didn't dare to make a comment. On the contrary, I pretended to take him seriously. "So all this is yours, president?"

"Yes, Ali. I, Daour Diagne, am a natural-born leader, and if you knew my family background, you would understand why."

We may well have been driving around for six or seven hours without a clear destination. I remember us passing the El-Hadj cinema in Gueule-Tapée several times. Very near there, Daour showed me the house where he used to go for Koranic studies when he was five or six years old. Then he drove on to the Corniche, turned left, and continued toward the Plateau district.

"Where are we going?" I asked.

Even after I asked him that question, my voice kept trembling, so afraid was I of what I was going to hear. Full of mischief, he replied, "To the palace, of course."

"Which palace, Daour?"

"Listen, Ali, my house is your house. You're my friend, aren't you? Let's go and help ourselves to a decent bit of breakfast, and then I'll have you dropped off in Niarela."

My heart was racing and I called out: "I'm not hungry, Daour. I'm really not the slightest bit hungry!"

He pretended he hadn't heard me. I thought my last hour had arrived, and with sadness in my heart I saw the images of my adolescence in the small village of Ndimboye, near the Forest of Kagne, coming back to me. This was the first time Daour Diagne had invited me into his palace. "That's very fishy," I thought. I remembered all those dreadful human sacrifices. They're terrible, those witchdoctors. When a powerful person goes to see them, they only have one thing to say: slit the throat of a vagrant lunatic during full moon, extract all his blood, boil it at a very high temperature with some honey and herbs, drink seven large glasses of that, and wash your face with what's left over, facing south or whichever direction you like. I swear, that's all they ever say, these charlatans.

And that makes us incredibly insecure, you know. Luckily, we, the vagrant lunatics in this city, know each other very well, and news spread fast in our circles. Our children know, for example, that it's dangerous to loiter in the streets near election time. We take this kind of thing very seriously.

Those were my thoughts while Daour Diagne was parking the car. He then said, "Here we are, Ali."

He saw me flinch, and smiled. "You seem preoccupied, my friend."

"Daour, a palace isn't really the place for me. In the name of our old friendship, please let me go back to Niarela."

That's when his mouth became distorted in a sudden fit of rage and he roared, "Am I your president or am I not?"

"Yes, Daour, we only have one president in this country and that's you."

"Well then, Ali Kaboye, get out of this car! This is an order from your president, who happens to be me!"

The breakfast wasn't bad, I have to say.

Perfectly trained servants came and tiptoed around us juggling platters of cheese, pastries, liver pâté, all sorts of juices—orange, strawberry, pineapple and grapefruit; then there was yogurt, different types of jam, smoked ham, scrambled and boiled eggs, and, last but not least, all those lackeys who were incessantly running around us, surreptitiously looking me up and down, pretending not to see me, and cooing "A little more coffee, Sir?" or "Still without milk, Sir?". I don't often get the chance to eat as much as I like, and I sure took advantage of that mountain of food.

"Long live the president!" I joked, punctuating my remark with a loud burp.

Daour Diagne wanted to say something, but his mouth was too full. So without giving him enough time to recover his freedom of expression, I continued, "Daour, you never stop complaining about being president, but I am telling you—and I should know!—a meal like this every morning is worth all those sacrifices!"

He burst out laughing. Daour Diagne loves to hear me tease him like this about the imaginary hardships of his position. He knows perfectly well I'm not a fool.

And there wasn't only food to eat, Badou.

Throughout our breakfast, a brass band was playing. Every now and then, the soldiers stopped to click their heels and growl two or three sentences while lifting one hand up to their temple in a rather comical salutation. Their boss, a corpulent officer in ceremonial dress, seemed quite interested in me. Initially, I didn't pay much attention to him. There are times when ordinary people like him—the waiters at a cocktail bar, street musicians or inspectors on the train—just form part of the decor, and one isn't even aware of the fact that one doesn't see them. That's pretty much how it was with this brass band. I was listening to Daour Diagne telling me juicy anecdotes about foreign heads of state. Some of these foreign presidents—I promised Daour Diagne not to leak any names, Badou—are of an unbelievable stupidity. I don't know why, but every time I took my eyes off Daour Diagne, I noticed that the officer was looking at me intently.

I stared back at him and after a few seconds, I heard myself murmuring: "Captain Baye Ndéné . . ."

Daour Diagne—not even the smallest movement or gesture among his entourage ever escaped him—had seen everything. He said, "Well, well, well! Do you perhaps know each other, Colonel Camara and you?"

"For us folk from Niarela, he will always be Captain Baye Ndéné, even after he's been promoted by you!" I said cheerfully.

Captain Baye Ndéné tried to speak to me, but he could not move his lips; not a single sound escaped from them. I suppose he simply wanted to say hello to me, but that proved much more difficult than expected.

I teased him, as you do when you bump into an old pal you haven't seen in many years. "Bloody hell, it's you, Baye Ndéné! Who would have guessed our paths would cross right here, at my friend Daour Diagne's place!"

He was still as dumbfounded as before, incapable of getting a single word out.

I casually turned round to Daour Diagne. "He's not a bad chap, your Baye Ndéné, but what a nasty temper he has, that fellow! If you want my advice, Daour, beware of offending the Colonel. Otherwise he might just decide to stroke your pretty bald skull with a broken bottle!"

"Watch out, Ali! If you don't stop dragging my colleagues through the mud, I'll have you locked up immediately," Daour Diagne said jokingly.

Well, right there and then and without any further ado, I started singing my song about the Warrior, that bloke whose belly was full of shit and who had so, so much of it in his interminable intestines that wherever he went, he left a wonderful smell, oh my God, how pleasant it was, the smell given off by the Warrior's anus that filled the air all around him! Baye Ndéné didn't know what to do with himself anymore. I asked him to join in the singing. He complied with alacrity. He looked as if his head was about to burst, and I found that madly amusing. I started clapping my hands, and, with a quick, nervous gesture, he ordered the band to play along. The cooks were tapping on plates with knives and forks and in the end, everybody was shouting and dancing around the banqueting hall with sweeping, boisterous steps.

Sadly we had to end the festivities after an hour. Daour Diagne asked us to accept his apologies—unfortunately, he had this millstone of a bloody country around his neck.

Before getting ready to go back to Niarela, I did something I still cannot understand to this day. I went up to Baye Ndéné and held out my hand to him with a friendly smile. He embraced me. Then he put his head on my right shoulder and burst into sobs.

■   ■   ■

One sunrise in the year 1619, in the Cayor, we, the grandees of the kingdom, are seated in a circle around a huge hole, dug out the previous day at the Damel's behest.

With his familiar, slightly rasping voice, the Damel says, "The Cayor, that's you, and you alone. Therefore you understand the significance of this meeting."

Of course we understand. The gathering is so secret we are not even allowed to look at each other. Our words die and fall into the hole where they will soon be buried forever.

Twittering birds flutter from tree to tree. They make the branches of the tamarind trees quiver, and the dew drops feel cool and refreshing.

The Damel continues, "If any one of you sees me batting an eyelid, he will know what he has to do if he is a man of honor."

Not one of us lifts his head or opens his mouth.

He says: "My patience is running out! You are all aware of the difficult decision I have to take. Our people's destiny is at stake, you are aware of that, too. I am planning to take action by sunset. I expect each one of you to tell me his opinion. Without you, this kingdom is nothing."

At that precise moment, I feel someone pulling the sleeve of my boubou, murmuring: "Ali . . ."

I discretely turn my head toward my neighbor.

It's Kocc Barma Fall.

An odd fish, this Kocc.

There is only one way to describe him: impossible to pin down. He looks at you with his small, inquisitive eyes and his mischievous smile jumbles up all your emotions, a smile that always seems to say, *I see right through you, you can't lie to me.* The truth is that nobody ever really feels at ease with him. You can tell it's him from a mile away, because he is so tall and incredibly thin. He pokes his nose into everything, especially when it's none of his business. Had I known he was coming to sit next to me, I quietly would have traded places. The day is not far off when this Kocc Barma fellow will be strung up on the gallows and his body tossed to the wild beasts; I definitely don't want that to happen to me. Surely I must be allowed to live my modest little life in peace. Challenging the overlords is his favorite pastime. When there is an audience at the court of the Damel, Kocc Barma always waits until the last moment before getting up to speak. We all listen to him with bated breath, because even the smartest among us never know what he is going to say. In fact, his general formula seems to be: I disagree with everything I have just heard, including what came out of the Damel's very own mouth! That is the true extent of Kocc Barma Fall's recklessness. He makes no distinction whatsoever between the Damel himself and me, Ali Kaboye, a simple dignitary of the Cayor.

Moreover, neither his words nor his deeds are ever straightforward. Everyone is wondering why he has kept his right fist permanently closed for years. Only recently did he deign to reveal to us at last that he was clasping nine monkey-bread seeds in his hand. So we immediately showered him with questions: Why precisely nine seeds? And why not corn or sorghum, for that matter? We got evasive answers that sparked off a thousand new questions with even more enigmatic responses and so on and so forth, ad infinitum. In the end, we begged him to stop explaining things to us.

The fact that a man like him should spend his time pouring scorn on the Damel will astonish no one. But when I turned round, I saw him pointing at our sovereign with a shockingly bold and provocative gesture. It almost made my heart stop.

And yet, I can't help being impressed by Kocc. He is so unlike the rest of us who never stop fussing and worrying about the interminable wars between Mboul, Lambaye and Nguiguiss. That man stems from a different era, I'm convinced of it. I am sure a few centuries from now, Kocc Barma Fall will still be remembered in the Cayor and people will extol his knowledge and foresight. And even if his words often strike us as outlandish and ludicrous at first, at the end of the day the facts nearly always prove him more or less right. All in all, you can accuse Kocc Barma Fall of just about anything, except hollow verbiage. For example, I remember the day when he arrived at the court of the Damel with his four tufts of hair. We had never seen such a hairstyle before and nearly killed ourselves laughing. We were certain he'd gone completely bonkers and that the Damel would cast him out into the forest.

The Damel asked him, "Kocc, what is the matter with you?"

Kocc Barma pretended to be surprised. "Why are you asking me that question, Damel?"

"What is the significance of your hairdo?"

"Is it my four tufts of hair you want to talk about?"

"Yes. What is the meaning of these four tufts of hair?"

"I have absolutely no idea, Damel. But if you insist, I can reveal to you what each one of these four tufts of hair is about."

"Are you properly aware of the risk you are taking, Kocc?"

"At nightfall, the hyenas and jackals will be fighting over my corpse in the forest."

"All right then, talk. Tell us what each one of those four tufts signifies."

Kocc smiled. Not only did he have the courage to lie to the Damel in public that day, but he also baffled us with his mind-blowing trickery. Today, more than ten years later, the Cayor still hasn't stopped talking about it.

With the dew dripping on us, we, the grandees of the kingdom, sat there that morning, listening to the Damel. We advised him on how to deal with the dangers threatening the Cayor. The words we spoke had no sooner slipped out of our mouths than they suffocated and died at the bottom of the hole. We covered them with sand. They will never be spoken again. The security of the kingdom dictates it.

Only one of us refused to participate in that ritual burial. Kocc Barma Fall.

On the way home, I expressed my amazement about this. "I didn't see you throw a single grain of sand into the hole when we were closing it up."

He seemed amused. "You didn't see me doing it, Ali, because I did not do it. What's so complicated about that?"

I realized he was about to embark on one of his famous little acts of intellectual acrobatics again, but I stopped him by going straight to the heart of the matter. "And why didn't you do what the rest of us did?"

"Because I didn't feel like it. When will you at last understand, Ali, that I only have one master, and his name is Kocc Barma Fall?"

To me, this was definite proof that this guy had lost his wits, and I should rather not appear in his company too often. But I was fond of him, and so I warned him, "You are playing with your life, Kocc . . . Since all that trouble started last year the Damel sees traitors everywhere. Why expose yourself to so much danger?"

His eyes sparkled with mischief. "Yes, he looks at me very strangely, your Damel. I suppose he thinks I am interested in his throne."

He didn't, on the other hand, seem very keen to find out what the Damel really thought of him.

This alarmed me. "If you actually believe that, then what are you still doing here? Surely you should hurry up and leave the Cayor before it's too late, shouldn't you?"

He burst out laughing, making it crystal-clear that he took me for a coward.

He then opened his hand, made me admire his nine monkey-bread seeds and offered me one of them.

I took the seed. When I looked up, he had vanished.

■　　■　　■

Even if you have never set foot there you must surely have heard about the Forest of Kagne. A traveler on the highway from Dakar to Thiès can just about make out its contours in the distance, either dark or milky white, depending on the season. He may even have a few vague memories of a local Robin Hood who simply called himself Kagne, and who during the era of the *Toubabs* imposed his own rules there—harsh but just. You might say that Ndimboye, my native village, was within his jurisdiction. People's views about Kagne are so contradictory that now, sixty years later, it's very hard to decide whether he really "took from the rich and gave to the poor" or whether he was just an ordinary highwayman. But for those of us who grew up in the shadow of this rebel, our fascination—encapsulated in the two words *Àllu Kaañ*—remains alive to this day. The ups and downs of his hard, lonely battle against the colonial powers form an integral part of my childhood. My story has many twists and turns, that's true, but that notwithstanding, I may well come back to this intrepid and magnanimous outlaw's exploits one day, should I feel so inclined.

Right now, though, I want to tell you what happened to a mirror in 1940 or thereabouts. Yes, it's a mirror I am talking about, a gigantic mirror that was put up in the heart of *Àllu Kaañ* the Forest of Kagne. All the details are verifiable and can be traced back to the year 1940, although they may well remind you of our legends from the earliest days of the world, when it was quite natural for a storyteller to make men walk on water or split a mountain with a single blow of their sword. Despite the fact that it has an important place there, the mirror is definitely not the only hero in my story. The railway line Dakar–Saint-Louis equally plays a very significant role, just like a certain André Castorel, the Thiès District Commander in those days. A fourth character completes the picture, but I prefer to keep him under wraps for the time being.

I was barely an adolescent when it all happened. Although I don't remember my exact age at the time, I cannot have been much more than ten years old.

It starts on a day like any other.

My playmates and I were roaming around the Forest of Kagne. We loved picking jujubes and cashew nuts and munching ripe mangoes straight off the tree, but our absolute favorite was hunting lizards and turtledoves with our slingshots.

That morning, one of us, Mbita Sarr, looked up into the trees, paying careful attention to the twittering of the birds. With a peculiar expression, he said: "Do you hear what I'm hearing?"

"What are you talking about, Mbita?"

"Strangers are on their way to Ndimboye. They're coming from Thiès."

We kept our eyes peeled for a moment, looking nervously around us. Then, a reddish dust cloud appeared on the horizon. A few seconds later we could hear the patter of horses' hooves on the dirt road to our left. They were getting closer.

Ndimboye in those days lived in constant fear of a surprise enemy attack.

I made a suggestion to my comrades. "Let's take the shortcut across the ravine so that we get back to Ndimboye ahead of those men on horseback!"

I got no reply, and that was because our group had a leader: Mbita Sarr. We hadn't elected Mbita Sarr, but he was our leader nevertheless. It always works like that with a gang of boys; when a big decision has to be made, everyone looks to one and the same person. So without wanting to admit it, we were waiting for Mbita Sarr's reaction.

He said, "No need to get so agitated about things, Ali. It's odd, but you don't seem to be able to keep your cool, my boy."

Hearing that, I felt humiliated, and I shot back, "And you, Mbita, you can't always pretend you know everything. I myself am determined to prevent those strangers from attacking Ndimboye!"

Mbita Sarr shook his head with an amused little smile. "Why are you such an idiot, Ali? Ndimboye has nothing to fear from those two men. One of these riders is the District Commander, the *Toubab* who is based in Thiès. I have forgotten his name, but I know he is with Baye Sèye, the interpreter who accompanies him wherever he goes. Let's go and hide."

We all climbed up into the trees. A few minutes later, the two travelers were riding past us below.

Incredible as it may seem, but Mbita Sarr was right again. André Castorel, the District Commander from Thiès. Baye Sèye, his interpreter. As inseparable as a man and his shadow. Two or three hundred meters away from us, they dismounted from their horses and tied them up near a mahogany tree, presumably to take a short rest before continuing on their way to Ndimboye.

Abou Sow turned to Mbita and said with admiration, "Are you an ordinary mortal like the rest of us, Mbita Sarr?" It was not the first time Mbita Sarr, with that prodigious intuition of his, had made us think he belonged to a different world from ours and that he was maybe in contact with supernatural, invisible forces. Mbita Sarr was still very young when he drowned in the Lake of Jooral, by the way, and his premature death somehow confirmed these suspicions. It seems an established fact that highly gifted adolescents like him never live long. On his way back from the cemetery, an old man said sadly, "Every day of my life I have spent praying for that boy, so he wouldn't be taken from us. But all was in vain, because that boy . . . they really wanted him."

We were still very young, but we understood perfectly why our friend Mbita Sarr would never hunt squirrels and shrews with us again.

But let's turn back to Commander Castorel and his interpreter. They had just arrived in Ndimboye. We ran after them, shouting as loudly as we could, "Long live the Commander! Long live the Commander! Com-man-der! Com-man-der!"

Everyone in Ndimboye knew that the arrival of the *Toubab* commander in a village was never a good omen.

André Castorel locked himself away with our village chief and the longer it took, the more worried everybody's faces became. I was eavesdropping on the adults' conversations and they were all wondering whether the *Toubab* had come, as usual, to talk about his famous Dakar–Saint-Louis railway line again, or whether he had even more sinister accusations in store for Ndimboye.

A little later, Mandiaye, the town crier, started doing the village rounds, with his drum on his hip. "People of Ndimboye, I salute you with my words of peace! Our chief has asked me to let it be known that the Thiès District Commander, Monsieur André Castorel, is ordering you to come and assemble in the Meeting Square! Old and young, men and women, people of Ndimboye, I salute you with my words of peace!"

The moment the town crier had got to the end of his village tour, there was a vague sense of relief. From certain subtle inflections in Mandiaye's voice we could tell that the topic of the day was still the Dakar–Saint-Louis railway line. That meant no beatings, no incarcerations in Thiès, and no one was going to be shot by the spahis on account of those common, extremely tedious tax-related incidents.

But still, a certain anxiety continued to hover in the air. We knew that all the *Toubabs* were at the end of their tether about this railway saga. If there was one thing they loved, it was definitely this long black thing that looks like a caterpillar. The fact is, they have crossed oceans and killed thousands of us solely to be able to hear the train whistling in the savanna, marvel at its smoke rising up over Mékhé or Sakal, and then go back home to France! At any rate, the repeated acts of sabotage on the line between Dakar and Saint-Louis infuriated them. This had been going on for almost two years now, and the scenario was always the same: the railway workers carried out their repairs during the day and by the following morning, everything had been ripped up and smashed to pieces again. Nobody knew who the perpetrators were. There had to be a large number of them and they had to be very strong. You should have seen the terrified expression on the faces of Castorel's workers every morning. Screaming and shouting, the Commander would slap their faces, threatening to kill them. It really was total chaos, that's what it was. And we in Ndimboye were afraid the *Toubabs* would accuse us of being in cahoots with their enemies.

∎   ∎   ∎

At the appointed hour of the meeting, our chief and the top dignitaries of Ndimboye took their seats, flanking Castorel. I noticed how some of them were surreptitiously trying to get as close to the Commander as possible. He was dressed in a jacket and matching khaki colored shorts, but most striking to me were his helmet and his clogs. Making no secret of the fact that he was already fed up with being there, he was distractedly tapping his thigh with his short bull's pizzle.

Being young doesn't mean you shouldn't keep your eyes open. Nothing was known about this short white man with his thin lips and steely gray eyes except that every time he paid a visit to Ndimboye, our relatives stopped being their normal selves. Our chief had never been particularly heroic, but on that day, he was even more nervous than the rest. All this was so painful to me and my childish heart that I wanted the proceedings to be over as quickly as possible. I wished the adults would stop being so pathetic.

Over time, I have managed to work out what happened, of course. I now have a fairly clear idea of Castorel's life story. After leaving home somewhere on the other side of the ocean, he embarked on a long, meandering journey before he ended up sitting right here in front of us in Ndimboye, almost like our Damel on his throne. He had raised armies against us and sowed death and destruction wherever he deemed it necessary to do so. He ruthlessly burned down villages, raped women and thrust his dagger into the chest of newborn infants. A century passed. Then another and yet another one. And now there we were, obediently lined up in front of him in the Meeting Square of Ndimboye, but the key issue had actually been decided centuries earlier. I have to say that I am still at a loss what to think of it. I frequently ask myself why your grandfather Nguirane—may his soul rest in peace!—reproached Castorel for having crushed us with his army. Can one reasonably expect the conqueror to apologize for having achieved his aim? There is no doubt that Commander Castorel acted with unspeakable cruelty, but in this business, Badou, the most abhorrent crimes pale in comparison to a small tactical blunder or a few potential scruples—highly improbable at any rate—that might stand in the way of subjecting the other to one's will. The fact is this: Castorel may be guilty of a thousand atrocities, but he did not commit any errors. And that's why Ndimboye is now at his beck and call.

In brief, the end point of Castorel's path coincided with the birth of the absolute present for us. Ndimboye's past, whether it was glorious or insignificant, has dissolved into thin air.

But do I have the right, I, Ali Kaboye, a penniless vagrant lunatic, to get embroiled in this story? It would be quite reckless of me to ask you to choose between Nguirane's opinion and mine. He, at least, was personally involved in bringing about the end of André Castorel's tyranny. Your grandfather was one of the people who demanded liberty by clamoring, "*Moom sa réew*!" You may remember how Castorel, who knew he was holding all the aces, exclaimed, looking down on us from his elevated position, "So it's independence you want, eh? What are you waiting for then, take it!" What that meant was, *We will see whether you, being who you are, have the guts to take control of your own destiny.* And you know what happened next, don't you: we did not have the guts.

Of course there was chanting and dancing for several years to come, and there was a lot of flexing of muscles and all that laudable enthusiasm about our imaginary tomorrows. Independence, blah, blah, blah! Beating his chest, Daour Diagne proudly proclaimed it was him and him alone who tossed André Castorel to the sharks. But once all the partying and reveling was over, life started becoming a bit of an uphill struggle. And, according to those in a position to know, this whole circus was in vain, because André Castorel, who is no longer either totally black or totally white, continues to prescribe the path we must follow from behind the scenes.

■　■　■

Ndimboye was waiting in silence under the scorching sun.

Commander Castorel let his eyes wander over the crowd and beckoned to his interpreter with a barely perceptible movement of his chin. Baye Sèye's posture, when standing in front of him, was humble and attentive at the same time. His hands were meekly folded at the level of his khaki jacket pockets. Castorel spent many minutes talking to him.

Then the interpreter turned to us. Initially, he spoke in measured tones, but soon his voice got louder, more jerky. After a few sentences, he was so worked up that he seemed angrier to us than the *Toubab* himself. What he said was that very generous white men had come from Castorel's country to build the railway and that bandits were destroying the tracks every night. "Who suffers the most from this situation?" he asked. "We know it perfectly well," he exclaimed with an anguished, dramatic gesture, "for since all this has started we have been deprived of fresh fish and all the good things the train used to bring us from Dakar and Saint-Louis. It is due to those evildoers that Ndimboye has remained such a god-forsaken little dump, ignored by the train of progress and civilization. It's an iniquity!" he thundered, and then he asked us to help the Commander fight our common enemy. He paused and scrutinized the audience, as if trying to read I-don't-know-what at the bottom of our souls, before going off on a completely different tangent. Having looked round the circle, he pointed his finger at each one of us and said, "Unless . . . unless . . ." deliberately leaving his unfinished sentence hanging in the air. He repeated "unless" several times, while moving from one group of people to the next. Finally, he erupted, "Unless it's you who are the Commander's enemies?" He shook his head and smiled, as if wanting to apologize for even contemplating such a monstrosity.

Proud of having made us face our responsibilities in this way, Baye Sèye wiped his forehead and went to sit down next to Castorel. The latter started talking to him for the second time. When he had finished, Baye Sèye walked into the middle of the circle again and baffled us greatly by repeatedly referring to the Damel Lat-Dior, who had died half a century earlier. "You need to know," he declared, "that he who thinks of nothing but destruction will always end up being destroyed himself. Where is he now, your Damel who said that Malaw, his thoroughbred, would never see the railway built by the whites with his own eyes? In Dékheulé, Malaw's blood tinged the earth red, while you are dead and forgotten by all, my poor old friend. Don't waste your time trying to convince me that you can reappear on the treetops of Kagne after having been reduced to dust in Dékheulé. Since you are so afraid of death, it's best if you stay quietly in your grave instead of sabotaging the work of our loyal railway workers!"

At the end of this, Baye Sèye was utterly exhausted. He had to catch his breath before he was able to ask us whether a man as generous as Castorel deserved so much ingratitude.

Just when he was asking this question, the chief jumped up from his seat, calling out to the interpreter, "Make it known to the white man that the railway sabotage pains us even more than him. We promise the day is not far off when we will bring him the heads of the perpetrators, impaled on the tips of our swords!"

Baye Sèye started translating for the Commander, but he had hardly pronounced the first few words when Castorel, seething with rage, looked like he was going to hit him with his bull's pizzle. The interpreter moved out of the way to dodge the blow, fell to the ground, and then yelled at the crowd as he was getting back up on his feet, "It's your fault that he is in this state, you dimwits!"

He then turned to our chief. "I know my master well, and I can tell he is very angry with you! This *Toubab* can read your thoughts, and he knows you are a liar and a hypocrite!"

André Castorel had turned as white as a sheet and was biting his lips nervously. Looking at his watch, he stood up.

After that, Commander Castorel spent several days traveling to Binkering, Mindal and Tinkis. In each one of these villages, which, like Ndimboye, are in the vicinity of the Forest of Kagne, he had very hard things to say against the enemies of Progress. Everybody promised the perpetrators would soon have their heads cut off.

Commander Castorel returned to Thiès.

The very next day, the saboteurs were at it again. For André Castorel, this could not be a coincidence. It was in fact a perfect example of organized political subversion to him and bore the hallmark of Lat-Dior's henchmen. Within a few hours, his Spahis had wrought bloodshed and devastation in Ndimboye, Tinkis and Mindal.

After that punitive expedition, no one messed with the railway for several months. The inhabitants of Ndimboye were just as happy about this as Commander Castorel himself, since this affair had already cost them so many human lives.

Then one day—according to some of the chroniclers it was a Wednesday and close to sunset—Baye Sèye gently opened the door of his boss's office in Thiès. The moment he saw him enter, Castorel murmured, "I know what you have come to tell me."

"Yes, my Commander."

"Yes . . . Yes, what?" roared Castorel.

"Lat-Dior, my Commander."

"Lat-Dior . . ." Commander Castorel repeated, sounding preoccupied. "Where did he strike this time?"

"Everywhere," said Baye Sèye.

The trains had been brought to a standstill again.

The Governor-General called André Castorel to Saint-Louis. He had barely walked through his office door when the Governor started shouting abuse at him. "You are utterly incompetent and you have been lying to me for the last three years! I was warned but paid no heed to that. I was convinced your enemies were maligning you out of jealousy. Oh well, I was wrong! The next time I hear someone talking about your little Negro king and that railway line, you're on the boat back to France!"

André Castorel felt completely misunderstood, and the Governor's threats didn't make much of an impression on him. He was one of those people who willingly endure any ordeal for their harebrained schemes, and he was quietly jubilant at the thought of himself as a martyr of the great Civilizing Mission. On the other hand, he found it much harder to swallow that a bunch of Negroes should have managed to outsmart him. He went to live in the Forest of Kagne for an extended period, and there he could be heard yelling his threats at the saboteurs day and night, calling them cowards, challenging them to come out of their hiding place and face him in a loyal fight. No one dared to go into the forest anymore. Castorel, on the brink of insanity, pulled his trigger on anything that moved. He shot deer and jaguars, but also two palm wine harvesters and even fruit falling off the trees.

Then, another day back in Thiès, there was a timid knock on Castorel's door. It was Baye Sèye. When the *Toubab* saw his dejected expression, he stopped him with a movement of his hand. "I don't want to hear what you've come to tell me, Baye."

Never before had he addressed the interpreter by his first name only, in a friendly and almost affectionate tone of voice. Baye Sèye gently closed the office door behind him and sat down in the courtyard again.

A few hours later, shots rang out from behind the door. The District Commander of Thiès had lodged two bullets in his head. He was found lying on the floor, propped up against the sofa, with his blood and brains spilled all over the piles of documents next to his body.

■　　■　　■

André Castorel was replaced by another *Toubab*. Luckily for us, this one did not turn the sabotage of the Dakar–Saint-Louis railway line into a personal affair. He seemed content to take note of an incident when it happened, without showing any obvious emotional involvement.

The new District Commander never even visited Ndimboye in person, but he simply sent one of his deputies instead. To our enormous surprise, he too, barely displayed any interest in the railway. He was one of the youngest *Toubabs* we had ever seen in Ndimboye during that time, since he could not have been more than thirty years old. He wasn't very tall, rather taciturn, and one of his feet was larger than the other, which made him hop in a peculiar way, but not without a certain elegance, or that's at least how we saw it from our childish perspective. Apart from that slight handicap, Robert Langlade—this was the foreigner's name—had a skull so flat on top that one could have put a small calabash of milk on it without having to worry it might tip over.

Mbita Sarr gave him the nickname Boxhead. He is still called that in Ndimboye even today, more than fifty years later, whenever the events that follow here are discussed.

We had never dealt with anybody as gentle and even—if that word makes any sense at all, regarding our relationship with the *Toubabs*—as sweet, as Robert Langlade. With his eyes always peeled straight ahead of him, he was clearly preoccupied with something we knew nothing about, and more due to his natural absentmindedness than arrogance, he barely seemed to take notice of our existence. He didn't meddle with our lives and that, too, was new, since we were used to the sort of *Toubabs* who just pitched up and quite unashamedly asked us all sorts of indiscreet or preposterous questions, similarly to the way some people are interested in the habits of sea turtles or praying mantises.

But be that as it may, we were intrigued by his presence in Ndimboye. As a rule, *Toubabs* only tended to live in the big cities. These people, who were so scared of just about anything—leopards, snakes and mosquito bites, for example—were especially afraid of the water in our rivers, and avoided our company as much as they could. So what was he doing in our midst, this Robert Langlade? We just couldn't believe how different he was from his brothers, and the most far-fetched theories were going round. Because he wanted to put an end to all the guesswork, the chief called the notables of Ndimboye to a meeting and said, "For several days now, a *Toubab* has been coming and going among us. He was sent here to Ndimboye by the new District Commander."

"We are aware of that, but we want to know the reason why he's here."

The chief responded with a despondent gesture. "He told me he has decided to come and live in Ndimboye."

"Since when have *Toubabs* been allowed to take up residence in Ndimboye?"

"I tried to sound him out discreetly, and he gave me nothing but evasive answers," said the chief, shaking his head. "He's very clever, that chap."

"And are you, our chief, just going to leave it at that? What you are telling us doesn't make sense!"

The person who said this was a sworn enemy of the chief. We all knew he was prepared to do whatever it would take to usurp his position. There was a brief silence, then the chief said, "I told you this young *Toubab* doesn't want us to know why he is here. I have never been able to get a clear answer out of him. So I simply don't know what he is up to."

"You should have insisted. He is on our home ground here."

"I did that. After each one of the rainy seasons he told me he has come here to help us achieve better millet and peanut harvests."

With these words, the atmosphere immediately became more relaxed, and someone said facetiously, "They must be mad, these *Toubabs*! The last one kept talking to us about Damel Lat-Dior, and now this young boy pretends to know our millet fields better than we do."

"I also didn't think what he was saying made sense," observed the Chief, "and that's why I haven't spoken to you about it sooner."

"A *Toubab* here in Ndimboye . . ." muttered an incredulous voice.

"And can we really not send him back to Thiès?"

"No," said the rival of the chief. "The *Toubabs* are stronger than us. They do whatever they want, and we just have to obey."

Boxhead stayed in Ndimboye for almost a year—nine months, if I remember correctly. It was relatively easy for us to tolerate his presence, since he did not take any liberties with us. If, for example, he came across one of our young girls in the Forest of Kagne, he didn't force her down onto the grass to quickly have his way with her and then walk on, just as one might taste a piece of *màdd* that has fallen off a tree, without even giving it a thought. Even though he didn't bombard us with idiotic questions, Boxhead was very nosy. He had started learning Wolof, and he wrote down everything we told him about the plants and animals of Ndimboye and its surroundings in a small notebook. What was still more surprising was that he always took his meals with us. Let me just mention in passing, Badou, that this *Toubab* was absolutely crazy about *cere baasi*. I, Ali Kaboye, have never seen a *Toubab* devour our *cere baasi* with a healthier appetite than he did!

At any rate, there was something that continued to intrigue us: this quiet young man seemed to have forgotten long ago that he had come to teach us how to get better yields from our cassava and peanut fields.

From time to time, he would disappear in the Forest of Kagne without warning for several days and several nights. He never told us what he was doing there, until one morning, Mbita Sarr and I managed to surprise him in Kagne. We were hiding behind a bush and very softly, Mbita whispered into my ear, "Ali, have you noticed anything?"

"I don't know what you are talking about, Mbita, but this *Toubab* seems quite intrepid to me! To stay in this forest completely alone . . ."

"That's not it, Ali. The foreigner is looking for something on the ground. I have the feeling he is following tracks."

Just for fun, I said Boxhead was probably descended from a long line of hunters.

"You're obviously not taking me seriously," said Mbita, slightly irritated. "But you will soon see that I'm right. What this *Toubab* is looking for is on the ground. I, Mbita Sarr, am saying this, and it's true."

Then the rainy season started and the attacks on the railway line became more vicious than ever before.

At the first opportunity, Mbita Sarr put on his most innocent expression and questioned Boxhead about this. Robert Langlade replied that he knew what was going on, but that it didn't form part of his responsibilities.

He added, "You, Mbita, are the smartest of all the children in this village. I am going to take you back to France with me. You will see, life over there is very pleasant, and you will be happier than here in Ndimboye."

Then he invited Mbita to accompany him into the Forest of Kagne. He said he needed help, because he wanted to install a big mirror there.

"A big mirror . . ." repeated Mbita, sounding surprised. "For what purpose?"

"It is to attract the rays of the sun."

"To attract the rays of the sun?"

Mbita Sarr couldn't make head or tail of this. Then Boxhead said, "Yes, this gigantic mirror is first going to capture the heat of the sun, then it will be sent back into the sky by the wind. Once it's up there, the heat will transform the clouds into raindrops, and they, in turn, are going to water the fields of Ndimboye. You will see, Mbita. Famines in Ndimboye will soon be a thing of the past."

Mbita Sarr seemed so impressed that Boxhead said to him, "When we're in France, you, too, can learn how to make rain fall on the soil of Ndimboye!"

Not long after that, we were woken up at sunrise by deafening howls coming from the Forest of Kagne. Because it was so early in the morning, we first assumed it was another Spahi attack, but we soon realized that this cacophony was unlike anything we had ever heard before. All the animals of Kagne were shrieking and howling in unison, which reminded us of those ancient fables where giants uproot trees and hurl them at the sun, plunging the world into darkness.

The chief dispatched a few young men on a reconnaissance mission. When they got there, they were surprised to find just two gorillas right in front of Robert Langlade's gigantic mirror, completely sozzled, staggering around and gesticulating strangely. There they were, bellowing and furiously beating their chests, clearly outraged about the other two gorillas they had found trespassing on their territory, and no doubt planning to pounce on them and give them a thorough hiding. They only stopped their antics to pick up a demijohn that was standing nearby, greedily inebriating themselves even more with gallons of palm wine. That made them even more aggressive. One of them became so exasperated that he tried to stab his opponent in the eye, but he missed, and only managed to injure his finger instead. The second one obviously couldn't tolerate very much alcohol. His eyes took on a malicious glow and he gestured to his companion to follow him. They disappeared into the thicket and returned a few moments later, armed with iron bars.

Then the fighting began in earnest.

The two animals were endowed with prodigious physical strength, but the mirror was clearly designed to withstand their blows. However hard they tried, it was exceedingly difficult for them to make that first breach in order to get at their enemies. Gripped by an uncontrollable rage, they kept attacking the mirror until they were covered in blood all over. The splinters of glass made them howl with pain, and we could tell they were utterly exhausted and on the verge of collapse. And yet, it was out of the question for them to abandon their territory to a couple of strangers.

Then came the moment when—incapable of distinguishing between their own bodies and those of the intruders—the two gorillas turned on each other. The second one was seemingly the more irate and also the more determined of the two. He tore off his opponent's head without flinching, uttered a sinister cry of victory and then proceeded—with us as his stupefied onlookers—to piss on the inert body with obscene gyrations of his loins.

There was no time for him to enjoy his triumph though, because another gorilla, brandishing an iron bar, immediately appeared in the mirror in front of him. He pounced on the impertinent fellow and the fight resumed, more savage and ferocious than the one he had just won. Within a few minutes, the gorilla had gravely lacerated his chest, his thighs and part of his face. While blood spurted from his gaping wounds, he clobbered his chest as a sign of victory. We watched him as he staggered around, punching the air more and more feebly—perhaps he was irritated by his failure to make even the slightest impression on the enemy—before slumping heavily to the ground.

After twitching for another two or three minutes, he soon lay motionless next to his companion. Their bodies, streaked with red and black, exuded a smell of blood, palm wine and urine.

We came out of our hiding places.

The gorilla had taken a long time to die. The worst part wasn't his death in itself, but the fact that he knew he was dying. Yes, Badou, sometimes when I am alone in my shack here in Niarela at night, that infinite sadness in his eyes comes back to me as though it was a dream. Then I immediately ban that image from my mind. It's a memory I find just too painful.

The moment the animal had expired, someone touched my elbow. I turned round. It was Mbita Sarr.

He murmured, "Ali, everything we have just witnessed here is Robert's doing."

"You mean Boxhead?"

"Yes, the very same," Mbita said confidently. "He tricked them."

"Who did he trick?"

"It was these two gorillas who sabotaged the railway line," Mbita said.

Distractedly, as if he were talking to no one but himself, and with a slight pang of regret—or was it admiration?—in his voice, he said, "He tricked them . . ."

"And what's become of him then, where is he?" I asked abruptly.

"Look over there, Ali."

Boxhead had made himself comfortable in the branches of a Baobab tree, and was overlooking the scene. I don't know why, but the top of his head suddenly struck me as even flatter than before. We looked at each other, and he smiled and tried to tell us something by using sign language. For the first time since his arrival several months earlier, he seemed relaxed.

On that day, Robert Langlade, alias Boxhead, did not spend the night in Ndimboye. He went to deliver the two gorilla heads to the Thiès District Commander and was never heard of again.

■   ■   ■

When you go near them, they get confused, and their sense of shame makes them fall apart. The bodies are drowning in blood. Your children avert their eyes.

■　　■　　■

One day, the Holy Man saw them overcome by doubt and he told them: "Don't be afraid. I am not the one who makes empty promises. I am the one who gives in abundance."

May the ignorant and the doubtful perish in the solitude of frosty mornings.

■　　■　　■

Badou Tall, your grandfather chose me to tell you the most improbable and therefore the most truthful part of the story of Yacine Ndiaye and her two children. He had good reason to trust me: my ears hear everything, and my memory never fails. And now I am going to absent myself in order to repeat to you—exactly as you are going to read them on your return in his *Notebooks*—the last lines Nguirane Faye wrote with his own hand. My voice will reach you. Yes, my voice is clear, it travels over the hills and across the oceans.

■　　■　　■

The next day, well before the time Yacine Ndiaye was supposed to leave for the airport, I sat down under my mango tree as I always did. I couldn't help feeling pleased, because her presence in the house had become stifling. Soon, a taxi would arrive, and we would be saying our good-byes to each other, with pleasant words and benedictions. Appearances would be kept up, and I would at last regain my peace of mind.

Toward midday, Yacine Ndiaye walked past me with an enormous red suitcase, but, instead of putting it down in the middle of the courtyard and going to fetch the rest, she did something utterly astounding. She sat down on a chair and started emptying the entire suitcase. She was much less relaxed than the day before; she was quite nervous, in actual fact. I watched her picking up every single garment, unfolding it, patting it with a mystified expression, and then dropping it at her feet. After that, she went back to her apartment, muttering to herself, and brought out a second suitcase which she inspected just as scrupulously. Gradually, Yacine Ndiaye got more and more worked up and let slip some rather vulgar swearwords that she repeated over and over while hitting her thighs at the same time.

I felt very intrigued by all this, but since I had promised myself to stay out of her business, I didn't ask any questions.

A little later, a taxi pulled up outside the house, and I could hear a car door being slammed shut. It was Bigué Samb, who had come to accompany Yacine Ndiaye into town. When she saw the clothes scattered all over the ground, she covered her mouth with her hand in shock and exclaimed, "What's going on, Yacine?"

Sweating and frantic, incapable of uttering a single word, Yacine Ndiaye gave your mother a blank stare. Her lips were trembling.

Bigué Samb continued, "Weren't we supposed to call on Sinkoun Camara before I take you to the airport tonight?"

Sinkoun Tiguidé Camara. There is a name you'll do well to remember, Badou. This servant of Cheytan is someone you will soon come across again in my Notebooks.

"I can find neither my passport nor any of my other papers," Yacine Ndiaye said in an utterly pathetic voice.

"Your passport?"

"I can't find any of my papers. Neither my passport nor anything else. Nothing."

In her state of distress, she seemed to be relying entirely on Bigué Samb for help, almost begging her to perform a miracle.

Bigué Samb started checking the suitcases all over again but gave up very quickly.

Yacine Ndiaye, still profoundly dejected, turned ever so slightly in my direction as she declared, "I'm sure my thief is right here in this house."

Did this mean she suspected me, Nguirane Faye, of having something to do with this? This was so absurd that I didn't waste any time on it.

Bigué Samb sounded warm and affectionate when she said, "That's my girl. Always ready for a fight, my Yacine!"

"Take a good look at me, Bigué," Yacine Ndiaye said with despair. She pointed at her left forearm. "Can't you see that with this black skin and without my papers I cannot prove who I am? I don't know what to do, Bigué."

After a brief silence, she burst into sobs.

"Don't worry," Bigué Samb said with resolve. "Just follow me."

Yacine Ndiaye stood up. They climbed into the taxi, and I realized then that Bigué Samb hadn't even seen me. But I knew exactly why I was suddenly so unimportant to her: she was far too busy homing in on her prey.

She was behind the mysterious disappearance of Yacine Ndiaye's passport. I didn't have the slightest doubt about that.

■   ■   ■

Bigué Samb took Yacine Ndiaye to a witchdoctor called Sinkoun Tiguidé Camara. When they got there, he was alone in a dimly lit room, surrounded by all his rams' horns, wild animals' tails, and magic potions. Yacine Ndiaye, "La Marseillaise"—that's what Bigué Samb used to call her for fun—was not very familiar with that world anymore. She sat down on an old wooden chair and looked around anxiously, clearly wondering already what had possessed her to come to this weird and dubious place.

As usual, the formal greetings seemed to her to go on forever, and she found their host's pose bewildering: with one arm propped up on his right knee, which was raised, he was absentmindedly stroking his left ankle while staring fixedly at his mat. Why on earth was he refusing to look at them? At brief intervals, he addressed himself to Bigué Samb in a barely audible voice, with trivialities like: "Is your mother Rama Gueye getting better? I have heard that her diabetes has made her very tired lately. Sugar is certainly wreaking havoc in our country, or did Ngoné Thioune go to buy some *bogolan* in Bamako this month?" He acknowledged all Bigué Samb's answers with "You are welcome," punctuated by brief and rasping repetitions of "Hun-hun, hun-hun," which came from deep down in his chest.

After these long-winded preliminary exchanges, Bigué Samb said to him, "Sinkoun, I am here to see you in the company of Yacine Ndiaye, the friend we talked about a few days ago."

Sinkoun Tiguidé Camara looked up for the first time and glanced at Yacine Ndiaye before lowering his head again and saying in a solemn voice, "I will do what I can for you, Bigué. The friendship between our two families goes back so far that you have become my sister."

When a friendship has withstood time for so long, it becomes stronger than blood ties. Bigué Samb agreed warmly.

"So says Wolof Njaay, and he is quite right, Bigué. I welcome you both."

"The way the world works," Bigué Samb continued, "means that we could have been the worst of enemies, Yacine Ndiaye—you see her here, sitting right in front of you—and I. She has had two God's-bits-of-wood with Assane Tall, who is also the father of my only son, Badou—you know him well. But Assane Tall was called home to God, and we have decided to forget all the bad things that happened."

"Of course, Bigué," said Sinkoun Tiguidé. "Your heart is pure."

"If we are like two sisters today, it is entirely thanks to Yacine," corrected Bigué Samb.

"May God the Almighty help you to persevere in that vein."

"Our plan was to come and seek your prayers before her departure for Marseille. But Yacine won't be able to travel today anymore, since she has lost her passport and the rest of her papers. I want you to assist her in finding them again. If anybody has stolen them, tell us his name and beat him up mercilessly, Sinkoun Tiguidé."

The man handed Yacine Ndiaye a small bowl filled with sand, asking her to focus on it while making her wishes. She, on the other hand, was beginning to feel distinctly uneasy, thinking all this was completely beyond her. She was like a little girl who is taken to the dentist by her mother and is looking anxiously at all the instruments of torture around her.

In a slight panic, without really knowing why—this place was so strange to her!—she started rattling off all sorts of things in French.

Bigué Samb said with an uneasy smile, "You must excuse her, Sinkoun Tiguidé, but Yacine doesn't remember much about our customs after living in France for such a long time."

Then she turned to Yacine Ndiaye. "Yacine, nobody in this room needs to hear what you want Sinkoun Tiguidé to do for you. He can hear you exactly like you can hear me right now, and there's no need for you to even open your mouth."

Sinkoun Tiguidé Camara appeared equally bemused by Yacine Ndiaye's behavior and asked her, "Do you speak Wolof?"

"Only a little," she replied, pleased to at last be able to say a few words to Sinkoun Tiguidé since her arrival in his house.

No doubt irritated by this answer, Sinkoun Tiguidé baffled her a bit. "If you want my Friends to understand you, it will be helpful to speak to them in Wolof, Diola, Sereer, Pulaar or Kikuyu. No human language is foreign to them, of course, but they are such cunning creatures! I wouldn't be too surprised if they tell me they don't know what you want from them!"

He kept quiet for a moment, his eyes riveted on Yacine, and then he added, "My Friends are strong, impetuous young fellows. They enjoy getting drunk, having a good time and poking fun at everything, but you should beware of their wrath, for that is always terrible."

"My Friends . . . My Friends . . . Who on earth are these Friends he is constantly talking about?" Yacine Ndiaye asked herself. What little she had understood led her to believe she would have to confide her innermost secrets—and possibly even her destiny—to these strangers. She therefore had the right to know a bit more about them. But rather than putting this question to Sinkoun Tiguidé, she suddenly realized she was talking very softly to the sand-covered bowl. When she had finished, Sinkoun Tiguidé said simply, "That's fine. Come back alone tomorrow, after the prayer of *tisbaar*."

■　　■　　■

To start with, Sinkoun Tiguidé Camara asked her for ten jujube leaves and three *ditax* nuts.

When Yacine gave them to him, he said, "That's good. And now I need some roots from a three hundred-year-old *kàdd*."

That tree wasn't easy to find. Bigué and Yacine went to look for it in several remote villages, and on one occasion they even ventured across the border into Mali. Eventually they heard about a particular *kàdd* near the small town of Kébémer.

For weeks on end, Sinkoun Tiguidé Camara made her bring him all sorts of strange and unusual objects. A parrot's tongue soaked in honey for an entire night. Five pairs of monkeys' eyes. Ostrich eggs. Fragments of a mirror. A tuft of hair from a blond woman. Some green grass and some rotten turkey eggs.

All that was so obviously nonsensical that more than once Yacine Ndiaye very nearly gave up her secret dreams. The simplest solution was perhaps to contact the French embassy. After all, she was entitled to new documents. But thanks to her friend Bigué, who never left her side and encouraged her to persevere, they finally managed to bring Sinkoun Tiguidé everything he had asked for.

A few days later, he asked Yacine Ndiaye to come and see him.

"Sit down," he said, pointing to the same rickety old chair.

Yacine Ndiaye's heart was pounding. Sinkoun Tiguidé, who was looking at her strangely, seemed less friendly than he had been during the previous days. His eyes were like glowing coals and cut right through her while he was talking to her in a bizarre manner, as if he had never seen her in his life before. "Yacine Ndiaye, are you quite sure you are the person who wants to be transformed into someone else?"

She thought she could sense a hint of irony, or perhaps even sarcasm, in Sinkoun Tiguidé's voice and was too shy to respond.

"I am talking to you, Yacine Ndiaye!" Sinkoun Tiguidé said harshly, without taking his eyes off her, in a voice that sounded vaguely reproachful. "Do you want me to transform you into another person? Is that what you want?"

"Yes, that's what I want," she stammered.

"And I, Sinkoun Tiguidé Camara, I can actually do it. Yacine Ndiaye?"

"Yes."

"I don't like people who just say yes. I want to hear you say loud and clear that you can hear me—me, the man whose name is Sinkoun Tiguidé Camara."

"I can hear you, Camara."

"God Almighty, He who gives and who takes away, has given me these special powers, and I know that I will not be able to keep them forever. This is why I like to help my human brothers as much as I can."

On the day when Bigué first mentioned Sinkoun Tiguidé Camara to her, Yacine Ndiaye had been extremely doubtful about his so-called supernatural powers. Now she regretted that. The man right in front of her really did strike her as an unusual being—as if he had come from another world.

Her musings were interrupted by Sinkoun Tiguidé Camara's voice. "What do you want your name to be, Yacine Ndiaye?"

"Marie-Gabrielle," she answered without hesitation.

Obviously she was well prepared. Who knows, but perhaps that name had a particular significance for her, all those many miles away in Marseille.

"Marie-Gabrielle," Sinkoun Tiguidé murmured without comment. "And what will be your new surname, Marie-Gabrielle?"

"Von Bolkowsky. I want to be called Marie-Gabrielle von Bolkowsky."

Yacine Ndiaye's sense of unease persisted—there was nothing she could do about it. She had no idea where the feeling came from, but she was convinced that Sinkoun Tiguidé thought she was either an imbecile or insane. She had an inkling that from now on she would be irresistibly swept along by the course of events. She was heading straight for the precipice, knowing full well there was no way back.

Sinkoun Tiguidé gave her a piece of paper. "Write your name down here."

With a trembling hand, she scrawled the letters on the white sheet of paper.

"Read your name out aloud. Read it seven times," ordered Sinkoun Tiguidé.

Yacine Ndiaye was floating in empty space and found it hard to recognize the sound of her own voice or to control her gestures.

She heard Sinkoun Tiguidé telling her calmly, "You can go back to Niarela. What needed to be done has been done."

Yacine Ndiaye opened her wallet, ready to hand Sinkoun Tiguidé a big pile of banknotes. Barely able to control his anger, he said coldly, "You can keep your money."

Yacine Ndiaye was quick to apologize. "I hope I didn't upset you, Monsieur Camara."

"I don't want you to call me either Mr. Camara or Mr. Diallo or whatever else! And stop flashing your miserable banknotes!"

He was so furious that Yacine Ndiaye was afraid of being transformed into a deer or a snake right there and then and not, as she had specified, into a brunette white woman with green eyes.

She returned two days later and Sinkoun Tiguidé Camara pointed to a large mirror at the other end of the room. "Look at yourself in this mirror."

Sinkoun Tiguidé's voice sounded as if it was coming from so far away that he appeared to be talking to another person. It didn't even occur to her to reply to him. At any rate, she couldn't have because her head was swimming and she didn't dare stand up, for fear that she might faint on the spot. So she stayed glued to her chair, thinking that this whole story seemed at the same time totally absurd and far too simple. She was forced to admit that since her arrival in Niarela, she had basically been like a ball of clay in Bigué Samb's hands. She recalled some episodes of their friendship, and Bigué Samb's beautiful words left nothing but a bitter taste in her mouth. Everything struck her as false, including her smiles and the advice she had received from this so-called older sister. Right there, under Sinkoun Tiguidé Camara's nose, she had walked into a trap that had been laid a long time ago. "I have allowed them to trick me like a silly little girl, and all of this is nobody's fault but my own," she thought. She should have been more careful; more than once already, she had caught in Bigué Samb's eyes a glimpse of her deep, unfathomable hatred for Assane Tall. Why did she want to take revenge on her and her two children? She, Yacine, had nothing to do with what happened after Badou was born. She and Assane Tall met in Marseille when they were very young. What could have been more normal? It was something that occurs all the time between girls and boys of their age. He never told her anything about his previous life, least of all that he had left a son behind in Niarela by the name of Badou Tall. And now she was going to have to pay for a story she had known nothing about. That simply wasn't fair.

The imperious voice of Sinkoun Tiguidé Camara abruptly brought her back to the present. "Didn't I tell you to go and look at yourself in the mirror, Yacine Ndiaye?"

She stood up with less difficulty than she had anticipated.

In the big mirror, she saw her face, dreadfully burned by the *xeesal*. Several years ago, she had tried to lighten her skin at least slightly, since that was all she could do. It ended up being a real disaster. My God, wouldn't the world be a wonderful place if everybody could choose the color of their skin! Ah! If only Sinkoun Tiguidé could grant her wish! She did not want to be black anymore. There were demagogues who claimed this was a totally irrelevant issue, or at any rate, that things were all right as they were. She wasn't afraid of the truth: filth always has one and the same color, and until the end of time, that will be black. It was as simple as that.

There were several knocks on the front-door, followed by Sinkoun Tiguidé Camara's voice. "Come in."

The curtain was pushed aside, and she saw a tall, slim young woman standing in the middle of the room. Yacine Ndiaye was surprised she hadn't even heard her greeting Sinkoun Tiguidé. "She obviously has no idea who she's dealing with, that impertinent woman," she said to herself. "But maybe there's some hanky-panky going on between these two." Apparently sorcerers, charlatans and miracle-makers in general were known for their lack of scruples in that regard, and it didn't surprise her. The women who consulted them were so fragile, more or less crushed by life. Clearly, they could do with them whatever they wanted.

After mulling this over for a long time, she finally became convinced that the newcomer had to be Sinkoun Tiguidé's mistress. She couldn't imagine that anybody would knowingly dare to provoke this terrifying fellow. All the while, Sinkoun Tiguidé had kept his eyes firmly fixed on the floor. He had sunk into a profound meditation and most probably hadn't noticed someone else bursting into the room. This other person, by the way, suddenly appeared to Yacine Ndiaye to bear the features of a *Toubab* with thin lips and bright blue eyes. Had this visitor undergone a surprise metamorphosis? Or else, had Yacine Ndiaye, in her troubled state of mind, not realized straight away what she was really like?

There were more knocks at the door.

Again, she heard Sinkoun Tiguidé Camara's voice. "Come in."

A second woman pushed the curtain aside, and Yacine Ndiaye exclaimed, "And now there's another one! Where has this one come from? And what's happened to the first one? Am I perhaps going mad? My God, how beautiful you are, my friend! How white your skin looks against that black dress! How I envy you your beautiful, long, blond hair and the way it falls onto your shoulders!"

The stranger stood behind her, gazing at her silently across the mirror.

Without any obvious reason, Yacine Ndiaye thought, "Hello, you! Why do I have the feeling that you hate me or despise me? What's the reason? I don't even know you, so how can I have wronged you?"

She looked at her with a disarming smile.

The white woman's face remained cold and closed. Suddenly, an idea crossed her mind: "Could it be that I am already dead and have arrived in the afterworld, although I actually believe I am visiting Sinkoun Tiguidé Camara?"

She turned round abruptly, so as to surprise the white woman, but she was gone. Only Sinkoun Tiguidé Camara was in the room with her.

This alarmed her. "Where is she, the lady I have just seen?"

"She has returned to the place she should never have left."

"What do you mean, Camara?"

"You are she, she is you."

"I still don't know what you are trying to say, Camara."

"You are beginning to irritate me, Marie-Gabrielle von Bolkowsky. Who can she be, if not you yourself? You are black, she is white, but you are one and the same person. I order you one last time to look at yourself in the mirror."

Yacine Ndiaye didn't dare. In fact, there was something at that very moment that made it impossible for her to look at the mirror. She shuddered. The earth was opening up under her feet. In the distance, almost as high up as the sky: rows upon rows of buildings embedded in the clouds, as far as the eye could see. They were enormous and minuscule at the same time. Where had they come from? They were floating above the water. They were floating in the bright blue air, all neatly lined up one behind the other. Jumping over the abyss. Getting to the other side. The abyss was there, very close, so tempting. But she sensed that after the first step, her left foot would never join up with her right foot again. The void: a sort of bottomless well. She wouldn't even be floating, no, she saw herself slipping and sliding in empty space, endlessly, from one second to the next, until the end of time, on the same rock face. Where was the endpoint, though; where exactly was that point toward which her body was being pulled so irresistibly? She didn't have the faintest idea. All she knew was that, for want of a better name, she would have to call that place—always close but forever out of reach—*Elsewhere*.

She closed her eyes and opened them again immediately. When she did look into the mirror, the woman reappeared behind her. Yacine Ndiaye slightly moved her left hand, then lifted it up. The other one did the same. Now she had understood that the white woman standing behind her in the mirror was herself.

She smiled, bewildered, and said resolutely, as she turned to Sinkoun Tiguidé Camara: "Ask me for whatever you want, Sinkoun Tiguidé, and I will give it to you. If I don't have it, I swear I will find it, Camara."

Sinkoun Tiguidé Camara simply said: "Get undressed."

She stretched out on the mat, and he penetrated her several times.

When they had finished, he confessed to her that it was the first time he had done this with a *Toubab*. He also asked her in a mocking, conniving tone of voice what she had been shouting all the time in the language of her new race.

"Who cares! I can't remember!" Yacine Ndiaye said cheerfully. "In any case, it was great! You are a dirty old pig, that's what you are!"

Sinkoun Tiguidé Camara smiled, pensively stroking his goatee, and said: "There is one last detail to sort out, Marie-Gabrielle. Come back on Wednesday after the prayer of *timis*."

Something in the man's voice put Yacine Ndiaye on alert: "What's the matter? You suddenly look so serious, Camara . . ." she said as she was putting on her pants.

"You asked me to do this job. I did it, but there is a price to pay. Next time we meet, we will talk about it."

When she came back, Sinkoun Tiguidé said to her: "Now listen to me very carefully: you have two children . . ."

"Yes. Mbissine and Mbissane."

"I need one of them."

"What do you mean, you need one of them?"

"You will let me have either Mbissine or Mbissane."

"I still don't know what this means, Camara."

"What I have told you is clear. I could have taken Mbissine or Mbissane without asking you first. But I prefer to let you choose which one you want to part with, because I know about a mother's heart. That's not an easy decision. I am aware of that."

"You are stark raving mad!" exclaimed Yacine Ndiaye, suddenly gripped by rage. "I am not going to let you have either of my children, and now stop your stupid nonsense, my friend!"

She could have killed him on the spot. Sinkoun Tiguidé observed her for a few moments and then said in an icy voice: "Don't forget who you are talking to."

Yacine Ndiaye dismissed his threats vehemently.

"I am not going to do it!" she shouted, more for herself than for Sinkoun Tiguidé. "No, no, and no again! I'm never going to do that!"

"You will do it. These things do not depend on our will."

"If you go anywhere near my children, you will end your life in prison, you miserable little charlatan!"

"You make me laugh, Yacine Ndiaye. Are you really so unaware of the true nature of things? Could it be that you are totally ignorant of the Lake of Oblivion? Every single God-given day, the Sons of the Earth are both attracted and frightened by it. You have been bold enough to cross it from one bank to the other. Not one day dawns when the Sons of the Earth do not go there in order to contemplate their shadowy side and their most monstrous desires. They all flee in terror, whereas you have faced that divide without fear. Marie-Gabrielle, you have crossed over to the other side of Life. And let me tell you: the place where your body is going to rot has no name."

"What's that gibberish you are telling me now, Camara?"

"There are no traces left on the bodies, because all the signs have dissipated. Entire cities are perched on the clouds, and the bottom of the lake is sprinkled with stars. It's chaos, Yacine Ndiaye. Pure chaos. Yesterday and today never stop chasing each other and time is biting its own tail. Time has left a trail of blood in its wake. Can you see it?"

"Oh my God, this man is mad! This man is completely mad! What's going to happen to me?"

"It's your fault that all the faces have become smooth, Yacine. It's a bad omen when the lines in a human face disappear just like that. I am asking myself what on earth I have done with all those fissures that used to protect us against the bush fires and enemy armies, but I don't even know. In His infinite goodness, the Almighty has admitted me to the secret of the Good. I have turned it into the key to Evil. God will never forgive me for what I've done. And down there, the forefather of the Son of the Earth will spit in my face and call me a vile creature. In the Kingdom of the Dead, all that awaits me is shame and suffering. I want everything right here and right now. Give me Mbissine or Mbissane."

"Have pity, Camara! Kill me if you like, but spare my children!"

That was more than Sinkoun Tiguidé could tolerate.

His piercing eyes went right through her. "You can talk to me about your love for Mbissine and for Mbissane all you like, bad mother that you are! How can you hate your own blood and pretend at the same time to love the children that have sprung from your entrails?"

Marie-Gabrielle von Bolkowsky started sobbing.

"What do you want to do to my children, Sinkoun Tiguidé? Do you really believe I will give them to you? What are you planning to do to them?"

"Nothing," said the man. He had calmed down but still bore an expression of profound contempt on his face. "I don't want to do anything to them."

"Is that true? Nothing?"

"The truth is that your children are useless to me. It's my Friends who want one of them."

"It's his Friends again!" Yacine Ndiaye grumbled to herself. And yet, at this very moment she was suddenly sure no evil would ever befall Mbissine and Mbissane. The feeling she had was rather odd and even slightly disconcerting. These events that were real and utterly absurd at the same time were going to self-destruct on contact with everyday life, just like certain chemical elements dissolve when they are exposed to air. She had accidentally slipped and trespassed into a world that was normally taboo to her. It was the world of magic but not necessarily the world of madness—that belonged to Sinkoun Tiguidé Camara and his mysterious Friends. All she had to do was leave this room and take up her normal activities again once she was back in Niarela—she was planning, for example, to have a new passport delivered—and this whole saga would be forgotten.

She almost managed to put a bit of irony into her voice when she said to Sinkoun Tiguidé Camara, "Who are they, these Friends of yours?"

"They assist me with my work. Without them, my voice would never reach the Seven Heavens. Are you really so ignorant that you don't know how it all works?"

"I have no idea," she said, flustered all over again.

"They take a lot of trouble to make your dreams come true, dreams that are often quite absurd, by the way, and afterward they say to me: Sinkoun Tiguidé, 'We are thirsty'—"

"Liar! Impostor! Filthy cannibal! You should be ashamed of yourself when you say things like that."

She was so hysterical that Sinkoun Tiguidé just smiled while stroking his ankle. "Are you really as naive as you are pretending to be? You used to be called Yacine Ndiaye and now your name is Marie-Gabrielle von Bolkowsky. It was your own wish; I have granted it to you. This isn't just any old name, that one, even in your country over there, where the whites live. One might say you have set your sights pretty high! When you return to Marseille, the city where, before, you had to keep a low profile, nobody will think you're not a local; it will be as though you had always lived there. Then it'll be your turn to ask people, just by the way, 'Where are you from? Oh, of course, Africa, I went there on holiday once—what a great place! The people down there are so simple and happy by nature! I can't wait to go back there one day!' No longer will you see repugnant little phrases dancing in their shifty eyes that they themselves are ashamed of."

France, you know, either you love it or you leave it. Don't bore us with your colonization and your slavery, it's OK, we realized long ago that you have nothing else to talk about. Parasite! Social Security racketeer!

"And as for you, Marie-Gabrielle, the whole world will be your backyard, and you'll be free to wander around there exactly as you please. Isn't that just great?"

"None of this is worth as much to me as the lives of my children."

"Let me finish, please. I don't know which one of your children you will choose to give to me, but the other one will have a lovely, peaceful life. Will it be little Mbissine? Or perhaps her brother, Mbissane? What can be better than growing up far away from our horrific tribal wars and all those awful epidemics? And maybe when the little sonny boy has grown up he will even come back here to lend us a hand one day as one of those big-hearted little soldiers for the humanitarian cause, someone who-hasn't-forgotten-his-faraway-roots, because those people, you know, if we don't do anything to help them dig wells, they'll just let themselves starve to death to the last man. Still, they're fabulous, those blacks!"

Sinkoun Tiguidé's infernal calm—his eyes with that evil glow very clearly belonged to a deranged brain—didn't leave the slightest doubt in Marie-Gabrielle's mind. She read in them the definitive, undeniable proof that her life was ruined forever.

All of a sudden, she screamed, "Where are you, Bigué Samb? Are you happy at last? You vowed to destroy me and now you have succeeded. I would never have thought you capable of hating me as much as that."

"Mbissine or Mbissane," said Sinkoun Tiguidé. "I am waiting for your answer."

"Why does everybody hate me? You, Sinkoun Tiguidé, can you at least explain to me what I have done to you?"

"If you don't give me one of your children, my Friends will take both of them away from you. They are greedy fellows, you know."

Sinkoun Tiguidé stubbornly repeated the same words over and over again. For Marie-Gabrielle, the last glimmer of hope was lost.

In the midst of her anguish, her memories were one of the few things she had left.

How tortuous life's paths could be . . . How strange that the sequel to her very first encounter with Assane Tall at the Bar des Trois-Frères, Rue des Récollets, should take place so many years later, in this room, with Sinkoun Tiguidé Camara demanding the flesh and blood of their two children. Assane Tall. A handsome young guy when they first met, and a highly talented soccer player to boot. How proud his compatriots in Marseille were of him! What she had liked most of all about him was his joie de vivre. And then, the abrupt end of his career because he loved partying too much. He ended up practically penniless and she had to support him while he was looking for a job. But after that, even the smaller clubs were no longer interested in such a volatile player. She had to find work, of course. What did she do? Her body, that was nobody's business but her own. And besides, it didn't bother Assane. On certain nights when he was drunk, he even said he felt turned on by the thought that so many strangers were doing it with her all the time. Although they were seemingly so close, Assane, who was sly and deceitful, had never stopped lying to her. He had muddled her up completely, to be honest. She never really knew much about him. Until the day when she arrived in Niarela with her husband's body. She was forced to live in a miserable abode in a slum where the only person waiting for her there was Nguirane Faye, that senile, toothless old man who did nothing but talk drivel all day. And since she came from France, he imagined she was going to take care of him. Just like that. No problem! And all those people in Niarela who were constantly slandering her . . .

"Are you going to leave without letting me know your decision, Yacine Ndiaye?" Sinkoun Tiguidé Camara asked her with icy calm.

She flinched and wanted to reply but lacked the necessary strength. The next moment, she was assaulted by thoughts so brutal and unexpected that she didn't dare to let them transform themselves into clear and intelligible sentences inside her head.

To give it to you in a nutshell, Badou: Marie-Gabrielle was beginning to feel tempted by Cheytan, who set her skull on fire. She became more and more troubled, and was dreadfully torn between *After all . . .* and *Why not?* Somehow she had to put an end to this abominable affair. Mbissine? Mbissane? Perhaps it would be better if she resigned herself to making the painful choice. *You are powerless. You are not in control of the situation. God knows that you never wanted this, you have fallen into an infernal trap. A brief moment of pain and it'll be over. We have seen far worse things happening on this earth. Everything has its price; you always knew that. And then one has to be logical, even if this story doesn't make sense at all. If you resist, all three of you will be annihilated. Is that what you want? Do this madman's bidding and go far away from this country, a country you have definitely never been able to understand."*

Marie-Gabrielle stood up, eyeing Sinkoun Tiguidé intensely, and said, "Monsieur Camara, your Friends and you . . ."

"I am listening."

"I want you to know that you and your Friends can go to Hell."

She was quiet for a moment and then started again in an even more violent fit of rage. "Can you hear me? You can go to Hell!"

Sinkoun Tiguidé dismissed her with a quick gesture of his hand.

He's furious, but I really couldn't give a damn! Yacine Ndiaye thought with satisfaction as she was leaving his house.

She couldn't remember when she had last been so proud of herself.

■ ■ ■

Badou Tall, Niarela is waiting impatiently for your return. Very odd things are happening here in your absence. Even Nguirane Faye would have had trouble narrating them to you.

I actually don't know where to start.

Since their mother, who has now completely lost her marbles, started claiming that her name is Marie-Gabrielle von Bolkowsky, Yacine Ndiaye's two children are no longer the same. If anybody goes near them, they immediately run away screaming and terrified, and then they start clambering up into the trees to hide themselves. Then they try to talk to us from up there, but all we can hear is shrill, confused sounds. Maybe their words get stuck at the bottom of their narrow throat, maybe they're all topsy-turvy and when they come out, they're totally muddled up. That might end badly. Trying to speak makes the two little ones choke, then they start grimacing and they vomit a bit of blood.

■ ■ ■

One day, Nguirane Faye was seized by an unbearable longing and he asked you, *Which sunrays caress your eyelids when you wake up in the morning, Badou Tall?*

That night, my shadow was hovering above Nguirane's *Notebooks*. His end was not far off and that made his separation from you even more difficult to endure. I didn't want to break his heart by telling him about your new life with its sufferings and humiliations in a foreign country, far away from home. Instead of trying to embellish reality, I chose to keep silent. One doesn't lie to a man like him. So that's why your grandfather has left us without knowing where you are now.

Yesterday, I paid you a visit over there.

I spent a long time following you silently up and down those steep, narrow streets of the old town, your Sudanese friend Abdelkader Mahjoub and you.

And now I am looking down on you again.

You are just walking into a small grocery shop in an area close to your workplace. The shopkeeper recognizes you but doesn't show it. "The two young security guards who work for the director of the Royal Tapestries," he says to himself. Abdelkader buys tea and milk, and you buy some peanut butter and a few vegetables. You have promised Abdelkader to cook *mafé* for dinner. A few days ago, you feasted on *Naemia be Dakwa* from his country together, and now it's your turn to introduce him to our cuisine. The shopkeeper's gestures are neat and precise. He always seems preoccupied with other things while serving his customers. This morning, too, you get the impression he wants to start a conversation with you but lacks the courage in the end. He's probably too shy. To start talking to people can be more difficult than one might think. But you should at least be able to get along with each other. He, too, is just a small guy who is dreaming of moving to new shores—that's obvious from the melancholic look in his eyes. Very different from your boss, who is basically a multimillionaire, they say, and who has put you up in that cramped little shed with its musty smell, right next to the entrance gate of his luxurious residence.

Back in the street, you hurry along with bent backs, shoulders hunched, and eyes riveted to the ground. In this country, a foreigner has to remain invisible. Just in case. You may not be quite as undernourished and emaciated as the people back home, but you don't seem to be in glowing health either.

All the buildings in this town are made of red brick. A dismal place where even the main avenues are treeless and barren. It's an arid town, burnt and blackened by the sun. The wind full of sand and dust prevents the inhabitants from standing and chatting at street corners or forming a colorful, noisy crowd. Their eyes never meet.

Leaning against a billboard, you open the paper. You love the news briefs about all sorts of weird and wonderful facts, usually totally improbable, but which, due to our mysterious desire to be amazed, we all want to believe. For example: "A white woman whose husband is black has for the second time in eight years given birth to twin girls, one of whom is black and the other white. Little Miya has the dark skin and eyes of her dad, while her twin sister Leah has light skin and blue eyes like her mother, Alison Spooner, a redhead. In 2001, their older sisters Lauren and Hayleigh were also born with different skin colors. 'I still can't believe it,' said the father, Dean Durrant, thirty-three, on the Sky News channel on Wednesday."

But what you've discovered in the newspaper is not only bewildering—it concerns you personally, and much more closely than you might think.

You frown, turn the page, and then you look at your friend. "This is truly mind-boggling," you say.

Abdelkader first gazes at the paper, then at you. "What's the matter, Alioune Badara?"

Let me say in passing that he is almost the only one who calls you by both your given names. Probably because he enjoys the beauty of the sounds. I, at any rate, love hearing him modulate the words "Alioune Badara" with such a melodious intonation. I am not sure why, but it makes the bond between you even stronger.

You can't hold back a smile. "A little dispatch about the country . . ."

"Your country?"

"Yes. It's really amazing. They say two young children have been transformed into monkeys!"

Abdelkader Mahjoub had probably feared some sort of serious disaster and seems relieved. "So that's all it was," he says to himself. He doesn't look like he is going to get too excited about something he regards as irrelevant hearsay.

But you insist. "And that's not all, Kader. While the people were making a big fuss about the little monkeys, a white woman, apparently very rich and very elegant, arrived and asked to be given back her children!"

"Her children?"

"Yes, she claims to be their mother!"

Abdelkader's eyes are sparkling with mischief; he tries to keep his voice down but fails. His smile turns to laughter, which gets louder and louder. He is slapping his thighs and nearly splits his sides laughing. An old lady looks at him sternly. *They have no manners, these foreigners.* You, on the other hand, are pleased, because you haven't seen Abdelkader in such a good mood for a very long time.

Then he becomes doubtful. "You're pulling my leg, Alioune Badara. You must be kidding me, right?"

You hand him the paper. He reads, then looks at you. He wants explanations but doesn't want to offend you. Before you became friends, you had some big rows. Like everybody almost anywhere, he thought you came from a different world full of huge trees, wild animals and naked giants armed with bows and arrows. You had a hard time trying to explain things to him—things that are basically so simple. After months of nightly quarrels outside your master's residence, he finally understood.

He plucks up his courage and says, trying to stay aloof, "It's just crazy, all this, Alioune Badara . . ."

"No, Abdelkader, it's not crazy."

"What is it then?"

"It's poverty, Kader."

Kader is very fond of you. He can tell how embarrassing you must find this. "Why are you taking this story so seriously? It's nothing."

"Serious or not, I know the whole country is talking about it. I know my Djoloff."

"Yes, but you also know what journalists are like. They are prepared to invent just about anything if it helps them sell paper."

At that point in the conversation I really wanted to say to your friend, "I hope you don't mind my butting in here, Abdelkader Mahjoub. How can you pretend to know what's going on in Niarela when you have never set foot there?" The man seems unaware of the fact that I alone, Ali Kaboye, have been given the power to traverse time and crisscross the seas. I hear everything. I see everything. My skull harbors past centuries and those still to come. They are lying there, slumbering, but at my behest they will jump up and cower at my feet.

And you are spot-on, Badou: this child-monkey story has really turned the whole country upside down.

Hundreds of keen young reporters have taken up residence in Niarela. I see them shouting into their microphones all day long and interviewing endless numbers of people. I, Ali Kaboye, am the only one they forget to question, of course.

Never since his exile and subsequent death in Marseille has the name Assane Faye Tall dominated our radio waves to this extent. A weekly magazine has published an old photograph of him with the following caption: *Is the former striker of the national soccer team the father of the two child-monkeys?* One also hears people talking about you. The mysterious older brother of the child-monkeys. In Niarela they say nobody knows where he is, or whether he is still alive. *However,* says a reporter, *according to reliable sources, Alioune Badara Tall, alias Badou, has drowned near Arrecife on the island of Lanzarote in the Canaries when a boat full of illegal migrants capsized.* I know the evil tongue that leaks these rumors to the journalists. That man has always hated Nguirane and he goes round everywhere saying that your family has been an eternal disgrace to Niarela. "What goes on in Nguirane's house," he often says to his friends and family, "doesn't surprise me one bit! God's punishment is to first turn them into monkeys and then toss them into the flames of Hell!"

Well, he has a surprise coming to him, that guy. I, Ali Kaboye, am going to settle the score for Nguirane Faye when the time is right.

As far as your mother Bigué Samb is concerned, she never rests for a single moment. She goes from one group to the next, questioning all the busybodies. "This white woman, Marie-Gabrielle, have you looked at her carefully?"

In Niarela, everyone listens to Bigué Samb, since she appears to know more about Yacine Ndiaye's tricks than anyone else.

"What do you think of all this, Bigué?" people ask her.

"The way she walks reminds me of someone . . ." she says.

That's all she will ever say about it, but everybody knows what she means.

■　　■　　■

It is a Wednesday afternoon, not long before Nguirane Faye's lingering death. He has just returned from the mosque and is rolling out his mat under the mango tree in the middle of the courtyard.

Mbissine and Mbissane have turned the TV up to the top volume. Normally, he tries to avoid scolding Yacine Ndiaye's children in any way. They love noise, and even if it gives him excruciating migraines, he is resigned to suffering in silence. But on that day, two neighbors have come over to complain politely about it. That's why he has decided to call Arame, Yacine Ndiaye's maid. "Arame, go and tell the children to switch off the television or at least turn down the volume."

He sees the young girl's confused expression and immediately corrects himself. It's true, even the slightest reprimand from Arame will make their mother pounce on her, and she may even get fired.

"Sorry, I forgot," he said. "All right, let them do whatever they want."

Arame knows she can trust Nguirane Faye and complains about her mistress, "Grandfather Nguirane, Yacine Ndiaye isn't bringing up her children well enough and I don't think she is a good person."

"The whole of Niarela knows this, Arame. If it wasn't for me, our young people would have taught her a lesson long ago. We don't like arrogant people here. Niarela is Niarela."

"You were right to protect her, Grandfather Nguirane. Anyway, she is soon going back to France with Mbissine and Mbissane."

"Has she found her papers?"

"I have heard her say that that's no longer important."

After this conversation, Arame quickly returns to her work and the music stops almost instantly.

Then Nguirane Faye opens *The Book of Secrets*, the red notebook in which he whispers words into your ear all the way from here.

While he is thinking about the first sentence, the sound of soft footsteps to his left attracts his attention. There is a whiff of cologne in the air, and he automatically looks up but cannot see anybody. A possible reason for this is that his eyes have started letting him down lately. His eyesight has deteriorated since he never found the time to do anything about it. And anyway, what could he have done? At that age, you wonder whether a cataract operation is actually still worth it. "A female visitor," he thinks, as the footsteps are becoming more distinct and the scent intensifies. For a few moments, Nguirane Faye remains on the alert, ready to respond to the new arrival's words of greeting. Nothing happens. The newcomer is like a shadow walking around the courtyard. Was he perhaps hallucinating? He wonders whether he should go to his bedroom and rest a little, but he has trouble collecting his thoughts. *Someone has just walked past me, I have heard her steps, smelled her perfume. A lady's perfume. It still lingers in the air. But where is she?* He looks around, lost in his thoughts. He knows very well that it is nothing of great significance, he just wants to be sure that his senses are not deceiving him. He is relieved when he sees a tall, slim woman with dark hair outside Yacine Ndiaye's apartment. A foreigner. Actually, a *Toubab*. The word "Marseille" is taking shape in his mind at that very moment. When he sees the woman putting a key into the lock, Nguirane Faye gets up and walks up to her. He wants to know what she is doing in his house. This is the first time he has seen a *Toubab* coming to Yacine Ndiaye's door. After all, he is the head of this family: he has the right to know how this stranger has managed to get hold of the key to the apartment. The young woman doesn't answer. She turns and looks at him in silence, and the moment he has reached her she slams the door in his face.

Less than a second later, little Arame starts crying. She comes out of her employer's house, seemingly in total disarray and running for shelter. Several times she falls over and gets up again, still uttering terrified screams with her hands folded on top of her head.

In no time, the courtyard has filled up with people. Everyone asks, "What on earth is going on in your house, Nguirane?"

He has no idea. He hasn't had time to wrap his head around it. It has all happened too quickly. The shadow that skimmed his face just a minute ago. The gaze, as from another universe, of this foreign woman. Little Arame, who still hasn't stopped crying and is running back and forth from one end of the compound to the other. And now all the neighbors are crowding around him.

"I don't know," he answers, getting more and more upset and probably feeling rather afraid himself.

"So, is that the way you run your house, Nguirane? Do you really not even want to know why Arame is crying like that?"

And then I hear someone mentioning my name. "I wouldn't be surprised if this was Ali Kaboye's new trick!"

For once, Badou, I had nothing to do with Niarela's misfortunes, but these people simply can't stop maligning me, that's how they are.

In a serious and almost aggressive tone of voice, another one says, "Nguirane, who is this young white woman we have seen get out of a car and walk into your house? Do you know her, at least?"

"I have never set eyes on this white woman in my life before," Nguirane sighs with a mixture of weariness and despair.

His one and only wish is to be left alone. He is even strangely pleased that he has no idea what is happening, and he declares, as though the whole thing had nothing to do with him, "Why don't you go and see Yacine Ndiaye and check for yourselves what is going on there?"

At that precise moment, Arame's screaming stops.

The silence strikes everybody as even more disquieting than the chaos that preceded it.

Straight afterward, soft murmurs are running through the crowd. Some of the neighbors are whispering into each other's ears, and one head after the other turns to the gate. Bigué Samb has arrived, with a worried, inscrutable expression. Everyone is aware this is a significant moment. For whatever reason, Bigué Samb is clearly the center of attention. She is also the only person with whom Yacine Ndiaye has had any ties that could even remotely be described as friendship during her stay in Niarela.

"I greet you all," she says, sitting down near Nguirane Faye.

She first asks the old man and Arame how they are, and then requests that she and Nguirane Faye be left alone. The whole of Niarela respects Bigué Samb as a woman of sound character and nobody would dream of disobeying her. Slowly but surely, people start leaving the courtyard, although a few stragglers, the notorious busybodies, drag their feet. Bigué Samb notices this and almost apologetically, she tells them, "Some of you are my elders, and some of you are my friends. I have never kept any secrets from you. If I have said what I had to say to you today, it's because I need to speak to Nguirane in private."

This has the desired effect and at last all the remaining visitors leave the house. There is silence again, but quite soon this silence starts becoming oppressive. Looking at Bigué Samb, Nguirane Faye asks, "Where is your friend, Bigué?"

At first, there's no reaction. Bigué Samb seems lost in her thoughts, keeping her head slightly bowed and her gaze fixed on the ground. When she finally responds, her voice sounds so different that Nguirane Faye barely recognizes it. "Stop asking yourself that question, Nguirane. No human being will ever set eyes on Yacine Ndiaye's face again."

"She came a few days ago to say good-bye to me," observes Nguirane, "but I know she never left. What's going on?"

"You haven't listened to what I said, Nguirane. What I have told you is this: no human being will ever set eyes on Yacine Ndiaye's face again."

"She cannot be dead, or else we would know about it."

"She isn't dead."

"Well then, what is going on?"

"Well, it's like this: Yacine Ndiaye is neither dead, nor is she really alive anymore."

Nguirane Faye suddenly perks up. "Who on earth is this white woman, Bigué?"

"Which white woman?"

Bigué Samb pauses. Without looking at Nguirane, she says in a barely audible voice, "It's her. It's Yacine Ndiaye. That's her you saw walking past here just now."

Nguirane Faye can't suppress a nervous little chuckle. "You, too, don't really listen anymore when I am talking to you. Are you feeling quite well these days, Bigué?"

"Don't worry, old Nguirane, I definitely have all my wits. The woman you mean is Yacine Ndiaye."

"Bigué Samb, what is the matter with you? Are you perhaps ill? I am talking about Assane Tall's widow who arrived here from Marseille with the body of my son."

"And I, Nguirane, I can only repeat the same thing to you all over again. The person you have just seen walking past you is Yacine Ndiaye."

At that precise moment, Nguirane Faye's face turns to stone. He, for his part, is averting his eyes from Bigué Samb. He picks up a yellow twig lying in front of him, twirls it between his fingers for a few seconds and says quietly, "Do you have anything to do with all this, my daughter?"

"You want to know if I, Bigué Samb, have anything to do with this? At last you're asking me the question I have been waiting for! That's why I chased the neighbors out of the house. Yes, Nguirane, it is all my doing. You remember the day Assane Tall left for Marseille?"

"It was long ago, but I remember it as if it had been yesterday. I was proud of him, because he was one of the first sons of this country to go and play for a great soccer team in Europe."

"I was proud of him too. I loved him like only a mad woman can love her man. Our good-byes were heart rending, we were both crying and the whole airport was staring at us. Some people were moved and others were slightly irritated, but Assane and I didn't care."

"I even saw some tourists taking pictures," adds Nguirane Faye. Despite everything, there is a hint of affectionate irony in his voice. Bigué Samb, by contrast, sounds cold and unemotional. "Old Nguirane, I spoke to Assane Tall just before he boarded his plane."

"What did you say to my son on that day, Bigué Samb?"

"I simply told him this: Assane, we have come here today to say good-bye to you, your son Badou Tall and I. I wish you a great career in Marseille, but you know me, I am not a woman who forgives. If you betray me, I will take revenge. I swear on the head of this child that I will take revenge."

"Did he answer you?"

"Our eyes met for a fraction of a second, and my blood froze, Nguirane."

She pauses again. Nguirane Faye remains silent. He waits for Bigué Samb to continue: "It was then, at the very moment when he was about to leave me, that Assane Tall's eyes told me he had been lying to me all along. Since that day, I have been waiting patiently for my hour of revenge. As things stand, you know everything, Nguirane. I have one last request: this conversation must be kept between us."

To Bigué Samb's great surprise, Nguirane Faye refuses. "No, I am not going to keep this to myself."

"Does this mean you want to tell Badou Tall about it?"

"Yes, because it concerns him very, very closely. It is important for all of us to know these things about ourselves."

Bigué Samb still looks pensive. Nguirane Faye can tell she is upset, so he quickly asks, "Don't you agree, Bigué?"

Just as she is about to reply, they hear a noise. Yacine Ndiaye's door is opening slowly, and Marie-Gabrielle sticks out her head.

Bigué Samb's voice bristles with hatred as she says almost inaudibly, "It's her. My very own pet monkey. Sinkoun Tiguidé is the best."

Nguirane Faye still hasn't looked up. Bigué Samb smiles maliciously. "So you don't want to see her?"

"May the Almighty protect me against having to look at her," says Nguirane.

Marie-Gabrielle von Bolkowsky opens her door wide. She comes out and stands outside her apartment, then takes a few steps in their direction, hesitates briefly and dashes back inside.

Nguirane Faye is murmuring verses from the Koran and tracing signs in the sand. He turns to Bigué Samb.

"Bigué Samb?"

"I hear you, Nguirane."

"Bigué Samb?"

"I hear you, Nguirane."

"Bigué Samb?"

"I hear you, Nguirane."

"Bigué, I have called you three times, and you have answered me three times. Here is what I have to say: these children haven't done you any harm."

"Which children, Nguirane? Do you mean the two little offspring of this monkey?"

"You must regain your self-control, Bigué Samb," says Nguirane Faye in a voice that suddenly sounds tense and shaky. "You must get a grip. Mbissine and Mbissane are *my* grandchildren."

There is a long pause. Nguirane Faye has never spoken to her with so much intensity. Suddenly, Bigué Samb is overcome by emotion. She's understood that he is bidding her farewell.

"I have heard you, Nguirane," she says.

"They are your children, too, Bigué. Look after them well. Turn them into human beings."

"I have heard you, Faye."

"Yes. Nobody can be a child and a monkey at the same time."

They are silent once more. Bigué Samb suddenly feels like she might faint at any moment.

"I am going to take little Arame home," she says, with a lump in her throat, and gets up.

■   ■   ■

I will finish Nguirane Faye's story where he started it, at the Léopold Sédar Senghor airport in Dakar. Two worlds revolving around each other: they are always close, but they never meet. I would like to end this second cycle with your grandfather's own words. I am doing this since it gives me pleasure to hear them myself, knowing that you will read them one day in his *Notebooks*. I love the idea that his voice and mine intermingle in this way and that he will briefly come back to life just for me alone.

Here are the first lines of *The Book of the Winds*:

It was on a Thursday, just before nightfall, when I went with a group of friends to collect Assane Tall's mortal remains. When we reached Ngalla Diop Street, the last junction before the airport, we found ourselves stuck in the middle of a huge crowd. There were thousands of people there, mostly youngsters—some on motorbikes, others crammed into overcrowded mini-buses, shaking their fists, but the majority were on foot, running around aimlessly in all directions. All were in a state of great excitement, shouting and clapping their hands or drumming on car bonnets: "Moo-dou Cissé! Moo-dou Cissé! Long live Modou! Long live Modou!" Loudspeakers were turned up to the max, blasting music, and we repeatedly saw pedestrians stopping briefly, tapping the ground with their feet and performing a quick little dance, twirling around four or five times before they vanished again into the seething cauldron of the streets of Dakar.

. ■ ■

Today, several years later, the area surrounding the airport is jam-packed with people once more. As the saying goes, the crowd is so dense that even the waters from heaven would have trouble finding their way to the ground. The number of people that have congregated here from all over the country could easily be between fifty and a hundred thousand. The journalists are out and about, dripping with sweat under the scorching sun and filling the air with soundbites that every member of the crowd will soon know by heart. *Niarela, a popular district. Yacine Ndiaye. Marie-Gabrielle von Bolkowsky.* About the latter, one might say the whole world is doing its best to mispronounce her name. I cannot tell you, Badou, how hilarious people find such a name. Of course they never stop talking about the two little monkeys with their sad, fearful eyes, the two little monkeys they all think they can hear rustling in the trees, but who have so far never been sighted. Actually, should one think of them as monkeys or rather as normal children? Nobody really seems to know.

It's total chaos.

Someone is posing the question to all and sundry, "Where did she go with her two children?"

The person next to him says, "They're hiding in the trees."

"Well, there sure are a lot of trees around this airport! That could well mean they'll never be found."

"The trouble is they can see us, but we can't see them. That makes me shudder, to tell you the truth."

"Oh come on. Monkeys, especially small ones like these aren't very dangerous."

"To me it feels like they are pulling faces at us this very moment."

"And if we were to cut down this tree?" suggests a fat man with a mustache. He looks very determined.

Another one takes a stroll between the trees and comes back with a new idea. "Why don't we throw pebbles at them and see what happens. That might make them come out of their hiding place."

He immediately acts upon his words and about a dozen youngsters, delighted at the opportunity to create a racket, start hurling pebbles into the branches.

The chief of the airport police is informed straightaway and comes to put an end to this game: "Throwing stones is strictly forbidden around here."

He looks stern, but he cannot hide a certain guarded benevolence that impresses everybody. He may well be a policeman, but he's a decent fellow nevertheless; you can see that immediately.

"Sorry, Chief. We didn't know," says one of the stone-throwers.

"It's all right," replies the policeman, who is eyeing a smoker and asks him for a cigarette.

The arrival of a public officer relieves the tension and the debate starts anew. A lady asks him, "What has this woman actually been accused of?"

"She's a foreigner who tried to steal two Senegalese children and take them home with her," he replies.

"Really?" exclaims a gentleman somewhere in the crowd, which is getting bigger all the time and closing in on the officer.

"She wanted to take them to Marseille," explains the policeman.

"She probably wanted to sell them over there. I have heard there is child trafficking going on between here and Europe."

The policeman smiles. You can tell the man is quite proud of himself in his faded blue uniform. In our current state of confusion, we are all looking to him for guidance. That's probably why he sounds so neutral and rational that he seems slightly blasé, which can be frustrating for those who are constantly seeking thrills and excitement.

"Yes," he says, "we are in the process of investigating this trafficking. That's exactly what happened today. Thanks to the police informer who tipped us off, it wasn't difficult to nab the woman. We had her description, and besides, she was extremely agitated. As soon as she knew she was exposed, she fled."

The man who offered the policeman a cigarette is surprised. "So it's in fact not true that she turned into a female monkey?"

He seems both disconcerted and profoundly disappointed.

The policeman takes a few puffs of his cigarette and while watching the rings of smoke rising slowly in the air, he says to him with a wry little smile, "You don't actually believe in such fairy tales, do you, my brother? People don't turn into monkeys or butterflies or whatever, just like that!"

Some members of the crowd burst out laughing. They all want to show they're not stupid and have never taken seriously what the man in the uniform has so rightly referred to as "fairy tales." But the other one is offended and seems ready to fight it out with the policeman. "Hold on, hold on! It doesn't mean you know everything just because you're a policeman, my brother! This lady is called Yacine Ndiaye, she used to walk the streets in Marseille and when her husband died over there, she came and wrought havoc in Niarela! That's the true story for you! This is what happened, and the fact that you're a cop doesn't change one iota of it!"

Now you could almost call what he said insulting a public official, couldn't you? He was certainly quite rude. Luckily, the policeman finds it amusing and fires a proverb by Wolof Njaay point-blank at the rebel, which sparks off more laughter: *Why accuse one another of having a testicular hernia? Wouldn't it be best if those concerned just took off their pants?*

Having said this, he takes some documents out of his pocket and waves them at the troublemaker. "Look here, my friend, these are the papers of this lady. She was born in Burgundy, and our French colleagues have informed us that her parents are very prominent members of society over there. She may not in fact belong to the French aristocracy, as some of us think, but just look carefully at her incredibly long name and look equally carefully at this photograph, and don't then come and tell me this woman is called Yacine Ndiaye or Coumba Sy!"

Can you tell, Badou, the sparks are flying in this debate! I absolutely love it when the ordinary people get embroiled in those street fights downtown! The policeman has managed to score some points, that's obvious from the expression on the faces all around me. But two or three renegades still aren't convinced. In a way, they feel cheated. First, they are told they're going to see child-monkeys—as if they were at the movies!—and then a guy suddenly turns up who doesn't even look like a proper policeman and sows confusion in their minds. What other information is this damn government withholding from the gullible man-in-the-street, one wonders?

■　　■　　■

Then, literally out of nowhere, the rumor started that a she-monkey and her two kids had gone into hiding back in Niarela by leaping from tree to tree, just as a raid around the airport was going on. On hearing this, thousands of busybodies dropped everything and came rushing to our area. Those who managed to get there first grabbed the best vantage points, hoping to get a good view of the apartment where Marie-Gabrielle von Bolkowsky had barricaded herself, a small concrete structure with a tiled roof. The waves of spectators that followed had to make do with tents pitched several hundred meters away. But none of these less lucky ones seemed to mind. What mattered to them was being at the heart of the action, talking to strangers as though they were old buddies, reveling in stories that were as far-fetched as they were contradictory and listening to pranksters trying, with fake clumsiness, to pronounce Marie-Gabrielle von Bolkowsky's full name before admitting defeat and drowning in the general mirth. Many of them really couldn't care less whether this young woman was a she-monkey, a blonde with pink eyes, a mixture of fenugreek and extra-virgin olive oil or just a crazy lady who had forgotten who she was.

More than once, pickpockets were caught red-handed, beaten to a pulp, and then handed over to the police who did their best to keep the crowd under control. Near the jewelry shop right next to the Empire cinema I came across a group of small-town thugs harassing a girl in a faded denim suit. They were drunk and wanted to be taken straight to the "witch," threatening in a very crude manner that they would finish her off.

At every street corner crooks were making bets. "How much r'ya gonna bet she'll eat those two kids?"

"I'm not betting anything, my friend."

"I'm prepared to put down five hundred. Those poor little ones, she's going to drink their blood."

"Heads or tails?"

"Tails."

"Tails you win, heads you lose. Heads. You've lost. My five hundred francs, old pal. Anybody else wanna place a bet?"

I have heard some of the Elders in Niarela say that those in the know had been expecting this to happen for a long time. "Shut up, you ignorant fools!" they shouted as they were pushing their way through the crowd with a wild and unfathomable glint in their eyes.

And there were those who got carried away and started throwing stones into Nguirane Faye's courtyard. They were targeting Marie-Gabrielle, but they could easily have hit the old man instead, who seemed to be in a daze and hadn't budged from his mat under the mango tree the entire time.

The following morning, he withdrew to his bedroom.

All those thousands of families preparing their meals out in the open and at night going to sleep on mats or cardboard boxes was a terrible sight. A few minutes before the early morning prayer, there they all were, washing and getting dressed in a hurry, sneaking to the makeshift toilets to relieve themselves. They seemed happy with a simple breakfast—a tuna sandwich with *kenkelibaa* tea or coffee with milk—and that's when the latest news started circulating from one group to the next. By around ten o'clock in the morning, an audience of hundreds of listeners would have crowded around preachers who almost all let it be known, amid the most deafening noise, that the end of the world and the Last Judgment were nigh.

One of these preachers was particularly ethereal and accomplished. He was tall and thin and his goatee and ardent gaze made him look like a recluse. He actually seemed to be hovering above the ground. Instead of gathering the bystanders around him, he walked away alone, with measured steps, apparently talking to himself or to some invisible power: "Almighty Father," he used to say, sounding grave and full of irony, "what more do they need? What do they actually want? The abundance of proof in front of their eyes is only exceeded by the stars in Your sky, and yet these villains and skeptics are still in doubt."

After a short pause, he would add, still as solemnly and as though he were in a trance, "I trust you will not forsake them in their ignorance."

■　　■　　■

Photographs of Marie-Gabrielle von Bolkowsky are for sale everywhere.

The bargaining is tough: "Six thousand francs."

"I'm prepared to give you three."

"Then beat it."

"I'm adding five hundred francs."

"I told you to beat it."

"Don't talk to me like this, please! You obviously have no idea who I am!"

"No, I don't know who you are, and I don't want to sell you my photograph, you punk."

The pitch is rising and blows are falling thick and fast.

Fortunately, in our country, one can always count on an old man walking past who, without fail, will help to restore calm. "What is happening in Niarela is an act of divine grace. Everyone has his part to play in it, but there is really no need to overdo things, my children."

There is noisy approval from the crowd. "How right you are, old man! We agree with you!"

•   •   •

With every passing day the tension in the air continued to rise. Some rowdies armed with petrol cans tried to set Marie-Gabrielle's apartment on fire. Luckily, the Niarela inhabitants quickly took control of the situation, and order was restored. But the heat, the noise and the dust had put everybody on edge, and people got irritated again, for no apparent reason.

For some, the time had come to settle old scores. "These people really stop at nothing," they roared. "They lock their borders and then they come and steal our children! This can't go on—we're not going to let them trample on us like that, for heaven's sake!"

And the delirious crowd chanted, "Those times are well and truly over!"

A big, strongly built fellow in combat uniform, who claimed to be a former paratrooper, aggressively declared, "In case there's any hostage taking, we have to go in."

You could tell that the boy was hungry for action. The crowd responded to his words with cheers.

"We have no choice," someone said, "we simply can't leave those kids in the clutches of a foreigner!"

An elderly gentleman tried to calm them down, but people started mocking him. "You're talking nonsense, old man!"

The paratrooper didn't want to give in. "If you refuse to defend your children, who is going to do it instead? I'm telling you, we have no choice but to go in."

While this discussion was going on, a group of youngsters came running toward them. One of them stopped, completely out of breath, panting and with panic in his eyes. Curious onlookers crowded around him as he let himself fall to the ground, muttering very faintly, with one hand pressed against his chest, "The soldiers . . ."

"What soldiers? What's going on?"

Instead of answering, the young man pointed in the direction he had just come from.

I immediately thought he must have witnessed atrocities and went to check it out.

There were bodies covered with sheets piled up against a wall. Some well-meaning individuals were caring for the wounded, and one woman was desperately looking for someone to help her take her little brother to the hospital. Everybody was complaining that the emergency services were taking too long to arrive. A man dressed in a red and blue jogging outfit tried his best to keep the crowd under control. "Don't block the passage, please! The paramedics won't be able to gain access to the wounded!" As so often in such cases, some of the onlookers, still in shock, couldn't stop talking about what they had seen. They went from one group to the next, describing how the catastrophe had happened. Cross-checking a few of these reports I realized there was no way all this bloodshed could have been prevented. In fact, Captain Dabo's men hadn't fired a single shot that day. As they were driving to Nguirane Faye's house, they had made a point of avoiding any sort of clash with the locals, who, for their part, had also made a special effort to stay out of their way. They even seemed to have received some applause, rather timid at first but then increasingly enthusiastic. I am not surprised. I have done my military service, and I know how much our compatriots love the spectacle of marching soldiers, their handsome uniforms and shiny helmets. Unfortunately, about two kilometers away from Nguirane's house, two young men, who, by the way, were never seen again after this, started yelling, "The soldiers! Daour Diagne's soldiers!" Soon, the same shouts started coming from every direction, and that's what sparked off a general panic. Nineteen unfortunate victims had already perished in the stampede, and, considering the state of many of the wounded, more casualties were to be expected.

We will never know whether all this was the consequence of a nasty joke or the work of professional troublemakers. Only one thing is certain: thanks to the sangfroid of our army, a veritable bloodbath has been avoided.

Despite this grave incident, Captain Dabo eventually managed to get to Nguirane Faye's house. When Bigué Samb saw him entering through the front gate, she got up to greet him.

"Is this where Mr. Nguirane Faye lives?" the Captain asked.

"Yes," she said, "you are at the right address."

"Captain Lamine Dabo," the officer introduced himself. "May I have a word with him?"

Bigué Samb told a barefaced lie. "He is sick and had to go to the hospital. But I am his daughter-in-law and can speak on his behalf."

Captain Dabo didn't reply. He already seemed to have forgotten all about her. Holding his walkie-talkie very close to his mouth, he rattled a few short words into it in the typical staccato speech of soldiers on duty, so reminiscent of a machine gun salvo.

He was quiet for a moment, listening to the person at the other end with the device pressed to his ear, then nodded his head and said, "You've got it. A stampede."

After listening again, he continued, "Okay. Just put your foot down and get here fast, my brother."

The conversation over, he switched off his device and looked around the courtyard. It was almost empty, but people were sitting on top of the enclosure and even in the trees and on the roofs of the neighboring houses.

Half an hour later, other soldiers—*Toubabs* in this case—arrived. Jean-Louis Préval, their commander, walked straight up to Captain Dabo. The two officers must have been old buddies, since they slapped each other affectionately on the back and exchanged a few jokes before moving on to the business at hand. Having listened to his colleague, Captain Préval turned to Bigué Samb. "We have orders to retrieve a certain Madame von Bolkowsky."

With her chin, Bigué Samb pointed to a door and said, with deliberate indifference but in very clumsy French, "She stays to the other side. She and her two children, they are inside there."

The *Toubab* seemed surprised: "Her two children . . . ?"

Bigué Samb turned to Captain Dabo. "Tell this *Toubab* to stop bothering me. He must take his compatriot and go where the heck he wants with her."

From the bathroom, where she had taken refuge with Mbissine and Mbissane, Marie-Gabrielle heard Captain Préval kicking down the door to her apartment. When she peeked through the shutters, she realized her saviors had finally arrived.

With a deep sigh of relief, she literally threw herself at Préval and the two young soldiers who were with him. "I was beginning to think you'd never come!"

She was relieved but too distressed—and also still quite worried—to show

how delighted she really was. "This hasn't been easy," said Préval. "There are people everywhere. We need to be careful when we leave here."

"These people wanted to burn us alive! Do you realize that, Sir?"

"Are you ready, Ma'am?"

With a triumphant smile, Marie-Gabrielle went back to her hiding-place, calling, "Mbissine! Mbissane! Come on my little darlings, let's go, we're leaving!"

She returned with her children. After living in a state of panic for so long, they were hanging on tightly to their mother.

"Who are these two kids?" asked Captain Préval.

"They are my children."

Immediately, the officer's expression changed, and he said harshly, "They may well be your children, Ma'am, but I cannot take them along."

"I am not going to leave them behind," said Marie-Gabrielle with determination.

"Sorry, Ma'am I have my orders."

Thanks to his long experience in dealing with emergency situations, he managed to stay calm, but Marie-Gabrielle could tell he was extremely irritated and close to losing his temper.

She realized right there and then that Bigué Samb and Sinkoun Tiguidé Camara had won the battle. All she could do now was to stand by helplessly, witnessing the spectacle of her own downfall.

She was clutching her stomach with both hands, and her face bore an expression of excruciating pain. She said, more to herself than to the *Toubab*, "But Mbissine and Mbissane came out of here, Sir . . ."

"Oh, you mean those two? Are you quite sure it's them?" Préval asked, rather sarcastically.

He was clearly getting totally fed up with this saga. The two kids were desperately clinging to their mother, who, for her part, seemed to be on the verge of a nervous breakdown. She went down on her knees before Captain Préval. "Don't you have any children of your own, Sir? How can you possibly expect me to leave Mbissine and Mbissane behind?"

The *Toubab* gave her a scornful look before barking at his men, "Go on, grab hold of her, what are you waiting for?"

And then, turning round to Marie-Gabrielle, he said, "Ma'am, my orders are to remove you from here safe and sound, and that's precisely what I am doing.

When you get to the embassy you can tell them any cock-and-bull story you like, but I can assure you that all they'll do is laugh!"

Two young soldiers took hold of Marie-Gabrielle. While she was trying to fight them off by hurling insults and trying to scratch them with her nails, Mbissine and Mbissane kept clinging to her dress, sobbing inconsolably. Préval's men found this quite touching and couldn't bring themselves to hurry the two little ones up. That made Préval even angrier. He separated Mbissine and Mbissane from their mother, threw them callously onto the sofa in the living room and shut the door behind him. Their crying continued, and they hammered their little fists on the windows with all their might.

In the courtyard, a man wearing a turban walked up to Préval and Marie-Gabrielle. It was Sinkoun Tiguidé. Seeing him standing in front of her, Marie-Gabrielle froze. For a few seconds, they looked at each other in silence. Préval and his men were baffled and kept looking from one to the other, no doubt trying to put two and two together.

In total disarray, Marie-Gabrielle said slowly and quietly, "Sinkoun Tiguidé..."

"Sinkoun Tiguidé Camara," the other one said simply.

"What have I done to you, Camara, to deserve so much hatred?"

Quite apart from her distress, her genuine desire to understand this at last was palpable.

"You cannot say you haven't been warned," Sinkoun Tiguidé replied. "Do you remember that day in my house when I heard Cheytan advising you to give me one of your children? You almost did, but then you didn't go through with it at the last minute. You offended us—my Friends and me—and insolence is anathema to us. And now you've got no one left to turn to."

"Have pity on my children. They haven't done anybody any harm, and they don't really know this country very well," she sighed in a voice that sounded distant but at the same time quite level-headed, as if she was sure she could rely on Sinkoun Tiguidé's help to take care of her children.

"What is happening to you is my doing," Sinkoun Tiguidé said coldly. "Farewell, Yacine Ndiaye."

After this brief encounter, she suddenly felt robbed of all her strength. She climbed into Préval's Land Rover without any further resistance. She did not even notice the thousands of people watching her departure in complete silence, visibly fascinated. The car drove off in a small dust cloud, sped along Blaise Diagne Avenue and disappeared.

Sinkoun Tiguidé turned to Bigué Samb and gave her a questioning look. She responded with a quick nod of her head and he understood that she had set him free.

Sinkoun Tiguidé adjusted his turban and started walking toward the gate, tossing back the tails of his boubou in a grand, theatrical, almost comical gesture.

．　．　．

Three months after Marie-Gabrielle had returned to Marseille, Nguirane Faye died alone in his modest little bedroom.

I was called to his side, since he wanted to entrust his last wishes to me. Just as he was talking to me about Mbissine and Mbissane, we heard a loud noise coming from the street.

I went to check what was going on.

Daour Diagne's soldiers were busy cordoning off the entire area while some of their colleagues carried out a search in Captain Baye Ndéné's house. Apparently they were looking for arms caches. This was worrying, but nobody in Niarela seemed to take it very seriously. "Arms? Here in Niarela?"

"That's what they say."

"Oh well, they're not telling the truth. And besides, not a single radio station has mentioned it."

"That means our area will be invaded again by the whole world!"

"God forbid! As far as I am concerned, I can tell you right now that I will go and live somewhere else if that nonsense starts up again!"

At this point, a neighbor comes back from downtown and says, "This is no joke! It's a story that could end badly. President Diagne will be on TV tonight. People say that Baye Ndéné wanted to stage a coup and take over."

Everyone roars with laughter. "Do you mean our Baye Ndéné?"

"The very same. The whole city is talking about him. Apparently he and his accomplices were planning to take control of the television headquarters and the presidential palace by the end of today."

I find it hard to believe that Baye Ndéné, too, dreamed of pissing on our heads and I mutter to myself, "President Baye Ndéné . . . Oh well, that's just what this poor country needs right now."

■   ■   ■

When I get back to Nguirane, I try not to make any noise because I don't want to wake him. In fact, he is not asleep and, as soon as I sit down next to his bed, he tilts his head slightly toward the door.

Calm gradually returns outside.

The muffled sound of detonations coming from the area around the Youth Center, just opposite Koussoum beach is audible at regular intervals, but very feebly. Each explosion seems to rock Nguirane Faye's body back to life for an instant.

I tell him that soldiers are looking for arms stockpiles in Niarela and I add—by miming them, like in the theater—a few of Baye Ndéné's typical little gestures as he is hatching his plot and then firing random shots into the crowd.

Baye Ndéné . . . Bang—bang—bang.

He opens his eyes and looks at me. His lips are twitching slightly, and I detect a gently mocking smile on his face. That's his way of drawing my attention to *their* madness—the madness of power. I am just as distressed by this as I was on the day when a gorilla, during his agonizing death-pangs in the Forest of Kagne, whispered the thousand and one tales of life and death into my ear as if it was the most normal thing in the world.

But even the small effort to speak silently to me causes Nguirane intense pain. Now he gets agitated and he rattles off swearwords that are sometimes so obscene that I find it difficult to believe they are coming out of his mouth. I have to admit that nothing has been as upsetting for me as seeing your grandfather lose his composure like this, so close to his death.

Perhaps I should add that it all started in a rather strange way, one night when he was suddenly talking to me so lucidly again that I thought some kind of miracle had cured him. But I quickly realized I was wrong, since from the next morning onward, he lost his grip for good. The names of Ninki and Nanka were constantly on his lips; he scolded them and sometimes complained about them in the harshest terms, until one evening he even hurt himself trying to jump out of bed in order to chastise them. I initially thought that was his way of continuing the fight—with the typical stubbornness of old men—against the two little monkeys of *Ninki-Nanka, a Fiction.* But I was mistaken. He rather wanted to tell them how much he loved them, and you must know, Badou Tall, that lately Nguirane had suffered a lot from the fact that he never found a way to open his heart to Mbissine and Mbissane. In mysterious ways, Marie-Gabrielle's departure for Marseille had given him back his grandchildren, and he was overcome by emotions that were extremely harsh and confusing for him. Yes it's true, he really felt very bad about never actually showing them his affection.

In the last few hours of his life he questioned me about people and places I had never heard of before. After listening more closely to him, I understood that he didn't know them either. That Nguirane Faye had become totally delirious was as true as it was unbearable to me. I couldn't help it, but I wanted him to die as quickly as possible. He certainly shouldn't have had to go like that after leading a life that was so simple, so impoverished, and yet so dignified. Every second more was a second too many.

Worst of all, though, was the fact that Nguirane was perfectly aware he was crumbling, Badou. A part of him was fighting desperately against his own decline. He would gladly have shut up and left quietly, but somehow he was dragged in the opposite direction, which meant that, in-between two bursts of laughter, he was talking total nonsense.

I sat down on the edge of his bed. Never before had I dared to get so close to Nguirane. I know who I am; I never forget about my filthy, stinking body. I took his hand and told him calmly, with words coming from very far away, "Nguirane, just cling to my voice. Forget everything and just do that, I beg you. Hold on to my voice. That's all you need to do. Do you understand?"

He said yes with his eyes and I could feel he was beginning to relax.

But what stories did I tell him? I honestly can't remember, and maybe it's better that way. I simply allowed myself to be carried along by the words that came to me, and I would never presume that I repopulated his memory with familiar faces. I am pleased to say that, unlike a number of other authors, I feel no need to make apologies for any potential resemblance—entirely coincidental, of course—between the figments of my imagination and any persons who are or have been actually alive. I invented creatures for Nguirane Faye at the time of his death so surreal that I feel neither the need to prove their nonexistence, nor to apologize to anybody for them. I kept talking to him until the very last moment, not as one would talk to a child or to a senile old man, but in the most normal way in the world, with respect and with love, exactly like he did to you in his *Notebooks* year after year, knowing full well you would never be able to respond to him directly.

He became very peaceful and a faint glimmer of light illuminated his face. I felt happy to see him at last looking so serene and radiant. Nguirane Faye gave me the gift of his last breath, and I gently closed his eyes.

▪   ▪   ▪

His body has been prepared for burial, and the hearse is on its way to the cemetery.

I am at the front of the funeral procession, quite far ahead of the rest. I am searching for the two little monkeys, and they are definitely there, just as I expected. Since their return to Niarela the day before, they have only emerged from the trees to hang around the area between the market and the Roxy cinema. And there they are, on this early afternoon, just beneath the poster advertising the famous film *Mother India*, totally absorbed in a ferocious fight about a moped. Every time one of them has managed to sit down on the saddle, trying to start the engine, the other one brutally throws him off. I get the impression that theirs are not just the harmless games most other animals play at their age. They are really getting carried away and seem quite determined to fight it out to the bitter end. I have a good mind to go and tell them to be careful and make sure they don't hurt themselves with the handlebars. But I miss the chance to do that, since as soon as we get closer to them, the moped is forgotten. They are standing side-by-side now, stock-still and peering at us attentively. Seeing them suddenly look so concerned, so serious, as if wanting to tell us something very specific, fills me with dread. It reminds me of those gorillas in the Forest of Kagne. It's a sobering thought that animals have their own ideas in their heads, and we will never know exactly what they are. One of the little monkeys turns to its companion, pointing to Nguirane's coffin, and I think I can detect a nasty glint of satisfaction in their eyes. Then, without any warning, they start jumping up and down and twirling around, simultaneously clapping their hands and stamping their feet in a crazy kind of circus act. One thing is clear: they're pleased Nguirane is dead and they want us to know it. Soon their jubilations are all you can hear on a large section of Blaise Diagne Avenue.

You must remember, Badou, that our procession is on its way to the cemetery. It is a solemn occasion, and none of us wants to pay attention to those antics, no matter how outrageous they may be. After all, we wouldn't expect animals to weep and mourn the death of our nearest and dearest. And yet, for the inhabitants of Niarela, these little monkeys are no ordinary animals. They bring back too many bad memories, and on every single face I detect a mixture of anxiety and bewilderment.

This feeling of irrational fear must largely be due to the fact that the two monkeys appeared in Niarela right in the middle of Nguirane Faye's funeral. That cannot be pure coincidence. Niarela does not want to get caught up in yet another battle involving the forces of darkness. These tiny little creatures that have suddenly appeared out of nowhere, might easily be seen as harbingers of a shadowy, threatening world.

But there was one person—Bigué Samb, your mother—who was prepared to take them under her wing, and by doing that, she gradually succeeded in allaying Niarela's fears.

These days, everyone is perfectly used to seeing the two little monkeys obediently perched on Bigué Samb's shoulders while she goes about her daily chores. She feeds and delouses them, and sometimes she even takes the time to carefully brush their bristly fur. We frequently see the three of them wrapped up in a lively conversation. In actual fact it's usually Bigué Samb who, with a lot of fun and laughter, talks to her little ones, as she likes to call them. What does she tell them? She alone knows. They, of course, have no idea what her words mean. They are content to look at her with those mischievous, melancholic eyes that their species is so famous for. Whether they reply to her or not is irrelevant to Bigué Samb. She never stops chatting to them, and maybe she even amuses them with entertaining stories of her own invention. It would take a lot more than their stubborn silence to throw a woman as opinionated as her off her path.

I am the only one who knows that this is her way of keeping the promise she made to Nguirane Faye.

■　　■　　■

At the cemetery, I listened patiently to the mourners. Despite their moving words, you could easily see they were all in a hurry to be done with Nguirane and get on with their trivial little lives. I made my voice boom while they were walking toward the exit. Their heads were turning this way and that, but they couldn't see me. There was silence, and I knew their hearts were pounding, because they are afraid of me. After listening to what I had to say, they walked away, ashamed and confused.

As for you, Badou Tall, we can't wait to welcome you back to Niarela. It doesn't matter much when you return—I, Ali Kaboye, will always be here, waiting for the day when I can hand over to you the words your grandfather wrote in his *Notebooks* with so much patience and care. They are buried under the canary, securely wrapped in one of those *turkis* he liked to wear. And then there is the *The Book of Secrets*, hidden even deeper underground. I don't know what's inside, because that concerns no one except Nguirane Faye and you, Badou Tall.

But the day you come back to Niarela, before you have even had a chance to start reading Nguirane Faye's *Doomi Golo—The Hidden Notebooks*, I will take your hand and we will go and pay him a visit. And if you say a silent prayer at his grave, don't worry, he will still hear your voice and see your face. I know that of all the prayers that will have been said there, yours is going to mean be the most to him. He is patiently looking forward to your homecoming, and the day you shall meet again in the next world will be the most beautiful of all the countless days of his death.

GLOSSARY

Àllu Kaañ (Allou Kagne) forest located 60 km northeast of Dakar

anango loose-fitting cotton top

àttaaya tea prepared according to the Moorish tradition

bàkk singing and dancing performed by wrestlers for the purpose of self-glorification

Baobab-of-the-Initiates a special tree under which the newly circumcised boys/young men gather

bogolan fabric originating from Mali

boroom saret cart driver

bunukabu home-brewed beer from the south of Senegal

caaya baggy pants

ceddo a pagan

cere baasi millet couscous with peanut sauce

Cheytan name derived from Arabic for the devil or Satan

daxin rice with mutton tripes in peanut sauce

daara Koranic school

ditax a fruit

fonde millet porridge with milk

Gaynde Njaay, mbarawàcc! Go for it, Lion!

God's-bits-of-wood a deprecating way of referring to people in order to keep away bad luck

Gueule-Tapée a popular district in the city of Dakar

Gouye-Ndiouli (*also* **Guy Njulli**) a special tree under which the newly circumcised boys/young men gather

HLM moderately priced, government subsidized housing, and the name of many popular districts in Senegal

jujube a wild berry

kacuupa dish originating from the Cape Verde Islands—a kind of French bouillabaisse

kàdd a tree, *Acacia albida*

kel extremely hard wood from the eponymous tree

kenkelibaa herbal tea

laax millet porridge with soured milk

layu a small dish made out of wicker and twine

màdd a wild fruit

mafé rice with peanut sauce

Man ràkkaaju naa! Waaw, man ràkkaaju naa! I am on tenterhooks, I am so excited, I can't wait!

mbapat nighttime wrestling match for amateurs

mbëggeel love

mbuum couscous prepared with leaves from the eponymous tree

Moom sa réew this is my country

Naeamia be Dakwa a Sudanese dish

ndënd a big drum

ñeleŋ Senegalese dish made from millet

Plateau district in the city center of Dakar

sabadoor caftan, boubou

salamalecs customary greetings in Senegal

Serer second-largest ethnic group in Senegal

tàkkusaan Muslim prayer at the end of the afternoon, around 5pm

talibé little beggar boy

tangana cheap restaurant

tengaade conical straw hat

timis Muslim prayer at the end of the day, around 7:00 p.m.

tisbaar midafternoon Muslim prayer, around 2:00 p.m.

Toubab white person, European

tulukuna very bitter medicinal potion

turki shirt split at the sides

xeesal intentional depigmentation of the skin in order to lighten it and make it look white